A thought-provoking work that stimulates and challenges ones mind. Filled with wisdom, The Avatar Syndrome is an intriguing and fascinating book. I recommend it.

F M J Clouatre, Amazon.com

From just a few pages, the Avatar Syndrome draws you in and doesn't let go. Just after a few paragraphs, I was part of the story, I befriended the characters, I had to read the next page. I just couldn't stop. However this book is not only a good read, but allowed me to reflect on my own life and look deep into my soul. This is a fantastic book, and I recommend it to anyone with heart!

Bogumila Gierus, on Amazon.ca

I loved the story of Anne. Many will be able to relate to her story, especially parents.

Roy E. Klienwachter, on Amazon.com
author, "Your Life Was Never Meant to be a Struggle"

I will start out by saying that this book was not for the casual reader. It is intense and heavy reading. With that said, I want to mention that I thoroughly enjoyed it.... It is thought-provoking and will stimulate and challenge you.

Patricia Chadwick,
Book Bargains and Previews, New York on Amazon.com

This is a subtle and intriguing mix of psychology, love, fame, faith and futurism. It feels like a rolling, slowly churning sea, where pieces come together and fall apart only to meet other pieces.

On a deeper level it is an exploration of the human potential that springboards forward from science and technology to a paradoxical return to ancient mysticism.

Bryn Symonds, writer, Barns & Noble

Also by Stan Law

Novels
IN SEARCH OF FREEDOM
GIFT OF GAMMAN
ONE JUST MAN
THE PRINCESS
ALEXANDER
SACHA – THE WAY BACK
YESHUA
[Missing Years of Jesus]
ENIGMA OF THE SECOND COMING
HEADLESS WORLD
[Sequel to The Avatar Syndrome]

Short stories
THE JEWEL AND OTHER SHORT STORIES

(by Stanislaw Kapuscinski)

Non-fiction:
VISUALIZATION
[Creating Your Own Universe]
KEY TO IMMORTALITY
[Commentary on the Gospel of Thomas]
BEYOND RELIGION
Volumes I, II and III
[Collections of essays on Perception of Reality]
DICTIONARY OF BIBLICAL SYMBOLISM

Poetry in Polish
KILKA SŁÓW I TROCHĘ GLINY
WIĘCEJ SŁÓW I WIĘCEJ GLINY

To read excerpts from any of the above books please enter:
http://www.inhousepress.ca
or email: inhousepress@sympatico.ca

THE AVATAR SYNDROME
The Messengers of God

A novel by

Stan I.S. Law

INHOUSEPRESS, MONTREAL, CANADA

Published in Canada in 2006 by
INHOUSEPRESS
7-1460 St-Jacques
Montreal
H3C 4J4
inhousepress@sympatico.ca   http://www.inhousepress.ca

Design and layout
Bozena Happach

Cover design after a sculpture by
Bozena Happach

This book is a work of fiction.
Names, characters, titles, places and incidents are either the products of the author's imagination or are used fictitiously.

LIBRARY AND ARCHIVES CANADA CATALOGUING IN PUBLICATION

Law, Stan I. S.
The Avatar Syndrome: The Messengers of God: a novel by Stan I.S. Law.

ISBN 0-9731872-5-5
ISBN13 978-0-9731872-5-0

I. Title.

PS8623.A92A92 2006   C813'.6   C2006-904234-9

Printed and bound in the USA

Dedicated to all the relatively unknown
Messengers of God

"Whatever is received,
is received according to the nature of the recipient."

Thomas Aquinas

PROLOGUE

"Two things are infinite: the universe and human stupidity; and I'm not sure about the universe."

Albert Einstein

The MNI

"Billions, my dear Minister, billions, not millions. Millions are what a baseball player gets for spitting on artificial turf, chewing gum and hitting a ball with a stick. We need billions!" Dr. Brent spoke with a sense of urgency.

The conference was the third of its kind. The Montreal Neurological Institute and Hospital, already the world epicentre of neurological research, needed funds, big funds, to resolve the problems of the foreseeable future. Until recently, only diseases of the aged such as Alzheimer's and other more benign forms of senile dementia had threatened to place an increasing financial burden on the allocation of funds. But lately, a range of benign as well as malignant intrusions had begun to accelerate within the young as well as the aged.

"We're scraping the bottom of the barrel, doctor," the Minister of Health tried his best to put a caring, concerned expression on his rotund face. The Minister glanced surreptitiously at his watch. He had a lunch appointment with his new assistant at one of the best restaurants in Hull. If it hadn't been for her extravagant hair and voluptuous proportions, the Right Honourable Jean Courtier would have sacked her weeks ago. Fortunately for her, Miss Mimi Whatshername was more than willing to share her generous amplitude with her boss, the Minister, in the room he had already booked above the restaurant. But she didn't like to be kept waiting.

"Sir, we are not dealing with a mere probability." Dr. Brent was at his most earnest. "After the age of sixty-five, the number of cases of senile diseases double every five years. Recently, the ground base of a mere sixty-four percent of ninety-year-olds with senile diseases had risen to over ninety percent for the centenarians. If we don't find a solution to the problem, Medicare as we know it will cease to exist."

"Surely, my good doctor, you are exaggerating?"

"Sir," Dr. Brent was becoming exasperated, "the population is growing old. Older as we speak. By the time you retire, the cost of maintaining any form of medical care for the elderly will have doubled. Doubled, Mr. Courtier. Doubled!"

For the second time the Minister glanced at his watch. The good doctor's problems would be the problems of his successor. Why should he care? It was his job to maintain the budgetary guidelines.

Dr. John Brent, MD, FRCS, had been Director of Montreal Neurological Institute long enough to know that threatening the Minister with future problems would be of little interest to him. He had saved his trump card.

"Minister Courtier," he said, leaning over the immaculate surface of the mahogany conference table and lowering his voice to a conspiratorial level, "I must confide in you."

The Minister unwittingly began to listen. Secrets were always good for business. It kept one ahead of the game.

"We have hard evidence that the Federal Government guidelines bear a direct result on the sanity of the whole nation.

The Whole Nation," the doctor capitalized the last two words
with exaggerated facial expression.
"What do you mean, doctor?" The Minister stirred uncomfortably. This didn't sound good. Mimi might have to wait
a minute longer. Life could be really tough in politics. Even
Canadian politics.

Dr. Brent allowed himself a quizzical smile. To describe it
as smug would be too much, but there was a touch of satisfaction
in it. Many changes had transpired at the Montreal Neurological
Institute since Dr. Wilfred Penfield had sketched, on a napkin in
the New York Biltmore Hotel, his dream of a Neurological Research facility. He had convinced the millionaire, J.D. Rockefeller, to underwrite his dream. In April 1932 the Montreal Gazette had reported a grant from the Rockefeller Foundation of
$1,232,562. Construction began almost immediately. Since
then, it had grown to more than thirty distinct neuroscience laboratories with a vast gamut of interests, ranging from molecular
mechanisms of neuronal growth to neuropsychology of human
behaviour. Further, the Montreal Neurological Institute had
close ties with the Royal Victoria Hospital, and in addition to the
120 tertiary-care neurological hospital treatment units of its own,
it had access to the 300-bed General Hospital. Such scientific
collaboration between scientists and physicians was unparalleled
throughout the world.
    "You might become known as the Tommy Douglas of
neurological science, Minister," Dr. Brent put in smoothly.
    Dr. Brent's choice of name was sneakily premeditated.
Only recently, Tommy Douglas, often referred to as the father of
Canadian Medicare, had been voted the Greatest Canadian of all
time. All Time! The suggestion was not lost on the pink-
cheeked prospective benefactor.
    For a moment the Right Honourable Minister basked in the
pleasure of his forthcoming fame. He could see the headlines
now: The Father of... Then he shook his head, cleared his throat
and looked down on the mortal sitting across from him.

"Just what do you mean, Doctor Brent?" This, the Minister thought doing his best to hide his sudden interest, was well worth digging into a little deeper.

"Well, Tommy Douglas...."

Courtier waved him away. "What do you mean by the, ah, sanity of the whole nation?"

So he took the bait, thought Dr. Brent. "Well, Minister, I am not free to tell you everything, you understand. We are still at the experimental stage. But..." he looked around to assure himself they were not being overheard, "but there is considerable evidence that the Ministry of Agriculture is indirectly responsible for approving certain food preservatives which have been linked directly to a substantial deterioration of the human brain."

To Dr. Brent's surprise, the Minister appeared to have exhaled a deep breath of relief.

"So it's not directly related to my department?"

"Well, not directly, sir. But... well, you are the Minister responsible for the health of the nation. "

Courtier seemed to be weighing the pros and cons. He had a real problem to resolve. And judging from the pained expression on his indulgent face, subjecting his grey cells to undue exercise was something he neither enjoyed nor did very often. One couldn't trust these scientists, he thought. If I do nothing, he'll claim that he'd informed me of the dangers looming over the general population. If I tell the Ministry of Agriculture about the news, they'll ask me for hard evidence and I'll be stuck.

"The clock is ticking, Minister. We are really running out of time. It is not just a question of advising the Ministry of Agriculture; it is a question of throwing all our resources behind research that we, at the MNI are conducting. And the resource we desperately need is money. Only last week I lost two of my best researchers to Uncle Sam. We are in no position to match their salaries on our present budget."

He recited this little speech practically in one breath. He didn't want the Minister to interrupt him, to have a chance to think. He had to instil fear into the Minister's subconscious.

"The nation is reaching a point of no return," he added lamely.

At least half of what Dr. Brent had said was true. The physicians in Montreal, indeed in Québec, were the worst paid professionals of the Canadian Medical establishment. As for the deterioration of the human gray matter, well, that was true also. Mostly due, he suspected, to the overwhelming preponderance of Canadians choosing to live in urban centres. The pollution in our big cities does have adverse effects on our cellular structures in general, our neurons, in particular. He needed money to hire the best staff to do the best work possible.

The Minister appeared to have reached some kind of conclusion.

"You realize that I cannot infringe on Provincial Jurisdiction?"

This indeed was a problem. The Provincial Jurisdiction, with the P and the J always capitalized, was the Holy Cow of the Confederation. John Brent was ready.

"Minister." He did his best to look the politician straight in his shifty eyes. "Doctor Penfield never thought of the Neurological Institute as a Provincial Institution. Not even a Canadian one. He thought of it as an Institute doing work for humanity. I believe it would be in accord with his thoughts, indeed with his wishes, to declare the MNI the World Institute for Neurological Sciences. Funded not just by Provincial or even Federal money, but by the United Nations."

This scored another point. The Right Honourable Jean Courtier saw himself addressing the United Nations, in New York, urging them to support the Canadian effort to save humanity. To save the World!

"I'll see what I can do, Doctor Brent."

The Minister bestowed upon the good doctor one of his effusive, benevolent smiles, the kind he normally reserved only for the higher echelons. "Leave it with me, Doctor. You can count on me or my name isn't Jean Courtier."

John Brent's narrow face broadened in a vaguely facetious smile. That was part of the problem, he thought. You son of a bitch! You promised me the same thing the last time I spoke to you. Dr. Brent extended his hand.

"I know I can, Minister," he said. There wasn't a trace of sarcasm in his voice. Rather – a smidgen of admiration. He found it hard to believe that a man of such limited intelligence could have become a minister. Or maybe that was why he had. Maybe... John shrugged inwardly. Maybe politics is simply a field of imponderables. Like religion, or quantum mechanics.

The Minster again glanced at his watch.

'MIMI!' his thoughts screamed. He shook Dr. Brent's hand as though it were red-hot and was out of the door in three steps. For the second time John Brent was filled with admiration. He'd never imagined that a man with so many extra pounds supported by such short, stumpy legs could move with such alacrity. He must have been drawn by some marvelous incentive, he mused.

Alas, The Right Honourable Minister's incentive had already left the restaurant.

* * * * *

THE BEAST

*"The mind is its own place and in itself
can make a heaven of hell, a hell of heaven"*

John Milton
PARADISE LOST

Chapter 1

The Flies

There were three of them. Three wingless flies moving slowly as though burdened by some invisible load in concentric circles across the kitchen table.

"Anne?"

"Yes, Mommy?"

Anne or Annette, as her father liked to call her, was a bundle of joy. Five at her last birthday, a mass of richly curled naturally red hair bounced with each of her jaunty youthful steps. She presented a picture of health and happiness. Diana Howell normally had to hold herself back from picking her up and squeezing her for all she was worth.

"Yes, Mommy?" Anne repeated as her mother stood over her, her hands clasped tightly together as though holding something small but precious.

"Please explain these?" Diana pointed to the three de-winged flies still performing their gyrations on the table.

"The flies, Mommy?"

Her mother didn't answer. This was the third time in as many weeks that she'd asked her daughter the same question. "Please explain these...."

"They like honey, Mommy. I gave them some..."

"Anne?" Diana's voice sounded more stern.

Anne's mop of hair bounced up and down as she danced around the table. "If I didn't take off their wings, they would fly away before they ate all the honey, Mommy!"

The first time she had claimed that the wings fell off all by themselves. "They take them off, Mommy, when they sit down," was that story. The second time she tore off their wings to see how high they could jump without them. Each time she had been told, sternly, that hurting animals, insects, or any living creature was wrong. Very wrong. She promised she'd never do it again. She didn't. Not for a whole week.

Diana had spoken to her friends about it, not mentioning Anne by name, of course. She had asked if their children ever did such things. "I never noticed, my dear. But I wouldn't worry about it. Children do strange things all the time. Besides, they're just flies." The answers had sounded quite candid.

But this was the third time.

Michael wasn't much help. In his eyes Anne could do no wrong. "You're imagining things," he'd said. "All children do odd things at times. It's their innate curiosity."

Fathers are like that, she'd learned early on. They would come back from the office and go all gaga over their daughters. Not that she could blame him. Barring these odd exceptions, Anne was wonderful. A bright, generally obedient, thoroughly nice child. In fact, if Diana hadn't seen the flies herself – now crawling even more slowly as they began to die – she would hardly have believed it.

For the next few weeks all was well. Anne continued to be a punctilious girl. Her room was unusually orderly for a child her age, her hands washed properly before meals, even before Diana had a chance to remind her. No flies, maimed, dead or otherwise tortured, were in evidence anywhere. Diana was beginning to relax. "Michael was right. Just innocent curiosity."

But she had relaxed her vigil all too quickly and dismissed her instincts much too easily. One autumn evening she found a jar full of flies. The jar itself was nothing special: just left over from some marmalade Anne particularly liked. But the flies? Some were alive, some dead; some looked on the verge of dying. Keeping vigil over their fate, to Diana's horror, were a half dozen large, black spiders. The lid was not screwed on tightly but lay loosely, allowing some air to get in, but with not enough space for any of the captives to escape. The jar appeared to have been carefully hidden behind some toys neatly stashed on low shelves in Anne's bedroom. Almost as an afterthought she noticed that all the flies had wings intact. At least those that were still alive.

After overcoming her initial disgust, Diana tried to rationalize that the flies had found their way into the jar on their own. That the spiders had followed in the hopes of a tasty meal. She knew she was lying to herself. This was deliberate and malicious. And worse, it had been done by her little girl. The joy of her life.

To her relief, this time Michael did not try to justify Anne's behaviour with some inane excuses. He studied the jar, emptied it into the toilet, and flushed twice. It never crossed his mind that he had merely accelerated the process that Anne had begun, while depriving the spiders of a decent meal. Next, as though in a dream, he walked to the window overlooking their rear garden. Anne was playing in the yard with the next-door neighbour, a girl two years her senior, making garlands of autumn multi-hued leaves with which they proceeded to crown each other's heads. The laurels were truly beautiful.

"We have a very talented daughter," he said.

Michael, being a no-nonsense structural engineer, recognized any colourful arrangement of almost anything as symptomatic of talent. There was a deep, underlying reason for his prosaic ineptitude. It reached back to his early boyhood.

Not that little Mike lacked cultural upbringing. His family home displayed a veritable if uncoordinated cocktail of who-is-who of modern art, or, to be more precise, of modern artists. Michael's father specialised in very modern art. And that was, at least partially, the problem. His father never took time to explain to him the inner meaning of the paintings. The Borduas and Riopells, or even an early Lichtenstein or his contemporary Rauschenberg, remained squiggles or blotches of colour framed in rich gilt frames, as though underlying their intrinsic value. For Michael, those works of art forever remained squiggles. And blotches. And little more.

When Michael had asked questions, he had been told that these were famous artists, who expressed esoteric concepts through their paintings, much too deep for a little boy to understand. By the time Michael turned fourteen, he was deeply convinced that art is on a par with Greek philosophers, Eastern mystics or equally incomprehensible religious tractates which the Jesuits attempted, as unsuccessfully, to instil in him. He didn't know that his parents didn't buy art. They bought 'names'.

Years later, Michael learned to see the world essentially in black and white, solid, structurally sound, even if, on occasion, at the very limits of inherent stability. At this very moment he felt at that limit himself. Whatever he also felt, at the moment, was that in spite of his 20/20 vision, art was as incomprehensible to him as to a man born blind.

"What a pity..." he added after a long pause. She, little Annette, truly was the apple of his eye. Who else had a daughter who never cried?

"What shall we do?"

"John Brent. Doctor Brent," he explained. "He and I went to school together. Upper Canada College. A nice guy. He's at the MNI, the Neurological Institute. The 'Neuro' I think he calls it. Running it, I suppose? I'll call him tomorrow. No. Tonight... He must know a good psychologist. He'll know someone." Michael was rambling, probably to avoid thinking. "He'll recommend someone," his voice trailed off.

Michael's prematurely greying hair spoke of a life that had not always been easy. His mother died at his birth, and even though his father had tried to make up for the loss in little Mike's life, it was hardly possible. No one really could. His youth was lonely, in a state of hunger for something unknown. He'd become a structural engineer mainly because of an unconscious need for stability. To build things out of concrete and metal that were permanent and tangible and never disappeared. Finally, he had married late, as if afraid to expose himself to even a remote possibility of yet another painful loss. Then he was equally afraid to have children. When Diana got pregnant, he would lie awake at night thinking that he would never forgive himself if his wife died just to bear him a child. Now he'd recovered sufficiently to lead a normal life, but nothing would induce him to have more children.

"Once lucky," he told himself, "twice shy. Or stupid."

He loved Diana very much. Anne, Annette, he worshipped.

That night John Brent was again in Ottawa, but he returned Michael's call early the next day. He said he would make some inquiries and call him back. They didn't talk long. They were both men of few words. Precise. Exact.

"Well?" Diana wanted to know.

"He'll call me back. He's not a psychiatrist. Nor a psychologist, for that matter. His specialty is neurosurgery with some MRI and even nanotechnology connotations. He's also working on stem-cell research. But that's nothing to do with behavioural disorders. At least, not at this stage."

For some reason the chat with John snapped Michael out of his despondency. John was an eminently practical man. "For every action there is an equal and opposite reaction," he'd said. "For every behaviour there is a reason. A cause. Remove the cause and you're home free."

Now that was the sort of talk that appealed to the engineer in Michael. It was logical. In engineering, if the calculations didn't follow the laws of logic, your calculations were wrong. He felt better already.

The next day there was no call from Dr. Brent, but a very youthful voice asked Diana if she would be willing to bring her daughter to the Montreal Children's Hospital, next week, on

Thursday, at 2.30 p.m. Dr. Schneider would be waiting for her, for both of them, in her office.

Time dragged on. Finally, the following Thursday at 2.25 p.m., Diana and Anne presented themselves in Dr. Schneider's waiting room. The place looked more like a tiny kindergarten than a doctor's office. Some toys had been stacked neatly in an étagère by the window, but an equal number were scattered about the room. Anne immediately began picking the toys up and arranging them in what seemed obviously, to her at least, appropriate places. The need for order was as strong in her as in her father. She needed order to be happy. Likewise, her curiosity was never sated until she felt order had been restored. Whatever it was had to be examined until it fit into the pattern. Everything had to be just so.

The door opened and an eye peeked through the crack between the hinges and the door.

"I can see you..." a voice whispered enticingly.

Anne was up and scanning the crack in the door.

"I can see you too, ha!" she announced triumphantly.

"Then come and get me," the hidden voice said.

Dr. Schneider's playful manner in no way diminished her powers of observation. She invited Anne into her office, and shortly but firmly asked Diana to remain in the waiting room.

"Just for a minute or two, Mrs. Howell. I don't want her distracted. Do you mind?" She didn't wait for an answer, closing the door silently behind her.

During the last few months, Diana had read anything she could lay her hands on about child psychology. Most books dealt with subjects like ADD: Attention Deficit Disorder, learning disabilities in general, parents' – rather then children's – inability to stay within limits of good behaviour, and masses of stuff on autism, which included checklists for initial diagnosis. Diana was sure that Anne was in no danger of being or becoming autistic. Her grasp of reality was as firm, as normal if you must, as... well, as her own.

But then again, maybe the problem was hers. Maybe her own grasp of reality wasn't as good as all that. Not if she, a mother of a five-year-old, couldn't discover what made her one and only daughter do horrible things to helpless insects. But surely, don't all, or most, children experiment with all sorts of things in search of knowledge? Don't we all?

Almost in desperation she had turned to the Internet. There, the thought of having a choice of some 435,000 books and articles at her disposal was enough to drive her slightly insane. More than slightly. There was nothing she could find about signs of sadism in children. There was a great deal of sadism being perpetrated on children; nothing on children being the perpetrators. And at any rate, the subject was banded together into Sadism and Masochism, Hatred and Cruelty, together with Sexual Deviation. She had shut off the computer in disgust.

"My daughter is not a deviant!" she had said out loud.

It was then that she decided to leave the diagnosis to the professionals. Arriving at the door of the Montreal Children's Hospital was more a relief than a hardship.

And there she was. Palms slightly sweaty, a little nervous, a little relieved. As soon as Anne went into the office with Dr. Schneider, she realized how very tired she was. Even just sitting there, while someone else, hopefully more proficient than she, was taking care of her little Annie, was a rest in itself. Her initial anger at not being allowed into the consulting room turned to gratitude. Poor Annie. Please, God, let it not be anything serious. Let it be just a passing phase. A child thing....

She dozed off.

"Mrs. Howell?"

Diana sprang to her feet rubbing her eyes. Apparently Dr. Schneider was used to exhausted mothers taking five while waiting for their little ones. "Would you come in, please?"

Diana was amazed to see Anne squatting on the carpet, not two feet away, playing quietly with some toys. Diana rubbed her eyes again. She obviously hadn't heard Anne come into the waiting room. I must have really been far away, she mused. She smiled at Anne and followed Dr. Schneider into the consulting room. Actually, it looked more like a small, intimate living room than any hospital consulting room she'd ever seen. There were fresh flowers on a low table, some toys placed apparently at random, perhaps left behind by some other patients. Patients? Was my daughter a patient? She sat down.

"Mrs. Howell?"

Diana brought her scattered mind into focus. She looked up at the Doctor sitting at her desk, smiling, inspiring confidence. "I'm glad you brought your daughter to see me. She's such a charming and bright girl. It was a real pleasure to meet her."

Diana remained silent, waiting for the worse to come.

"There is nothing wrong with your daughter that I can find. At least, not immediately." Dr. Schneider smiled again. "You know, Mrs. Howell – may I call you Diana?" Registering a nod she went on. "You know, Diana, there are psychoanalysts who have their patients on a couch for five to ten years. I defy anyone, psychiatrist or otherwise, who would not find something wrong with any one of us in such a length of time, don't you think?"

Diana smiled feebly.

"But to be serious. You have a wonderful daughter. Her desire for knowledge, her curiosity, might run wild, on occasion, but what of it? We all have secret dreams that we wouldn't admit to one another. The difference between adults and children is that children have not developed a sense of propriety. They haven't defined the boundaries. Not yet. We must give them time."

"Time?" Diana echoed. She wasn't quite sure if the Doctor was approving Anne's behaviour or merely explaining it.

"As much time as they need." Dr. Schneider smiled yet again, then she leaned forward. "Diana," her tone studiously serious, "there is nothing wrong with your daughter. If such things as Dr. Brent described to me occur again, ah, more than once or twice, then by all means, come to see me again. I don't think they will, though. The important thing is not to build boundaries too early. If we do, we might stunt an eager mind from growing."

The Doctor got up, walked around the table and shook Diana's hand warmly. "I have a daughter, too," she said. " I know what it is to worry...."

With that she walked to the door and invited Anne to join them. There were some other people in the waiting room. Diana could only hear them. A minute later Diana and Anne left the consulting room by a different door. Diana felt a lot better. At last a professional had confirmed her own hopes on the subject. All would be well now. Or soon. Very soon.

Michael took the rest of the afternoon off to celebrate the good news.

"I told you, darling, you shouldn't worry so much." His eyes were literally sparkling with joy. His only daughter was all right. Finally they knew. They could be certain.

Together they drove up Mount Royal and spent the late afternoon walking in the park. Anne was running in circles, spreading a kaleidoscope of colourful leaves all around her. She seemed to have completely forgotten the visit to Dr. Schneider.

The next day Diana couldn't find one of her kitchen knives. As she walked to the garden to get some herbs, she saw it lying on the ground, half covered by some leaves. She didn't recall taking it out. As she picked it up, she gasped. There was what appeared to be blood on the blade.

Doctor Brent returned from Ottawa more tired then he'd ever been after a long day's work in his office, his laboratory, or even after hours of intensive neurosurgery. At least at the Neuro, after a day's work, he took with him a sense of accomplishment. A trip to Ottawa, on the other hand....

This had been his third meeting with the Right Honourable Minister Courtier in the present series, and John Brent was getting fed up. The Minister was seldom 'Right', and John had no idea whether he was 'Honourable' or not. He lied well, if that meant anything. The Minister was much more concerned with the effect his decisions might have on his constituency than about the mental health of the constituents. He liked making statements such as: "I'm only thinking of the people, my good doctor. Only of the *people*," he would stress, usually glancing at his watch at the same time. What a buffoon. John strongly suspected that the Minister's concern for the people was directly related to his own well-being. The better he felt, the more flamboyant his speeches. The more flamboyant his speeches, the further they drifted from the matter at hand. Sometimes John thought he was flogging a dead horse. Dead from the neck up.

John Brent needed money. All of his departments needed money. Desperately. The idea of making the MNI an International Organization was hardly his dream alone. Back in the 1930s Dr. Penfield had not only began to draw a detailed map of the brain's motor functions, but he had initiated the idea of an interdisciplinary approach wherein daily medicine and pure science would pool their resources to learn from each other. A great idea whose time had come.

But it, like most things, needed money.

"Patients suffering from Alzheimer's disease, Parkinson's, stroke, spinal cord injuries . . . they could all benefit greatly from stem-cell research, Minister." Recently John's colleagues had made enormous strides in this field at the Neuro.

"Isn't that rather, ah . . . unethical?" The Minister's face assumed angelic innocence.

"No more so than masturbation, Minister," John fired back. He was getting fed up.

The Minister's face reddened. Mimi flashed through his mind.

"This is not a laughing matter, Doctor."

John shrugged. He didn't care if the Minister tossed himself off the top of the Peace Tower crowning the Houses of Parliament, or to hell and back, for that matter, as long as he got the funds he needed. But there was a grain of truth in the Minister's concern. About the moral rectitude, but, more immediately important, about the political repercussions of the research.

Scientists had to contend with religious fundamentalists who, while claiming to be temples for spirit, seemed eminently concerned about the molecular structure of their bodies. Or elements that might, just might, be capable of producing a body. They murdered each other with religious zeal in their eyes, waged wars against women and children in the name of some puritanical interpretations of biblical parables, but refused to allow scientists to derive any benefits from research carried out on discarded placentas. As far as John Brent was concerned, the research could be a boon for all humanity. Not just for the 'righteous', if indignant, members of the Moral Majority – a vocal Christian group in the United States. Soul, by whatever definition, seemed of little concern to those moralists.

But the religious fanatics notwithstanding, the research needed money. John Brent just couldn't understand the contradictions in their positions. The logic that said some executions and murders were justified but using a discarded placenta for research was immoral. Why? Because, they claimed, genetics on the whole was playing God.

Since Francis Crick and James Watson discovered the double-helix blueprint of DNA, the science of genetics had exploded like a nova in the field of interstellar gray matter. Recently, at the Neuro, scientists had successfully manufactured artificial or copy genes that, in specific combination with other genes, could be loaded into the deteriorating fibre. This technique had the potential of curing muscular dystrophy – a neuromuscular disease. And glioblastoma, a fast-spreading brain tumour. And other incurable diseases. Of curing the incurable!

In rats....

Yes. So far the new methods had given fantastic results in rats. The genes had been manufactured to the most stringent Federal standards, and most people involved felt they were ready to be applied to human subjects. Alas – money was the determining factor.

"The material for just a handful of patients runs into half-a-million dollars, Minister."

"Isn't that a trifle expensive, Doctor?"

"The Governor General of Canada spent six times as much on a single trip to Russia. For each of her flings, we could cure two or three dozen people," John said very quietly.

It was true that the technique was almost absurdly expensive. Perhaps, in time, given *money*, we would learn to streamline the process.

"That is not in my jurisdiction," the Minister said brusquely.

"In whose jurisdiction is human life?" John countered.

Suddenly the Minister had an important meeting to attend.

When John returned from Ottawa, a message from Michael was waiting for him. God, people have problems! A knife covered with blood? What did that have to do with me? I'm not a pathologist. He called Michael later that evening.

"How was the trip?"

"Don't ask. Red tape is the colour of blood. My blood. They suck it out of me by the gallon. Which brings me to your problem...."

"I'm sorry, John. As I told you, Diana found it and we are worried stiff where the blood may have come from. Is there anything you can do?"

"Drop it over, tomorrow, and I'll pass it on to the lab. They're bound to come up with something."

"I don't know how to thank you, John."

"Then don't. That's what friends are for."

Dr. Brent hung up. He was more tired than he'd imagined. Even talking to John felt like an effort. He didn't go home. He'd never married. Or at least, had not married a woman. With a doctorate in physics, which he then followed with studies in medicine and neurosurgery, he was a natural choice to run the MNI. He was married to his work. She was a very demanding mistress. Day and night, he thought as he loosened his tie and collapsed onto the couch in his office.

Within seconds he was fast asleep.

* * * * *

Chapter 2

Cats, Dogs and Rats

For the next few days after finding the knife, the Holwells lived in a self-induced hell. They imagined frogs, squirrels, maybe even a cat or, worse, one of the local children being carefully dissected by their daughter. They both remembered playing doctor, when very young, though hardly as surgeons wielding kitchen knives. The fear of violence that Dr. Schneider had dispelled returned in force. Diana began watching Anne like a hawk. The poor girl couldn't take a step without her mother tensing just a little around her mouth and eyes and across her shoulders.

Finally, toward the end of the third day, John Brent called back. Michael wasn't home yet. Diana picked up the phone.

"I have good news and I have bad news," John started without any preambles.

Diana's heart missed a beat.

"Please John, I must know," she said weakly. She had to sit down. She was in no mood to enjoy John's rather oblique medical sense of humour. None of this was funny from her point of view.

"The results have just arrived. The good news is that the blood is not human. And it's not a rat's." He chuckled at his private joke. Since he had taken office as Director of the Institute, rats were the only experimental animals allowed in his labs. "The bad news, my dear Diana, is that we have no idea whose blood it might be."

Diana remained silent. Not human. NOT HUMAN. That was good news indeed. The rest didn't matter.

"It could be a dog or a cat, I suppose. They tell me it's some kind of a mammal. We really couldn't give it too much time. Busy, you know. Terribly busy."

"I understand," Diana managed at last. "Thank you, John. Thank you for calling so promptly." Three days. Three long days....

They hung up.

Not human. Whose then?

Diana decided to make discreet inquiries in the neighbourhood to see if anyone was missing a cat or a dog. Or had an injured one. God forbid she might be successful. It took a week, but finally she relaxed. No one complained of a freshly reincarnated Jack the Ripper murdering meandering bitches. Or felines.

She did ask Annie, of course, about the blood. At first, it was her intention to confront Anne directly, with the knife still dripping with blood in her hand. Not that there was ever more than just a smidgen of the offensive fluid on the blade, and even that was already dry. But the following day she'd dismissed the idea as soon as it had crossed her mind. The night before, she'd had visions, she dreamed of a tiny Lady Macbeth following her in the garden, among the roses bushes. As they walked, tiny rivulets of red liquid had run down Anne's long, voluminous hair – for there was little doubt in her chimerical mind who Lady Macbeth really was. Each time a drop descended upon an autumn leaf, it turned into a tiny pool of blood. She, Diana, had run up the terrace steps to escape the red slime that threatened to draw her back among the bushes that, by then, reached out for her with thorny, convoluting arms. The air itself turned red and sticky and smelled sweet, like honey.

She woke up covered in sweat.

A direct approach, she realized, was out of the question. Frankly, Diana was afraid to mention the subject at all.

Nevertheless, two days later, she did muster enough courage to face her daughter. Not directly, but repeatedly approaching the subject from different directions. The gentle inquisition yielded nothing. No concern, not a smidgen of embarrassment nor even a suggestion of a white lie. While remaining her usual, joyful self, Anne expressed no interest whatsoever in the matter of the bloody knife.

Two days later, Diana had given up. Either Anne had nothing to do with the knife, or she refused to discuss the matter. Diana, though not at the conscious level, preferred not to know which was the truth. If there was harm, the harm was done. If not? It was probably too late to do anything about it. Whatever 'it' was.

Since October, Anne had been picked up by a school bus at 7.45 a.m., and returned home a little after 3.00 p.m.. This gave Diana ample time to check all the nooks and crannies for evidence of Anne's past interests. There was none. Gradually, things got back to normal. By first snow, all was forgotten.

After school, Anne stayed indoors – most of the time. There were no more flies. They went wherever flies go during winter. Diana hoped they would fly south, and stay there. There were spiders, of course, which seemed to prefer the indoors at this time of the year, but Anne expressed no interest in them either. And even spiders seemed to disappear quite quickly. Perhaps they knew they weren't welcome here. Anne focused all her energies on her homework.

By mid-December, Annie was getting bored. The lessons, she said, were too easy.

"We've done that already, Mommy. Lots of times!" she complained repeatedly.

Other children were not as fast on the uptake. Diana tried to engage her daughter in extracurricular activities. All to no avail. She needed a more challenging schooling. After a month of repeated complaints, Anne found a new interest. She'd decided to bully other children into a sort of intellectual submission. She would ask them questions on schoolwork assignments, and then ridicule the boys and girls when they didn't know the answers. She seemed to enjoy her mental superiority.

The children began calling her the Brain. She called them Morons. The children didn't mind. They didn't know what the word 'moron' meant. The teachers didn't like it, though. They said so, first to Anne, then to Diana. That teacher – the one who had spoken to Diana – found a collection of spiders in her coat pocket a week later. Her hysterics were heard all the way down the corridor. Anne knew nothing about it, of course. That day she discarded the extra jars from her locker and forgot all about it. The teacher didn't. She had nightmares for weeks afterwards.

No one seemed to suspect Anne. It would have been too horrifying to consider. A girl of five? A revenge? A lesson? No. No one suspected. Except for her mother. Somehow Diana knew the truth without a shadow of a doubt.

That Christmas, Anne was given a puppy. It came with its own soft crib, a bunch of toys and a retractable leash for Anne to take it for walks. On Christmas Day Diana and Michael sat spellbound watching as Anne talked to the tiny Labrador – if any Labrador can be considered tiny. She talked to him, for it was a he, as though the dog were human.

"What will you call him, pet?" her father asked.

"He doesn't have a name?" Anne sounded surprised. In her reality everyone had a name. Even if some were called just Morons.

"He's been waiting for you to give him a name, Annie," her mother helped.

There was deep hesitation in Anne's voice. "But everybody has a name. Everybody," she insisted.

"Well, where he came from they called him Fluffy. But you can change that if you like."

"Did you change my name when you got me?" Anne asked, still looking at the puppy.

She asked questions like that. Often. You had to be pretty careful what you said. It had to be logical. Grounded in the reality with which she was familiar. Otherwise, you were in trouble.

That night, Anne and Fluffy, a name she'd refused to change, slept together. Fluffy peed on Anne's bed. She didn't mind. She had been told that she also peed in bed when she was little. Very little, of course. Fluffy was very little. She accepted it at face value that all who are little pee in bed. Or on the floor, for that matter. Or anywhere. Until they grow up.

"When will Fluffy be as grown up as I am, Mommy?"

"You must teach him where he can pee and where he shouldn't, pet."

She did. In less than two weeks Fluffy was perfectly house-trained. Anne was very proud of herself. "He's all grown up now, Mommy. Like I am." She glanced at a full-length mirror. "Like me," she added as though to reassure herself.

For Spring Break, Michael wanted to fly south. For the first time in her life Anne indulged in real tantrums. She stomped her feet, banged her fists on the floor, and generally raised Cain. It stopped the moment Michael agreed that they would cancel the air tickets and drive to Florida. Now, Fluffy could and would go with them.

Anne had won again.

There was a moment when Diana wondered what Anne would have done had she failed in her plan to take Fluffy with them. Would she have taken Fluffy and disappeared? Run away? Would she have devised a way to punish them as she had punished her teacher? Diana felt a shiver running down her back.

The holidays were as blissful as holidays should be. Long days on the beach, Fluffy being the centre of attraction. Anne wouldn't leave him for a moment. They walked, ran, bathed, and slept together. Anne was a perfect mother to the puppy. A perfect friend. Fluffy sensed her affection and likewise wouldn't leave her side. They were inseparable.

Time passed quickly. Tanned and rested, they drove back, Michael and Diana taking turns at the wheel. They stopped only to walk Fluffy and for small snacks. The parents sat in front, Fluffy cuddled in Anne's arms. Or else they were both peering through the same window. It wasn't that bad.

The snow melted early that year. The moment the lawns had cleared, Michael went out to rake the autumn leaves he'd neglected to remove last year. On the third stroke of his rake, the leaves uncovered a fluffy bit of string. He picked it up and dropped it with disgust. It was a tail. Probably of a squirrel. As he raised it again with the tip of the rake, it had begun losing moisture quickly and was regaining its fluffiness. Poor beast, he thought. They were a nuisance but, well, he just shooed them away. He'd heard somewhere that the poor animal was capable of re-growing its lost appendage. He hoped they were right. And his next thought was of Anne. What have I done wrong, he wondered? What have we done wrong?

The following week he received a leaflet from one of his neighbours warning pet owners about some deviant who was poisoning dogs. Apparently he'd found their dog moaning on the front lawn. It seemed in dire straits. They'd saved him, at the cost of more than a thousand dollars. The poor animal had spent a week on intravenous support, and had to have his heart rate increased with a number of injections. He'd spent another two weeks being force-fed semi-liquid food with an enormous syringe. Michael had never actually 'met' the dog, a Great Dane, but he felt sorry for both the animal and its owners.

Actually, they were wrong. The next day the same thing happened to a cat belonging to people across the street. The cat died. They couldn't afford the veterinary fees.

"Something is rotten in the state of Denmark," he told Diana. "Who on earth would do a thing like that?"

"And why?"

They both refused to allow their own doubts to reach their frontal lobes. To surface. To escape. They pushed their dark speculations to the deepest corners of their minds.

"Daddy," Anne asked without taking her eyes off Fluffy. Her glorious green eyes were filled with innocence, her tone suggesting casual interest only. "If someone attacked me, would you kill him?"

Michael was stunned.

"Why would you ask such a thing, dear. Of course I wouldn't kill him. We have police to take care of such things."

She pondered her father's words for a little while and then she pursued, "Would the police kill him?"

Doctor John Brent divided his time equally between the very young and the very old. The first were disorders grouped under the general heading of Autism, the latter dealt with incapacitating Alzheimer's disease and more mild forms of senile dementia. There were now more than 4,000 Canadians over the age of 100. In the United States, the figure was much larger, although recently that had decreased a bit, owing, he suspected, to the unparalleled rate of obesity, which cut the Americans' lives in relative prime.

Basically there were more old people because they had been maintained artificially alive by pharmaceutical conglomerates which, by keeping the old alive, if incapacitated, reaped vast profits from their magnanimous endeavours. Some groups of people were becoming progressively more fed up with the stories they heard about the increasing number of the negative side effects that the drugs appeared to cause. The problem was that a great many of the side effects only came to the fore after ten or even fifteen years, when irreparable damage had already been done; but no one was willing to test the drugs for fifteen years before launching them into the market. John, hardly surprisingly, held strong views that the answer lay, for most such diseases, in the field of genetics, and if genetics didn't work, in surgery. Particularly in neurosurgery. There was ample evidence that the human body was equipped with a magnificent immune system which, given half a chance, could heal the patient. Provided the brain sent the right signals, and provided the body hadn't been poisoned by years of chemical interference.

Egyptians in 2500 BC believed the heart was the centre of thought. For mummification the brain was scratched out with a hook through the nose and thrown away. The heart was separately mummified and kept in a jar. 500 years later, the Pre-Incas drilled holes in the middle of the skull to perform brain surgery. Evidently, the centre of thought migrated upwards. In 450 BC Alcmaeon, the Greek physician, affirmed that the brain not only controlled our thoughts but also our emotions.

The modern era really began around 1662, when an English surgeon, Thomas Willis, conducted the very first detailed study of the brain's anatomy, defining the brain's inner working. He also connected the brain to the nervous system and coined the term 'neurology'.

Modern scientific proof of Alcmaeon's claim came in 1848, after an iron rod pierced the frontal lobe of an English railroad worker. Following the accident, the worker retained his speech, hearing and motor skills, but his personality changed radically. He became a completely different man. Scientists of the day had just connected the brain to personality.

This marked the beginning of the long journey towards the identification of the workings of specific parts of the brain. The Polish-born neurologist Carl Wernicke, studying stroke victims, identified the left hemisphere of the brain as controlling speech. Canada's own Dr. Penfield studied and identified motor functions and drew a detailed map of our brain.

Dr. John Brent continued to expand the same field. The precision of this strange cartography was vastly enhanced by the development in 1974 of a positron emission tomography scanner that allowed him to study the reactions of various parts of the brain in conscious patients. No more laborious dissections of corpses in deep caverns akin to Dr. Frankenstein's subterranean endeavours. Out of the realm of science fiction horror and obsessions of the deranged, neurology became the most fascinating profession of the century.

"I think, therefore I am," mused Descartes so many years ago. "Now we can study the machine that translates our thoughts into words," John affirmed in one of his lectures.

"'The brain struggling to understand the brain is society trying to explain itself'," wrote Colin Blakemore in his book, *Mechanics of the Mind*. John Brent had tried hard but failed to explain these concepts to Minister Courtier – that neurology, the study of the machine of thought, was the study of the machine of society. "Surely, you as a public official can see the benefits to that kind of knowledge, Minister?"

"I don't believe society is trying to do anything very much, doctor, as long as their bellies are full and they can afford to winter in Florida," the Minister replied with a straight face and profound, if self-appointed, authority.

Sometimes John thought that perhaps the Minister was right. It usually took him a day or two to recover from the effusion of wisdom the Minister spewed at him on each occasion. Only then could he dive headlong, once again, into the work he loved and lived for. John was as fanatical about helping people as the Minister about creating an impression on the masses. Perhaps this was as it should be. John Brent dealt always with an individual, the Minister with a group, determined to mould them into his own image and likeness. Into a homogeneous group whose actions and reactions would always remain predictable. It was easier to control them that way.

There had been moments when John, listening to the Minister's pronouncements, thought that the Minister was a near ideal subject for experimental neurosurgery.

"If I could make a human being out of him, I could do anything," he told Michael at the next dinner they had together.

John was becoming a frequent guest at the Howells. He liked their open, direct approach to life. Both his hosts, Michael and Diana, were scrupulously honest. They were direct, devoid of any iota of posturing. What you saw was what you got. And in his case, he got close friendship.

"Just how much do we know about the structure of our brain?" Michael asked over deep ruby Porto they sipped after dinner. Porto was as strong a drink as John Brent could be induced to taste. He was the nearest man to a teetotaller Michael had ever met.

"I know very little, but there are some guys at Princeton...."

"...who know everything about everything," Michael finished for his friend.

"Ah, so you've heard?"

There was a standard joke circulating at the Neuro about Princeton.

Before the invention of the MRI, the CT and other electronic equipment, the only way to acquire knowledge about the brain was to perform an autopsy. Back in 1955, when Einstein died, a Princeton pathologist Thomas Harvey had performed the autopsy on one of the 20th century's most influential brains. There had been stories that Harvey had stored the disembodied brain in the trunk of his car, chopping off occasional chunks of it whenever moved by scientific curiosity. Everyone assumed that he must have learned something that no one else knew. Alas, the supposition had proven erroneous. Thomas Harvey contributed little to neurology. Hence, the joke.

"Well, Michael, we now know a great deal more than we did a few year ago," he said slowly.

Michael and Diana waited for him to continue. They didn't bother to explain their sudden interest in the secrets of human brains. Anne continued playing on the carpet, Fluffy following her every move with his big, liquid eyes.

After another tiny sip, John shrugged.

"All right. Here goes," he began. "We know that the human brain is divided into two distinct hemispheres, each busy doing its own thing. The left is principally involved with logical and rational processes, while the right hemisphere tends to control the creative, intuitive, and all that which is unspoken. It reacts to rhythm, gestures, and images – particularly as pertaining to depth perception. Is that what you wanted to know?" John paused, not sure if he had said too much or too little.

"Go on... please." This was Diana.

"Well, the left hemisphere also governs words, as in reading and writing, math, and all skills requiring reasoning." John smiled. "But it's not always so...." he left the sentence hanging.

"So that would make me a left hemispherite," Michael offered.

"Well, people who process information step by step, like engineers or journalists, or lawyers for that matter, tend to keep their left hemisphere more active. The right hemispherites, as you choose to call them, would tend to use the right half that deals in music and other forms of art. In fact, all aspects of creativity which call for spontaneity, which might be experimental, which rely mostly on multiple choice or that is absorbed randomly – is done on the right side."

"But there must be an exchange?" asked Diana.

"Of course, take Michael, for example. As an engineer you must be good at math, say algebra, but also at geometry, which belongs on the right side of your brain."

"So there is an interchange?"

"Of course. We couldn't function otherwise. Sometimes I think that it is the interchange, the pons, the bridge between the left and the right hemisphere, which is truly responsible for the mental power of a person: how well the two sides work together." Dr. Brent glanced at his watch. "But that's as far as we can go tonight. I've got a plane to catch at seven tomorrow morning," he said rising to his feet.

"The Right Honourable...?" Michael began.

"The very same. Sometimes I think if I weren't such a coward, I'd turn him into a vegetable, or kill him, painlessly, of course, or render him harmless otherwise. Maybe his successor might be better."

Michael shuffled over to John, "Master, the body is waiting for you in the laboratory, Master."

"Not now, Igor. Not now, I say!"

And with that he kissed Diana on both cheeks, shook Michael's hand and made for the door. As he reached it, he spun around, walked quickly to Anne, bent over double and kissed her hand.

"Please forgive me, my lady. May I take my leave?"

"I forgive you, Uncle John. And you may go now," she acquiesced magnanimously.

John walked away backwards, bowing all the way to the door. Anne looked up briefly, waved and continued with her deep if silent conversation with Fluffy. Yet, the moment the door shut, she looked up again.

"Would he really kill him, Daddy?"

"Who kill who, pet?" Michael was taken aback.

"Uncle John, that Ritorable man...?"

"No, dear. Of course not. Why would you think such a thing?"

"He said if he was only braver that he could easily...."

"Anne! You don't even think things like that!" Diana stepped in.

"But wouldn't it be good for everybody if...."

"No it wouldn't. Older people say things when they are joking that shouldn't be taken exactly." He wanted to say *á la lettre*, but thought better of it. Anne's French was quite good already, but he wanted to drive the idea home.

"Killing some, Daddy, is not a joke. Uncle John should know that," Anne affirmed strongly and left the room.

When she's right, she's right, Michael thought.

But why did it still make him feel uncomfortable? After all, don't all children regard life and death merely as abstract concepts? Surely, it is only when we reach the top of the hill that we seem perturbed by the very idea of killing. Or death. Isn't this why we try so hard to turn our inner, a trifle more bloodthirsty desires, into a joke? But the word 'kill' coming from a child still sent chills down his back. Am I the only one who feels that way?

He glanced at Diana. She looked as white as a sheet.

* * * * *

Chapter 3

The Grant

They grow up so quickly. Only yesterday Anne was rolling on the carpet with Fluffy in hot pursuit, and then, as if overnight, she was a proper young lady of eight. She was no longer an innocent girl with starry eyes, even if she did, at times, still try to play the part. Every few months there had been incidents, but gradually those incidents diminished – if not in nature, then at least in frequency. Either Anne was truly growing out of her childish duplicity, if one could call it that, or she was getting better at hiding it. There had been unexplained things happening to boys and girls at school, but none ever pointed directly to Anne. A bunch of cockroaches had been found crawling all over the locker of a boy who had attempted to ridicule her in front of other pupils. Blood – of no apparent source – had been smeared on the textbooks of a girl who had thrown a stone at Fluffy. A round hole had been cut, neatly – presumably with a razor blade – in the seat of a winter coat of a professor who once said that Anne should be spanked for bullying other pupils.

There was no evidence whatever tying Anne to any of those events. Furthermore, there was always a time lag of a few weeks between the presumed cause and the apparent result of the incidents. Everyone had forgotten about the first, and so never connected it to the latter. There was no hard evidence that Diana could take to Dr. Schneider.

Diana called the psychologist every once in a while. Just to be reassured.

"Can you be sure, Diana, that your daughter is responsible?"

Diana stammered and stuttered, only to admit that no, there was no solid proof that pointed specifically and exclusively to her daughter being the perpetrator of a particular misdemeanour. Or even to an overblown prank gone a little wild. She never thought that passing judgment on her own child had to conform to the legal code governing a prosecuting attorney.

"No, Doctor, I cannot. But doesn't mother's intuition count for anything?"

"It certainly does, Diana. But if we were to cast an errant stone at the innocent, we would never forgive ourselves, would we? And let's not forget what irreparable damage we could do to a child if...."

She went on.

And yet....

Whenever Anne was scolded, particularly in school, she stood facing the accuser, looking him or her straight in the eye, never answering back. When the castigation was over, she would sit down and keep very quiet. Her usual boisterous behaviour would return a few hours later, but would seem to evaporate should the offensive teacher come close.

In her relation to other pupils, she gave an impression of being easygoing, to the point of conspicuous indifference. Yet should anyone encroach on boundaries she defined in her own mind, the errant boy or girl would learn in no uncertain terms where those boundaries lay. Her own 'things', her private possessions, lay within the clearly defined, inaccessible no-man's land. The desk at which she sat was not to be tampered with, not even touched, or brushed against, by anyone. Her locker was out of bounds even to casual scrutiny. Should anyone inadvertently cross such boundaries, he or she would hear a single warning. An even-toned comment. If such were ignored, something unpleasant was bound to happen to the offending party. Later. Sometimes, a week later.

To be fair, she treated others, including their personal possessions, with the same deference with which she expected to be treated herself.

Apart from imposing, or trying to impose, her will on all that she deemed stood in her way, for whatever reason, she was an ideal pupil. Even if this particular weakness of hers, particularly her lack of tolerance, was a manifestation of her innate strength.

"In time this energy, this inner strength, will be channelled in the right direction," said Dr. Schneider echoing Diana's thoughts. "Give her time, Diana. Surely she deserves a little time."

Her grades were excellent. Whatever her other foibles, Anne was an exemplary student. She went far beyond the minimum requirements set by the curriculum. And yet Fluffy invariably took priority over all her other interests. She never forgot to take him for his morning walk, regardless of the weather, and well before 7.45 in the morning when the bus picked her up for school. Just before boarding she would talk to him, whisper things in his ear, and then turn and walk to the bus without looking back.

And so three years passed without a serious incident. No poisoned cats or dogs, no bloodstained knives hidden under the autumn leaves. Michael and Diana tried hard not to notice certain things which, if it hadn't been for Dr. Schneider's assurances, they would have taken more seriously. And then, just before her eighth birthday, two things happened within a week of each other. Anne was expelled from school for bullying other girls, and John Brent got the first instalment on a $3 billion grant. He called Michael to share his good news only to find out about Anne's latest misdemeanour.

"She'll grow out of it, Mike, trust me," he tried his best to cheer Michael up.

"That's what Dr. Schneider said more than once. Only she doesn't. In fact, it's getting worse."

There was little more John could say. They agreed to meet later that week and compare notes.

As had become more and more common among the frustrated, not to say unorthodox, pupils and parents, Diana had decided to school Anne at home. She would be able to keep a much closer eye on her, at all times.

"Perhaps it's for the best," she told her husband, her voice begging for confirmation.

"I'm sure it is, dear. I am sure it is," Michael sounded as reassuring as he knew how. He was actually aware that the extra responsibilities would fall squarely on Diana's shoulders.

He kept his doubts to himself. If Anne needed anything, it would be contact with other children. How else would she learn to control her temper? Michael was sure it was a question of temperament. Anne was bright, kind to Fluffy, obedient to her parents. There was only that one thing which distorted her vision of the world. She thought she was its centre. She refused to compromise. She was like a bull which, having sighted the matador's cape, couldn't stop until it gored the red cloth, or even the matador himself. She also seemed to have an absolute conviction about her inherent righteousness. She took criticism well enough, always politely, but if she sensed that her accuser wasn't fair, fair by her own stringent standards, she took it upon herself to inflict punishment.

Anne was evidently the judge and the executioner of her sentences. Luckily, Michael and Diana seemed exempt from her inordinate judgment. Michael wondered if she ever thought herself in the wrong.

"Do you ever make mistakes, Anne?" he asked her in as offhanded a voice as he could.

"You mean like the wrong answer in school, Daddy?"

He tried again, "Like doing something you shouldn't."

"Like what, Daddy?"

He was already sorry he'd started this conversation. There seemed no way to elicit from her an answer without mentioning her presumed pranks, or youthful indiscretions, which had never been proven. Dr. Schneider warned them both, repeatedly, about making such a mistake.

"Do you think you are always right, pet?"

"About what, Daddy?" she looked up at him with those sweet, wonderful, emerald eyes, filled with utter innocence.

"Never mind, dear," he gave up. "I was just wondering...." he tried to dismiss the subject. Suddenly Anne came to his rescue. At least it seemed so.

"I was wrong about all people being nice to Fluffy. Is that what you mean, Daddy?"

He preferred not to ask further.

"Yes, pet. That was what Daddy meant."

"Not any more, Daddy," she added as an afterthought.

"Not any more," she nodded affirmatively.

They wouldn't dare, Michael thought. And then, though not for the first time, Michael realized that no matter what happened to Anne, she never cried. There had been times when her anger manifested itself with some foot stomping, even a raised word or two, but never tears. The last time she had cried to get her own way, he'd convinced Diana not to give in. Since then, those gorgeous emerald eyes hadn't shed a single tear. He wondered if that was healthy.

Doctor John Brent was on cloud nine. His plans for the expansion of the Montreal Neurological Institute went into high gear within hours of receiving the Minister's call, almost immediately confirmed by email and fax. Apparently the Minister wanted the news to leak out far and wide, to assure an optimum audience for that evening's news. The press release had been sent out simultaneously. Not just to the national media. Three billion dollars warranted international coverage. With the Right Honourable Jean Courtier in the starring role.

Actually, to give Courtier his due, he had done his best to convince the Prime Minister about John Brent's vision.

"If I may say so, Prime Minister, Canada has been accused, of late, of having lost her clout," he began. "This would put us on the world platform," the minister coaxed his superior with a knowing expression on his pudgy face. "We would become world leaders in the field, and..." here he lowered his voice into a liquid honey of confidentiality, "...and let us not forget the votes the aging population would bring us. They tell me they can get rid of Alzheimer's, you know, Prime Minister?"

Canada's non-existent clout notwithstanding, this last was a profound exaggeration, unless one omitted the element of time, which Jean Courtier did with his usual affinity for wrapping the truth in a woolly blanket. They played politics within politics. Wasn't that what the inner caucus was for? A sort of circling within the inner circle. Or perhaps, just walking in circles....

John Brent didn't care who took the credit. What mattered was that he would double his electronic scanning capacity in the new wing. Since the first informal discussion about the possibilities of clinical electroencephalography in England in 1929, the EEG had become an indispensable tool in examining the rhythms of the brain. The next big step took place in 1974, when positron emission tomography, or PET, provided computer imagery wherein a single selected plane, or a cross-section, of a brain could be photographed. The patient remained conscious throughout the procedure. Now, in addition to the above, the researchers had at their disposal the fMRI, or functional magnetic resonance imaging which had become the workhorse of modern neurological research. Diagnostic neurology was now almost completely non-invasive.

With three billion, they could double the present capacity. Hundreds of people's brains could be scanned, fully conscious. Work on the reactions to various stimuli administered to autistic children, the study of the rare savant syndrome, the Mongoloid dilemma, and many other abnormalities, would now be allotted their rightful place in the research labs. To date, the Neuro had only been able to afford to concentrate on the disorders identified as diseases, such as Parkinson's, Alzheimer's, or dementia. Diseases of the aging. And, of course, the malignant and non-malignant intrusive growths. As of now the Neuro would be able to give equal time to the young. To the children.

"Surely they deserve no less than those who, for all we know, have themselves contributed to their conditions."

Michael hadn't seen his friend this happy in a long time. John Brent was definitely on cloud nine.

He had accepted Michael's invitation to watch the Minister's official proclamation on TV that same evening. The Rt. Hon. Jean Courtier was given equal time with the winning goal in the Canada and Russia hockey match. Well, almost equal. John had arrived at the Howell residence around six-fifteen, only to find that the Minister had already made the announcement preempting the six o'clock news. Well, not actually preempting, but basking in the limelight of being the lead story of the evening National.

In a way John was relieved. Even the act of watching the pompous minister's presentation might well have proven painful. John had too many unpleasant memories of that man, spanning a period of almost six years. Six years of haggling with Courtier and his predecessor. John was glad he had missed the broadcast. Alas, he missed the winning goal also.

"You were mentioned, John. Courtier spoke highly of you," Diana told him.

John bowed deeply. *"Non dignus sum,"* he replied gravely. While Latin did little to advance his scientific career, medicine still leaned heavily on the ancient language.

"Non understandum niente," Michael tried to emulate his friend. Engineers had no use for Latin at all. "But I gather that the $3 billion represents a record for research in any field. At least in this country."

"He'll get his money's worth, Mike. Many times over. Besides, it's good for business. People are screaming for more money being allotted for Medicare. This way he shuts them up. For a while."

"And I suppose it won't do any harm for the upcoming General Elections?" There was speculation the Prime Minister would call them by February of next year.

"It won't reduce the waiting lists in the hospitals," Diana sounded doubtful.

"Not immediately. But in time it will cut the lengthy medical procedures by ninety percent. With virtually all the preliminary procedures being reduced to non-invasive diagnoses, and even treatments, the recovery time can be taken out of the equation. People will come, be treated, and go within hours. Not weeks like they do now," John assured them.

Anne was listening to the adults' discussion through an open door. Since her expulsion, she had shunned company. There was some sort of a battle going on inside her youthful head. Diana was worried. What mother wouldn't be? She'd tried to break through Anne's defences but so far with little success. It was as though she were closing in on herself. Apart from with Fluffy, she hadn't initiated a single conversation.

Diana had tried to get her own version of the headmaster's accusations. The way he told it Anne's behaviour had been getting worse over the last few months and that during the recent weeks Anne had torn up the homework of six pupils because she didn't agree with their answers.

Initially, according to the headmaster, the six pupils had been punished for failing to do their assignment. Their accusations against Anne sounded too absurd to be believable. The teacher had even charged the pupils with conspiring to punish Anne for her previous bullying.

After repeated questioning, it finally dawned on him that Anne had really been the culprit all along. Yet, when facing her accusers, the six boys, she had said nothing. Not a single word in her own defence. She had been told not to return to school until she was willing to answer questions.

So far, Anne had remained silent.

It was about that time that Diana had begun to suspect that she, too, was being punished. That the Deity she had visited in churches as a young girl had turned against her. The Father and the Son, without whom she had learned to cope quite well, were now beginning to exact their dues. Vengeance would be too strong a word, but, at the convent she had attended when little, she had been told, daily, that God is infinitely patient, but also infinitely just.

"What do you want from me, Lord?" she would ask when sitting alone thinking about Anne.

In her mind a child had to be innocent; 'be ye like little children', she remembered. If Anne did have some serious psychological problems, then she must be suffering not for her own sins, but those of her parents. As delicately and obliquely as she could, she raised the subject with John and Michael after dinner.

"But, darling," Michael smiled broadly, "Annie is not suffering, surely."

"Are you sure, Mike? Are you sure she's not missing all her friends from school even now?"

John kept judiciously silent. There was little he could add to this conversation. Having no children of his own, and being a confirmed agnostic, both issues raised by Diana were beyond his expertise. Alas, he was not to get away with it.

"What do you think, John?"

Evidently Diana was expecting reinforcement for her theory. None of them was qualified to be called Practicing Catholics, but she knew all three had been taught, at one time or another, by priests or nuns.

There was a prolonged silence. Finally, John realized that they wouldn't continue until he'd had his say. "You are asking me to talk on a subject that is both subjective and speculative. If you raise the question of God, as taught by various religions, then I am definitely an atheist." He looked at his hosts as though weighing in his mind how far to go with his personal beliefs.

"Go on," Michael said. He was sure that John would agree with him. God was just fine on a Sunday morning, particularly around Christmas, or maybe Easter, but of little use the rest of the week, or the year, for that matter.

"Well, I find no evidence of a deity wielding a carrot or a stick over our heads to extract or enforce any type of behaviour. There is too much evidence of very successful mass murderers who benefited from such a deity's munificence as there were men and women who led quiet, normal, and generous lives."

"So you don't believe in God? Not at all?" Diana was studiously examining her white knuckles.

"Not in the personal God of the religious. Too many wars have been conducted in the name of such a deity. Still are. In many ways, the world would be a better place if religious leaders left people alone."

In spite of his stated beliefs, John looked uncomfortable.

Michael and Diana waited. Obviously there was more.

"As you know, I am both – a scientist and a neurosurgeon. No day passes without my being amazed that the human brain is, as Isaac Asimov once said, 'the most complicated organization of matter that we know'. I would go further. I believe that had such an organization of matter been left to 'accidental' if natural selection, then even ten billion years on Earth would not have sufficed to produce it." He spread his arms in utter helplessness.

"Divine intervention?" Michael offered. This time his smile was more whimsical.

"Again, not in the religious sense. Not in the sense that an outside agency, a Divine Agency, brought it about. But as I study the structure of this complex biological organism, I cannot help wondering not just *how* nature put such an 'organization of matter' atop our necks." He paused momentarily, "but *why*."

"You mean we don't need such complexity just to sustain together our body and . . . and what? And soul?"

John didn't answer.

Just then Anne and Fluffy walked in. She stood in the middle of the sitting room, head held high, as though ready to make some momentous statement.

"God makes me do things!" she announced triumphantly. And, with a winning glance at all present, she left the room without another word.

Michael chuckled. Anne's oratorical stance gave it away. She'd obviously overheard something said on TV that, of late, was a veritable goldmine of pseudo-philosophical balderdash. Come prime-time, the gurus came out in force blaming God for just about everything. It was a new twist. We used to be sinners, destined to pay dearly for our transgressions. Lately, we became mere pawns in the hands of the Almighty.

"So there you are, John," Michael said with a straight face.

"I most certainly am," John confirmed, rising to his feet.

He seemed relieved at the interruption Anne had provided. He thought the subject of personal belief should be, and should remain, just that – personal. One could hardly speak the unspeakable, explain the ineffable, discuss the incomprehensible. If God were as simple as the various religions described Him, or Her, or It, there would be no need for any religion. On the other hand, surely the religions created the only God they could understand, and thus by definition denied His existence. Wasn't it Spinoza who had said, 'to define God is to deny God'? Whatever is definable is no longer infinite. Thus the act of defining denies the fundamental property of God.

"So there you are, folks. At last we know," John smiled.

Anne's whimsical posture provided an incongruous contrast to the tone and the gravity of her announcement. It made any further serious discussion virtually impossible. Yet, there was little humour in John's expression. In fact, they all felt that the subject was far from over, and that maybe they just never should have raised the topic.

* * * * *

Chapter 4

Private Schooling

It was not nearly as simple as it sounded. It sounded like ABRA-CADABRA. In fact they all did. All the support groups seemed to specialize in acronyms. And that made everything, at least for Diana, seem unnecessarily complicated. Diana had no experience with home study. She soon discovered that the AQED, *L'Association Québecoise pour L'Education a Domicile,* would be of little help. Diana's French wasn't bad, but she and Michael had long ago decided to educate Anne in English. It had something to do with blood being stronger than water. Presumably, blood of their ancestors.

Next there was the ACHEQ – ACEFQ, the Association of Christian Home Educators of Québec. While this body represented all home-schoolers across the province, regardless of religious affiliation, every member of the Board of Directors had to sign a Statement of Faith and a detailed constitution. Yes, their constitution. As in Magna Carta, or 'We, the people....' What of parents, she thought? What do I have to sign?

She kept looking.

Only then had she discovered that there was an English branch of the AQED, the QAHBE, the Québec Association of Home-Based Education. There were a number of support groups in Montreal. In addition, she had to study the Québec's Education Law, which had its own requirements.

Nevertheless, in three weeks she had it all sorted out. At least the QAHBE – AQED offered support for all parents who chose to educate their children at home, regardless of language, religious affiliation or education philosophy.

Anne settled into home study. In fact, she took to it like a bee to a field of clover. It fitted her personality. It wasn't that at school she had wanted to be better than others. She wasn't really competitive – except with herself. It was more that she suffered from a low tolerance for wilful stupidity. A term which, like most things for Anne, had a very strict definition. At home she seemed happy, if a little restless.

Anne was eight when she embarked on home study, and for the next two years she conducted herself beyond reproach. There were some childish pranks, now and again, but nothing that could be defined as sadistic or in the bullying category. They were childish pranks, even if of a slightly unorthodox nature. Whatever her questionable past, she seemed to have developed an affinity for animals. Maybe she saw herself as a caped crusader, seeking justice for all her mistreated, adopted charges.

On a few occasions she unleashed dogs which had been tied to the trees or guard rails in the park, while their masters went for a hamburger or a pop. It offended her concept of freedom. The errant owners were forced to spend hours looking for their pets. At other times she would tell Fluffy to chase away teenagers who were being rough on squirrels. This sort of thing happened more than once in Mount Royal Park. Fluffy was almost six now, and as big as a Labrador can get. And that's pretty big.

Once, Anne chose to mete out her justice to a pair of very fat boys. They were walking down the street, dragging their obese bodies with them, while munching on double cheeseburgers. Again Fluffy was told to teach them a little exercise by scaring the wits out of them. The two lumps of corpulence dropped their cherished junk-food while Fluffy chased them for half a block. Actually, Fluffy would never have hurt anyone, let alone children, no matter how fat or tasty looking. The big lug was kindness incarnate, but the fat boys didn't know that.

Diana was vaguely aware of her daughter's little games. She invariably accompanied Anne on her walks on Mount Royal; but once there, Diana would sit back with a good book while Anne continued on her escapades. As Fluffy followed her wherever she went, Diana had no qualms about Anne's safety.

Every few minutes, Anne would return with a nebulously triumphant look on her face. When Diana questioned her, she would
give precise half-answers.

"Yes, Mommy, we played with the squirrels," she'd say,
defying Diana to say otherwise.

Fluffy confirmed this statement with vigorous swinging of
his tail.

"But why were the boys running so fast away from you?"

"They weren't, Mommy."

"But I saw them, dear." Diana no longer allowed herself
to become exasperated by her daughter's denials. "I saw you
and the boys. And the boys were running...."

"They were running from Fluffy, Mommy," Anne corrected severely. Of late she did not take kindly to being accused
of misrepresenting facts. Evidently, low bushes had hidden
Fluffy from her mother's line of vision.

Only sometime later did Diana connect the boys and Fluffy
to the squirrels. Learning about any of Anne's pranks was like
pulling teeth. Diana strongly suspected that, in her daughter's
judgment, these were not pranks at all. It was becoming evident
that Anne took on the function of the caped crusader very seriously.

During the last year or two, there had been fewer than a
dozen such occurrences, which appeared to have pushed the envelope of Anne's self-control. And even those incidents
dropped off in frequency once Diana filled Anne's time with
extracurricular activities. They went swimming together. While
Diana was happy splashing in the shallow end of the pool, Anne
insisted on being taught the various strokes. Then she would
practise them until the bell announced the end of the session.
The same was true of her tennis lessons. She didn't have to beat
others, but she had to be the best she was capable of being. She
repeatedly demonstrated an obsession with perfection. But her
critical approach, which at school had been directed at others,
had now swung a full hundred eighty degrees, to point directly
at herself. Or mostly so.

And then, one day, for no apparent reason, Anne complained of a headache. She'd never done that before. After she complained a few more times, Diana took her to their family physician. He didn't help. The headaches continued. Diana decided to call John Brent.

"Without any reason," she said. "We would be walking along and suddenly she would grab her head and tears would run down her cheeks. Don't forget, John, she never cries."

"How often does this happen, Diana?"

"Not once for a whole week, and then two or three times in a row. For the last three days she's been complaining of nausea."

"Did she fall down or hit her head on anything?" he sounded obscurely hopeful.

"No, John. Not that I know about. She'd have told me or there'd be some sort of a bump or scar, wouldn't there?"

"And your physician threw no light on the symptoms at all?" John's tone indicated growing concern. He had had many neurological cases that had begun with unpredictable and unexplained headaches.

"No, John. He thought it might be some sort of allergy, but didn't suggest any treatment other than some analgesics." Diana had much greater faith in John's diagnostic abilities than in those of her family doctor. "You know those quacks only treat symptoms, never the cause."

John didn't say anything for a while. Time dragged on as though he were trying to make up his mind. Finally it came out.

"I can't promise anything, but, if you like, I can arrange a brain scan for Anne. It might not be conclusive, but it might exclude certain possible causes." He consulted his diary. " I could see her tomorrow at six. Would that be all right?"

"I knew you would help," Diana sounded really grateful.

"The fMRI will not heal anything, Diana, but it might help us form a diagnosis."

"Thanks, John. We'll see you tomorrow?"

"Tomorrow then." With that, he hung up.

This was strange about John Brent. He would take as long as needed to help a person, but the moment the matter at hand was done – he would be gone. No good-byes, no see-yous, or good lucks.

John Brent had good reason not to waste time. The new expansion of the hospital was not entirely his to supervise; the purchase of the specialized equipment, however – the selection of the very latest models, examining their specifications that changed almost daily – was his to decide. His daily routine started a little after six a.m. He would clear his paperwork by seven, make a round of the wards, have a quick bite, and spend the rest of the day in the labs or in the operating theatre. Unless he had to attend some meetings, which, of course, he did his best to delegate to his deputy.

The neurosurgical wards were only part of his realm. There was important work being carried out in the nanotechnology wing, of which he liked to keep abreast. This new branch of science advanced knowledge in stem-cell technology. Their results were astounding. John had been asked to allow experiments on primates. He had refused categorically.

"They are the nearest kin we've got. It would be like experimenting on your cousin. Which might not be such a bad idea, at that," he had given the doctor a stern smile. "I met your cousin at last year's Christmas party. He might benefit greatly from your expertise," he'd said with a straight face.

The poor cousin had had one drink too many. John had very low tolerance for people who, though perfectly healthy, tried hard to become his patients. Or anyone's patients. As for primates, John was quite serious. The genome of a chimpanzee was as close to a human as it could be without actually being human. As such, he held, they should be treated as equals. John still allowed some experiments on rats. But that was his absolute limit.

"You have hundreds, perhaps thousands of sick people who might well volunteer to take part in your experiments. People who would die unless you could save them. Put ads in La Presse. The Gazette. In all the papers. But primates? No."

Within two months the research scientist had assembled a respectable group of volunteers. There were a number of strenuous objections from some church groups, bellyaching about the sanctity of human life and such like. Those objections, paradoxically, came from the fundamentalist groups that most vocally supported what our friends down south called 'preventative wars', with their attendant 'collateral damage'. Even more inconsequential, and certainly more entertaining for John, was the fact that the most vocal of the critics appearing on TV abused the sanctity of their own lives by allowing their bodies to become pathologically bloated through evidently uncontrolled overeating. They weren't just fat – they were grotesque. The hypocrisies of their positions didn't seem to matter much to them or their supporters.

"Let the will of the Almighty run its course," a crimson balloon announced, his cheeks almost matching his regalia.

"Ours is not to question why," added his companion sporting an oversized gold cross dangling over his portly paunch. Apparently, penicillin was fine, radiology for cancer was fine, but – no more. Science had gone far enough.

There was also a summons from one family who claimed that a particular volunteer was not capable of making his own decisions. The case was thrown out of court. The young lad in question had a perfectly sane mind. What he also had was a malignant tumour that would guarantee to take his life within months, if untreated. Not that the treatment would be necessarily successful, but at least there would be a chance.

John was kept busy on all fronts at the same time.

Anne's inexplicable headaches brought Diana, once again, to question her own moral fibre. She seriously wondered if she oughtn't to begin, or really resume, attending the local church. She visited it one day, just to see what it felt like. The silence was inviting. But for a tiny sacral red light, there was no sign of divine intervention. Real or imagined. The church could be filled with whatever she chose. With hope, or faith, or prayer. Or utter indifference. She wondered why the latter was the strongest sensation she had felt.

She eased into a pew close to the middle of the nave. She wanted to be surrounded by the Presence. Instead her nose picked up the remnants of incense mixed with a whiff of stale perspiration. Apart from that, there was a sensation of mildly damp coolness. No love. No passion or compassion. No forgiveness. She wondered if any of those exuded any aroma. If they could be detected by the sense of smell? Or any other sense?

The last time John Brent had come to dinner, he had told her about Dr. Richard Axel, who had just became a Nobel Prize Laureate for his work in physiology and medicine. Apparently the good doctor had said that at the tip of each cell in our nose there are molecular receptors which pick up tens of thousands of chemical smells. He'd called it chemosensory recognition.

"Doctor Axel tells us that individual olfactory sensory neurons express only one of a thousand receptor genes."

She had no idea what that meant.

The usual receptors, John had explained, those dealing with food or predators or possibly mating, convey information to the cognitive brain for analysis and responses. But there is a vast array of chemosensory receptors that are connected to the emotive brain. This input bypasses our conscious awareness. It reaches and controls our subconscious. Or something like that.

Smell controlling our subconscious? Are we just puppets serving our body? Mere observers, destined not to steer but to shut up and listen?

Diana couldn't believe that. She'd often had memories or emotions triggered by smells. Unremembered associations that made her feel nostalgic for something she'd never normally think about and couldn't begin to put into words.

Now, sitting on the hard pew, polished to a high gloss by years of human bodies, Diana wondered what inputs her subconscious was getting right now. Perhaps Spirit also exuded some sort of aroma, directly to her chemosensory receptors in her subconscious. Perhaps saintliness discharged a pleasing smell, and evil reeked of vile decadence. Perhaps people exuded a multitude of odours which only some of us could pick up with our olfactory equipment.

Michael smelled good. So did Anne. Even Fluffy was pleasing to her nose. But here? Here there was a smell of yesterday. Of something long gone.

Once, the church served to build my dreams. As a little girl, I asked for whatever I needed. It didn't matter if it worked. If my prayers failed, maybe it was not meant to be. 'Thy will be done....' Thy will be done. It was a statement of resignation. Of submission, like the Moslems are supposed to offer to their Allah. No matter how inconvenient. How seemingly cruel. Am I a wimp swaying in the wind, the breath of an Almighty Monarch, the King of Heaven, whose Will overrides all I've ever desired? Is this what God is supposed to be? Are we just pawns swaying in the currents at the discretion of a God who allows murder and mayhem throughout the world? And what of the starving children? What of the tens of thousands murdered in the name of collateral damage? What of . . . there are so many imponderables. So many....

Perhaps Dr. Axel was right. We just follow our noses. Wherever they might lead us. Gravitating towards eventual death, like dung beetles towards piles of manure.

But I'd gladly return to this, prostrate myself before that central cross suspended over the altar, and beg for Anne to get well. To be well. What's missing is faith. I lost that when my father died. Died unnecessarily. In an accident that could have been so easily avoided. I never prayed so ardently as then. If there was such a thing as Divine Intervention, as Infinite Love, my father would be alive today. No. Faith is lost irretrievably. I didn't give up on God. He gave up on me. No faith and very little hope. What remains is this lingering, churning sense of guilt. It would come in the early hours, when Michael turned over in bed... Those times when I shut my eyes tight and see myself drifting without a rudder, being carried by a stream, a river against my will. In such moments I scream silently for guidance, for a sign of which way to go, where to go....

Next morning the dreams are a shallow memory. I get up, shower, get dressed, prepare breakfast. And look after Anne.

*All day. All my waking moments. Annie's the only reason for
my life. Even Michael is sometimes a distant second place. But I
can always count on him. Michael's the only stable element in
my life. Without him?*

She refused even to think about it.

At ten-to-six in the evening, Diana and Anne entered the ornate
door at the west entrance of the Montreal Neurological Institute.
At the mention of Dr. Brent's name, a young man detached
himself from the reception desk and approached Diana.

"My name is Doctor Brown. Doctor Peter Brown. Doctor
Brent asked me to take you up to his office."

John was not in. Dr. Brown left them in the Director's office and went in search of his boss. The interns were always glad
to ingratiate themselves to the Director.

"I'm sure he won't be long," he said before departing.

He wasn't. John burst into his office like a gust of wind,
picked Anne up in his arms, kissed her on both cheeks and said:
"Let's go and take a picture." He then spun on his heels towards Diana. "You want to come along, Diana? Only please,
don't touch anything," he added half seriously.

Usually he would delegate the fMRI to one of his assistants,
particularly Dr. Brown, who was certainly competent. But this
was Anne. And Diana might feel very uncomfortable to see
someone else peering into Anne's brain. Michael was one of his
oldest friends. And a good one. Mike had helped him when he
was cramming for exams, had been like a brother to him. They
had shared their digs. Mike did most of the shopping, the cooking and the cleaning up. Now it was John's turn. He was glad
he could help. He only hoped that the gods of Olympus would
be kind to the little girl. John knew that Anne meant the world
to his friend.

The magnetic resonance imagery equipment was located
two floors below John's office. Rather than wait for an elevator,
John led the way down the stairs, practically sliding the last three
in each flight. Diana'd never seen him so agile. At dinners in

her home he seemed to switch to a different gear. Or perhaps he just idled in neutral. But at the rate he moved through the hospital, she understood why he didn't need any sports or exercise to keep fit. She was sure he climbed the steps two, probably even three at a time.

The lab looked impressive.

Diana looked so nervous that John asked her to stay behind the glass partition. She could see and hear Anne examining the machine, while Uncle John explained to her how it worked. On occasion parents were allowed to come into the actual examination room, but today it wasn't the patient but the parent who showed signs of acute nervousness.

"Relax, Diana," John had whispered to her just before following Anne inside. "MRI uses radio waves and a strong magnetic field rather than X-rays to provide a detailed scan of the brain. There is absolutely no danger, no side effects. Take a deep breath and relax." With that he'd disappeared through the door, only to reappear on the other side of a glass partition.

Dr. Brown had already made sure that Anne wore no braces, nor partook of the peculiar habit that girls had – even at Anne's age – of piercing their faces, eyebrows, noses, lips or even tongues with scraps of metal. Any such would affect the magnetic resonance of the device. In no time at all Anne lay down on a sliding table, her head held in a brace designed to hold it still.

Diana looked away. She still thought that computers were evil, or at the very least untrustworthy, monsters designed to confuse people; and hospital equipment, these days, looked and felt even more so. Even though she was fully aware that her attitude was quite irrational. Emotional? She vaguely heard Anne being asked to tap the thumb of one hand against each of the fingers of that hand, and then rub a block of sandpaper. She then seemed to be answering a few simple questions.

What was the point of all this? If we are puppets of an invisible, uncaring God who plays with our bodies, our minds, even our hearts, then what is the point of all this? We can try, do our very best only to end up at the other end of the vicious

circle. We are born, we suffer and we die. Buddha was right.
Life is defined by the suffering one undergoes. When you stop
suffering, it only means that you're dead. And in itself, if a beast
lurks within us, such must be the will of Him that created us.

"Mrs. Howell?" Dr. Brown was leaning over her.

Unwittingly Diana shook her head. "Yes, doctor, what is it?
Is it over already?"

"Not at all. We just thought that you might want to watch
the procedure inside?"

Diana stood up and followed Peter Brown inside the scanning room. John was staring at some instrumentation, another of
those infernal computers. 'There I go again,' she thought. 'Infernal machines that might save her....' she couldn't finish the
thought. Anne was lying, perfectly still, her head inside a round
tunnel. She must have heard them come in.

"Hello, Mommy?" she said and wiggled her toes.

"Don't move, Anne. Not yet, would you?" John asked,
sounding serious.

"All right, Uncle John," she confirmed.

"She can talk during the examination?" Diana was aghast.

"She has to. We are also checking her speech centres," Dr.
Brown told her. "Please sit down. Make yourself comfortable."

Hardly. There were two straight-backed chairs and a simple
table next to one of them. She sat at the table and followed John
Brent's movements. After the display of agility a minute ago, he
now showed an amazing economy of motion. His head didn't
move while his arms and fingers played with a large console in
front of him. He was all concentration. Diana wouldn't have
been surprised if he hadn't even noticed her come in.

"Hi, Di. Won't be long now," he said, still without moving
his head. Apparently he was very much aware of everything
around him.

Diana hated being useless or inactive. In one of Joseph
Campbell's books she'd read that women must *be* while men
must *do*. As far as she was concerned, Campbell was wrong.

She definitely needed to *do*. *Being* she left to holidays, when lying idle in the sun didn't fill her with guilt. She realized that all too often, recently, she experienced unpredictable pangs of guilt. She wondered if they might be genetic or imposed on her by her upbringing or even the environment. She didn't steal, or lie, or do any of the things forbidden by the Mosaic Law, yet she was persecuted by this unrelenting sense of guilt.

"That will do for now," John said, getting up from his stool. At long last the furrow of concentration left his forehead. "There you are, as good as new," he joked, picking Anne up and putting her on Diana's lap. "How about you, Diana? Would you like to have your picture taken?"

"I would like to be home, John. I'll thank you properly the next time you come to see us. Now I must run. Don't be offended, but your place," her arm swept the room, "gives me the creeps. I'm expecting Dr. Frankenstein to walk through the door any minute, followed by his creation, the monster."

Anne smiled, then laughed.

"Dr. Frankenstein didn't create the monster, Mommy. The monster created Dr. Frankenstein. Without the monster, no one would ever hear about Dr. Frankenstein. He would just be a doctor. Like Uncle John."

"Have heard, dear. No one would ever have heard...."

John Brent smiled his farewells.

Diana took Anne by the hand and walked towards the elevator. Even as she pressed the down button, she saw John running for the stairs. He was in a hurry.

* * * * *

Chapter 5

Escape

Michael Howell was an excellent engineer. As a partner in a firm of structural engineers, he was instrumental in many Montreal buildings looking light, elegant, and eminently stable. He had once read that architecture could be defined by three attributes. It had to have firmness, commodity and delight. The first was his domain. He was responsible for its firmness, its inherent stability. As for delight, well, the architect couldn't achieve much of that if he, Michael Howell, the engineer, didn't provide him with the means to achieve his ends. If an architect dreamed up delightful shapes, Michael had to make them work.

He loved his job.

Physically, Michael was the antithesis of John Brent. John was tall and lanky, athletic, with hair dishevelled unto the image and likeness of a long line of Einsteins. Michael didn't have an ounce of athleticism in him. A little too short, with the promise of an early stoop which further diminished his stature, not fat but already a trifle paunchy. His hair, graying at the temples, was cropped to within an inch of his scalp. Had the two friends had comedic proclivities, they would have made an ideal duo. Like Abbott and Costello, or Laurel and Hardy. John was spontaneous, outgoing, a bundle of energy, wry humour exuding from every pore. Michael was a confirmed introvert. He tended towards silence. An ideal straight man. Sharing his innermost feelings was painful to him. Even Diana had a problem finding out what was really eating at him, on occasion. "It's nothing, darling," he would say, dismissing the matter out of hand.

Whatever he felt was invariably hard to tell. For strangers, near impossible. He did have his moments of spontaneity, but rarely. If you were to meet him at a party, it would be difficult to get a feel for who Michael really was.

Notwithstanding all of the above, there were times when Michael would toss and turn all night, unable to sleep. Those were the moments when Diana, woken in the wee hours, would also drift into her nether lands, in which her apparently inherent sense of guilt came to the forefront of her mind.

At the conscious level, Michael never allowed his gloomy side to come to the foreground. He kept tight reins on the beast that lurked in the dark corners of his mind. He had to. For him the world was pretty much black and white. It was either good or bad, either right or wrong. Since, apart from his professional life, he did not consider himself competent to pass judgment on most things, he preferred to give problems a wide berth, and suspend his judgment until evidence presented itself to make an informed decision. This philosophy had served him well until recently.

Anne's behaviour, or suspected behaviour, did not lend itself to black and white interpretations. She was so good at so many things, yet there had been moments that threatened to wipe out all her achievements, all her beautiful, positive traits, and move her to the negative side of the equation. For Michael, life was an assortment of equations. He applied the expertise he had developed in his professional life to the rest of his reality. A building would either stand up or fall down. Sure, there were a number of different structural systems he could design, but ultimately, the equations had to add up to stability. There was no room for error. For compromise. No question of 'maybe' they will stand up. Anne just wasn't that simple.

Thanks to Diana, he was kept once removed from the day-to-day problems which Anne had created. All too often, seeing how hard Michael took any of Anne's presumed transgressions, Diana kept them from her husband. She chose to share such with him only when a ready-made counter-argument was available.

"Dr. Schneider insists it's only a passing phase. It's nothing to worry about."

Michael believed her. He had to. The alternative would
have destroyed him. In business, Michael could be as tough as
any man, but when it came to his only daughter, he was that
fragile. He didn't just love her. From the day she was born, he
was in love with her. And lately, somewhere at the back of his
mind, there was that recurrent nagging question. Why doesn't
Anne ever cry? It seemed unnatural.

Home schooling was a godsend to him. He could call
home during the day, morning and afternoon, hear Anne's
voice, and return relaxed to his work. Diana also seemed happy.
The system worked well enough for almost two years. Next year
Anne would start her first year in high school, and the immedi-
acy of contact inherent in home schooling would be gone.
There had been moments when Michael hoped his daughter
would never grow up. He imagined, as do many parents.

"You will always be Daddy's little girl," he told her. "Always," he would stress again, as if anyone could ever doubt it.

And now Anne had had her brain examined at the MNI.
Thank God John was there to look after her. Michael knew he
could trust him. He would never admit that he was afraid to go
to the hospital. Afraid of what? Of his weakness? Of not pre-
senting to strangers the strong father image Anne and Diana
must have expected of him? He wasn't sure. He tried to dismiss
self-analysis till later. If ever. It wasn't really in his nature to
dwell on his own shortcomings. He would concentrate on Anne.
On positive thoughts. It was indeed lucky that he had taught
himself to suspend judgment until hearing the complete results.
But this time it was much harder not to speculate. He forcefully
dismissed the matter from his mind by burying himself in his
work. All would be well, he kept telling himself. It had to be.
Though Michael would never admit it, he held a strong conviction that the world was a benign place, that universal laws were
not designed to make life hell on earth, but rather to guide people towards order and compatibility. A single look at a night
sky proved that. The stars would have smashed into each other

long ago if it hadn't been for such order. And, at his level of
perception, there was also beauty. A black and white sort of
beauty. Derived from the order inherent in the universe.

And then, in spite of all that was good and orderly, his
world collapsed. On the morning of November 17th, exactly a
week after Anne's 10th birthday, and three days after her visit to
the Montreal Neurological Institute, his only daughter disappeared. She had gone out with Fluffy for a walk, as she had
every morning and, an hour later, Fluffy had come back alone.
Diana walked the local streets for hours trying to find her. She
imagined the worst. Anne had been hit by a car, she thought.
Someone had found her body and taken it to the police. She
had been kidnapped. She was....
    At last she called Michael.
    "I don't know what to do, I just don't...."
    "Did you call the police?"
    "You think I should?"
    "Yes, dear. Call me back after you give them all the de-
tails. All right? I'll hang up, now. Do it right away, all right,
Di?"
    It took all his will not to slam the receiver down and speed
home. Instead he sat back and took a deep breath. He had to
reason this out. The ever cool and collected Mike didn't feel
cool and collected at all.
    Why would a ten-year-old girl, taking a walk with her fa-
vourite dog, disappear in the early morning on a dull November
day? There is a reason, a cause – for everything. All he had to
do was find it. Each action has an equal and opposite reaction.
He picked up the phone and dialled John Brent's number. His
friend wasn't in. "I'll call you as soon as I can," said the message on John's very private answering machine. He didn't leave
a message and hung up.
    The phone rang; it was Diana. She had reported the inci-
dent, and had been promised that if Anne didn't come back
within a few hours, they would come round to speak to her.
Would Mrs. Howell prepare some recent photos for them? A list
of friends she might visit would also help. Also a list of Anne's

favourite places, of friends she liked more than others. Things like that.

Diana said that she would. That she had them right here. Now. Why wait a few hours? We have no one available right now, Madam. Please call us again if there are any changes.

The next two hours were the toughest in Michael's life. Four times he left his desk to go home. Four times an urgent telephone stopped him short. As he got up for the fifth time the telephone rang again. This time it was his friend. Had Michael been more relaxed, he would have detected the strain in John's voice. But his subconscious smelled a rat.

"I was going to come round tonight, Mike. I was hoping you would feed me?" His tone sounded hopeful.

"Anne's disappeared," Michael said outright.

There was a momentary silence. "Explain."

"She went out for a walk with Fluffy and didn't come back. That was somewhere around eight this morning. About five hours ago. Diana's called the police."

"I'll come over tonight," John said. There was little else he could do at this moment.

"Thank you John, I appreciate your concern. I'll see you later," he said and hung up.

Anne had told Fluffy to go straight home. Not to bark at any-one, nor stop to talk to any other dogs, nor to chase any cats, but to go straight home. With that she'd turned on her heels and walked down the street.

For three days she'd been accumulating money. She was as methodical in this endeavour as in anything else she set her mind to. She found cash in the kitchen drawer, in the jar behind the cans of soup on the lower shelf in the kitchen, and in the drawer of Mommy's bedside table. She put together over $200 and thought it would last her for a good long time. She would eat very little and she could sleep in the warm nooks of buildings like banks and churches and even in some office buildings. She was little and would fit into a broom closet before anyone even noticed.

She had decided to run away when she'd overheard Dr. Brown and Uncle John discussing drilling a hole in her head and extracting something bad; she didn't understand that part.

What she also hadn't understood was that the two surgeons had been discussing someone else's head.

"No one is going to make holes in my head," she'd decided there and then.

She had to act quickly. She didn't know how long Uncle John would take to decide about when to drill a hole, but she assumed she had a day or two. She'd heard her parents discussing the ever-growing waiting lists in all the hospitals, all waiting for operations. Weeks and weeks, they'd said. Sometimes months. She assumed that Uncle John would find a way to fit her in sooner; after all, she still had a relatively small head, but a few days would allow her to organize her escape.

In addition to the money, she'd squirreled away lots of nuts, a few roughly put together sandwiches, two apples, long, warm underwear and an extra scarf in case the wind blew too hard. She recalled how, last winter, mother had wrapped an extra scarf around her mouth and forehead, leaving just a gap for her eyes. She carried all her belongings in a backpack. She had no idea how long she would have to stay away from home, but she suspected that after a few days, weeks at most, they would forget all about drilling some silly holes. In her head or anywhere else. She liked herself just the way she was.

It seemed simple enough.

It wasn't.

Anne walked till she descended to Sherbrooke Street, an arterial route running practically the whole east/west axis of Montreal. There she hopped on a bus. So far, for some reason, whenever her mother took her to visit someone, they'd always travelled west. Diana had friends in NDG, or Notre Dame de Grace on maps, where Anne had played with some of her friends while her mother compared notes on raising children with other mothers. Today Anne went east. After a dozen bus stops, she decided she'd ridden far enough not to be traced by whoever might look for her. She was going to protect her head at all costs. She remembered her address in Westmount, where she could return when she felt sufficiently safe. She got off the bus at St. Urbain, and walked another two blocks further east, just in case someone had decided to follow her. Just before 9 a.m., she arrived at another Montreal axis, St. Laurent. The Main, as some call it, which runs north/south. For no reason, she turned north.

Functional Magnetic Resonance Imaging is a very precise method applied to a very inexact science. To procure exact results, the scientists are faced with a set of challenges. No amount of reading material can substitute for hands-on experience. The neurosurgeon, who ideally should be a physicist as well as a physician, has to relate abstract concepts to clinical applications. The technology, which forced its way into the realm of medicine, was literally overwhelming. The old fashioned stethoscope, still proudly dangling from physicians' white collars, was now little more than an intern's toy designed for very preliminary examinations. This invaluable instrument of the recent past has been replaced by an army of complex electronic applications that no one short of an expert in physics and computer sciences could begin to understand. Tests, countless tests and analyses, performed by specialised equipment replaced the old diagnostic tools. All too often, they replaced common sense.

One of the simpler things the attending surgeon has to do is control the table the patient is lying on. It has to be adjusted constantly to assure an even distribution of blood, compensating for any of the patient's physiological or emotional changes.

The human brain requires 15% of total blood flow, about 700 millilitres per minute, although the whole brain accounts for just 2% of our body weight. To confuse the things still further, the gray matter in the brain receives several times more blood per gram of tissue than white matter. Unless the blood flow is maintained, the reading might well produce erroneous results.

Three days after Anne's scan, Dr. Brown presented Dr. Brent with his conclusions. Anne had a minor tumour in her frontal lobe, just behind her left eye, in the part of her brain that deals with problem solving, emotions and planning.

That evening, after drawing no new information about Anne's disappearance, John was forced to add to his friends' problems.

Michael and Diana sat speechless while he made his announcement. Their daughter? A brain tumour? It can't be. It just cannot be! There had to be some mistake. Anne was as normal as... just how normal was Anne? They each recalled the long series of events that did not follow the, so-called, normal behaviour of a child. And then, there was that strange absence of tears. Anger, even what seemed cold methodical revenge, but no tears.

Michael recovered first. He swallowed hard before asking in a reasonably steady voice: "Is it malignant?"

"We don't think so. It is still very small. We have a good chance of getting rid of if. Anne could be as good as new, in no time at all."

John lied, just a little. Between 30 and 40 percent of benign tumours were curable. There were many treatments possible. They included surgery, radiation therapy and chemotherapy. Alone or in combination.

"To tell you the truth," John leaned forward, "what we should do is to take a complete medical history and perform a thorough neurological examination. I'd also like to narrow down the odds by taking other scans. A computed tomography and, if possible, the PET scan. That's the positronic emission tomography which takes x-ray pictures of the particular area of the brain," he added unnecessarily.

Unnecessarily, because Diana and Michael weren't really listening. They were still trying to recover from his first announcement. Yet, what else could he have said?

If left unattended, benign tumours had a nasty habit of turning malignant. He certainly wouldn't tell them that, of patients with malignant or cancerous growths, only 60% survived over five years. But time was of the essence. The brain is a very delicate instrument. There was no need to worry his friends unnecessarily. Certainly not at this stage. Only a biopsy would provide the final answer. In Anne's case the area of the brain was critical. It would have to be a needle biopsy. A stereotactic biopsy would allow him to take a sample of the tumour while disturbing very little of the brain tissue. An experienced pathologist would determine the exact type and grade or aggressiveness of the tumour.

Even as he finished telling them about the treatment options, a single tear began to descend, in absurdly slow motion, down Diana's cheek. Michael sat down next to her, on the settee, and held her head close to his chest. John had had this conversation countless times with patients he'd long since forgotten, but tonight he felt especially helpless and awkward. He sipped his tea and kept his eyes down.

"There now, Di. John will take care of her. Anne's in the best hands possible."

But she wasn't.

About this time Anne was beginning to feel the cold of the evening. She was walking down *rue St. Laurent* looking for a spot to hide herself before the approaching night. By now, the police had been given all the information they needed to conduct a citywide search. They had pictures, even some of her clothing for the police dogs to sniff, should the occasion present itself. So far, no one had thought of looking for her anywhere near St. Laurent. After all, she'd never been there. And it seemed too far for a ten year-old to travel alone, especially one who had spent the last two years in home schooling, only leaving her immediate neighbourhood with her mother. Why would she want to hide in a place so strange, so unfamiliar? And that was assuming she was hiding and hadn't just been kidnapped. Perhaps a ransom note would come. Soon. In a way, it would make things easier. The Howells were reasonably wealthy. Most people in Upper Westmount were.

"We all pay for our lot in life," the sergeant in charge of the search thought. There was a time when he was jealous of the

Upper Westmounters. Now he knew better. Fate had a strange way of extracting particular payments from people for the life they led. It seems impersonal, uncaring; yet, in a peculiar way, it also tended to equalize our modes of life. Like nature. The bigger your house, the more you lose in a fire. The more assets you have invested, the more you lose if the stock market collapses.

Even then, on that first evening, Anne began to have doubts about her decision. What's a hole or two extra, she kidded herself. I've already got... she started counting her eyes, nose, mouth and ears. I already have seven holes in my head. Although eyes are not really holes, she decided. Even so, perhaps one more wouldn't do much harm. She was almost ready to give up when a nice-looking man put a very gentle hand on her shoulder.

"Would you like a warm cup of cocoa, dear?" he asked. His face was round and angelic, with rosy cheeks. His open smile inspired confidence.

"I think I would like that, sir," Anne admitted. It really was getting cold and she had already eaten two of her three sandwiches.

"Then come along, deary. Come along, now."

And she did. She had never been called 'deary' before. And a hot chocolate was a very tempting offer. By that time, she'd been outdoors for more than eight hours, and her toes were beginning to hurt. In fact, she was tired all over. She really wanted that hot chocolate. And this man seemed nice, and getting out of the cold sounded so nice. She knew she probably shouldn't, but perhaps the isolation of home-schooling had made her too trusting or, with no enemies to fight, she had become too confident of her own powers.

The man who picked her up said his name was George. "Like Saint George," he said. "The man who slew the dragon, remember?" His smile was wide, showing none-too-white teeth.

"Do you have biscuits?" Anne began to feel better.

"Lots and lots," he assured her.

In no time at all, they had arrived at a three-story walk-up. The man led the way and Anne followed obediently. "Let me take your coat, deary." The man reached out for her outer clothing. "There – you sit yourself down and don't worry about a thing. Your Uncle George will look after you."

She wondered again why he continued calling her 'deary'. It sounded foreign, but it also sounded friendly. Right then, Anne was ready to tell him that he was no Uncle of hers, but she thought better of it. I'll tell him after the hot chocolate, she thought. Then I'll take a few biscuits and go back home. Perhaps they've forgotten about making a hole in my head. It was a silly idea, after all. Who ever heard of making holes in people's heads?

But she didn't go back. Not for quite a while.

One other thing happened about that time. Lately the media had been full of articles and TV programs about the International Chemical Combines making billions of dollars from feeding people pills which had neither been thoroughly tested, nor proven to be free from long term adverse effects. The result was a very profitable but vicious cycle of more drugs to counteract the side-effects of the original drugs. Earlier that day there had been actual street riots in front of the Pharmaceutical Conglomerates by people whose families had suffered from these side effects. There seemed to be an incredible number of them. People, that is.

"The do-gooders," Peter Brown mused, "or the social activists, I believe they call themselves."

Dr Brent, after dining at the Howells', was taking a rare quiet moment. He and his assistant were watching the late news in the cafeteria while Peter ate his supper.

This particular series of events will have a very direct effect on Anne's future. But that comes later. Much later.

* * * * *

Chapter 6

Surgery

When the police broke into the St. Laurent walk-up apartment, Anne was already gone. That was in the first week of March. For almost four months, Anne had been kept there, against her will, and forced to satisfy the perverse fantasies of the sad, depraved, sick man, Saint George.

To make sure she behaved, George told Anne that he and his friends had kidnapped her mother and would do terrible things to her, including kill her, if Anne tried to escape or didn't do as she was told. To play safe, the room she was kept in had a sheet of thick plastic screwed to the window frame, and the door was double-locked. There was no toilet in the room, so she was given a ceramic chamber-pot, decorated with an elaborate flower design. The first thing George did each and every day on his return to the apartment was to check the content of the pot and, if used, he would transport it with flourish, as though carrying a relic of a dear departed saint, to the bathroom. He would return a half-hour later and place it with reverence next to Anne's bed.

Evidently George's sickness had many facets.

Once a day George escorted Anne to that same bathroom and would watch her like a hawk while she brushed her teeth and washed, or used the toilet. The single stroke of luck for Anne was that George was principally a voyeur and, more often than not, was satisfied with just observing Anne's naked body while she moved according to his instructions. To move seductively, in front of his hungry eyes.

All days were about the same. The same breakfast, the morning rite with the chamber-pot, repeat of the same on his return, another meal and finally the long, protracted ceremony of Anne undressing for bed. Often she would be told to dress again and again, only to remove her clothing before him afresh. The days all ended with the bathroom ablutions under his supervision. Days passed without George touching her, as though he were afraid of catching a disease from her tiny body. She was quite unaware of the demons that tortured his mind. When driven by them, he forced Anne to watch him while he masturbated himself. Apparently her presence stimulated and ultimately mollified his insatiable hunger. He needed her innocence, her youth, even her very presence. Her vapid stare seemed to stimulate him still further, as though driving him to find a way to extract a reaction from her. Had Anne been older, she would have realized that she had been held prisoner by a man as lonely as she'd felt when first becoming aware that the door to the outside world had been shut. Yet in that same moment, she entered a state of mind she hadn't felt since her early schooldays, when she imposed her will on some of her peers. It was in that moment that she started plotting, methodically, her eventual escape. She made a careful note of the limited means at her disposal. She scrutinized objects in her room, in the bathroom, even those lying about in the kitchen, though she had no access there. She knew intuitively that only total detachment would guide her to freedom. It never crossed her mind that George, Uncle George, would remain forever in the dungeon ruled by his demons.

Anne escaped on her own. Practically naked, she walked up to an officer who happened to be smoking a cigarette in a police cruiser parked in front of a doughnut shop. She told him that she was cold. The officer's first reaction was that the girl was soliciting. He was ready to arrest her, when he glanced up at his dashboard, where a photocopy of Anne's likeness was still pinned with three others. His jaw dropped. He invited her into his car, gave her his own jacket, and telephoned his precinct. Half an hour later he knocked on the Howells' front door.

In the meantime, three squad cars with six policemen surrounded the front and back of the address Anne had given them, only to find George practically bleeding to death. The police had saved his life, but he would never harm another child. Anne had made sure of that. She was quite unaware that, in the exact sense of the word, he'd never physically abused her at all. Yet, at the time, she saw no other object on which to vent her injured sense of justice. He was lying on the floor in a pool of his own blood. The portion of his anatomy, which he used to satisfy his cravings, now lay some distance away, looking quite harmless. A single, rusty razor blade was also lying on the floor, next to the door. A razor blade Anne had found in a small waste-bin in the bathroom, over two weeks ago, in that rare moment when George had turned his back on her. She palmed scraps of toilet paper, wrapping single sheets of tissue around the blade into a semblance of a handle. She was very patient about it. Her loathing mixed with fear gave her strength. For nineteen days she'd awaited her opportunity to seek justice.

"Serves you right, you son of a bitch," the sergeant said, delivering a kick to the man's bloody crotch, now deprived of its most sensitive element. "Serves you right, you creep," the sergeant repeated through clenched teeth. He was a father of a girl about Anne's age.

There was no warning, no call, no inkling of what was about to take place. The police thought it best to let the mother identify her lost daughter, lest they'd made a mistake and raised false hopes. Diana stood at the door, her mouth open, allowing the policeman to lead Anne inside. Stupor and relief. Fluffy let out a yelp, halfway between a bark and a wail, and ran to hide under Anne's bed. He'd spent a lot of his time there during the last few months.

For the first few days Anne refused to discuss any aspect of her absence. She had been an unusually taciturn child before,

and now she had turned into a mute. She would say all the perfunctory phrases like 'good morning' and 'good bye', even
'please' and 'thank you', but little more. She didn't seem to
have been injured, in any way, though Diana took great care to
inspect her, surreptitiously, during her first long soak in the
bathtub. She considered taking her to the hospital, just in case.
But the look in Anne's eyes discouraged any such idea. Anne
needed to be home. Her home, and nowhere else.

Anne hadn't even lost any weight. What was really missing
was the sparkle in her eye. Her glorious eyes were now shaded,
as though dwelling some distance away, extant in a half-life of
an elusive reality. Outwardly she appeared fine. Quiet but fine.
To Diana and Michael, she was a small remnant of the daughter
they'd once had. The larger part was still missing.

"She'll be back," Michael repeated daily, stroking Diana's
hair. In a way, his wife had also become a child. "You will see,
Di. She'll come back." But after three weeks he also began to
lose hope. Neither Diana nor Michael thought about the tumour. It was too real, too scary. They'd only just gotten their
daughter back; they certainly weren't ready to put her at risk
again.

"You really shouldn't delay," John Brent told them. "At
least let me finish the diagnosis," he begged.

"No, John. Not yet. Let her get settled again."

John Brent continued to telephone the Howells daily. He
spoke to Diana or Michael, whoever picked up the receiver. He
didn't always talk about the proposed treatments, but he always
hoped to hear that there was a change in Anne's behaviour. Dr.
Schneider had been consulted three times. Each time she'd said
that Anne needed time.

"Time – and lots of love," she repeated in her kind, sym-
pathetic voice designed to relax wrought-up nerves. "That's the
best you can do. I could give her pills to relax her, but, as you
can see, she's almost too relaxed.... Give her time," she repeated.

Dr. Schneider had had two previous cases of child abuse.
One improved after two years. The other committed suicide.
She didn't tell them that.

By the end of March, Anne hadn't improved, and her lack of emotional engagement was starting to wear on her parents. They went through the motions of everyday life but had put their feelings aside. They did what they ought to, as well as what they thought they should, and left the rest of their private world to unfold itself. If Anne needed time, she would get it. If she needed love, she got all the external manifestations of it. She was held, cuddled, her hair was stroked, her cheeks kissed, her every desire granted. But there was never any response, and she hardly had any desires. She was nice, she almost smiled. Like a mask smiles on an android in a science-fiction movie. She wasn't quite alive, she wasn't quite dead. She was in abeyance. Only Fluffy seemed content to have Anne back, but even he kept a precautionary distance. At least he'd stopped wailing.

On April 3rd, Diana took Anne to the Montreal Neurological Institute. Anne raised no objections. When Diana asked her if she was sure she wanted to go to see Uncle John, she only nodded.

"Are you quite sure, pet?" Diana pressed.

She nodded again.

John Brent came down himself. It broke his heart to see Diana in such distress. Her face was lined; eyes appeared to have sunk deeper into her face. She seemed to have aged by a decade during those five months. John knew he couldn't cure Anne of her ailment, but at least he could try to extend her life, and allow her youthful resilience to heal her. To enable her to heal herself. Isn't this what ultimately we all do? We just help our bodies do what they have to do. We can give them the ammunition. The strength.

"Medicine cures, the body heals," he recalled one of his professors from the final year of his medical studies. I must help her to heal herself, he thought with determination.

This time Anne was admitted to the ward, though he told her that she could come and play in his office whenever she wanted to. He needed Anne to be under professional observation, twenty-four-hours a day. At least for a little while. He had to be 100% sure of his diagnosis.

During the next few days, Anne underwent all the available tests. By the end of the week, John and three of his colleagues had confirmed their preliminary suspicions. Anne's left frontal lobe had developed a minor tumour. It was of a magnitude that could be practically ignored in any other part of her body but, regrettably, it was located in the most active and important part of her brain. Even its nominal pressure could be responsible for mood changes, unpredictable behaviour, or any number of personality disorders. They decided to perform the operation as soon as possible. That evening he visited his old friends. He brought Anne back home with him.

"I've brought you a surprise," he said, trying to lighten the mood. He was hiding Anne behind his back.

Anne smiled the perfunctory smile. "Hello," she said.

Diana embraced her and hugged her, and Michael did the same. But there was little joy in their reunion. The motions were all there, all correct, yet all lacked spontaneity. They both looked exhausted and heart-broken that Anne wasn't happier to see them. Poor bastards, John thought. He was a surgeon. He had no idea how to help them.

The moment supper was over, Anne looked at her mother who nodded, allowing Anne to leave the table. Fluffy also rose from under the table and escorted her dutifully to her room. It all happened in a total silence that dragged out for a minute or two. In fact, during the entire meal hardly anyone had spoken. John had made a few feeble attempts to raise any number of subjects, only for each of them to trickle into apparent indifference. Finally, with Anne disappearing into her bedroom, John raised his arms in a dramatic gesture.

"We have very good news," he announced. "We are ninety-nine percent sure that the tumour is benign. We have very little to worry about. And a great deal might be gained."

For a moment Diana's eyes lit up with long pent-up hope. Then another cloud passed over them. "Ninety-nine...?"

"That's what surgeons always say. Only God is one-hundred percent right!" This was again an attempt at humour. No one laughed.

"Will she recover from her..." she stopped when she saw Anne sitting curled up on the settee in the living room. The double doors to the dining room were wide open. Anne must have returned almost immediately, her steps deadened by the pile carpet. Fluffy remained at the doorway, some distance from her. His placid eyes followed her every move, but he still didn't curl up with her as he did before. His tail gave half-hearted wags: occasional signs of life.

"We really can't be sure," John lowered his voice. "If you're talking about her, ah . . . present condition. We don't really know." He was searching for the right words. "We have no way of knowing how much of this is being caused by the tumour and how much by the abduction." He glanced nervously at Anne. She hadn't heard. "What we do know is that removing it can only help her, and that time is of the essence." He let that sink in.

"When?" Michael asked.

"We could take her next Tuesday. Would that be all right?"

Michael looked at Diana. Her eyes rested absently on Anne's face, who in turn was looking at Fluffy. She didn't react.

"I suppose so, John. I suppose so." He felt helpless. It seemed as if in spite of Diana and Anne and even John, he was all alone. Deserted by those nearest to him.

Anne's tumour was of the meningioma variety, which is non-malignant, and which arises from the membrane that lines the skull and encloses the brain. It would be a particularly delicate operation because of its hazardous location, not its type per se. Any damage to the frontal lobe could result in severe personality disorders, impaired thought processes, and even interfere with the ability to cope with ordinary, everyday events.

John's team included physicians with expertise in neuropathology, neurosurgery, neurology, neuroradiology and radiation oncology. Those last were only needed if there was any chance of latent malignancy. Following detailed examination of all the evidence, they were ready to remove Anne's tumour. Dr. Brent would be the leading neurosurgeon, with four physicians in attendance. For John, this was a very special case.

The next time the team met, Anne was stretched out motionless on the table, already anesthetized, her metabolic rate at an acceptable state of equilibrium. On the side there were all sorts of strange-looking instruments. A few days before the operation, Michael had asked John to describe the operation to him. With his methodological mind motivated by the left hemispherical half of his brain, Michael thought that the more he knew about the surgical procedure, the more he would feel a participator and not just a spectator in his daughter's fate. John had started by describing some of the instruments.

"There are so many of them, Mike. There is the Slightly Curved Obwegesero Zygomatic Arch Awl, the Sympathectomy Dissectors – bilaterally calibrated...."

He didn't get much further.

"I suppose you don't know much about the stress calculations in high-tensile steel, either," Michael commented wryly. From that moment on he left the surgical gobbledy-gook and paraphernalia to the experts. He had a good idea of what was going to happen and that was enough.

Dr. John Brent took a deep breath. This was no longer his best friend's daughter. This was a case. Total concentration. Total commitment. Once started, there was no way back.

An hour later he placed a patch of gelfoam in the craniotomy and sealed the edges with fibrin glue. He carefully closed the incision in successive layers. He had done his job. Now, nature had to do her part. The results were always unpredictable. Every brain was like a fingerprint. Entirely different. A little prayer wouldn't hurt, he thought. He wished he knew how to pray.

Back home, Anne wasn't quite sure what all the fuss was about. After a few weeks, the single puncture in her forehead was hardly visible. As far as she was concerned, all was back to normal. She resumed her home study, and was determined to get sufficiently good results to be admitted to a good high school. She knew she could pass all the exams. It was funny, she thought, until recently she hadn't cared one way or another. She knew she was smart. She could do anything she put her mind to. But now she thought it would be nice to get the best results possible.

Almost overnight, her emotions, held back for such a long time, almost a lifetime, were now demanding to be acknowledged, to be recognized as part of her being. As part of being Anne Howell. She found these emotional stirrings strange. She was not used to them. She hardly recognized them.

"It's all right, darling," Diana would try to reassure her.

At first, Diana couldn't believe her good fortune when Anne threw her arms around her neck and said, in a voice filled with youthful directness, "Oh Mommy, Mommy, I do love you!"

Anne repeated this assertion two more times that same day. They talked a lot. They had so much to catch up on. So many months, which seemed like years. Yet in all their chats, Anne's four-month absence – just like the knife – was left alone.

"There's nothing to say," Anne replied.

And Diana, not wanting to upset her, moved on. "Nothing to say about what?" She never asked.

Perhaps, Diana thought, Anne suffered from a blissful amnesia that selectively excluded those months from her memory. Perhaps there really is nothing to say. Maybe it is really gone. Perhaps all is for the best, she thought. She had no choice but to accept things as they were.

Michael likewise found it almost euphoric to observe the sudden change in his daughter. He took time off from work just to be with Anne, to take her for walks, to the cinema, shopping, whatever her heart desired. A few times he just sat there, in the living room, spellbound, watching her through a half-shut door as she was doing her homework. How glad he was that all of Anne's work was just that. Homework. Things always turn out for the best, he echoed his wife's conclusions.

But the greatest beneficiary of Anne's awakening was Fluffy. He, with senses that had not been given to humans, was the first to know that Anne had returned. Even before any exterior signs of her new personality became visible, Fluffy's tail had announced the birth of Anne's new persona.

"Just look at that tail," Michael had said. "Surely that's good news!"

It was.

Anne was hardly aware of how great a change had taken place in her behaviour. And not just behaviour. Her attitude, her reactions to events, to the people around her, to Fluffy, all these were no longer impersonal. What others thought or did began to matter to her. She felt part of a group, linked together by an unspoken common interest, wrapped in a blanket of emotional well-being. She felt her parents' love as one feels the first rays of sun touching one's skin after a long winter. For the first time she wanted them to feel hers.

Spring was truly upon them.

As for the past, Anne wasn't pretending when she told her mother that those months had never really happened. Had she been older, she would have said that the matrix of time had bent upon itself and excluded whatever took place during her absence. She was aware of an unexplained void in her life. She knew she had been away – her body was aware of the passage of time – but she had no real strong idea of anything between the day she spent on the street and the day she came home from the hospital after her operation. None of it really mattered anyway, she thought. And didn't really worry herself about it.

Around the middle of May, she and Fluffy ran out to the garden to chase around the bushes, to lose themselves in the exuberance of spring's awakening nature. They chased each other, even rolled on the still wet grass together, laughed and barked, to their heart's content. As Anne finally sat down on the rear porch to catch her breath, a picture flashed into her mind: a man, short and tubby, naked to the waist, doing something she hated. She was scared but didn't know why. She shook her head to destroy the vision. It came and went, as though recorded on a tape running around a VCR, in circles. It came and it went. The next moment she felt an acute headache.

An hour later, Diana called her to come in for lunch. When she didn't respond, her mother came to the window and called again. Anne was sitting on the bottom step, her body reclining against the steps rising behind her. She was motionless.

"Anne, why don't you answer me? Are you asleep?" Diana suspected that Anne was playing some sort of childish game.

"Anne?" she repeated. This time there was a touch of anxiety in her voice. "Anne!" She called out loudly.

But Anne didn't move. She was gone again. But this time it was worse.

For the next two weeks Anne remained in a deep coma.

* * * * *

ENNUI

"The most beautiful experience we can have,
is the mysterious."

Albert Einstein

Chapter 7

Recovery

Since the Right Honourable Jean Courtier, the Federal Minister of Health, had made the official announcement about the windfall for the Neuro, John's long hours had become even longer. Most days he slept at the office. There was the usual political storm about Federal encroachment into Provincial jurisdiction, by assigning funds to a specific project, and not allowing the Provincial bureaucrats to determine where the money was most needed.

"Or could be most efficiently wasted," John quipped to Michael when they were alone.

Such puerile political storms occurred with nauseating frequency, more often than not, about the lack of equalization payments rather than about fiscal generosity.

Nevertheless, the Rt. Hon. (etc., etc.) Premier of Québec found it necessary to elegantly stomp his feet and display the usual tantrums as publicly as possible, before he began boasting that Montreal not only already had, but would have even greater hegemony in the important, overwhelmingly important, field of neuroscience. Indeed, he bragged quite unabashed by his previous histrionics, "Québec is finally recognized as the World Leader in the field of Neurology."

"Be that as it may," Dr. Brent mused at this meeting with the Provincial Minister, "will it not be embarrassing if people learn that the Québec Government did not contribute an equal, if not greater portion of the funds to such an important cause?"

The Minister wiped her receding forehead completely covered by an exorbitant overhanging coiffure. Don't those people ever have enough, she wondered? Three billion... On the other hand the Director had a point. We have to find a way to grab the limelight. What would people say indeed? They might even begin to enjoy the benefits of federalism. Not that they hadn't for years, but at least they had been, quite successfully, kept ignorant of the fact. The threat of separation was a marvellous card to flash in front of the Federal eyes. All in the name of French culture, of course. Just for the people. For the *Québecois* and *Québecoises*. *Culture Française. La langue française, et cetera, et cetera, et cetera.* The usual *foutaises. Connerie.* Or as our Mexican friends would say, *excramente del torro!*

There was once a time when the French language, in North America generally, and in Québec specifically, deserved all the protection the Federal and the Provincial Governments could command. That was years ago. Nowadays, as it was with the trade unions, the most vocal defenders of their imagined cause were men and women whose overblown physiques matched their overblown bank accounts. Most of them had little command of the decent, let alone the beautiful, melodious French language. They spoke and worked in a goulash of English and French, which no real Frenchman could understand.

"You need more money?" the minister stuttered. It didn't come out the way it was meant to. "You have already spent your..."

"*Cher Madame la Ministre,*" John Brent was fluently bilingual, "it is not a question of money. It is a question of French Culture! French Science! French..." Two could play at this game. John was flapping his arms in a truly French style. It seemed to create an air of unequivocal honesty.

Was that why so many people did that? Flap their hands as though ready for take-off? John replaced his quizzical expression with ardent seriousness. He was getting very good at this sort of thing. He could maintain a poker face for minutes at a time, hours if need be, or paint any number of expressions without the slightest difficulty. It came in useful, nay expedient, when dealing with politicians. He was playing their game. What he hadn't told the minister was that since at least half of the research projects at the Neuro were conducted in close cooperation with his colleagues in the United States, the working language at the Neuro had to be English.

"*C'est vrai*," the minister conceded grudgingly.

"We could build another ward with ah, the minister's name on it, perhaps?"

"I'll see what I can do," the Minister replied. Judging by her expression, she'd begun warming to the idea.

John managed to conceal his smile of satisfaction. It always worked with those politicos, he mused. Don't they ever think about anything other than their own egos?

"I know I can count on your generosity and commitment to Science, Minister," was John's parting shot. He'd stressed the words Science and Minister. They belonged together like S&M.

A month after this, Premier of Québec made an announcement that a new wing would be funded by the Provincial Government to commemorate Québec's great contribution to the field of Neuro-science. No date was given. Just a lot of hot air. TV air. Photo ops. But no money.

"Oh, well," thought John. "*On n'a rien sans risque!*" He had taken a considerable risk pushing the Minister. He was well aware of the linguistic liberties he had taken, and continued to take, at the Neuro. Bill 101, which demanded not only equality but also visible superiority of French, everywhere in Québec, was quite explicit. Even if eminently impractical.

In the meantime, the Deputy Director of the MNI had prepared a surprise of his own. For whatever reason, John Brent was by far the most popular figure at the Institute. It may have been his directness, the unquestionable evidence of his total commitment to the needs of the Neuro, or perhaps just his personal charm, but from his Deputy Director all the way down to the floor cleaners, he was both liked and respected. A rare combination, indeed.

The last time John was away on one of his trips, the Deputy took it upon himself to have the contractor, working on the new wing, install a full bath, with a whirlpool and a shower, the latter fitted with an extra powerful jet. When the bathroom was almost ready, the Deputy had the contractor cut through the wall into John's office and install a connecting door, obviously, while John was away.

"We all thought you should have a shower before you go to work, John," he mentioned *en passant*, when he saw John, once again, about to stretch out on his sofa. It was close to midnight. He opened the door to the bathroom, ran the tap to the whirlpool bath, and left with a smirk on his face.

John had been utterly flabbergasted. As he was making his rounds the following morning, the staff looked at him with surreptitious smiles, occasionally pretending to take equally as surreptitious sniffs in his direction. It was apparent the installation of the bathroom had been, for quite a while, a public secret.

"All right!" he announced at last. "I take a shower every morning." He swept the pretty nurses with a leery eye, "*wherever* I sleep," he added, staring pointedly at one nurse after another.

The giggles died out immediately. The Director didn't have a reputation as a philanderer. On the other hand, no one could know for sure. That day John Brent, the bachelor, became the hottest topic among the female staff. Physicians and nurses alike.

Anne remained in a coma or, for want of a better expression, 'a near-coma condition', for sixteen days. Within minutes of finding her slumped on the steps of the back porch, Michael had taken her to the MNI himself. There had been no question of waiting for an ambulance. He picked her up in his arms and placed her on Diana's lap on the front seat of his Buick. Both Michael and Diana had been so distracted that they forgot to call ahead. They arrived at the Institute unannounced. For once, they had to wait in line to be seen like other ordinary mortals.

They both forgot how taxing it was to have to wait with a sick
child. Twenty minutes later Dr. Brown was examining her. John
Brent was not available. The MNI, while specializing in research and neurosurgery,
also had a contingent of psychologists and psychiatrists. One of
each was summoned to look at Anne, even as Dr. Brown carried
her to Dr. John Brent's office. There were no available beds, let
alone private rooms. Dr. Brown did what he thought his boss
would have wanted him to do. He knew what he did was highly
unorthodox, certainly unconventional, but he reasoned that special cases called for special measures. As for Anne's parents, he
sequestered them, temporarily, in the conference room adjoining
Dr. Brent's private office.

Within fifteen minutes Dr. Brown had organized a preliminary session at Anne's bedside, or more accurately settee-side.
There wasn't that much they could do, but the preliminaries
would help John, when he arrived, to attempt a diagnosis. They
were almost finished when the Director returned. A single
glance sufficed to assess the situation: Anne lying on the sofa, a
fresh IV in her arm with a group of doctors and nurses huddled
around her.

"You'll make a good physician, Peter. You place the patient first," John complimented Dr. Brown. Peter thought this
must have referred to his presumptuous occupation of the Director's office. No matter. At least he hadn't been scolded.

"Forgive me," John added after a moment's hesitation.
"You *are* a good physician."

Dr. Brown smiled. The Director was known to be a very
fair man, but hardly generous with his compliments. He expected the very best from himself and from his staff. It wasn't
easy to meet his high standards, let alone to exceed them.

"Thank you, Sir. I assumed you would want me to bring
her here," he said in a tone hardly above a whisper.

Despite her medical condition, Anne looked as though she
were sleeping. During the period before her operation, Peter
Brown had grown attached to the girl. Now lying on John's
couch, she looked so utterly helpless. He was too young himself
to know that most, if not all, girls looked like that when they

were ten years old. They invoked latent paternal feelings in most men. She looked perfectly at peace.

A Sleeping Beauty, Peter thought. A little princess....

The moment John had assured himself that Anne's condition was stable, he went to see Diana and Michael. Both looked pale, yet seemingly, if strangely, resigned. After a brief chat, he sent them home.

"There is absolutely nothing you can do here," he urged them. "I would rather you got some rest." They both looked ready to collapse.

John had a folding bed installed behind the settee and moved Anne onto it. Probably more comfortable than the couch and half-concealed behind it, she was a little less obtrusive. Anyway, until a bed became available on a ward, there was hardly any choice. As expected, John refused to have Anne out of his sight. When he left his office, a nurse remained in his stead. Often she would remain even when he was there also, just so that he could get on with his paperwork.

These were trying times for all.

Later that evening, John called Michael.

"You and Diana are welcome to come and see her, if you like." He looked down at the tiny body on the small cot behind the settee. "Although, she's sleeping, so to speak. Perhaps you should rest and I'll call you tomorrow..."

"Do you know what it is? What happened?"

"I've discussed her condition with our psychiatric staff. They agree that the most likely diagnosis is that this is a direct result of the experience she had during her . . . absence. It is as though she is determined to block out some memories. Even at the expense of remaining unconscious."

"She will come out of it?" Michael's whisper was unsteady. It was a statement framed into a question.

"Of course!" John put on his most persuasive tone of voice. "Such things happen all the time, Michael. You and Diana have a good rest, and I'll call you, all right?"

As Michael thanked him, John hung up. He, too, was dead tired. What he'd just told his friend was not a medical opinion.

It was a friend talking to a friend. It wouldn't help to tell Mike that he, as a surgeon and as the director of the Neurological Institute and Hospital, had no idea what had happened to Anne. Her vital signs were completely normal. Her pulse, heartbeat, temperature, even the electroencephalogram he had taken, did not show any abnormal brain waves. Medically, Anne should be able to get up and walk. Right now. Only she didn't. Not for another two weeks.

"You cannot pour new wine into old skins," he said. His tone suggested that he was stating the obvious.

Anne walked to the car under her own steam, sat quietly in the back seat, nestled close beside her mother while Michael drove home. She then got out, again with no apparent problem, and walked to the house from the driveway unaided. Fluffy met her at the door. She stroked his shaggy head absentmindedly. His tail wagged uncertainly, as though hoping for more.

There was no more.

Externally, Anne was completely normal. She looked fine, could move about but she seemed detached. Detached from what they all recognized as reality. She spoke little and didn't really seem engaged in her surroundings. Even less so than before. Almost as if she were terribly preoccupied with solving a riddle.

Then, two days after Anne returned home, Diana collapsed. It was a case of extreme exhaustion. The nervous tension of the last six months had been just too much for her. Michael, in consultation with John, hired a retired male nurse. Not retired from the MNI, but from a hospital that John rated highly.

"He's a good man," John assured, "and what he really wants is not so much a nursing job, but a sort of major domo position. He wants to help out."

Gabriel Morton was as good as stated on the label. In his early fifties, tall, much taller than Michael, well-spoken and polite. What else do we need? He must have already earned a decent pension after some thirty years as a registered nurse, Mi-

chael presumed. Why else would he accept such a small re-
tainer? He didn't need much money but, he said, he needed a
family who needed him. Gabriel Morton believed that life without being needed was not worth living.

"He will be a great help to Diana," Michael told John the
very next day. "Thanks again. I seem to lumber you with all
my problems."

"Your time will come," John quipped. "By the way, can
Gabby cook?"

"Gabby? Ah, Gabriel. Are you worried about your palate
or mine?" Michael asked.

"Both!" John said and hung up.

Gabriel Morton fit into the Howell family from day one.
His only vaguely unnerving habit was to come up, repeatedly,
with peculiar statements, like about this wine business, and it being a small price to pay. "You cannot pour new wine into old
skins," he'd said a few days after he arrived. And having said
that he then mentioned something about Anne's sickness being
the price, and went to the kitchen before anyone had a chance to
ask him what he was talking about.

At the time of this assertion, Diana was trying, probably
belatedly, to sound out Anne's views on the intangibles. Of
matters that dealt with the cause, not the effect. Most mothers
had it easy, she thought. Their children grew up in an atmosphere of either a church-going environment or of abjectly laic
attitudes towards the world at large. She could never reconcile
herself to the concept of good and evil. She vaguely recalled
such sayings as 'do not resist evil', or the Rumi statement about
'meeting in the field that lay beyond the doing right and doing
wrong'. Somehow these two notions complemented each other.
She couldn't accept the dichotomy of ethical duality. Neither
she nor Michael attended any church, but both had been raised
in families in which an allegiance to a particular denomination
was not only cherished but held to the exclusion of all other religions, or even other Christian sects. This total lack of tolerance
towards other faiths was one of the reasons that had led Diana to
reject her upbringing. This very attitude also had drawn her to

Michael who, at the time they met, was facing similar problems with his own family and with his parish priest.

"Only the Catholics have access to heaven," the emaciated padre had declared from the elevated pulpit. "Only those who recognize Christ as their Saviour."

This sounded like a contradiction. There were many that were not Catholics yet recognized their salvation in Christ. Christ being the state of consciousness not limited to the one man who'd achieved it some two thousand years ago. But this was only part of the problem. Michael had found it more and more difficult to accept that he must die in order to experience bliss. He felt that there might well be different degrees of bliss.

Right now he would be more than happy to recapture the bliss of Anne being healthy. Or that experienced during the first few months with Diana when they'd first met; or even the bliss of an afternoon stroll with his family on Mount Royal. A healthy family, he thought, a grim smile twisting his regular features. Lately, his previously ruddy cheeks had become more sallow, and his stoop a little more pronounced.

What was more, both he and Diana were great advocates of life. Of the 'here and now'. Diana had once read a book that stated, quite adamantly, that the soul has existence only in the present. The concept had appealed to both of them, and from that moment on their apostasy had taken a giant step forward. Unfortunately, they did not replace that which they'd lost, their religious affiliation, with anything new. Only now, now when no temporal powers seemed to wield any protection for their daughter, they both felt empty, useless, and particularly unable to help. Diana, after so many years, began to pray. Though Michael wouldn't admit it, he envied her for whatever elusive, if fragmentary, peace it might give her.

"Let Thy will be done," she uttered in a half-tone, looking at the swirling clouds over the horizon.

"What's that?" His thoughts were evidently as far away as his wife's.

"There is so little we can do, Michael. We are so helpless..." Her tone was resigned, but there was a suggestion of a glimmer of light over some distant horizon. "Perhaps we don't have to be?"

He let that go.

The very next day, Diana began delving into Anne's mind, trying to understand her daughter's attitudes towards – what can only be described as – the tangible and the intangible. She simply had to know what motivated her daughter's behaviour. Not its outward manifestation but what lay at their root. She was trying to puncture the barrier that Anne had built around her inner sanctum. Always taciturn, particularly on the subjects that Diana wanted to discuss, Anne would not commit herself at all. It was as though what she believed was hers and hers only to enjoy.

About a week later, Diana began to suspect that it wasn't Anne's reticence that held her from any discussion of her beliefs. Perhaps Anne had no beliefs. Maybe her actions had always been little more than reactions. She seldom initiated anything new. But she was very fast and stubborn in reacting to whatever affected her presumed well-being.

And this was where Gabriel came in.

Gabriel, or Gabby, as everyone soon addressed him, explained that Anne did not have any mechanism to form abstract notions. The portion of her personality which would cope with such problems had been totally taken over by her subconscious reactions.

"There is no room there for anything new," he added after Diana wouldn't let him get away with more biblical quotations. "Usually people have to give up their old beliefs, go through a period of adjustment, and only then taste of new wine."

Gabriel talked like that. It was as though he'd spent years studying metaphysics. Or at least, the Bible.

"But she has no previous beliefs that I know of, Gabby." Diana insisted.

"That seems true. But she doesn't know that one needs them. That one cannot live without any beliefs. Even avowed atheists believe in all sorts of things. In money, or their inherent superiority, or in power. We cannot survive in a vacuum. A spiritual vacuum. It would be like denying life itself."

She decided to talk to Michael about it, but she had no idea how to tackle the subject. Michael was such a practical man. He had deep faith in some sort of benevolence that saturated the world intrinsically. He'd never explained what he meant by that.

Diana didn't know how seriously she should take Gabby's pronouncements. 'Gabby', she knew, happened to be the colloquial expression for one who liked to talk. For one that was overly talkative. But this couldn't really be said of Gabriel. He answered readily when asked, but seldom volunteered. He gave the impression of being a man of his own convictions, who didn't mind sharing them, but would never impose them on anyone. The exact opposite of everyone she'd ever met who held convictions on matters of faith.

Perhaps, she reasoned, there is that elusive universal benevolence, as Michael called it, and perhaps Gabby had arrived on their doorstep at a propitious moment. Anne seemed to take to him with unusual trust. Gabriel's overwhelming 'extra-large' size seemed in direct contradiction to his disarming smile. Not a wide grin, but a slight, gentle smile evidently inspiring trust.

There was also an array of new problems.

While most of the time Anne was her old self, or nearly so, there were other moments when she appeared to cave in under an onslaught of emotions. After such a bout, she retreated into the security of indifference. The beast within her was putting up a royal battle.

It was after one of those, what can only be described as attacks, that Diana learned to truly appreciate her new major domo. She saw Gabriel sitting directly opposite her daughter, holding her hands, looking into her eyes. They were both completely motionless, silent, as though in a world unto themselves. After some ten minutes of such silent communion, Anne's face showed a suggestion of a minute smile. Unfortunately it faded as soon as it came. Gabriel got up and slowly moved away, leaving Anne on her own.

"Why did you stop?" Diana had asked.

"Stop what, Madam?"

"Stop whatever you were doing!" Diana did not know how to explain the soft smile and peace she had seen on Anne's face, but her maternal instinct wanted him to continue to bring it back. There was that suggestion of a smile. "I couldn't, Madam," Gabriel replied. "She couldn't absorb any more."

And no matter how hard she prodded Gabriel, at that moment he wouldn't say any more. The next few days Anne spent in a detached state. Then, just as slowly, she recovered. In another few days she was playing with Fluffy. Dear old Fluffy. He seldom left her side.

* * * * *

Chapter 8

Awakening of an Angel

Michael was at the end of his tether. No matter what he tried, all came to naught. His firm had begun to have problems finding new contracts. Construction in Montreal, so vibrant at the beginning of the new millennium, was running out of steam. Not that Michael really needed work. The good years, the seven fat years as Gabriel would call them, served to assure his financial independence. He'd invested his money wisely, not searching for a quick profit from quarterly returns, but rather a steady growth from firms which showed stability, offered value now and hopefully in the future. Actually, fate had been kind to Michael for more than thirty years. He continued working because he loved working. Not because he needed the income.

His real problems were not work-related. Diana, of late, had become lethargic; unable to make any decisions, particularly if such concerned their daughter.

"You know best, dear," she'd say, smiling, utterly trusting in his judgment.

Michael remembered when she had been a tower of strength. He would go to work and be confident that whatever

Diana did with Anne would be the best possible for both of
them. Now he wasn't so sure. And he needed to be.

He didn't want to carry the whole weight of Anne's welfare
on his own shoulders. Anne, particularly of late, needed a femi-
nine touch, a woman's intuition. And he needed the same to
help him in supporting his daughter with the guidance she so
badly needed. Diana did what a good wife was supposed to do,
but there was little joy in any of her endeavours. She went
through the motions: smiled at the appropriate moments, showed
concern when Michael described his office problems, but
seemed to freeze into a peculiar sort of numbness when he mentioned Anne's name. Michael was sure that Diana loved her
daughter as much as ever, but she seemed to harbour a strange
kind of fear that whatever she decided might have adverse effects
on their only child.

There was Gabriel, of course. But whatever hidden talents
he may have had, Gabriel always deferred to the parental judgment. It was as though he were there in case Michael or Diana
failed. He was there to assist, not to replace them.

"We all inherit our karma," Gabriel had once told him.
"We must justify or repeat it."

The Gentle Giant, for he truly towered over everyone, refused to clarify his enigmatic statements. Yet in spite of
Gabriel's apparent reticence to get involved in philosophical discussions, Michael was developing great faith in the tall man's
judgment. He had to admit to himself that he felt much safer
having him around: better than leaving Anne in just Diana's
care. She would never hurt Anne, but he wasn't confident that
she would stop Anne from hurting herself. For some time, Michael had begun to feel that he had not one but two dysfunc-
tional members of the family. Only John, still a regular visitor,
provided a lighter note in his routine.

"I'll tell you one thing, Mike, I know of many people who
are a lot worse off than you are," he'd say.

"Are you sure...?" There was real doubt in Michael's
voice.

"Trust me. What I see, almost daily in my profession, you
wouldn't want to see even on your worst days. People with can-

cers. Parents who must be told that their children have six months to live. Patients with Parkinson's disease so advanced that...."

"I get the point, John. Thanks." Michael knew that John was right, but, for some reason, it did not make him feel any better. 'We are all born with our karma,' he recalled Gabriel's dictum. It appeared that he had to wade through his, no matter how treacherous the stream he had to cross.

The construction on John's New Wing was progressing on a fast-track contract. By the time Anne turned eleven, they had the topping-off ceremony. The whole building was now under one roof. He was looking forward to the time when the new, bright walls would be filled with children who needed his help, rather than with decrepit senior citizens. That was not to say that he didn't care for the elderly. During the last twenty-five to thirty years, John had allotted the vast majority of his time to the sufferers of diseases that almost exclusively afflict the very old.

Fortunately or not, during those same years, the term 'very old' had changed its meaning. Until relatively recently, men and women of sixty-five were deemed to be elderly. Old. Probably senile. They'd been expected to retire, often by legislation. At this age they were assigned the job of quietly waiting for death, while placing minimum demands on society. No wonder they contracted innumerable diseases to which abject boredom, if not actual apathy, may well have contributed.

"Take it easy, dad," John recalled telling his own father when his 'old man' attempted to bring more firewood for the fireplace. "Let me do that for you...."

His father had been in his late fifties then. An 'old man', by all accounts.

John was rapidly approaching the same age and he had never been busier. He had colleagues in their late seventies from whom he still had plenty to learn. Times had changed, as had our ability to stimulate people towards more active lives.

Not all the sexagenarians and older senior citizens wanted such activity. He had met dozens, over the years hundreds of men and women alike, mostly his own patients, who seemed to have given up.

"We're old, doctor," they would say. "There is nothing we can do about it."

"You are as old as you feel," he tried to convince them otherwise. That it was up to them.

"The Lord giveth, the Lord taketh away..." they countered plaintively.

You are the Lords, he wanted to shout. You hold your future in your hands. But you must get up and do something. You must act. Live. LIVE!

"Wait till you get to be my age," the patient would whimper defensively.

"I *am* practically your age," he'd told some of them quite recently. They, the decrepit elderly, were only six or seven years his seniors.

"It is written in the stars..." the plaintive whine would continue.

'It is not in our stars but in ourselves that we are underlings,' he wanted to quote Shakespeare to them. But he didn't. He wasn't a preacher. The preachers had already done their job. They had told them to wait for a better day in heaven. After death. After a protracted process of dying like a vegetable preserved for a better day. Or a worse day. When both, you and the vegetable, became shrivelled and hard to stomach.

He had never said that to them, either. But the prospect of helping younger patients to face their lives; patients whose minds and wills were still directed to the here and now and still had hope for the future, filled him with enormous energy. Not that he wanted a single child to need his services. In some ways, he would be as happy if the new wing, with all its magnificent equipment, remained empty forever. No child should suffer the problems that he hoped to alleviate. But if they had to, he would be there to offer them life. A chance at life.

Just as he strove, as best he could, to give that chance to little Anne.

Only Anne he couldn't help. Not really. 'There's the rub', he thought of Shakespeare once more. And there's the rub, he mused, even as a deep vertical furrow formed on his high forehead.

In spite of Uncle John's dark thoughts, Anne had been undergoing profound changes. Long gone were the days when she would tear off the wings of common domestic flies, just to make sure that they ate all the honey. Whatever emotions were in the process of awakening in her young mind, by the time she had turned twelve, she was again reminiscent of a little angel. Her innocence was not that of a twelve-year-old, but a step closer to the sort of exuberant naiveté of a six-year-old. She seemed unable to understand that something, whatever it might have been, was evil. Had she been older, she would have asked: "We're all children of God. How can we do anything wrong?" Of course, she'd never put such a sentiment into words, but acted as though it were true. Now, unlike in her earlier life, if her mother attempted to swat that same fly's great-great-great-grand-son or daughter, little Anne would burst into a flood of tears. It would take a while for her to calm down.

Diana remembered when Anne used to stomp her feet, go through bouts of childish tantrums, even try screaming, which she seemed to think simulated crying. But she had never wept. Not in the deep, painful way, which heaves your chest and brakes down your breathing into a series of painful gasps. It was as though all her emotional outbursts had been premeditated, weighed for the effect they might have on her mother.

Now it was different. There were days when Diana would find her quietly sobbing in her bedroom. When asked what was the matter, she would turn her head away, as though ashamed of her weakness. Pride, apparently, was all that was left of the old Anne.

"We all must reach a state of balance," Gabriel offered when he saw Diana's face after one such display of sorrow.

"She's merely catching up with the tears she hadn't shed yesterday."

'Yesterday', in Gabriel's vocabulary, could mean the day
before today, ten years ago, or any time in-between. Gabriel's
concept of time was as flexible as his ability to adapt to changing
situations. As Anne changed, so did he. Not as such, but he
adjusted his point of view to understand her needs. Whether it
was his years of nursing, when he had to cope with different patients, all regarding themselves as the centres of their particular
tiny universes, or just an innate ability, Gabriel was an extraordinary man. A one in a million, and a godsend for Anne. By the
time Diana had fully recovered from her period of acute depression, neither she nor Michael would dream of letting Gabriel go.
He was as much a part of their family as each one of them.

"How on earth did we ever cope without him?" Michael
reiterated periodically. He wouldn't admit it outright, but he
lived in a grudging admiration of the major domo.

Gabriel not only refused to intrude on the paternal privileges, but was fully capable of making himself practically invisible; yet he was always there when needed. To an ordinary man,
the two functions he performed – those of a major domo and of
a dedicated nurse to all Anne's and, until recently, Diana's needs
– would, at least at times, come into conflict. Not so for Gabriel.
He had an uncanny ability to be at the right place at the right
time. And he did so in such an unobtrusive way that one was
hardly aware that he was there at all. What one really noticed, at
times, was his absence, more than his presence.

"You just can't have too much of Gabriel," Diana once
remarked. There was deep conviction in her voice.

On one occasion she had questioned if Gabriel wasn't an
angel in an elaborate disguise. After all, wasn't Gabriel one of
the seven Archangels? In fact, wasn't he the angel of the An-
nunciation and the herald of good news and comfort?

Diana liked to weave stories that took her back to her childhood. Those days had been so much easier. This particular tale
came to an untimely end when Gabriel admitted to her that his
father, having already sired two boys, had been desperately

hoping for a girl. Alas, out popped another, extra large, lad. And thus Gabriella had become Gabriel.

"Sad but true, Mrs. Howell," he confessed, wiping an imaginary crocodile tear.

Gabriel carried out all his uncalled-for tasks in a manner which seemed perfectly natural, effortless, in harmony with all his duties. Actually, within a year of joining their little family, Gabriel had grown to be the sole arbiter as to what his duties were. Yet whenever Diana or Michael would ask him if he could perform, for either one of them, some additional service, more often than not such had already been done. In spite of all that, had it not been for his size, Gabriel would have remained virtually invisible.

As for Anne, her gradual return, awakening might be a better term, was constant but slow. On occasion she would go emotionally overboard. Floods of tears came and went just as quickly, for no apparent reason. At the same time, she maintained a cool reserve towards all but a few of everyday events. Her relationship toward her immediate environment remained cursory, bordering on indifference.

Except for Fluffy. Fluffy and, in a strange tacit way, Gabriel. She seemed to share their divergent realities more so than that of her parents. They didn't find it easy.

Michael, especially when tired from his office work, had occasion to express his frustrations with Anne's relatively slow progress. The once precocious child had now become very selective in what knowledge she chose to absorb. For surely, John was convinced, her change of heart, her lackadaisical attitude towards most things, must have been an act of premeditation. He was wrong. At this stage, Anne had little or no control over her emotions. It was these emotions, and not her mind, that ruled her behaviour.

There was no question, of course, of sending her to High School. Her tutoring continued at home, as it had before her absence. Michael mentioned his disappointment to John. Like a good friend, John did his best to cheer him up. But, there was only so much John could do.

"She could be a late bloomer, Mike," he tried. "It happens all the time."

Michael remained silent. He'd thought of that himself. But at this stage, this notion was of little consolation. He began to regret not having had more children. At least Anne would have had some sort of yardstick with which, or with whom, to compare herself. It was too late now. Even if Diana, at forty-three, could get pregnant, the difference in ages would be too great to do either of the two children much good.

"Don't forget, Mike, Anne passed her PSAT exams with flying colours. You must give her time...."

Dr. Schneider repeated John's sentiments, word for word. She appeared to regard time as the panacea for all children's ailments. She'd added that there were many children less developed intellectually than Anne was.

"And many who don't cry their eyes out when I swat a mosquito sucking *my* blood from *my* arm," Michael muttered under his nose at their last follow-up visit to the Montreal Children's Hospital. Luckily neither the psychiatrist nor his daughter had heard him.

Anne managed to maintain relative equanimity when strangers were present. Only at home did she feel she could release the tight reins she held on her delicate emotions. She allowed herself this freedom more and more often. Any hurt perpetrated by anyone on another, human or otherwise, would release a flood of tears. Such actions seemed acutely painful to her. On many occasions she would burst into tears when watching TV news. An accident, of whatever nature, was more than she could bear to witness.

"But they'll be all right," Diana assured her.

"Yes," Anne would reply sobbing, "but her parents are so sad..."

Neither Diana nor Michael had noticed the parents standing next to the ambulance. Anne noticed things from a different point of view. She saw things everyone else missed. Yet, for all that, her personality still lacked the self-determining gene, that elusive element which, seemingly overnight, turns a relatively obsequious child into an obstinate teenager. After such a difficult, not to say stubborn, early childhood, she now was putty in Diana's or Michael's hands. For all her peculiarities, she was well on the way to becoming a real little angel. Obedient. Pliant. Having no demands of her own.

Indeed, having no demands at all.

By the time Anne turned thirteen, she'd become a shy, retiring teenager, unable to find interest in anything at all. Whatever happened during those four months of her involuntary incarceration, and her neurosurgical operation, served to rid her of all the impulses which guided her in her earlier life. But for all that, those young, strange leanings did not seem to have been replaced with any new traits defining a new Anne.

It was the absence of her ego that seemed most pronounced. Even when she cried, it was never for some real hurt that she experienced. It was always out of concern for someone else. But, in direct contrast to her earlier life, she never attempted to do anything about these injustices. Perhaps because they weren't about her anymore or perhaps she didn't feel like the vigilante she'd once been.

Diana recalled, once again, one of Gabriel's statements. "We all inherit our karma. We must discharge it or..." she forgot exactly what he'd said. Something about repeating it. Unless . . . then she remembered. 'Justify it or repeat it'. It seemed to Diana that most of us have been destined to repeat it. To repeat our karma. Round and round. The Hindus call it the Wheel of Awagawan. Could it be that Anne was trying, at some subliminal level, to discharge her karma? Were such things possible?

Nothing but goodness seemed to flow from Anne. But this absence of duality had also drained her of any desire. For anything. Like a kitten, an innocent kitten, happy to remain a kitten. Asking for nothing, accepting everything. Like a blade of grass, swaying in the wind with infinite patience, only to return to its point of origin.

The MNI was making great strides. With the publicity the Institute had received upon the announcement of the new funding, American institutions were clamouring, head over heals, to take part in the new research programs at the Neuro. Once the new wing was finished, some of the wards in the old building would also be updated. Anything and everything electronic seemed to retreat into obsolescence as soon as it had been installed. The equipment was still perfectly good, but... not good enough.

"It's perfectly good for a lesser Institution," John would say proudly. "But here, at the Neuro...?" He would leave the sentence unfinished.

The Neuro was no longer the best in Canada. It was rapidly becoming the best in the world. Our friends from down south knew that. There was also an avalanche of invitations for lectures, for research results, for the latest that the Neuro had to announce.

But all this meant extra work. John had hired a dozen new research scientists. It had not been that easy. For a physician, research work invariably meant a substantial cut in personal income. The extra funds John commanded were dedicated to research not to the researchers. Anyone who had abused their quota, or had lagged behind the other researchers, was called on the carpet. John had called for monthly meetings of all the departments. Everyone had to report on his or her progress. Not just the researchers but the physicians also. After all, ultimately it was the patient that mattered. Everything had been directed towards that single goal: the patient. It wasn't just a question of professional ethics. Of the Hippocratic Oath that, these days, all too often, seemed to have become lost in a bureaucratic quagmire. The MNI was now a world-class institution. The staff had to be no less.

Recently, the neurosurgeons had accomplished mind-boggling results at the nanotechnological level. During the 1930s, their predecessors had taken the first peek inside a cell with an electron microscope. This instrument was many times more powerful that any optical device. By focusing rays of electrons, rather than of visible light, the scientists could obtain vastly enlarged images of infinitesimal objects. Now, the scientists were splicing genes, which were later implanted into living tissue. Not into the living tissue of rats, or even apes, but, for the first time in history, into human flesh. The consequences were staggering. There was advanced theoretical evidence that the paralyzed would walk, the blind would see, the deaf would hear. Perhaps not tomorrow or the day after, but soon.

Very soon.

John Brent, as so many times in the past, was on cloud nine. If he died today, he would die a very happy man.

* * * * *

Chapter 9

Desperate Measures

It wasn't due to Diana's love of travel, nor to her need to escape her home which, if one could judge by appearances, she loved dearly; it was the direct result of her intense sense of guilt. This recurring symptom of an emotional unrest worried Michael deeply. He didn't have the courage to approach any psychiatrists. Diana might think that Anne's problems were hereditary. He had asked John if he, as a physician, had thought of any such possibilities. John laughed.

"I must say, you do begin to sound a little unbalanced, my friend, but really, don't you have enough real problems?" He stressed the word *real*.

"I gather your answer is no?" Michael was not offended. He was too worried to be offended.

Nevertheless, when Diana proposed that the three of them take a vacation in Europe, he'd agreed immediately. Regardless of what else may have been necessary, he also felt the need to get out of town for a little while. For an instant, his mind's eye saw scantily dressed *danseuses* high-kicking a boisterous can-can in

Place Pigalle, other delightful silhouettes in string bikinis strolling the Promenade des Anglais on French Riviera, perhaps a dash to Monte Carlo. For the briefest of moments he felt young, irresponsible. His enthusiasm faded considerably when Diana announced that she wanted to visit Lourdes and La Salette.

"Oh, well, beggars can't be choosers," Michael murmured and asked Diana to book the tickets for any time after the beginning of June. That left less than a month to make his own arrangements. He needed to delegate his office responsibilities to his partners. No one is indispensable, he had often said, but some of us are, at times, more indispensable than others.

His orderly mind also sought to fathom what may have attracted Diana to those particular destinations. He had heard, of course, about Lourdes. There was a time when miraculous cures, there, had been particularly *en vogue*. Not lately, though. At home, he looked up the two destinations on line from his cherished laptop. At first scan, he found little information on the subject of miraculous cures. There were many pages on visions, on the history of little children, even on the simplistic innocence that supposedly precipitated their fantasies. But not on healing. He drew the same blank in the healing department when he looked up Fatima, another holy site. Some of the information was undeniably interesting, but hardly a prescription for alleviating behavioural disorders. If Diana had designs on procuring a cure for whatever affected Anne, then he drew a total blank. Diana's purpose remained an enigma. For some reason, he wasn't disposed to ask her. Not then.

Diana's preoccupation with Lourdes, and possibly with the shrine of La Salette, may have sprung directly from her recently acquired passion for the occult. Everything mystical, esoteric, or even marginally related to magic, attracted her as never before. Michael considered himself lucky that his wife had not fallen under the spell of one of the many cults that had recently been attracting wandering sheep to their money-grabbing, mind-twisting fold.

Diana was lost, he reasoned. Not stupid.

Having lost the taste for membership in any church-going fraternity, the vacuum, which her change of heart had created over the years, now screamed to be filled with something. Anything. That's why, Michael reasoned, she might well have become so vulnerable. She needed to lean on something, anything that would remain reliable, permanent, not to say immutable. Certainly not as transient as everything that characterized the innumerable modes of physical, day-to-day existence.   No doubt, Gabriel had a lot to do with Michael's expanding horizons.   Concepts or concerns which a few short years ago would not even have crossed his mind, today seemed his own. Neither he nor Diana had learned from Gabriel. Not in the accepted sense of the word. Rather, like Anne, they metabolized Gabriel's wisdom by a strange unspoken osmosis. Gabriel influenced all their lives in a manner that was as profound as it was illusive.

"Life is change," she had said. "I need stability."

With the dramatic changes Anne was constantly undergoing, it was hardly surprising.

This, Michael felt sure, was the chief advantage of being a churchgoer.   You discharged your duties to your Maker in a single hour, once a week, and, in exchange you had peace of mind for the next six days. He had personal knowledge of people who cheated on their mates, did not pay their debts, never shared their considerable wealth with those in far greater need, but faithfully attended their local churches.   Those men and women, strange though it may seem, abided in a deep conviction that they were all good Christians, regardless of whether they were affiliated with Baptists or Presbyterians or Catholics or whatever sect they'd chosen to sate their needs.   Such people represented the majority. As an American professional buffoon had once called them: 'the moral majority'.

Michael did not entertain these thoughts in any critical way. If he judged people at all, his opinions were never based on their religious affiliations. They might have belonged to any church or any organization. He judged them as individuals. On their particular merits.   Decent people usually remained decent, no matter what ghetto they chose to adhere to. And most people did feel the need to attach themselves to some sort of a group.

They must have practiced the dictum of 'strength in numbers'. This had been true, once, Michael thought. Perhaps during the Middle Ages. But now? Now a single person could wield enormous power. Particularly 'evil' or destructive power. Assuming all power is not evil by definition. Today, a single individual can smuggle a 'dirty' bomb into a city and take tens if not hundreds of thousands of lives, of total strangers, just to make a questionable political or religious statement.

"We live in the Age of Aquarius," Diana had told him as though this sufficed to explain his own thesis. Only later had he learned that the Aquarians were people who tended each to his and her own garden. A 'garden' symbolizing a state of consciousness. An individual reality.

But the vast majority, moral or otherwise, still lacked the individuality to stand up on their own emotional and mental feet. Those people invariably expressed their opinions as 'we', seldom as 'I'. Michael thought it flippant, or even facetious, that particularly the churchgoers needed such an affirmation of their collegiality. They must have forgotten that, according to their own terms of reference, God created man in His own image. He had not created a church, nor *the* church, nor any church, nor any celebrated, powerful, or famed congregation – but an individual.

"Ye are gods..." he remembered from way back when. Funny that King David had known more, some 3000 years ago, than most people appeared to know today. Perhaps Diana was right. Perhaps we are regressing into the Dark Ages once again.

Michael was very sure of his ground. He was definitely an individual confident of his territory. Physically, emotionally, mentally and, yes, even spiritually. He felt no need to find spots of 'healing' radiation, or spiritual waves, or other mumbo-jumbo, in order to find his inner equilibrium. His world was replete with those very vibrations, those waves, which people, now apparently also his wife, search for so desperately in so many locations.

"God is ubiquitous," was his first reaction to Diana's proposed destinations. *"Omnipresent,"* he stressed the word. "You won't find Him in any particular place any more than elsewhere you could find Her absence." He looked at Diana sidewise. She hated when he referred to God as She, although she had never explained why. Nevertheless, at that particular time in their lives, Michael was just a little bit annoyed with his beloved wife.

On Saturday, June 10th, on the eve of their departure, John Brent attended the farewell dinner at the Howell residence. Due to John's commitments, the dinner was served rather late. Anne was already tucked safely away in bed. She'd gone without complaint or fuss. How strange, Michael mused. Children, as far as he knew, resented going to bed early. Particularly when guests were coming, and when they were already thirteen years old. Of late, contrary to her previous arbitrary disposition, Anne didn't seem to resent anything. As long as no one was hurt.

Michael held that, in spite of his frequent denials as regarding his psychological or psychiatric expertise, John still knew far more about the workings of the brain than anyone else around. He wanted to make quite sure that it was safe to take Anne so far away from possible medical help, from physicians who knew her medical history. Usually, they would sit down at the table as soon as John arrived. The good doctor hardly ever drank any alcohol, thus eliminating the need for cocktails. Also, his time was so precious that he usually arrived at the very last minute. On that particular evening, before Michael had a chance to ask John anything, Diana completely took over the conversation.

"Do you believe in miracles, John?" she'd asked even before they sat down to dinner.

John was taken aback. Michael had warned him about their holiday destination, but the question still came as a shock.

"My dear Diana, it is hardly my area of expertise..." he started but Diana waved him down.

"I think you are perfectly qualified to speak as a human being, regardless of your area of expertise," she said looking him directly in the eye. It was quite a while since Diana had sounded so combative.

"What exactly do you mean...?" John shook his head looking lost. "What exactly do you mean by a miracle?"

It was Diana's turn to look discombobulated. She had never thought of defining a miracle. But her determination led her on. She looked and sounded as though she were on a war-path; although it wasn't clear whom or what she intended to fight.

"I mean do you believe things happen for which there is no rational explanation?" She delivered this hypothetical quandary, this time much more slowly.

"Of course!" John smiled broadly.

"You do?" This time Diana sounded genuinely surprised. She knew John to be a hard-nosed scientist. He would rather trust his infernal machines than another human being.

"Of course, Diana. In my line of work there is a painful lack of explanation for a great many things. But they still are, exist, have effect on...."

"That's not quite what I meant," she cut him off, but this time gently.

"I know," John said. "I was just teasing you." He looked contrite. "You are referring to the influence of the intangible power, or powers, on our mundane existence for which there is no rational explanation. Like God, or Spirit or just, as in Michael's case, the Omnipresent Benevolence."

"You know about that?"

"We have been friends for a very long time, Diana. I suspect Mike could tell you things about *me* I don't know myself."

It was time for Diana to take a deep breath and relax. She was among friends.

Dinner was splendid. Until recently Diana had done most of her own cooking, but since her last breakdown, Gabriel had prepared the meals, particularly on special occasions. His years of globetrotting added a touch of the exotic, the unusual, and certainly of the cosmopolitan, in equal measure to his culinary expertise. He enjoyed mixing various ingredients that he purchased in oriental shops that neither Diana nor Michael had ever heard of.

When they were alone, just the Howells, Gabriel ate at the dinner table, as a member of the family. When the Howells had guests, or a guest, or even just John, who by then had also been adopted into the clan, Gabriel insisted on staying 'downstairs'. It so happened the Howells' residence was a cottage and Gabriel's room was *upstairs*, but Diana knew what he meant. At first she tried to persuade him to join them at the table anyway, but Gabriel dug his heels in.

"Surely, Madam, this is the only chance you get to talk freely about me."

There was no denying his logic, though the only thing anyone had to say about Gabriel could be said in front of him. She told him as much.

"No, Madam. It couldn't. It would make me blush!"

The very idea of a man, whose head barely cleared the doorways, blushing, was more than Diana could take with a straight face. She burst out laughing.

"This is exactly what I mean, Madam," he affirmed gravely.

To this day Diana wasn't sure if Gabriel had been serious or just jesting at his own expense. Normally he was very deferential but – he had his moments. Yet whenever 'strangers' were in the house, he remained aloof.

"I know my place, Madam," he'd said on another occasion. Diana wondered if he ever suspected how warm a place he held in her own, and Michael's, and most certainly in Anne's heart. Not to mention in Fluffy's.

Fluffy they would miss the most – on the trip. Thank heavens for Gabby. He would look after him. In his quiet, patient way, Gabriel seemed to be looking after all of them. At all times.

Over coffee, Diana returned to her subject. Evidently her need for some sort of confirmation of her conclusions was still preying on her mind.

"You know, dear?" This time she directed her line of attack at her husband, hoping to draw John into the discussion. "People get ulcers."

No one contradicted her observation.

"And if they don't mend their ways, they get bleeding ulcers."

"And they have to drink a lot of milk?" Michael asked.

Diana gave him a dirty look. She would have made a superb actress. For a woman well over forty, she had an amazing gamut of looks, winks, smiles and generally interesting facial contortions, ah . . . expressions. Not that age had anything to do with it, but in her case she could pout and look like a girl of fifteen and then, with but a single look, become a 1930s vamp. At some level of her psyche she must have been both. Even now, nearly fifteen years after they had tied the knot, she was perfectly capable of driving Michael wild with some of her salacious facial expressions.

"As far as I know, the medical profession accepts that ulcers are often brought about by stress. Bleeding ulcers – by lots of stress."

In addition to bad eating and drinking habits, Michael mused, but kept his counsel.

"Isn't that right, Dr. Brent?" Diana only addressed John as 'doctor' when he was supposed to answer *ex cathedra* of the Medical Establishment. As a sort of Infallible Medical Pope. Infallible in matters of Medicine with a capital M.

"That is the present school of thought, Madam," John replied gravely.

Diana's face lit up. A few years back she would have clapped her hands. "Then, my dear doctor, if the workings of the mind can affect the physiological balance of our organism, can we assume that an equal and opposite action would reverse the effect?"

"You are back on the miracles, aren't you, dear?" Michael asked, but John butted in.

"If you are asking if the mind can produce physiological changes in our body, then the answer is a categorical yes. And the reverse is also true. It has been well documented that laughter, for instance, has beneficial effects on our nervous system and even on our electrochemical balance. Even more so, the state of relaxation is definitely beneficial. The mystics of the Far East have known this for countless centuries."

Diana's eyes were growing larger. Michael was spellbound. His wife hadn't looked so lively, so beautiful, so young, in a long time. In years.

John, however, was on a roll.

"The brain releases endorphins, which are chemicals produced in the brain in response to pain and/or stress. They are known to be neurotransmitters, that is to say, they function in the transmission of signals within the nervous system. About twenty types of endorphins have already been identified in humans; in the pituitary gland, which is located at the base of the brain; in other parts of the brain; and still others scattered all over our nervous system. But I am ranting...." John looked embarrassed.

"Please, John, please go on," Diana implored him.

"Well, actually, we've come to the interesting part. We know that certain activities stimulate the increase in the release of the endorphin levels. Things like acupuncture, massage therapy, both directed at relaxation and," here he looked at Diana, "and meditation."

There ensued a prolonged wistful silence.

"And would it be ludicrous to say that certain particular locations might help to stimulate your ability to meditate, John?" Diana asked very quietly.

"You mean like a soft armchair, dimmed lights, or the gentle sound of surf washing a sandy shore?"

"Or like the atmosphere generated by thousands of believers in a secluded valley at La Salette?" She ignored the fact that the shrine of La Salette was on a mountain, not in a valley.

John didn't answer. Who could tell? He didn't have to look for miracles. They surrounded him all day long. For John Brent, the brain itself was the greatest miracle of all.

The 747 took off on schedule. These last few years they'd travelled together so rarely that Michael insisted on splurging on first class tickets. The moment they boarded, Diana and Michael were presented with a glass of champagne, at no time Michael's cup of tea. At ten at night, he equated it with poison. At any other time he would prefer to be asked, 'Olive or a twist, sir?' The last time he'd flown on business he'd almost replied, 'who cares?' before settling on an olive. This time he gracefully requested a Martini, a Scotch or a Cognac.

"Anything rather than aerated wine," he smiled sternly, controlling his exasperation. The slim attendant smiled back her understanding. She'd experienced men's tastes before.

Contrary to John Brent, Michael liked, on occasion, to wet his whistle. He didn't care if his Martinis were stirred or shaken as long as they were dry. Very dry. He didn't particularly care for Champagne, except on anniversaries when he drank a perfunctory glass to his wife's everlasting health. Once liberated from the need to partake in the bubbly, he settled down and lustfully luxuriated in the well-being which the first class compartment exuded. Whatever atmosphere Diana expected to find in the Holy Places, he had already found right here. Tilting his seat back, he closed his eyes. Moments later he saw Anne leaning over him, kissing him gently on his cheek. Then she embraced him and whispered, "Thank you, Daddy." As he opened his eyes, Anne was sitting quietly in her seat, her safety belt tightly around her waist. What a lovely dream, he thought. And then he realized that the plane had only just begun to taxi towards the take-off line-up. It must have been the shortest dream on record.

In little more than six hours they landed at Orly. He adjusted his watch to ten in the morning, local time. The Charles de Gaulle airport, not for the first time, was closed for repairs. Diana had already made it quite clear that they should start with Lourdes, then visit La Salette, before spending any time at all visiting the usual tourist attractions.

"First things first," she said sternly. "Then I shall be all yours." She looked seductively into Michael's eyes. "All yours," she repeated, stressing the word 'all'. She was well aware that the itinerary she had chosen did not fill her husband with effusive joy.

What could the poor man do? After all this time Michael still found this firebrand of many years damnably attractive. To shake off his rising blood pressure, he took Anne's hand and asked her quietly:

"And where would you like to go, pet?"

"Back to Fluffy," she replied with conviction.

Oh well, Michael reflected, looking at Anne's resigned expression, the things we do for our children....

A shuttle took them to Gare Montparnasse. In less than two hours after landing in France, they'd boarded a train heading south. It was good to be able to get up and walk around without bumping into other passengers. Not that first class had been crowded, but on board an airplane, Michael always experienced a lingering feeling of claustrophobia. He'd never felt that on a train. He took a walk of reconnaissance along the corridor.

When he got back, Anne was still sitting quietly, her eyes as green as the rolling landscape she was following through the coach window. She had become very quiet lately. Diana thought that she must be tired. There was plenty of space for her to curl up on and take a little nap, but she refused.

"I can sleep at home, Mommy. Now I must look," she declared.

When you must you must.

It wasn't exactly like that, but it was unnerving. For a start, the flashing sign, oops . . . *signs*, many, many signs, were all in French. Only some minutes later, Michael managed to discern eleven other languages before he'd stopped counting. He was partial to Vichi water, but Lourdes?

CERTIFIED HOLY HOLY HOLY LOURDES WATER
«HERE HERE HERE »
BUY BUY BUY

"Scotch and Lourdes water?" Michael smirked. Diana wasn't amused. She did, however, show vague signs of her recurring depression. Or was it disgust? Did everything have to appear in threes? "I thought six-six-six was the devil's number, not threes," he muttered to himself. "Perhaps it loses something in the translation," he said aloud, in an attempt to mollify the expression on Diana's face.

But it wasn't just the signs.

The first omen of what was yet to come surfaced about halfway out of Paris. Well, almost. For the last 30 kilometres, or at least as far north as Pau, the placards had displayed such crass commercialism that whatever beauty the landscape may have possessed was no longer visible to the human eye. Placards crammed one next to another, often atop each other, in all shapes and colours, flashing with heavenly lights. Some adorned with images of the Blessed Virgin advocating her wares to all comers.

It was truly miraculous.

Apparently Lourdes was completely dedicated to the wanton exploitation of some seven million Catholic pilgrims who passed this way every year. Back in 1858, when Bernadette Soubirous, then fourteen, had had the first of her eighteen visions of the Virgin, Lourdes had been but a small village.

Today, every square inch was dedicated to an astounding assembly of religious kitsch. Plastic ruled supreme. Bernadette, in all shapes and sizes, including in the shape of a bottle, which could be filled with miraculous water, if and when, purchased at a different distributor. Such a prize could be had just by stretching out one's arm, with a Euro or two attached to the end of it. Plastic souvenirs, also of all shapes and sizes, abounded everywhere. There were things you could stand indoors or outside, things you could hang on the walls or ceilings, there was a plethora of plastic grottoes, candles to be lit in front of those grottoes, plastic tree trunks, bellows, thermometers, barometers, key rings, pens and pencils, books, pamphlets, cameras and photographs...

You could have a photograph taken with the Holy Virgin herself in front of a brand new Holy Cave built unto the image and likeness of the miraculous *Grotte du Massabielle*. What better place to gain a miraculous cure for your incurable disease? And if you didn't, well, then maybe you could pick up at least some of the swirling viruses and bacteria which must have been brought here from far and wide. By the sick. The sick and the hopeful. If you weren't cured, you could at least offer your freshly acquired disease and the attendant discomfort, if not actual suffering, for your sins.

"Ça va purifier votre âme." It will purify your soul, Michael remembered having being told as a child.

Michael had never thought of himself as being in possession of a soul. If anything, it was soul that possessed him. Furthermore, his soul didn't need purification. He did. And anyway, he had never subscribed to the theory of the beneficial effects of suffering. Michael held that suffering meant that you had already lost contact with soul. His soul, if such a possessive pronominal could apply, let alone God, was a magnanimous entity.

"If anyone still believes in a personal God, this is the place to lose your faith completely," Michael murmured to Diana. "To think that I once believed in this sort of thing...."

"You never believed in this sort of thing, Michael. You believed in what you thought this place stood for," Diana countered.

She was right. Anyone who had never visited Lourdes could possibly imagine what little Bernadette had accomplished. Quite unwittingly. At the time, Bernadette had been only one year older than Anne was now. Poor girl, Michael thought. No one had believed her. The Church had to protect its domain from hysterical girls... "Visions indeed! Only saints are allowed to see the Virgin Mary in flesh and blood!" The bishop was quite adamant. No matter what the girl claimed.

It was getting late. For the last hour Michael had been carrying Anne astride on his shoulders. It was frankly expedient to do so in the milling crowd, seemingly growing by the minute.

She could so easily get lost. Michael thanked his lucky stars that Anne had remained petite. It also gave her a bird's eye view of the vicinity. He felt no need to see it. He wanted to sit down in his hotel room, switch on the satellite TV channel, listen to the News, and sip a glass of some decent Bordeaux.

Luckily the season was not yet in full swing. From a vast array of hotels, Michael had chosen Grand Hotel de la Grotte.

"How appropriate. If we don't get through to the actual *grotte*, at least we'll sleep in one."

Diana gave him a dirty look.

The hotel was one of the oldest in town. The original building dated back to 1871, a mere thirteen years after Bernadette had had the first of her visions. About the same time as the first flamboyant *Basilique du Rosaire et de L'Immaculée Conception* began its construction. The massive *Basilique St-Pie-X* came later. Neither he nor Diana had any ambition to share the latter's space with 20,000 other pilgrims. They'd seen it from outside. It was huge. Monstrous.

The Grand Hotel, thanks to constant updates, assured the pious pilgrims every luxury, while managing to maintain its original charm and elegance. It was the only place in town which did not display an overt appetite for the tourist dollar. Or the Euro. Or any currency. And the wine was as good as Michael had expected. The Claret was light in texture yet complex, with a lingering bouquet.

Early next morning, after a *petit déjeuner* of croissants with homemade jam and excellent coffee, they went to visit the *Grotte*. The streets were already filling with people. They didn't have far to walk. In no time Diana had reached her first destination. She stood, speechless, communing with her thoughts. Anne looked around, hardly impressed by her surroundings.

The only sensation Michael experienced at the moisture-darkened overhang which went under the name of *Grotte* was that of dampness. The white and baby blue statue of the Holy Virgin looked kindly on him, but that was all.

He hoped Diana found whatever she came looking for.

"That's what I came here for, Michael. You know that?"
She echoed his thoughts.

There was no conviction in her voice. She had to do it 'because she was there'. Like climbing the mountain. It was there. What else could you do with it? To do what wasn't exactly clear to him. Nevertheless, he suspected that if she had not 'done it', she would have accumulated an extra measure of guilt. For all that, Diana walked on stiffly, holding Anne's hand with a tight grip, looking straight ahead. Two hours later they walked back to the hotel to pick up their baggage. The railway station was not far away, either.

Soon Lourdes was but a memory with a vague if unpleasant aftertaste in their mouths. At least in Michael's mouth. Anne looked untouched by it all. By Lourdes, by the Holy Virgin, and hopefully by the commercialism. She continued to stare through the window. Diana grew even quieter during the next leg of their journey. There was some sort of struggle going on inside her which, quite evidently, she was not prepared to share. Later that day they arrived in Grenoble, a proverbial stone's throw from La Salette.

"It's good to be in a normal place, where normal people go about their normal business," Michael observed in a dry half-tone, minutes after arrival. "For now, at least."

Even setting aside the indescribable religious kitsch, he'd had his fill of shrines, churches, and mass hysteria.

Some twenty minutes later, a taxi brought them to a hotel lobby. *En route* from the station, they'd decided to spend at least one night in Grenoble and generally to take things easy. Since leaving Montreal, they'd been on the go non-stop. It was beginning to get to both of them. Anne didn't seem bothered one way or another. She looked relaxed.

She just . . . looked.

Perhaps it was just as well that Diana had not heard the comment Michael made on their arrival. It might have depressed Diana even more. Michael left her and Anne on an old, slightly worn leather settee and busied himself with booking a double room with an extra bed. His only other request was that he have access to the Internet. He'd never left Montreal without his laptop. He needed it to keep in touch with his office and to keep on top of his e-mails. It wasn't cheap, but he found it necessary. Satisfied, he leaned on the reception desk and glanced at his two ladies. Diana's arm rested protectively over Anne's shoulders, while Anne's head, in turn, reposed on Diana's lap. They were both quite still. Presumably, as tired as they looked.

Michael blinked hard, then shook his head.

For an instant he could have sworn that he had been looking at the Madonna with Child. Then the image metamorphosed again into Diana with Anne's head on her lap, a mass of bushy hair strewn in an array of red. They definitely looked exhausted, yet, for some reason, they also exemplified a deep sense of peace. Almost contentment.

Was it just being away from Lourdes? Admittedly, there had been tension there. The very pace of commercialism imposed an atmosphere of time speeding away. Here, just an ordinary lobby, in an ordinary hotel, offered haven from the hordes of people, from agitated movement, from noise. Perhaps also from unfulfilled hopes and prayers. There had been, in Lourdes, a number of inexplicable healings, attested to by professional physicians. But these had been few and far between. Perhaps this had brought about the aura of tension. After but a few hours in Lourdes, tranquillity was what they needed. The train had already helped with its staccato, unhurried rhythm.

Tratatatam . . . tratatatam . . . tratatatam . . .

Here the sense of peace was even more perceptible to all their senses.

"Could it be the influence of the shrine?" Michael wondered, and instantly felt embarrassed at his speculation. I'm a rational man, he told himself. I'm a civil engineer whose life is governed by facts. Hard facts. I'm a tourist, a Canadian on a wild goose chase.

And yet? And yet there was something in the air that seemed both palpable and intangible at the same time.

"But we're not even there yet!" he said aloud.

"*Pardon, Monsieur?*" The clerk at the desk looked up from his ledger.

Michael dismissed his question with a wave of his hand.

"Eet ees on ze sird floor, overlooking ze mountains, Monsieur," the clerk said, beckoning a bellboy, or bellman as they preferred to be called, to pick up their baggage.

"Zee, I mean the mountains? Ah, yes. Tomorrow," Michael thanked the desk clerk. Only after he'd turned towards his ladies did he realize that he'd spoken to the man in English. How silly of me, he thought.

For some reason the superficial sense of peace was being displaced by an undefined disquiet. Funny, he mused, that the girls look so very relaxed. He still had no idea what had prompted Diana to drag the three of them halfway around the world to visit a semi-forgotten shrine. It wasn't even fashionable any more, he had been told. No one goes there any more, others had said. Finally, up in their room, he asked Diana directly.

"I don't really know, darling," she replied, an enigmatic smile playing at the corners of her mouth. "I don't really know," she repeated. And then she turned away and nothing more was said about it.

Within minutes, all three were asleep.

* * * * *

Chapter 10

La Salette

After dashing from Paris to Lourdes, then, almost as fast, from Lourdes to Grenoble, Diana and Michael agreed to spend a day lazing around, doing nothing much, rather than charging, head-long, to yet another destination. Diana's actions, so far, had seemed like desperate measures. As though she had been driven to find something elusive, something that lay just around the corner yet remained outside her reach. For now, this relative lull, which the laid-back town of Grenoble offered, allowed all three of them to take a deep breath. It also allowed the world to un-fold itself at its own pace. For the first time since leaving Mont-real, Michael, finally, had a chance to relax.

They were all tired, but Michael also detected something else. He thought that Diana showed symptoms of something akin to stage fright. She wanted to go, soon, but she also wanted to drag out their stay in Grenoble. For a whole day La Salette wasn't even mentioned. Not even once. Nor the next day.

Nor the next.

They strolled along the ancient streets, bought some souve-nirs, visited the old Olympic installations, and on the third day went horseback riding in the adjoining hills. Later that day all three lingered in street-side cafés so typical of southern France. Tables wrapped in red and white chequered cloth spilled onto broad sidewalks. Colourful *baldaquins* jutted out from stone walls, undulating gently in the warm breeze like giant butterflies that alit over doors and windows for the sole purpose of offering protection from the sun for the ever-thirsty patrons. Throughout the day, the natives of this quaint town relaxed over exotic French cooking, elaborate *gâteaux*, scrumptious ice cream or just a traditional glass or two of *vin d'Alsace*. Even Anne's eyes registered a degree of interest in her strange surroundings. She looked more involved than she had been in anything during recent weeks.

At long last Michael felt that he was on holidays. Alas, he'd relaxed too quickly. The day after they had gone horseback riding, Diana decided that they could not delay any longer.

"I love it here, darling. I really do. But...." She left the sentence unfinished.

There was obviously something she was not willing or able to share with him. It was that same 'something' that had prompted her to suggest this trip in the first place, to hurry to their destination, to give her face a strained look of a person hungry for something intangible, something seemingly within her grasp but frustratingly elusive . . . he'd seen the symptoms before. Or she may have been hoping against hope to find herself.

A thought crossed his mind that Anne may have only provided a pretext for the trip. That, deep down, Diana . . . he dismissed the idea. Yet the fact remained that whenever he approached the subject of her apparent anxiety, Diana withdrew, giving some lame excuse, or simply changing the subject. Only once had she admitted to her inability of sharing her state of mind.

"I don't know, Michael. I really don't know. There are moments when I feel that I'm approaching an abyss that I am unable to span. It feels as though an ominous cloud is inexorably drawing from the East, obliterating the sun.... If it wasn't for the glimmer of a very bright light way beyond this dismal shadow, I don't think I'd have the strength to continue."

So much for explanations, he thought.

"Is there anything I can do? Any way I can help?" he tried nevertheless.

"Oh, darling! If you only knew how much you do help. You are the only help I've got!"

This explanation didn't enlighten him, either. He had no choice but to adopt a wait-and-see attitude. Or, as in the recent days, rush from place to place, and see. Or not see at all. 'To see or not to see, was that the question?' He shrugged.

"We really must go now," Diana repeated. She sounded as though neither she nor anyone else could avoid the inevitable.

That evening he paid the hotel bill and rented a car for the following morning.

On the evening before they left Grenoble, Michael read a brochure about their next destination. Apparently, La Salette was the antithesis of Lourdes. The visions that made La Salette relatively famous predated those of Lourdes by some twelve years. On Saturday September 19th, 1846, an eleven-year-old boy, Maximin, together with a fourteen-year-old girl, Mélanie, both from Corps – a small town south by south east of Grenoble – had been looking after their employer's cows, high up on the pastures above La Salette, a nearby village.

Michael tried to imagine their shock when, quite out of the blue, they saw a luminous globe of light hovering just above the ground. From this sphere of light emerged a woman. She sat down on a rock and hid her face in her hands.

There followed a long description of her appearance.

Speaking in a voice choked with tears, the beautiful lady told the two children that unless people repented, she would no longer be able to hold back her Son's heavy arm. Son was spelled with a capital S. Apparently punishment for our sins was imminent. In spite of this, it took four years before the ecclesi-

astical authorities had accepted the children's story. Or maybe
that was why.

"If my people do not obey," went on the ominous message, "I shall be compelled to loose my Son's arm. It is so
heavy I can no longer restrain it. How long have I suffered for
you! If my Son is not to abandon you, I am obliged to entreat
Him without ceasing...."

There was more about swearing and working on Sundays.
A lot more about suffering. Too much for my taste, mused Michael.

But there had been other revelations.

The beautiful lady had also confided a secret to each of the
two children, which they were to keep to themselves for a specific period of time. In spite of that, those secrets had been
made known to Pope Pius IX, a fact which may have precipitated
the Pope's declaration of the dogma of the Immaculate Conception of the Virgin Mary. The Pope could not have had much
faith in his own dogma, however, which in turn may have inspired him to also declare himself infallible. In spite of Michael's Jesuit upbringing, the logic of papal infallibility escaped
him. Nevertheless, if the Pope had coerced the children to give
away their secrets, judging from what Michael read further, the
Pope must have been sorry he'd asked. And having declared
the Virgin immaculately conceived, people would not dare to
doubt Her words. It's tough being infallible.

"Melanie," read the transcript, "what I am about to tell you
now will not always be a secret. You may make it public in
1858." Michael noted that by 1854 the Virgin had already been
declared immaculately conceived.

There was something peculiar here. Then he got it. 1858
was the year in which apparently the very same Lady chose to
appear to Bernadette in Lourdes. How the dickens could
Melanie know.... No matter. This was enough to make him read
on.

*"The priests, ministers of my Son, the priests, by their
wicked lives, by their irreverence and their impiety in
the celebration of the holy mysteries, by their love of*

money, their love of honour and pleasures, the priests have become cesspools of impurity. Yes, the priests are asking for vengeance, and vengeance is hanging over their heads. Woe to the priests and to those dedicated to God who, by their unfaithfulness and their wicked lives, are crucifying my Son again! The sins of those dedicated to God...."

And the church let this out of their Vatican bag? This was but a fragment. Michael recalled, from his youthful days, a similar sentiment expressed by the very same Son: 'Woe unto you scribes and Pharisees . . . ye fools and blind . . . ye serpents, ye generations of vipers, how can ye escape the damnation of hell?' Or something like that. Weren't the scribes and Pharisees the equivalent of priests and preachers of today? But if so, how could an eleven-year-old boy and a fourteen-year-old girl have known about it? They couldn't have made it up, he reasoned. And sure as hell the Church wouldn't have made up such a censure against itself. Would they? He skipped a few paragraphs till a strange sentence caught his eye.

"May the Pope guard against the performers of miracles. For the time has come when the most astonishing wonders will take place on the earth and in the air."

Michael switched on his laptop. He thanked his lucky stars that he hadn't cancelled the Internet access after he'd finished his communication with his office. This was their last day in Grenoble. Who knew if La Sallette would provide such a modern convenience?

As far as he could gather, the next 'astonishing wonder in the air' did not take place till 1917 when Our Lady of the Rosary appeared, again to shepherd children in Fatima. He read on.

"In the year 1864, Lucifer together with a large number of demons will be unloosed from hell...."

Ouch, was Michael's first reaction. How large a number?

*"...they will put an end to faith little by little... Evil
books will be abundant on earth and the spirits of
darkness will spread everywhere a universal slacken-
ing in all that concerns the service of God... People
will be transported from one place to another by these
evil spirits, even priests...."*

My goodness! That was 1846. Did the children have a vision of forthcoming aviation? But surely, the Wright brothers
hadn't flown anything at all till December of 1903! That's, ah...
57 years into the future. And what exactly happened in 1864?
Anything significant? Again he reached for his laptop. 1864...
Civil War was still going on . . . but it had started already in
1861... there was a plethora of insignificant events appended to
this date. He was about to give up when he spotted a headline:

**The International Workingmen's Association is
founded in London on September 28, 1864 and elects
Marx to its General Council.**

Now dear old Karl had never been a good practicing
Catholic. At least, not to Mike's knowledge. Would Marx qualify under the heading of demons?

Apart from this one juicy titbit, there was no sign of demons gallivanting about the world at large. In August 1864,
twelve nations had signed the Geneva Convention. Rather a decent thing to do, Michael thought. In September he found a
possibility. Nietzsche had passed his *Zeugnis der Reife*, or Final
Exams. While far from demonic, in his *Thus Spake Zarathustra*,
he had condemned traditional Christian morality as the code for
slavish masses . . . but that had been published only in 1883, and
in 1889 poor Friedrich had already gone hopelessly insane.
Way too late for the prophecy. As for Nietzsche's 'Beyond
Good and Evil' . . . well, his sentiments expressed therein had
been as close as you can get to Diana's favourite poet, Jalal-ud-

Din Rumi. The Persian sage had said: *Beyond the doing right and doing wrong there is a field. I'll meet you there.* Very close to the sentiment expressed by Nietzsche.

Michael kept digging.

In October that same year, 60,000 had died in Calcutta due to a cyclone. Michael could only surmise that there had been but few Catholics among them. In December, Pope Pius IX published an Encyclical Quanta cura (Syllabus errorum). Although Michael had no idea that Syllabus errorum was a document in which some eighty current doctrines such as pantheism, socialism, rationalism, Bible societies and suchlike had been condemned as heretical, it hardly seemed likely to be a demonic act.

All the other demons had apparently immigrated to the good ol' USA, which at that time wasn't very United, and partook in countless, literally *countless,* skirmishes and battles all over their God-given country. Many indigenous nations had expressed profound reservations about the assumed birthright of the European invaders. They, the natives, had previous claims on the Divine Munificence. Nevertheless, then as now, killing one's enemies was deemed to be a non-demonic activity – at least by our illustrious leaders, who invariably preferred to remain home. They probably deemed it safer to keep warm in front of their fireplaces or, some years later, nice and cool in the air-conditioned drawing rooms, than risk their lives on the battlefield. So while there may have been thousands of little demons, there was little evidence of any bigwigs having been unleashed from the Infernal Gates. Unless, of course, they'd all come incognito.

Michael tried just once more.

Engels had been born too early, Stalin too late, Hitler missed the critical date by twenty-five years. So that was that. And thus, search as he might, Michael failed to locate the principal demons of the secret revelation. A little disheartened, he read on.

"Extraordinary prodigies will abound everywhere because the true faith had been extinguished and the false light illuminates the world...."

Michael didn't like that. He always assumed that prodigies, extraordinary or not, were the favourite children of God. Surely, he reasoned, they were children in whom God found particular joy and thus endowed them with wonderful talents. No matter.

"France, Italy, Spain and England will be at war...."

Aha! He almost exclaimed. At last we are getting somewhere. But what about Germany, Italy, and the Civil War in the United States? Aah . . . I spoke too soon:

"A general war will follow which will be appalling...."

What war isn't appalling? Again Michael was ready to give up. He was getting depressed.

"...demons of the air together with the Antichrist will perform great wonders on earth and in the atmosphere, and men will become more and more perverted...."

Had the children been talking about our present-day priests, already then? Michael stopped reading. Had he wanted to get depressed, he would have returned to Lourdes. Which wasn't likely. Now or ever.

And all this talk of Antichrist and demons.... Diana had once told him that Antichrist was an invention of imaginative fundamentalist writers who specialized in making money out of scaring people half to death. According to her, the word antichrist had only been mentioned in the Bible four times, and only by John in his epistles. And even John defined an antichrist as anyone who denied that Christ is the spirit of God incarnate. That would probably account for some four to five billion antichrists walking the earth today.

Michael couldn't help laughing. He'd just had a vision of billions of horny people running around with pairs of horns protruding from their foreheads and cute little tails dangling from their hindquarters.

"What is it, darling?" There was a whisper behind his left ear.

"I hate prophecies, predictions and suchlike. They depress me," he said. A touch of sadness belied his smile. "Am I the only one who wants to live in the present?"

"I know. You look worried," Diana's whisper was a caress to his ears. "Anne's already asleep. Go to bed."

He hated it when she said go and not come.

"You shouldn't read about the nihilists before going to sleep. They upset your stomach," she whispered dreamily.

"Nihilists?"

He clicked on his laptop for the last time. 'Nihilism', he read, 'a doctrine that all the social and political institutions must be destroyed . . . the denial of any basis for the existence of knowledge or truth.' The church must have loved this . . . but how did the children know about it?

And then came the punch line. 'A political movement in Russia, starting around 1860.' By 1864 the gates of hell must have been wide open.

Children seem to know many things....

He got up and looked at Anne's deep, relaxed breathing. Her face retained a gentle smile. He thought that he had never seen a better representation of perfect innocence. 'Be ye like little children,' he recalled echoes of his younger days. Only now, after so many years, he was just beginning to understand why. Anne was showing him the way.

The road took them almost straight south, gradually veering to the east. At Vizille Michael took the *Route Napoléon*, which brought them all the way to Corps. They drove in near silence, soaking up the unfolding vistas. Anne looked unusually agitated. Until recently a bundle of uncontrolled emotion, she swung her head from one side of the car to the other. If Michael hadn't known better, he would have thought that she was recognizing certain spots, imbedded somewhere deep in her memory. That was nonsense, of course. To the best of his knowledge, Anne had never even seen a book about France. Let alone the road to La Salette. Nor had he, for that matter.

As they neared Corps, the road climbed until the views became more dramatic. The town was almost a kilometre above sea level, the village La Salette still higher, towards the northeast. From there a short steep, winding climb brought them to their destination. Michael parked their Peugeot behind the *Basilica de Notre Dame de La Salette* and went to inquire about accommodation. Behind the Basilica with its ancillary buildings, the mountain rose another 557 meters.

Diana's and Anne's eyes grew visibly larger and wider by the minute.

Also behind the church, but integral with it, there were a hotel and a monastery. Perhaps not in that order. Simple, almost austere rooms, not suitable for those who sought creature comforts. Usually one had to book a bed well in advance. This was no Lourdes with its innumerable hotels. But they were in luck.

Michael wondered why he was so happy about procuring a simple, Spartan room with three simple cots. This was no five-star establishment. The only stars they would see up here were those in the sky, above them. They even carried their own baggage to their cell. As soon as Diana arranged her clothing in the single wardrobe, she joined Anne and Michael outside. This room was for sleeping, not for living. Unless you were a monk.

Michael took a deep breath. They were standing at 1800 meters above sea level. The air was pure. Anne looked spellbound. Michael and Diana gazed at her, then at each other.

This was definitely not Lourdes. It was nothing like Lourdes. It didn't even smell like Lourdes.

"How did they manage to raise a building of this size, up here, nestling on the slopes of a mountain?" This was the engineer talking. "Would you believe it?" His arms swept the enormous stone complex. "Someone had to carry all these rocks from the quarry below. I bet there were no paved roads here then. I presume these are all local stones, but still, at this elevation it must have taken a lot of love and sacrifice." Indeed, the air was perceptibly thinner here.

Diana didn't comment. Her eyes continued to look dreamy.

They took a leisurely stroll to the rear of the main building. Due east, Mount Gargas rose another half a kilometre. For some reason, they both sensed a strange mystery that seemed to permeate the air all around them. For a while Michael and Diana stood entranced, unable or unwilling to move. Diana recovered first. She looked around. Anne was gone. A few steps later they saw her. She was walking down the path zigzagging across the hill. Diana pulled on Michael's sleeve.

"Let's follow her." For some reason she spoke in a whisper.

Anne did not lead them towards the top of the mountain. She made straight for the shrine. Michael and Diana continued walking some distance behind her. Once Anne reached the statue, she sat down on the grass and appeared to be staring at the Beautiful Lady. They observed her from afar. Now and again Anne would turn her head as though admiring the landscape. After a little while Michael got restless. Holy places had that effect on him.

"What's she doing down there?" he asked. "Aren't her lips moving?"

Diana smiled. "I wouldn't be surprised..."

"What on earth do you mean? Surprised at what?"

"They may have a lot to say to each other," Diana said, as though pointing out the obvious.

Whatever brought Diana to this place was still a mystery to him. Now it was getting deeper. Michael said nothing. What could he say?

Next morning they all got out of their cots before dawn.
By six, before breakfast, Anne led them outside. Actually, she
went outside and they followed. She pointed to the cross at the
very top of Mount Gargas.

"Take me there, Daddy," she pulled his hand towards the
footpath.

"Isn't that a bit high?" It was still grey, probably slippery
with morning dew.

"Mommy, will you come with me?" She was determined.

They went together, Anne a few steps in front. It wasn't
really a climb. The footpath wound at a reasonably gentle inclination. Still, the air was definitely thinner.

Thomas Mann had his Magic Mountain. Mount Gargas
claimed her own mystery. The air was so pure they inhaled it as
though it were an elixir of life. The magnificence of the French
Alps continued to unfold itself before them. Moments later, the
first rays of the rising sun kissed the very tops of the mountains
to the east, shimmering as though showing them the way to . . .
to where? Michael still wasn't sure. As they neared the top, he
was beginning to be taken in by the all-pervasive magic.

And then they stood at the summit.

A spectacular drop on one side, the panorama of the Dau-
phinés to the south, the peaks of the *Alpes Hautes* straight ahead
and beyond. Below and behind them, the vivid green of the lake
in Corps, seemingly a world away. Here, they were in a different
realm. Anne wanted to see everything all at once, as though her
life depended on it. Diana and Michael could hardly keep up
with her.

"You know, pet," Michael squeezed Diana's hand, "If I
were God, I couldn't have picked a better spot to reveal myself."

"Nor could the Beautiful Lady," Diana agreed. "I knew
we would find her here," she added as an afterthought.

"Mommy, does God live on this mountain?"

This was a little girl talking. Not at all like the Anne they
both knew. She was pointing at the large cross spreading its

arms far and wide. Though just a simple cross, it dominated the whole district like Cristo Redemptor atop the Corcovado.

"God lives everywhere, dear," Diana said stroking her flamboyant head. "But there is something special here," she added.

As they looked down, the only signs of civilization in sight were the Basilica with its ancillary buildings, a small cemetery and, of course, the Shrine. The rest of the terrain was green, the rounded hills protecting the holy place. The panorama was both rich and austere. It was as though the contrasts, or the opposites, merged here in serene harmony. Aren't all places holy, Michael wondered? Not as holy as this, came the answer from nowhere.

"Not as holy as this," he murmured.

"What, dear?"

He smiled. "I am beginning to understand why you brought me – why you brought *us* here."

"So am I, my husband. So am I. And I'm beginning to think that Anne does, too."

Michael looked at his daughter still staring at the cross.

"It was for her, wasn't it?"

Diana didn't answer, but it wasn't necessary. He knew. And he was grateful.

That evening they took part in the procession of candles. The wind died together with the setting sun. Not a sigh of air disturbed the stillness of the night. Then the stars moved. A long, winding path salted with flickering lights like a minuscule Milky Way, proceeded slowly down the gentle slope to stop momentarily at the statue and then return as slowly to the cathedral. Then the silence was broken as someone intoned a traditional tribute to the Beautiful Lady. Soon others joined her. Still others just inhaled the atmosphere that seemed filled with the magic of total dedication. Then with an air of having awoken from a lingering half-life, they retired to their narrow cots. The next morning, when Michael woke up, Anne's bed was empty. He assumed that she had gone to the bathroom. They shared one with four other cells along the corridor. After a while Diana opened her eyes. Anne still hadn't returned.

"Where could she be?" he pointed to her empty bed.

They searched the building. Two hours later they found her at the Shrine. She was sitting, as she had on the day of their arrival, facing the statue. Her knees were drawn up to her chest, her elbows resting on them. She was quite motionless. They didn't want to disturb her. It seemed wrong. She looked so very happy. So very much at peace with the world. With herself. Also she'd never looked quite so beautiful.

* * * * *

Chapter 11

Reunion

John Brent was, as he had been so often in the past, in seventh heaven. Or on cloud nine, depending how one chose to define his state of euphoria. It is true that his ecstatic states differed substantially from one another; nevertheless, he was quite content to increase the scale of his rapturous experiences as often as possible.

Usually, such states of ebullience were the consequences of specific incidents, such as procuring a grant for one of his many research projects, or a topping off ceremony – when the roof slab over the new wing's structure had been completed. Or even after individual successful neurosurgical operations, which lately seemed to follow one on the heels of another. His army of specialists had learned to derive and apply the full benefits the latest technology had to offer. What was more, the new discoveries enabled the surgeons to take gigantic steps in curing the heretofore incurable. There were moments when they felt like gods. Almighty.

There were a number of contributing factors. Giant steps in technology had been made possible not only by the unprecedented Federal stipend, but also by the funds that had suddenly begun to flow from unexpected quarters. Those latter boons may have resulted from John's refusal to use primates for even the most elementary experiments. Perhaps he'd awakened within us some sort of atavistic conscience towards our nearest relatives. Also, during recent months, the numbers of volunteers had swollen so much that even the new enlarged wards of the Neuro could not quite accommodate them. Such influx of patients willing to take a chance on new, experimental methods of treatment bore immediate results. Finally, there were hosts of long established, experienced neurosurgeons waiting in line to join John's teams. If necessary as interns.

Hardly surprising.

The success rate had tripled. Although the results had often been unpredictable, the developments were close to miraculous. *The Lancet* and other leading medical journals gloated about the Neuro's successes as if the publishers themselves had been responsible for the phenomenal breakthroughs.

This, in turn, fuelled the flow of yet additional funds. Various governmental agencies, individual millionaires, pharmaceutical conglomerates, even small businesses wanted to be associated with the growing accomplishments.

John felt a distinct sense of satisfaction. As he finished reviewing the 'in' basket, he leaned back in his swivel chair. He smiled at his thoughts.

"Like attracts like," Gabriel would comment dryly as though all John's successes had been a matter of course.

"Or in this case – success breeds success," Michael would add with equal equanimity. John closed the thick file and got up to go home. The empty apartment he visited less and less often.

And for the first time John became aware just how much he missed Mike and Diana. And Gabriel. Yes, and definitely he missed Anne. Only at the Howells, over those family dinners, had he felt sufficiently at ease to talk freely. Had he attempted such openness anywhere else, he would have been quoted, word for word, and all too often would have lived to regret having taken the liberty. He missed his friends all the more so, as he had never really developed closer ties with anyone else. His work commitments, upwards of seventy hours a week, were not conducive to an expansive social life. To any social life. Except for dear old Mike. When John's telephone rang on his desk, he picked it up automatically.

"Brent," he almost barked. He saved his suave manner for the bedside.

"John? What's wrong?"

"Mike! Is this really you?" The joy in his voice was reminiscent of a father greeting his prodigal son.

"Are you free tonight, by any chance?"

"When did you get back?"

"Last week. Are you?"

"Of course. I'll make myself free." He glanced at his agenda spread open on his desk. My God, I really am free! The lecture he was to give had been cancelled.

"About seven?"

"Make it eight." He really needed to catch up on his paperwork.

Only after Mike had hung up did John realize that he had not asked how his friends were. Now that he thought of it, there had been a certain tension in Mike's voice. More so than usual. Not that Mike was in the habit of lapsing into melancholy. But he had had his problems lately. John hoped Anne was all right. Anne and Diana, of course. They both had fallen on hard times, these last few months. Mike had to carry the burden. Belatedly, John felt pangs of guilt that he had not offered Michael more help. Perhaps weekly dinners weren't enough.

"I'll keep closer tabs on them," he promised himself.

From what he knew, Michael had a number of other friends. Perhaps not as close. Mike had once told him that when he and Diana visited others, or had other friends over, they talked shop.

"They're all engineers. Mostly civil, occasionally mechanical, once in a blue moon electrical. If an architect joins us, it's a big deal. Of course, architects are meting out our jobs, but still, it's never like eating with you."

There was an elusive line between a close friend and even a good acquaintance.

John also wondered what had happened to Gabriel. He was glad he had steered old Gabby Michael's way. The tall man was still a mystery to him, but there was something very reliable about his demeanour. From the way the Howells had spoken about him, he was a godsend.

Michael was still mulling over the mysteries of La Salette. He'd spent most of his time in his study, not feeling up to showing his face at his office. He sat at his desk, pensive, brooding over what had really taken place in France. As usual, his laptop remained his principal source of information. He wondered, for the umpteenth time, about Mélanie's vision. He knew that she had shared the experience with little Maximin in 1846. Why did Mélanie only write it all down in 1878? Why had she waited so long? Who could tell what memory did during those intervening thirty-two years? He wondered if John would know anything about things like that. Probably, he concluded. John knew a great deal about a great many things.

Still....

Do we remember selectively? Does that which is dearest to us stay with us longer? Or is it only that which stirs in us the most vivid emotions that we tend to retain? Michael's own memories of thirty-two years ago were as hazy as the early morning mist rising over the rounded hills of La Salette. He tried to picture the two children tending to their cattle on the slopes. Would, one day, his mind's imagery become part of his memories?

He couldn't let go the nagging question. Why did Mélanie Calvat wait thirty-two years to write her impressions? Of course, she probably couldn't write, at first.

He left his study to get a glass of water. He found Anne sitting cross-legged on the floor, a book on her lap, her green dress contrasting with the autumn-leaf carpet. Fluffy lay curled up at her feet, both seemingly content to just be. Neither looked up when Michael came in.

I might as well be at the office, he mused. He became vaguely aware of a silence that permeated the whole house. Aren't children supposed to make noise? Don't dogs bark, run around, knock things over with their tails? The next instant he understood. It wasn't silence he'd heard. It was peace. An impalpable aura of inexplicable serenity. It was the stillness he'd heard just before people started singing at the procession of candles.

His mind drifted back to his quandary.

Unless . . . unless it hadn't been Mélanie who had authored those vengeful mysteries. One thing was sure. Unless this, too, was a miracle, there was no way a simple peasant girl could write such things on her own. Not even thirty-two years later.

He glanced at Anne.

Since that day on the mountain, when he and Diana had found her sitting in front of the statue of the Beautiful Lady, she hadn't said much. She hadn't done much, either. True, it had been only a week since they got back, but it seemed Anne, his little Annette, was in a state of semi-trance. Today was the first time he caught her reading. Usually, when left to herself, she would sit for hours, immobile, silent, staring straight ahead. A vague smile would hover around her mouth, as though something very pleasant was taking place in her mind. Pleasant but distant. Like a mental and emotional insensibility. Or the sweet serenity of a hypnotic trance. Could it be that Anne was still absorbing, making her own, whatever it was that had taken place at the statue of the Beautiful Lady?

With a wistful shrug he returned to his study. He'd forgotten about the water. His mind drifted again to Europe.

During the last week in France they had made a cursory tour of the main tourist attractions – mostly in Paris. Obviously, Anne always went with them. Diana wouldn't let go of her hand, even for a moment. Yet, in spite of Anne's apparent withdrawal, Diana didn't seem worried. He'd actually found her seeming indifference annoying. Each time he'd approached the subject, he'd heard the same story.

"She will be back, darling. You will see," she'd said.

She will be back....

How many times had he heard himself say those very words to Diana over the years? She will be back... Now he was the one who was worried.

Diana was beginning to sound like Dr. Schneider.

"Would you ladies like to go out for a walk?" he suggested the other day. His voice sounded unnaturally light, almost uncaring. But before Diana or Anne could answer, he turned and went back to his study. He needed to talk, and Anne and Diana seemed to communicate without words lately.

Perhaps it is I who needs treatment, not Anne, he wondered half seriously. Yet the smile he kept on whenever Diana or Anne were around left his lips.

As far as he was concerned, Anne was in some kind of emotional paralysis. It was as though, during those last two days in La Salette, the remnants of her personality had been drained out of her in a flood of emotions which she'd poured out in front of that statue. The Anne he had known and loved was lurking somewhere behind a mask of studied indifference.

"Or it might be that I am simply jealous of the emotional detachment which the visit to La Sallette has conferred on both, my wife and my daughter," he muttered to himself.

He thought of Gabriel. "Where the hell is Gabriel?" he asked out loud. He rose to look for him and as quickly sat down. "I've got to do this on my own," he thought darkly. Aren't we all alone in this world?

His eyes wandered around the room. Shelves filled with books, mostly to do with engineering. A broad mahogany desk, his open laptop and writing pad. Diana had placed a slim crystal vase with a single carnation on the left corner of the polished surface. She always did that when he spent more time in his study. "It will keep you in touch with the world," she would say. To his right, photos of a dozen of his major projects reminded him of his past. On the wall to his left, two paintings, which to this day he neither understood nor liked, demanded attention. They represented colourful squiggles. Or a hundred thousand dollars. Each. They were from his father. Behind him was a large window. He seldom looked outside.

"Is this the sum total of my life?"

The study always was his cherished escape. His den where he rebuilt his defences against the vicissitudes of business life. Today, it felt like a prison.

"I wonder where Diana is...." He swung his chair to face the window. Only the highest twigs of the maple trees moved. There must be hardly any breeze at all.

For some reason he kept thinking that Anne was almost exactly the age of both girls, Mélanie and Bernadette. Was there something about that particular age that was crucial to a girl's development? Maybe, would John know?

Officially, Michael was still on holidays. Just as well. He was still under the influence of La Salette. He was not used to sitting at home, doing nothing much. Diana took Anne for walks in the park. He could have joined them, but he needed to be on his own. The two weeks in which the three of them had been seldom more than a few feet apart was great, but he wasn't used to such constant proximity. Even of people he loved with all his heart.

In many ways, Michael was a loner. He was happiest in his own office, resolving complex structural problems on his computer. He delegated as much administrative work to his partners, or even assistants, as he possibly could without overtly abusing his seniority. He didn't feel guilty for doing so, because he had discovered long ago that many people thought that leaving the office and attending what, to him, were boring meetings – was fun. Smiling, shaking hands and trying to impress people was not his forte.

At the same time, Michael found holidays unnatural.

One Sunday afternoon, about a month before they'd left for Europe, John had dropped in unexpectedly. Michael had been busy in his study, trying to sort out old business papers. His heart wasn't in it. Diana, just as half-heartedly, was catching up with her correspondence. They both longed for an excuse to spend the afternoon lazing in the garden.

Soon Diana, John and Michael found themselves stretched out on reclining deckchairs. Moments later Gabriel served all three tall steins of homemade Australian lager. From the side of the house they could just hear Anne and Fluffy playing hide and seek.

"Surely, if people don't like what they are doing, they should be doing something else." It had been on that occasion that Michael began expounding his ideas about work ethic. "Or, if absolutely necessary, learn to like that which they do." Though John had never thought about it before, he agreed. The alternatives were too dismal to contemplate.

"Not all people have this luxury," Diana had said at the time.

"They would if their motivations were to do the best they can, rather than concentrate on how much money they could make," Michael had insisted.

Money was never discussed at the Howells. Not that there was anything wrong with it. The fact was that money was always a by-product of their efforts, never a foremost reason for working. Before Anne was born, and before her parents had retired to North Vancouver, Diana was a teacher.

When her parents still lived in Montreal, Diana had taught history and geography. She enjoyed teaching – she enjoyed children. She even enjoyed preparing for the lessons, afterwards correcting her pupils' homework and seeing the children's progress. And after all this, she was paid for having such fun. Yet she still held that not all people were, or could be, so lucky.

"There are some who cannot do what they really want. They'd already missed the boat. They are too old, or infirm, or...."

"Diana, I'm not going to base my philosophy of life on exceptions. If some cannot do what they really want to do, they should make a concentrated effort to learn to like what they are doing," he insisted.

"And what of the maimed, the chronically sick?"

"Like Stephen Hawking?"

"That's not fair, and you know it. He is a most gifted man." Professor Hawking suffered from Lou Gehrig's disease, which had trapped him in a wheelchair for two decades. The incapacitating illness in no way stopped him from rising to world prominence.

"I dare say he might well be willing to return some of the gifts fate has bestowed upon him. But again, we are discussing exceptions. I firmly believe that we are all born to be good at something. That we all have been dealt cards with which, if we play them wisely, and don't waste our chances, we can win."

"You wax poetic, my husband," Diana smiled. "It sounds like your famous theory of universal benevolence."

John had been listening to all this without butting in. Finally Diana remembered the deliverer from having to spend her afternoon writing letters. She nudged him to have his say.

"My point of view is biased," John said slowly. "I met people with half their brains missing, who were bright. I met others who had minor spinal injuries, who preferred to think of themselves as complete invalids. One threatened to sue me for not declaring him incapacitated just so that he could collect insurance for the rest of his life. I think we are all different."

"I'll drink to that," Michael clearly recalled raising his tumbler on one such occasion.

They had spent many an evening talking like this. That was in the good old days when Anne's biggest problem had been bossing around some kids her own age. Or so they had said. Michael had never seen Anne being unfair to anyone. Nor taking advantage of someone weaker than she. If you don't count the flies, that is. As for the rest of her misdemeanours, they had never been proven. Not to his satisfaction.

In those days, Diana would often pick up the phone to call her mother, or Dad, just to share with them her problems. Then, at the last moment, she would stare at the plastic receiver and let it be. It seemed so cold. Indifferent. She was determined to share with her parents only her joys. Not her sorrows. Her self-imposed discipline was testing her resolve.

Over the years, they'd shared many such discussions.

John embraced Diana and held her until Michael advised him to get his own girl to squeeze. Only then did the two men hug. John's eyes searched for Anne.

"In her room," Diana said. "She likes it there. She enjoys her solitude."

John disengaged himself from Michael and tiptoed to Anne's room. The door was ajar, but to enter he would have to step over Fluffy, whose considerable bulk was prostrated across the entry. Fluffy was a very effective sentry.

Anne and Gabriel were seated and staring into each other's eyes. Neither of them moved until Gabriel detected a movement behind him. He rose slowly, towering over Anne.

"Welcome back, sir," he bowed to John. "It is a pleasure to see you again."

"You too, Gabriel, you too," John offered his hand. "How is..." he directed his eyes towards Anne who still hadn't moved although now her eyes were closed.

"She's coming, sir. She has come a long way."

John had been told about Gabriel's enigmatic pronouncements, but this was the first time he found himself on the receiving end of one.

"Do you know where she is going, Gabriel?"

"Of course, sir."

"Well...?"

"We are all going there, sir. Only very few of us make it. I think she might."

"Care to expand on that, my friend?"

"She is going where the opposites meet," was the cryptic reply. With that Gabriel bowed and withdrew towards the kitchen.

For some reason, just then John recalled his early days as a physicist. He thought of the mathematical formula which had proven that two parallel lines meet in infinity. He couldn't help smiling.

It was a strange reunion.

Within half an hour they were all sitting at the dinner table. Gabriel slipped in and out of the dining room, as always impersonating the invisible man. The plates seemed to dissolve into the kitchen, new dishes arriving at precisely the right moment. If Gabriel hadn't had the reputation of being an excellent nurse, he could have made a fortune as a butler at any of the regal houses. He really was that good.

In spite of the lateness of the hour, Anne joined them at the table. These were still the holidays. Schooling would start only next week. She ate her food with measured determination. The movement of her hands gave an impression of being automatic, as did her chewing, as though she attached no importance to those actions. Only her eyes spoke of a dormant volcano, not quite ready to erupt. Her eyes, and an almost constant smile. It seemed as if she were privy to some wonderful secret that she was not quite ready to share with anyone. Not even her parents. After the soup and a mere taste of the main course, she asked to be excused.

"But we have Peach Melba, darling. Don't you want any dessert?"

Anne's head swung from left to right. Other than that she remained still, waiting for permission to leave the table. In fact, since La Salette, she often gave this impression of waiting. It seemed as though she had been emptied of all desires, certainly of all malice, even of past memories, and was waiting to be filled in, anew, with new life, new vitality. She was neither sad nor joyful. Not really. Not as a child her age would be. Or should be. She seemed watchful, expectant. Of what?

Diana recalled the parable about new wine and old skins. She glanced at Michael. He was looking at his daughter with raised eyebrows. Diana thought she detected a shadow of understanding smouldering in her husband's eyes. After a moment or two he nodded, as if some idea had just come to him.

"Very well, pet. I'll bring the dessert to your room," he said.

Diana gave up. There was little else to be done. Anne was perfectly polite, perfectly poised. Perhaps she just wasn't hungry. After all, what sort of company were three almost elderly people for her? "But," thought Diana, "she'd probably act the same way if she were with people her own age."

After Anne left, no one spoke for a while. Anne's inward orientation seemed contagious. Each one of them was lost in his and her own thoughts. At length John began fidgeting.

"Well, John?" Michael practically spluttered.

"It is most interesting," John said slowly.

"That's it? Interesting?"

"It is interesting because it's unique in my experience."

"Explain?"

"I have been watching her eyes. Her reactions were different from anything I've ever seen." John leaned forward. "Two things. First, her eye reaction to movement is twice as fast as in an average person. Quite amazing...."

"And two?" Michael prompted.

"And two, her peripheral vision seems wider than in anyone I've ever seen."

"That's it?" Michael sounded nervous.

"What do you mean, Mike?" John sounded surprised.

"What Michael means," Diana interceded, "is that we are, well, Michael is worried about her behaviour in . . . in general. That she is not her old self."

"And you are not, I suppose?" Michael stared at his wife.

"Not in the way you are, dear. I became an ardent believer in your theory."

Diana was referring to Michael's concept of universal benevolence. He wished he had never shared it with her. On the other hand, he could hardly blame her. It had kept him going during Anne's earlier unusual activities as well as when Diana had her initial breakdown.

"You really believe in that?" He didn't sound convinced.

"Like never before, dear." Diana reached over and placed her hand on Michael's arm. "Ever since the three of us stood atop Mount Gargas, remember?"

He remembered well enough.

"And just what is Mount Gargas?"

"It is a magic mountain, John," Diana murmured.

"I thought that was Thomas Mann's domain," John grinned.

"To each his own. But trust me, John. Mount Gargas *is* a magic mountain. As we all stood there, right at the summit, Michael said that God picked a marvellous place to reveal himself."

"I thought that was Mount Sinai," John murmured.

"That's not what I said." Michael gave Diana a stern look. He sounded on edge. "What I said was . . . never mind. What do you make of Anne's behaviour, John?"

"As you already know, Mike, behavioural analysis is not my domain. What I do recommend, however, very strongly, is a follow up fMRI. We should see what is happening now that the tumour is not effecting any pressure." John swirled the water in his glass. "The brain is a homogeneous entity. But each single brain is as different from all the other human brains as are our fingerprints, or the patterns of our retinas. More so. We keep our fingerprints for life. The brain, on the other hand, is not only an amorphous organism but is alive. It moves. It changes. It expands and it contracts. It develops new connections, new means of communication with its various parts, all the time. I suspect that Anne's frontal lobes are involved in some sort of reorganization. Fascinating. Quite fascinating," he added.

"Another MRI?" Diana never did like the fangle-dangle machines.

"fMRI," John corrected. "We can study her brain while she remains fully conscious."

"I remember," Diana admitted meekly. "Do you really think it's necessary?"

"I know of no other way to learn more, and certainly of no better way..."

"It's OK, John. We'll do as you ask." Michael glanced at Diana. "Benevolence, remember?"

For the rest of the evening they talked about the trip to Europe. John listened, occasionally asking pertinent questions. He didn't want to talk about his business. He came here to escape from his total immersion. In Diana and Michael's absence, he'd been talking nothing but 'neurons'. Yet, neither of his friends seemed in the mood for idle talk. Anne's condition, whatever it was, had cast an invisible cloud over the evening. Not

one of them felt fully relaxed. They didn't listen to each other
with full attention.

At ten-thirty John got up to leave. He tiptoed again to
Anne's room. She still wasn't asleep. She was sitting on her
bed, her back towards him, listening to something only she could
hear. He could just see Fluffy's tail protruding from around her
bed. John didn't disturb her. As he turned to go, he heard her
whisper, "Goodnight, Uncle John."

Wide peripheral vision was one thing, but this was ridicu-
lous, he thought. Could it be that she'd recognized his specific
footsteps? On a thick carpet? Somehow he doubted it. Anne's
hearing had not been tested. He made a mental note to do so the
next time they did the fMRI.

After John left, Michael returned to his laptop. He thought he
would take a look at Fatima. He'd already looked up the revelations at Lourdes. There was nothing significant that he could
find except that whatever little Bernadette had heard did not
seem to make her very happy. Perhaps Fatima would shed some
light on Anne's strange reaction to La Salette. In a way, it was
an absence of reaction. To the shrine or to almost everything
else. Or else, and this was more than likely, whatever reaction
there was, it had been completely internalized.

A moment or two later, his computer screen displayed 'The
Message of Fatima'.

Michael wasn't really interested in the actual events, but just
in the portion that he had failed to understand in La Salette. The
part about the Secret Revelations. Before even attempting to explain the fairly recent Third Part of this now famous Revelation,
Michael read a lengthy Theological Commentary which made
two *a priori* assumptions. This first set Michael back. It said:

> "...the single Revelation of God addressed to all peo-
> ples comes to completion with Christ...."

What, he wondered, no more Revelations? Visions? Surely, in terms of the universe we are still primitives. We are babes in arms. If we ever needed revelations – about which he had his doubts – then we would certainly continue to need them. But then the light dawned once again:

> "...even if Revelation is already complete, it has not been made fully explicit, it remains for Christian faith gradually to grasp its full significance over the course of the centuries...."

If not longer. Phew . . . that's better, he smiled. So the Revelation is complete but we are not. Nor are we ready as yet to understand it.

"I can buy that," Michael told Diana, who was busy trying to read a book. She much preferred Michael in his office. He interrupted her periodically to share his thoughts. Most of the time the interruptions were out of context, and poor Diana had no idea what Michael was talking about.

"Yes, dear," she muttered.

"In their incredibly confusing way, they occasionally make a little bit of sense." Michael, of course, failed to tell her who 'they' were. "To simplify it still further, they might as well have said that everything already exists, but it will take us a few billion years to begin to understand it. Rather like the super string theory."

He then turned to the Revelation itself.

The translation purported to be in accordance with the version presented by Sister Lucia in the Third Memoir of August 31st, 1941. The third part had only been put on paper in 1944, fully twenty-seven years after the three children experienced the vision in Cova da Iria, near Fatima in 1917. Pope John Paul II only allowed Sister Lucia to comment on the secret in April 2000, when the poor sister was ninety-three years old. For the most part, the visions had not presented a pretty picture.

In the first vision Sister Lucia had offered a vision of hell. The usual demons, burning embers, bodies floating in conflagration, flames, great clouds of acrid smoke, etc., etc. It would have made Dante proud. To repeat, not a pretty picture.

In a way it was pathetic. From what little Michael had read on the subject of religious imagery, fire always symbolized a cleansing process. Here, it was just a scare tactic. No carrot, just a big stick. He told Diana about it.

"That's because you're just an old heretic," she replied with a straight face.

"Thank you, dear. I cherish my freedom." He sounded smug.

"Of course you do, dear."

"Don't you know, Di, that heretic means 'able to choose'?"

"Must have been the Greeks," she said sweetly. When Michael looked up from his laptop, she added, "heretic comes from Greek *hairetikos*, meaning able to choose."

"That's what I just said." Michael forgot that Diana used to be a teacher. Gosh, how time flies.

At any rate, the second part of the Revelation did not shed much joy either. Apparently if all of us sinners did not mend our ways, we would find ourselves . . . you know where. In the meantime we would experience wars, destruction and all sorts of very unpleasant things, right here on dear old earth.

The Third Part of the secret seemed directed at the Pope himself. If one were to take the vision as prophecy, then the Pope, his attendant entourage and a bunch of other people, religious and otherwise, would come to no good. No good at all. They would all end up in a hail of bullets and arrows, no less. Rather a strange mixture of weaponry, Michael thought. It ought to be one or the other, surely. But that was not the point.

Michael wanted to find out what sort of experience Anne might have had at La Salette. It was certainly true that she had undergone some sort of experience. A vision? Perhaps. And it was also true that her behaviour had undergone a considerable change.

There was one fundamental difference, though. Whatever Anne had heard or seen, it had left her with the most beautiful smile that almost permanently adorned her youthful little face. A smile of pleasure, of contentment, almost of bliss.

Strange, that. Four girls. Three spoke of suffering, or at the very least issued warnings of impending punishment and disaster. Anne hadn't spoken of her experience at all. But what her demeanour did indicate was that the Beautiful Lady was not wielding a flaming sword. She must have been kind and loving to have left Anne with such an angelic smile.

* * * * *

Chapter 12

The Second fMRI

"**After** the removal of even a very minor tumour, the particular portion of the frontal lobe affected by such an excision has room to expand. Not necessarily to grow in volume, but to change its density, which in turn might affect the way existing or new synapses act." His eyes belied his relaxed manner.

"The human brain is an extremely complex organism. At birth, a baby is endowed with hardly 340 grams of brain matter. By the time he or she reaches the age of three, the brain has grown to about 80 percent of its ultimate size. By the time a youth is 15 or 16, the brain has reached its adult size of about 1400 cc, weighing around 1.4 kilograms, which is also the age at which the bones of the skull fuse, presumably stalling any further physical expansion. Evidently nature has decided that, for now, we must make do with about 100 billion neurons."

John was used to giving background information to parents who desperately tried to understand the mysteries that lurked in their children's heads. Periodically he glanced at his friends to be sure that he still held their attention.

"What is perhaps of equal importance," he continued, "is that our cerebral cortex occupies, by volume, about 77% of our brain. What might appear to be of much lesser interest is that some 78% of our brain is made up of . . . water. And 99% of our cerebrospinal fluid is also water. Not good news for people who insist on walking bareheaded, outdoors, during Canadian winters."

Michael grinned triumphantly.

"These," John concluded as Michael continued to dig into his friend's knowledge for more details, "are rough guidelines only."

"I always wear a hat," Michael affirmed with dignity.

Actually, there was a great deal more. John went on to explain that the size of the human brain varies even as does the human body. The brain size of the modern day 'geniuses' has been found to vary anywhere between 1000 cc and 2000 cc. Obviously there are factors other than size which influence the brain's efficacy. An adult elephant's brain weighing in at 6 kilograms and a sperm whale's at 7.8 kilos, attest to this hypothesis.

"Unless, of course, there is something about the elephants and sperm whales," he concluded, "which we, with a mere 1.4 kilos, still do not understand." John looked fascinated and mystified, simultaneously.

"Probably," Diana affirmed with a straight face. John chose to ignore the comment.

"Anne's brain is reaching its ultimate size, but there is still room for some organic growth. A good few billion additional neurons."

As regarding the tumour, the problem was much more complex. What John had not told Diana or Michael was that brain tumours were the most common form of cancer in children. For every 10,000 brain tumours diagnosed in Canada, 3,000 originated in the brain. The remainder started in other parts of the body and spread to the brain over time. While Anne's brain tumour was definitely benign, its very presence suggested a possible predisposition to such growths. The next one, should there be one, might not be so harmless.

The reason John was particularly fascinated by Anne's symptoms wasn't just his personal fondness, if not indeed love, for the girl. With no children of his own, Anne was the nearest he had ever come to watching a child grow and mature, practically from her birth to her present stage of development. He saw her very nearly on a weekly basis, and rejoiced with Diana and Michael in her scholastic achievements, her evident, if somewhat erratic, perspicacity, not to mention her joyful relationship with Fluffy – even if, lately, that relationship seemed slightly suppressed by her emotional upheavals.

John was well aware that the particular part of the brain affected by the removal of the tumour was reputed to be the source of, or at least the control centre for, our emotions, our sadness or happiness, perhaps our anger, frustrations, and even our sense of humour. It was the CPU, the Central Processing Unit, of the magnificent computer that we recognize as our brain. These were scientific suppositions still needing further research, and Anne was a superb subject for such research. Just watching her told John volumes about possible neural sources of her behaviour. An fMRI, he felt, would say considerably more.

Just before Michael had taken his family to France, he and John had had a chance to discuss the moral implications of certain brain disorders. John did his best to explain to Michael that moral implications were completely *non sequitur* to surgical applications. John insisted that his job was to do the best he knew how and not concern himself with ethical connotations.

"We do not judge, Mike. No one can," John insisted.

"But surely," Michael pressed, "you must ask yourself if it is better to be instrumental in the creation of an amoral vegetable rather than permitting an obviously evil person to continue untreated."

"I'm not sure there is such a thing as an obviously evil person. His or her morality may be the consequence of an abnormal genetic structure."

"Are you trying to tell me that our morality is derived from our genetic code?"

"What else?" John sounded surprised. "Our actions, reactions, our power to reason, to calculate, to employ our intuition, to draw on our experience, memory, even our dreams, as well as a million and one other everyday actions are controlled and influenced by the way our brain functions. Why not our morality?"

"And what of our conscience?"

"To discuss our conscience we would first have to define what consciousness is," John insisted.

"Why, consciousness is our awareness. It is being aware of our environment."

"And our subconscious?"

"Diana has strong views on this. On the subconscious, I mean. She claims that each one of us is an individualized expression of a single, universal unconscious, and the subconscious is the storehouse of what we did, over aeons of evolution, with this individualization. Don't ask me what she means by this. But I, too, always imagined that we are more than our flesh and bones." Michael scratched his head.

"I couldn't agree more, though I am not really competent to discuss any of this. But if we do regard our brains as computers, then Diana seems to suggest that our subconscious is equivalent to memory banks. Am I right?" This time John felt on safer ground.

"I suppose....?"

"Well, if she is right, then the subconscious must have developed a means of expression. Or communication. Of sharing information." John sounded excited while Michael's expression looked painful. John didn't want to confuse the matter still further by bringing DNA into the memory equation, let alone the specialized neurons.

"I suppose...." Mike repeated feebly.

"Look at it this way, Mike. You and I can communicate thanks to our subconscious having developed a means of communication. Poor Fluffy can't. It is not that a dog cannot speak because he is stupid. A dog understands a great many things, can find objects by smell and recall items from memory, which are beyond human capability. But he cannot talk. Why do you think that is so?"

"I suppose he lacks the mechanism necessary to produce various sounds?"

John smiled triumphantly. "That, too, although there are many dogs that produce a great variety of sounds. They should be able to utter ten or twenty words. No. The main reason is that the speech centre in their brain is not yet sufficiently developed."

"What you are saying is that even if God wanted to speak through a dog he couldn't because a dog couldn't translate the mental concepts into words?"

"Something like that. God, the individualized unconscious . . . whatever. Although, I am told that God is God because He or She can do anything He or She bloody well wants!"

"S o ?"

"So I do not believe that God would *choose* to speak through a dog when He has six billion people at His disposal. Although, in most cases, He might get fed up waiting for one of us to shut up, so that He might have a chance to say something."

Michael ignored that latter part of John's speculation. "In other words, whatever we are, over and above our physical enclosure, must have a mode or a means through which to express itself."

John remained silent but his grin provided the answer.

"I and my Father are one," he murmured after a while. "We cannot do the impossible. Nor can God deny His own divinity."

"Diana would call that 'as above, so below', although I've never quite agreed with her," Michael mused.

"It depends what you mean by 'above'. That which motivates me is omnipresent. There is no above or below. Rather like your benevolent predisposition."

"One day I'll be very sorry I ever said that!"

"Why?" John spread his arms. "It makes good scientific sense. If you don't believe me look up the Chaos Theory. It suggests the very same thing, or at least a predisposition towards order and harmony. Or at least order...."

"I've read it. Some stuff on it, anyway. I like it. And what of evolution versus creation?"

"Again, I don't really distinguish between the two."

"You mean you agree with the six days...."

"I am not an idiot," John smiled. "I meant that creation takes place all the time. Look at it this way. The purpose of a gene is to reproduce itself, the best way it knows how. That, by the way, is why we are still alive. Why the human race is surviving. But occasionally a gene makes a mistake. Let's call it a bad mistake. In science we would call such an error – cancer. If it were a good mistake, we would call it a mutation. Now if the mutation is not all that good, it dies out. If it is really good, it results in evolution...."

"So evolution is a series of fortuitous genetic mistakes?" Michael's eyes were growing larger.

"What do you think?"

Michael didn't answer.

"You see, Mike, only the religious people can be sure of anything. That's because they've never seen the object of their belief. A scientist is never sure. We deal in facts, or what we presume to be facts. A dogma is a theory that has never been proven. A scientific theory is one that has not as yet been disproved. Now ask me if I believe in God."

Michael's eyebrow went up. He chose to say nothing.

"Of course I do. I make too many mistakes not to!"

This time Michael smiled broadly. "You are a true product of evolution, John."

"I'll take that as a compliment. So are you, by the way. Isn't everybody?"

"Aye... we all make mistakes!"

Their laughter was followed by a moment of pensive silence. Then Michael, as though returning from a short but pleasant trip, repeated the original question. "And what of our conscience?"

John threw up his hands in mock desperation. "I strongly suspect that it is little more than a reaction to our awareness of who we really are. You'd better talk to Diana about it. I'm still searching."

They had met to discuss what might happen to Anne as a result of her operation. Instead they had veered into quasi metaphysics. Or were they really physics, only with philosophi-

cal connotations? Michael still drew a line between science and
religion. For John it was all one. Perhaps one with a capital O.

Yet for some reason Michael felt reassured. Even if John
did make a mistake, it might turn out to be an opportunity. A
step upwards. At least upwards on the scale of evolution. Poor
Annette. If only she knew. After studying all those apparitions
in Lourdes, La Salette and Fatima, Michael was no wiser. On the
other hand . . . perhaps Anne knew. Maybe she was just keeping
it to herself.

And then an idea struck him out of the blue.

"I'll talk to Gabriel about it," he said out loud. "First
thing tomorrow."

Anne walked into Uncle John's office and made directly for the
settee by the window. She was calm and seemed completely at
ease. Diana had brought her to the MNI at the appointed time.
As usual, Dr. Brown was there to receive them. Minutes later
Diana and John Brent were seated next door to John's office, the
private meeting room he used for intimate, one-on-one consul-
tations. Diana remembered the room from her last visit. She
didn't find it intimate at all. Once settled, John attempted to explain to Diana what he hoped to accomplish with the fMRI. He
thought it best if, at this stage, Anne didn't get involved. He believed her emotional condition should not be subjected to any
more stress than absolutely necessary.

As it happened, Anne didn't mind at all. She'd already
met Dr. Brown and remembered him well. She liked him. He
was much younger than all the other doctors she'd noticed at the
Institute. Some of them had grey beards. They must have been
really old. Older than her father. Peter was possibly no more
then twenty-five years old. Maybe even less. Anne thought that
Peter Brown was very handsome. He was also tall and had beautiful jet-black hair. And he smiled a lot. But what was most important, he had always treated her like an adult. He spoke to her
as one speaks to an equal. And he'd asked her to address him
by his first name. She liked his name. It was short and . . . well,

she just liked it. In fact, she couldn't think of anything she
didn't like about Dr. Brown. About Peter.

"I'll wait here for Uncle John," she told him.

He agreed. "Do you mind if I go and do my work?" he
asked politely as usual.

She did mind. Of course she minded. "Go right ahead,
Peter. I'll be quite all right here," she said with perfect poise. It
wouldn't do to show him that she minded. She watched him all
the way to the door. He moved so nicely. Like a dancer, or that
boxer she'd seen on TV. It was good thinking about Peter, she
thought. Yet, the moment the door closed behind Dr. Brown,
Anne's lids descended halfway down her eyes, and her body
relaxed into that peculiar state of being that could only be described as detached immobility.

Anne had returned to her private realm.

About that time John's beeper played a little madrigal. He
instantly got up and, with a little bow towards Diana, left the
room. As he opened the door, Diana heard hurried steps racing
down the corridor. She caught a whiff of anaesthetic. Or it
could have been just the smell of sterilized surgical instruments.
Or the floor. Or the green gowns the surgeons all wore. She
thought white gowns would have been more elegant. More
'medical', so to speak. But the smell was strong.

She shrugged. Frankly, she didn't care.

She felt distracted. Her mind refused to be quiet. She
wished she could find the detachment that Anne, apparently,
found so easy. Dear Anne. Was she really going to benefit
from La Salette? Two weeks had passed since they'd returned
from Europe. From France, to be more precise. In some ways,
Diana was glad they were back home. She had been quite ready
to make a quick dash to Fatima, if necessary, but there was no
need. She had found what she'd gone for. At least, she thought
she had. God, how she hoped....

As Diana waited for John to return, she thought of the conversation she'd had with Michael last night.

"You wouldn't believe, Michael, how many holy places are actually sanctioned and approved by the Vatican as places of worship," she'd told him, looking up from the book on her lap.

Michael nodded, waiting for her to continue. This was the fifth or sixth time she had raised the subject of 'holy places'.

"Just listen to this," Diana turned a page, "this book offers more than seventy of Christianity's more celebrated shrines and sanctuaries... Seventy! I bet there are many others which are not quite as celebrated."

"Why are you telling me all this?" Michael was attempting to read his own book.

"Just think how much money I've saved you by hitting the jackpot on my second attempt." Diana had said this in a serious tone of voice, though there was a twinkle in her eye.

It was at that moment that John returned, breaking into her thoughts. He glanced at his watch and apologized for leaving her alone for so long. Actually, only minutes had passed. Diana smiled her forgiveness. She told John about the discussion she'd been having with Michael the previous evening. Just to give him some background. John had asked her to tell him something of Anne's behaviour at La Salette. Diana was playing for time. What she felt about Anne's experiences and what she could put into words were two different things. She couldn't even explain most of it to Michael. For some reason she felt nervous. She wished they were at home, in comfortable arm-chairs, not here, in this sterile environment. John's conference room was too functional. Too rigid. Pale green walls. Thermo-plastic tiles on the floor. And those tiny windows with thin Venetian blinds. Not conducive to discussing the intangibles.

"I often thought that Anne was communicating at different . . . at a different vibration than other children," she started lamely. John didn't interrupt. "I felt that I had to look for conditions in which she would experience a similar resonance to that which was already in her. I mean...." she spread her arms. She had no idea how to continue.

"You thought that Lourdes or La Salette would do to the workings of her mind what they are known to have done to the bodies of many men and women?" John offered.

"Not really. People go to the various shrines hoping for a cure. To get healed. I never thought that Anne needed healing. I don't mean her tumour, but her state of mind. I just thought that she did not find familiarity with the way most of us think. That she was, in a way, on a different vibration or wavelength. Different resonance. I don't know how else to put it."

"I think you've explained it very well. And you think that Anne found compatible, ah . . . vibrations in La Salette?"

"Not so much found them as affirmed them. It seems to me that she no longer feels alone."

John remained silent. There is more to heaven and earth... he remembered Shakespeare. Or was it the Bible? While he wouldn't deny that Diana might have a point, he didn't really know how her assumptions, or conclusions for that matter, might benefit his diagnosis. Perhaps a psychiatrist could help, but Anne did not seem to manifest any overt signs of neurosis, phobia, delusions, nor any other pathological conditions of the mind. She did have moments during which she appeared to withdraw from what most of us recognize as tangible reality. But so do most poets, composers, or artists of one persuasion or another. Their condition was different from the so-called average, but so is a politician's, a CEO's of a large conglomerate, or the Queen of England's. They all have to be, and they are – unique. But so what? Aren't we all supposed to be distinct?

Anne was very distinct. More distinct than anyone he'd ever met. Behaviour patterns that in others would have been ignored, at most passed over as childish or adolescent idiosyncrasies, in Anne's case took on compound meanings. Compound overtones. Or was it just he who failed to reconcile them as normal or at least within accepted norms of behaviour? What was it that made Anne so distinctive?

An fMRI, however, was a different story. It did not draw conclusions, it merely reported what was happening. It was up to him, later, to draw such conclusions as might be of some help. If indeed help was needed.

"Would you say that Anne's behaviour is normal?"

Diana looked at him closely. "Just what do you mean by normal, John?"

To be quite honest, John was more curious than anything else. Apart from his professional obligation to follow up on Anne's operation, he had always been fascinated by deviations from the norm. Was Einstein normal? Or Newton? or Mozart? Or any of the great people of our cultural heritage? Surely had they been normal, they wouldn't have been able to accomplish what they did.

If normal meant average, then God save her from being normal, he almost said aloud. "I mean, is there anything in her behaviour which threatens her safety?"

"Absolutely not. Not in the least." Diana sounded adamant.

"I thought as much." He smiled to set her at ease. "We, in medicine, have a habit of judging people by their deviation from that which we consider normal. A normal person has such and such temperature, such and such pulse and so on. In a way, conformity to the average has become the yardstick for assuring peoples' state of well-being."

"How boring," Diana couldn't help herself. "But I see your point. You have to start somewhere."

"Precisely. At a deeper level, we are all different. But the more different we are, the harder it is to come up with the correct diagnosis."

He wanted to be reassuring, but there was a vague uneasiness in his voice he couldn't quite hide. He wasn't quite sure whether he'd come across an Einstein, a savant, or just a trifling departure from the boring norm.

"We have an opening for the fMRI in," he glanced at his watch, "...in about two hours. Let's go and talk to Anne."

As they walked into John's office, Anne was lying on the settee by the window. Her head rested against the side armrest. She looked asleep. There was a vague smile of contentment that made her face look angelic. Her hair formed a round halo of an almost perfect circle.

Diana walked up to her and stroked her forehead. Anne didn't move.

"Come, baby, Uncle John wants to ask you some questions," she said quietly.

Anne still didn't move.

Diana's heart missed a beat. For an instant she imagined that Anne had slipped again into a coma.

"Let her rest. There is nothing much we can do until after we take the scan," John proposed. Who knows what the Annes of this world do at night, he mused. Perhaps she has some catching up to do?

John's relaxed voice snapped Diana out of her momentary panic. Her nerves weren't what they used to be. She took a deep breath. They sat down, he behind his desk, Diana on one of the chairs in front of it.

They chatted about this and that. Diana told John about Michael's preoccupation with trying to dissect the prophecies of various shrines into some semblance of order.

"As far as I know, the more logic he applies, the less sense they make to him."

"He is, what we call, a left-hemisphere man. Left hemisphere of the brain. His mind is logical, orderly, well structured, rational and indeed analytical. Perhaps the very opposite of Anne's. She seems to experiment. To pick and choose. To absorb facts randomly. I wouldn't be surprised if she had a good ear for music." John was thinking of his tiptoeing to her bedroom two weeks ago. His own mind also leaned towards the structured and methodical.

"And...?"

"And thus Michael would always have difficulties with the spontaneous, the creative or the mystical. I would, too, had I not studied the subject."

"So one can study to . . . to use both hemispheres of our brain?"

"My dear Diana! We all use both of our hemispheres, all the time. It is only a question of intuitive priorities. It is like being ambidextrous but favouring one hand over the other. A sort of natural predisposition."

Five minutes before the scheduled time for her fMRI, Anne opened her eyes and favoured John and Diana with a beautiful smile.

"Shall we go?" she asked, as though nothing had happened. Frankly, nothing had. Her recurrent if unpredictable withdrawals from reality were becoming commonplace.

"We thought you were asleep, pet?"

Anne's smile was replaced by concentration as she led them to the door. "Sort of, Mommy."

As they walked along the corridor and down the main staircase, a number of doctors and nurses bowed to John Brent and smiled at Anne. She seemed to invoke smiles in most people. In – not from. On meeting or even just seeing her in passing, they smiled. Not specifically to her or at her but just, well . . . their smile remained on their lips long after they'd passed her.

How different Anne seemed from a few years ago, Diana thought. Then, still in school, children had tended to keep their distance from her. Diana recalled some annual parents' meetings she'd attended. It seemed like ages ago. Other parents, even teachers, had not been forthcoming in discussing Anne's behaviour. Her likes or dislikes. It was as though they'd been embarrassed. Reserved. On the few occasions when Diana picked Anne up at school, to go somewhere directly, the other children showed Anne a strange sort of deference. Not that they didn't like her, but there was a conspicuous reserve in their relationships. They lacked spontaneity. Diana suspected that they had also been afraid of her. Then as now, nothing had ever been proven, but, well, people talked. It must be in our nature, she mused.

"There is no smoke without fire," they must have said. Or probably whispered among themselves.

Then, there was that extended period when Anne hadn't talked at all. In rare moments of communication, Diana had gathered that, in some ways, she seemed unaware of right and wrong. Not that she'd ever talked about it directly. Later still, for a while, she was also very emotional. Rather than right or wrong, she seemed swayed by sadness or contentment. But

mostly sadness. As though someone had done something very
wrong to her. Of course, someone had. Michael had managed to
save Anne from having to testify in courts. Not that she would
have said much. In those days she talked very little. Even less
so than now. Only now she had that strange serenity about her.
As though she'd finally managed to get rid of whatever had
been bothering her.

She was certainly a complex child, and she appeared to
grow in complexity. This autumn she would turn fourteen, and
she'd already manifested a variety of different personas. She
exhibited but few symptoms of her old modes of behaviour.
She displayed a whole gamut of new ones. In succession. Albeit
no longer aggressive. You might call it the Anne Syndrome.

The functional magnetic resonance imaging procedure was
routine. Anne lay down, had her head strapped securely, and the
sliding platform slowly moved towards the dark opening. There
followed the usual questions, finger movements and other trials
to establish parameters. John and Peter were busy studying the
computer screens and manipulating various, to Diana completely
meaningless, knobs. After what seemed like a very long time,
Anne's limp body slid out of the dark tunnel and lay, helpless,
waiting to be freed from the restraining straps.

At least, that was how Diana saw it. In fact, the tunnel
wasn't dark at all, and the whole procedure took a little over
twenty minutes.

When Anne stood up, she thanked Uncle John, shook hands
with Peter, and asked her mother if she could go home now. She
seemed relaxed, though her voice sounded a bit wooden. As if
she spoke because she had to, or because it had been expected of
her. Diana felt that if she refused, or wanted to stay much
longer, Anne would have found a bench or a chair and departed
to her never-never land where she'd spent those two hours in
John's office. She didn't want to take that risk.

"Shall we see you tomorrow, John?"

"I'll be happy to come," he assured her. Then, as an afterthought, he took Diana to one side. "Would you mind awfully if I brought Peter? He's been a great help with Anne."

"Of course. He seems like such a nice young man," she said, also in half tone. Then she turned to Dr. Brown. "Do you think, Doctor Brown, that you might find time tomorrow to drop in for a bite with us and Doctor Brent?"

Peter took a deep breath. It's not often that a resident is asked to dine with the Chief of Staff. The Director, to boot.

"It would be my pleasure, Madam," he replied, bowing like a young man straight from a Swiss finishing school.

"See you both around seven, then," Diana said and made for the door.

For a moment she thought that Anne had changed her mind about going home, or else that she'd already succumbed to one of her frequent stances of total immobility. Then Anne blinked a few times in quick succession and followed her mother. Her mouth widened into one of her unique smiles, as mysterious as Mona Lisa's. Only much, much prettier.

Anne was very happy. Very happy indeed.

* * * * *

GENIUS

*"What does a fish know about the water
in which he swims all his life?"*

Albert Einstein

Chapter 13

Waiting

Waiting for the diagnosis of your child's suspected affliction is a painful time. It does not matter what the problem is. In a way, it's like visiting your doctor for an annual check-up. You hope he will find nothing, and yet, if there is nothing, then you wonder, what was the point of the visit? You always hope for the best, but then you think that if he is to discover something, anything at all, then at least whatever-it-is might prove to be easily curable.

The moment John had run over the entire set of computer images, he telephoned Michael to say that things looked OK. Diana listened on the extension. He heard them both take a deep breath in perfect unison.

"I'll tell you the rest over dinner? I just wanted to let you know that you have nothing to worry about," he assured them.

John could hardly hide the profound relief in his voice. What he still had to share with them hardly amounted to a pathological condition. It was certainly not a malady. It was an error. A genetic mutation. Only time would tell what might be its consequences. If any.

One of the challenges Diana had with her daughter was that, whatever her other faults, Anne was a very quick study. She seemed to have a knack for reading books very fast indeed. She memorized the essential elements only, which, nevertheless, enabled her to reconstruct the entire story or to elaborate on those elements, in great detail, at a later date. This coming November, Anne would begin her fifteenth year, and she had already completed the entire curriculum designed for girls finishing high school. She hadn't taken the exams, but was ready to do so at any time.

When Anne wasn't sitting still and withdrawing into her inner world, she was scanning rather than reading books, selectively, and then spending equal time looking for new material to read. Her main interest was autobiographies. She was interested in what motivated people to do things. Any things. What Diana and Michael missed most was that she very seldom deigned to discuss what she had read, or even express an opinion, let alone a judgment, on her voluminous literature. It was evident that Anne did have a distinct view of reality, if only by studying her facial expression. Yet those views remained internalized, perhaps stored for later reference. Of course, it was possible that she had dismissed the vast majority of her books as dull, not worthy of discussion.

"One day she'll open up and boggle our minds," Diana confided to John as they waited for Anne to finish Peter's 'newcomers' tour of the house. As both physicians managed to get away from the Institute by six, Anne had plenty of time to play the perfect hostess. Especially to Peter. To Doctor Peter Brown. She showed him every nook and cranny in meticulous detail.

Anne invariably took it upon herself to offer a sightseeing tour of the house to all guests who came to visit for the very first time. It had become a tradition. Although, to date, she had never been quite so attentive in her presentation of every element.

Diana was careful not to discuss either Anne's achievement or foibles in her presence.

"Our children always boggle our minds," John replied, " I speak from vast experience..." he grinned. His experience of 'our' children was a precise zero.

"You know more than you let on," Michael put in. "I bet you could teach us both a great deal about our own daughter."

Moments later Anne brought Peter back to the living room.

"Do we pass?" Diana asked.

"Your daughter, Madam, is a very gracious guide." Dr. Brown bowed a little stiffly. He wasn't quite sure how to behave: outside the confines of the Neuro, yet still in the presence of the Director.

"If you are going to be a visitor in our house, doctor, I suggest you address me by my first name," Diana proposed. " I am not as old as those two fuddy-duddy gentlemen make me look."

There was a peculiar paradox in the Howell family. Diana looked as young as Anne looked mature, for their respective ages. A few years from now, they would probably fool people by claiming to be sisters.

"Oh no, Mada . . . I mean, Diana. Of course not. I don't mean that Mister Howell and Doctor Brent is, I mean are, old, I mean...." He got completely tongue-tied. Doctor Brown had heard many an uncensored designation spoken behind Dr. Brent's back, but fuddy-duddy? Surely....

"Oh, yes, I am!" Michael assured. "I'm old enough to be your father. I think you should call me Dad." He was addressing Peter.

"And me – uncle," John threw in.

During all this, Anne was standing very still, as if weighing the pros and cons of joining the discussion. She looked radiant and not just because of her hair. There were signs, perhaps visible only to her mother, that she was in the process of waking up from a long rumination. Diana wondered if she would ever find out just where her daughter went for such long periods of time. Apart from the brief sojourn at La Salette, it had been years since Anne had looked or sounded really spontaneous.

After a little more jesting at poor Peter's expense, Anne took a step forward.

"If you would like to talk to an adult, I shall be in my room." With this she spun on her heel and walked out.

There was a moment of startled silence.

"I think, Peter, you'd better follow her. You might try apologizing for us all. It's just, you see, in this house we don't take ourselves very seriously..." Michael sounded contrite. " I do hope we haven't offended you."

"Of course not, Sir."

"That goes double," John butted in, making a penitent face. This was an aspect of the Chief of Staff that Peter Brown had neither seen nor imagined possible. At the MNI, Dr. Brent was the epitome of succinct efficiency. He may have cracked a joke now and then, but only after a difficult case had been re-solved and, Peter suspected, only to relieve the pent-up tension.

"Michael," Michael corrected. "There are no sirs or mad-ams in this house. Sirs are gentlemen who have been knighted by Her Majesty the Queen of England and her defunct colonies, and Madams are ladies who run disorderly houses. We don't qualify under either definition."

"Dinner is served, Madam," a deep voice announced.

"Except for Gabriel. He refuses to treat either of us like regular people."

As tall as Peter was, Gabriel towered over him.

"I'm honoured, Michael," Peter bowed again.

"You know, Mike, this lad does more exercises in a day just bowing than I do in a week running up and down the stairs at the Neuro," John said, his voice as wistful as the expression on his face.

"I'm sorry, Sir..." Peter began, only to have John cut him off.

"Sir? SIR? Didn't your host just explain to you the finer points of the English Language?"

"But... b-b-but...."

"It's OK, Peter, you can still call me whatever you like at the Neuro. But have the decency not to insult my best friend in his own house."

Peter opened his mouth, thought better of it, bowed stiffly again and went in search of Anne.

"Gentlemen, dinner is served," Gabriel repeated, this time raising his voice a little.

The three of them jumped to their feet. Peter met Anne halfway to the dining room.

"Are they always like that?" he asked her in a hushed voice. "Always?"

"No, Peter. Only on empty stomachs," Anne replied, walking past him. She almost said 'race you to the dining room', but thought it would be unladylike. The moment she'd thought of it she slowed down and walked the rest of the way in a dignified manner.

Peter followed her physically as well as with his eyes. He just couldn't believe what he saw. The girl wasn't even fourteen yet. And yet....

"Don't be bloody stupid, lad," he admonished himself.

After dinner, they all went back to the living room for coffee and some *bouchées sucrées*. Michael also took a Remi Martin, Diana and John sipped Cockburn's 1997 vintage Porto, a treat reserved for special occasions only. Peter had been about to join Michael when Anne asked him if he drank lots of alcohol. Suddenly Peter felt that he was being evaluated not as a physician but as a man, probably one displaying his vices.

"Why, no, Anne. I take a drink very seldom, in fact...." again he sounded a little flustered. His apparent state of confusion would have been easier to understand if Peter hadn't been the most efficient, able and articulate resident John Brent had ever had.

"Anne, this is not the sort of thing a young lady asks a gentleman. If you must ask him such things, you can do so when you are alone with him." Diana's tone was sterner than she'd intended. She didn't know how Peter would react to her daughter's overt lack of tact. Her directness carried echoes of her early childhood.

At this Anne got up and walked to the door. There she turned and waited.

"Well?" she said, looking at Peter.

"Anne!" Diana got up and was about to take Anne out of the room when Peter came to her rescue.

"Really, Diana. I don't mind. Really."

With that he got up and followed Anne into the garden.

"I don't know what's gotten into her. She never acted like this before."

"She wasn't aware of her hormones before," John muttered under his breath. Then he said aloud. "Actually, I'd asked Peter to take Anne out of earshot when he got a chance. I didn't know that Anne would be such a willing accomplice. I wanted to tell you about her latest fMRI."

"You mean you told Peter...."

"Just what I said," John reaffirmed. Then he took a deep breath. "We have a very interesting set of observations. They account for some of the symptoms which we, actually mostly you, both of you, have been noticing."

Diana and Michael put their glasses on the side tables and, as though on command, both leaned over towards John.

"Go on?" Michael sat on the edge of his armchair.

"There are two items. First, the excision of the tumour was complete. We can be sure that there are no residual cells which could initiate another occurrence." He looked at each of them in turn. "Sometimes, no matter how hard we try, even a minute remnant of tumourous matter can act as seed for another growth. Well, there is no danger of that."

"So what's so interesting, John?"

"I'm coming to that. The reason I dwell on this matter is that most tumours do not spread to other parts of the body. What they do is invade other parts of the brain. Had the tumour been deep inside the brain tissue, we would have had to resort to radiation therapy. Now we are reasonably sure that there is no need for such. Anne's brain appears as healthy as it was on the day she was born."

John felt that there was no need to tell his friends that there may be rogue cells that are not metabolically active. They would be a little like moles that might awaken to their subversive activity at some later date.

Diana smiled a knowing smile as though to say 'I knew that'. Michael was still anxious.

"Go on," he urged.

"Well, when we removed the benign growth, we created, for the want of a better word, a space. What normally happens is that the density of the brain matter gradually decreases as the existing cells fill the void – and all's well. The brain just spreads out and fills in the space. Well," he paused, searching for words that would be understandable to people not trained in medical terminology, "this has not happened in Anne's case. We have strong evidence that the space liberated by the tumour is already being filled in. But, and this is what made us wonder, it is not being filled in by reduced density of the surrounding area but by new neurons. And they must have grown at a fantastic rate to fill in the space so quickly."

"Is that good or bad?" Michael was fidgeting on the edge of his seat.

"To tell you the truth, we don't know. It is as though Anne's grown a billion or two extra neurons in the area of her brain that is at the very core of the nerve centre. It is also the part of the brain which controls emotional behaviour."

There followed a sustained silence. John couldn't possibly tell his friends that increased metabolic rate is usually associated with malignant growths. As best as he and his staff had managed to assess, the new neurons in Anne's frontal lobe appeared completely normal.

Some moments later they all heard a burst of laughter from the garden. Whatever Anne may have become, she sounded radiantly happy. This hadn't happened for some time now. Perhaps it never had. Not till this very moment.

Once again, Diana's face reflected her daughter's happiness. She got up, walked to the window and looked out. Anne and Peter were talking and seemed engaged in some peculiar, mime. She couldn't hear the words, but the scene was peculiar to say the least. Peter held a stick in his left hand, wedging its other end between his chin and his left shoulder. In his right hand he held another stick, which he rubbed vigorously up and down the horizontal one. As he continued to do so, swaying from side to side, Anne proceeded to jump in a show of joy. She then clapped her hands in apparent admiration. It's a strange way to start a fire, Diana thought smiling.

"Children..." she murmured, returning to her chair. "What imagination."

"You are quite sure?" Michael also got up, but he began pacing the room. He was still thinking about John's report.

"Mike, the brain is the most complex organism in the universe. Scientists are never sure. We only eliminate as many possibilities as we possibly can."

Diana wasn't worried. She knew, not hoped nor thought but *knew*, that Anne was all right. Perhaps more than all right. All of us were all right. Anne was more than just that. She was... she is my Anne, she concluded silently.

About then Michael stopped pacing.

"And the other item you were going to tell us about?"

"Ah, yes," John again seemed to have trouble finding the right words. "You probably know that the brain is composed of various parts. Basically of cerebrum, the cerebellum, the pons and the medulla oblongata." He looked at Michael who nodded knowledgeably. "As you probably also know, the cerebrum is the largest part, and it consists of two virtually equal parts known as the hemispheres, whose outer part is made up of neurons. These two hemispheres, the left and the right, are recognized as the parts of the brain that control man's conscious and voluntary processes. The cerebellum, which is located below and behind the cerebrum, controls our muscular movement, while the medulla oblongata, atop our spinal column, is the vital nerve centre that controls our breathing, circulation and so forth."

John stopped to take a tiny sip of Porto. "To the pons, the link between the two hemispheres of the cerebrum, I'll come back later," he added, as though not sure of his ground.

This wasn't easy. Few people could grasp the significance of knowledge that had advanced meteorically in recent years. Neither of them interrupted, waiting patiently for John to continue. As a matter of fact, since Anne's original fMRI, Michael had read enough on the subject to feel at home with the terminology. Diana didn't seem to mind missing a word or two. Her knowledge spanned quite different realms.

"As you already know, the two hemispheres work in conjunction with each other. A long time ago, around 1800, a fellow by the name of Franz Joseph Gall developed a system of analyzing human character, as well as other traits, by studying the shape and protuberances of the human skull. He called the method phrenology, which strangely has a double etymology. The Greek *phren* or *phrenos* means the mind, but also the midriff. At any rate, serious neurologists have long since discarded the theory, but I thought of it when I measured Anne's skull. That mass of glorious hair hides a little secret."

John was becoming increasingly nervous.

"Is there something wrong with her scull?"

"Mike, relax. Were there something wrong I would have told you straight away. Just bear with me."

Michael finally settled next to Diana, who seemed perfectly relaxed. She acted and looked as though she had known all along that there was nothing wrong with her little Anne's head.

"Whenever we examine a patient, do a PET scan or take an fMRI, we also measure his or her skull in great detail. The first time we measured Anne's was when she was barely eleven years old. This time we did it again and we found that the part of the skull that protects the pons Varolii, that is to say the bridge between the left and the right side of the brain, is more developed than in an average, ah . . . head. The fMRI obviously confirmed this observation." John glanced at Diana and Michael to see if they understood the possible consequences of this discovery.

"I suppose that would make her ambidextrous?" Diana asked innocently.

"That, too." John looked at Diana with surprise. "Frankly, we have no idea where this might lead. But we strongly suspect that she might develop an ability to vastly increase the communication between her two hemispheres. An interaction vastly greater than an average person is likely to enjoy. I suspect that people like Einstein and Mozart may have developed similarly enlarged pons, or pontes. Although it is too late to prove it."

There was real sadness on John's face. Whatever he felt for Anne, or his friends, he was first and foremost a scientist. The possibilities of Anne's latent potential, as defined by the latest fMRI, fascinated him more than he could say.

"Are you suggesting that my daughter is some sort of a genius?"

"Easy, boy." John couldn't help smiling. "Genius is defined as five percent talent and ninety percent sweat."

"By my calculation that adds up to ninety-five percent," the engineer in Michael pointed out triumphantly. It wasn't often that he managed to score one over his friend.

"That's right. The residual five percent is pure luck," John said, grinning. Then his tone turned serious again. "No. What I am saying is that if Anne is willing to sweat a great deal, then she appears to have the equipment to...." his voice trailed off into a broad spread of his arms. "The sky is the limit," he added quietly.

John could have speculated at length.... A scientist who could excel in theoretical physics with ability to confirm his findings in a laboratory? A scientist who was also a great artist? A master of art forms as yet unknown to man? A conductor who was also a great composer? A great saint capable of great evil? Or indifference? "The sky is the limit...." he muttered to himself.

He glanced at Diana and Michael. They too looked lost in deep thought.

"Oh, no, you don't!"

Anne, with Peter at her heels, burst into the room almost simultaneously.

"Mommy! Dad! Peter can play the violin!"

"Actually, I used to practice a little until a couple of years ago. Now Doctor Bre . . . now John has other designs for my time."

Diana smiled. "So that's what you were doing with those two sticks! You weren't rubbing them together to make fire at all!"

"Fire, no Ma . . . Diana." Peter had great difficulties fraternizing with his betters. Elders, he quickly corrected his own definition. It certainly wasn't due to his so-called humble milieu. In fact, his father was a respected oncologist in Toronto. It was mostly John Brent's presence that dampened his spontaneity. "Actually I was...."

"...playing the Sibelius violin concerto. He is brilliant!" Anne burst in with unaccustomed vivacity.

"Well, there is only so much you can do with a stick..." he continued to look embarrassed.

"I thought your rendering of the andante was particularly engaging, Sir," Gabriel said from the doorway, his voice as serious as though delivering a pontifical dogma. He filled the opening almost completely. "Will there be anything else, Madam?"

By now Diana had no idea what was going on at all. Her daughter a genius, Peter playing violin concertos with a pair of sticks, Gabriel applauding his performance!

"Can anyone tell me what is going on?" she asked lamely.

"I thought that you might care for me to brew another pot of coffee, Madam," Gabriel inquired gravely.

"Coffee, anyone?"

No one wanted any more. Gabriel bowed stiffly yet with all the attendant decorum and withdrew.

"Now you see me, now you don't," John murmured. "You sure he doesn't scare you?" he asked aloud.

"He is by far the gentlest man I've ever met," Michael assured him. "Although I wouldn't like to bump into him on a dark street if I hadn't met him before."

They laughed. There was no need to return to the serious subject of neurology. Anne was all right. Perhaps she was more than all right. They all wanted her just to be healthy. Healthy and happy. The rest was unimportant.

In the meantime Anne began, yet again, to demonstrate to everyone Peter's technique and describe how he had explained to her the finer points of the violin. Peter looked ready to give another command performance. Then he glanced at John and thought better of it.

In all this chicanery, John completely forgot to report on his examination of Anne's ears. Her hearing was perfect. Indeed, more than perfect. The range of decibels she could detect would make Fluffy jealous. Yet there was nothing to suggest that this exemplary ability of hers was in any way connected to her additional neurons or the mutation of her pons Varolii. It seemed like a bonus that nature had bestowed upon her in a whim of extravagant generosity. He gazed at Anne with something akin to love, as he would gaze at his own daughter.

"You're one lucky girl, little one," he almost said aloud. "One lucky girl...."

Just before they disbanded for the evening, Anne's face turned serious again. When Diana asked if anything was bothering her, she looked up with those marvellous green eyes.

"Do you think I could play the violin?" she asked.

"Of course you could, darling," Diana assured her. "You can do anything you set your heart on. You know that."

"Yes, Mother. I know that," she replied gravely.

This was the first time that she had ever called Diana 'mother'. Mommy was out – Mother was in. Anne had entered a new phase of growing up. How sad, thought Diana. How very sad, she smiled, though her eyes turned misty.

"And just what do you make of all that?" Michael asked Gabriel when the big man returned to clear the rest of the table. Diana and Anne had already piled the plates up to help out.

Incongruously, Michael thought that Gabriel's arms must be very long to allow him to pick things up from the table without having to bend over. For some moments Gabriel continued clearing the dishes, as though he hadn't heard Michael's question. Then he stopped right in front of Michael. Just stood there without uttering a word.

"Well?" Michael prompted.

"I presume, Sir, you are referring to Doctor Brent's comments?" And when Michael nodded, Gabriel bowed slightly and asked if Michael thought the garden was beautiful this time of the year. In spite of dinner being served an hour earlier, it was rapidly getting dark.

Michael got the idea. He excused himself and Gabriel under the pretext of examining the Ayrshire roses that Gabriel had found by accident at the Atwater market. He'd planted them only last week. Once in the garden, Gabriel stopped again. For another short while he remained silent. Michael knew him well enough not to rush him. For some reason, it had always been worthwhile waiting for Gabriel to talk in his own time.

"I feel, Sir, that Doctor Brent did not tell you everything. Or to be more precise, he suggested rather than imposed his own opinion."

Michael waited for Gabriel to continue.

"Perhaps you've had occasion to read Thomas Aquinas, Sir?"

"Can't say that I have, Gabriel. Should I have?"

"The great Dominican had interesting thoughts to offer, Sir. He said that whatever is received is received according to the nature of the recipient."

"Yes...?" Michael didn't follow the quiet giant.

"Well, Sir, it is apparent to me that the nature of your daughter has undergone a profound change."

"So, my friend, you heard all Doctor Brent had to say?"

"I am blessed with very good hearing, Sir."

And with that Gabriel bowed and directed his steps towards the house. He stopped at the top terrace step. "You'll forgive me, Sir, if I finish my duties."

So that was that. The nature of the recipient? Was Thomas Aquinas referring to our bodies? Our nature in the literal sense? Or would it be our spiritual or, at the very least, mental and emotional nature? As for Anne, surely, whatever means nature had provided her in the physiological sense would one day serve to manifest that which she was yet to receive.

Michael's eyebrows cut a deep vertical furrow.

Or was our physical nature inexorably interconnected with whatever we manifested in the physical reality? John seemed to suggest that there was, or might be, some sort of a gift that was about to be bestowed on Anne. Could it be that the mutations in her brain had been the result of the changes that took place in

Anne's personality? Or was her changing personality the result of the mutations?

Was my little Anne changing that much?

"I guess we'll just have to wait and see," he muttered, as he followed Gabriel inside.

The table was already cleared, which was more than Michael could say of his mind. The phrase 'nature of the recipient' kept mulling in his mind. Even in bed. And next morning.

* * * * *

Chapter 14.

Virtuoso

Two weeks before Anne would turn sixteen, she had her first solo violin performance. Diana, Michael, John and Peter all sat, side by side, in the front row of the Pollack Concert Hall on Sherbrooke Street. Not that acoustics were good so close to the stage, but they, all four of them, wanted to be close to Anne. To see her every move, every grimace, every twitch of her eyebrow, every nuance of expression that might be painted on her face.

Anne was much too old to be considered a child prodigy. Mozart was four when he composed his first symphony. He qualified to be called a Wunderkind, Michael agreed, but not Anne.

"No way," Michael insisted, "Anne is very talented, after all she's my daughter," he postulated with a straight face, "but she's no prodigy. She just works very hard."

Michael desperately wanted Anne to be, what he called, 'normal'. He had read about too many cases where the so-called 'wonder children' had their lives destroyed by success too early.

Peter tended to agree. He knew a thing or two about the fiddle. Also about child prodigies. But early success did not necessarily spell impending doom. Yehudi Menuhin had played solo violin with the San Francisco Symphony Orchestra when he was just seven years old. At eleven he'd made his debut in Carnegie Hall with Beethoven's violin concerto. When Einstein heard him two years later, he is reported to have said: 'Now I know there is a God in heaven!'

Peter smiled at his own thoughts. He loved that story.

On March 12, 1999, Yehudi Menuhin died in Berlin, Germany, ending one of the longest and most prestigious careers of any American violinist.

But he had to admit that Anne was no prodigy. And, for that matter, she was no longer a child. Not in the usual sense of the word. Biologically she exhibited signs of a sixteen-year-old, but in every other sense she was mature beyond her years. Well beyond. One could, or at least he could, conduct a normal 'adult' conversation with her. Precocious perhaps, but no Wunderkind.

She walked on stage with a long, confident step. The conductor, who had just received his MA in music at McGill University, walked four paces behind her. When she stopped just to the left of the conductor's platform, she bowed once, and without any delay checked the A string with the first violinist. She then made the usual quick check of D, G and E fifths with each other. The conductor tapped his baton on the lectern. The audience took a deep breath.

Peter knew the concerto by heart. After all, just two years ago he'd played it for her on two sticks in her very own garden. He was also instrumental, so to speak, in aiding Anne with the deeper understanding of the composer's intent. Technically, Anne was perfect. The coordination between her bow and the fingers of her left hand was nothing short of astounding. At least, to another violinist, who once went through the same paces. Not since Paganini, he often thought. Not since the man who had been accused of having been in cahoots with the devil himself – though Peter never understood how they had managed to credit the devil with such beauty. Well, technique wasn't all, but it sure was a necessary ingredient of beauty. Peter was sure that had Anne started ten years earlier, she would have made her mark as a prodigy. But there was a great gulf between technique and musical maturity. Especially when the pupil or student was virtually self-taught. Peter hardly considered himself to be a teacher, particularly of a concert violinist.

Incongruously, he became aware that, for the first time, he was dissecting Anne as an object, as an instrument for producing music. When alone, practising, he had always been under the spell of her physical beauty. He had been too close to her, then. Too close physically. He could smell her hair, observe the curve of her lips, pouting, as she added her inimitable legato to articulate a particular passage. Yes, even while keeping strict tempo with the Allegro Moderato. There, he'd been under her spell. And here? Here he was detached, set a distance apart, lowered to the stalls while she, at long last, was raised to the podium where all goddesses belong.

One doesn't place demands on goddesses. One can only admire them, worship from afar....

His detachment didn't last. Moments later the music swept him, consumed his critical faculties, leaving him, once again, mesmerized, enchanted, transported, fascinated.

Anne was coming to the end of the first movement.

Where did she find such depths of emotion? The intense longing for something ineffable, perhaps forbidden, still unknown... Could it have been a longing for love? Not as we humans define it but at a still deeper, much deeper level, something that had its source in the realm of the divine.

Peter's thoughts wandered, incongruously, to a song he'd heard as a teenager.

Where have you been when I've been standing yonder, blinking at a star?

He wasn't sure of the words. Her long dress of green taffeta clung to her girlish hips only just beginning to swell into womanhood, then flowed like molten emeralds down to her feet. The colour was a perfect match to her eyes. She looked taller in her gown. The high collar framed her face from below, while her fiery hair flowed freely, dancing with each movement of her head. Only her long arms were left bare. Bare and so incredibly talented.

Gigi... you're not at all that funny, awkward little girl I knew....

Actually, Anne was never awkward. Unpredictable. Sometimes quite impossible, but never awkward. It was he who often felt awkward. Anne was still, at least in the legal sense, a child.

He had to keep reminding himself about that. A funny, if not awkward little girl....

She really did justice to the *Adagio di molto*. Her legato was much smoother, much broader than anything he, himself, had ever been capable of. God knows, he had tried. He'd shown her the fundamentals. That was about all. All too soon she'd taken flight on her own.

Her music rose and fell in flowing waves, interwoven with the Finnish lakes and forests and the endless fields stretching into the distant, misty unknown. Here, her longing was filled with sorrow, or resignation. No, it was more like acceptance.... Or perhaps reconciliation? A question or two, then peace, serenity of a summer's day hovering over a lustrous lake....

Anne... when did your sparkle turn to fire?

The music no longer belonged to Sibelius. She took it from him, she appropriated it with such ease. There was no act of usurping this jewel. Anne and the music were one. A single entity. Both magical, both beautiful, both....

The Allegro (*ma non tanto*) snapped him out of his reverie. Peter sat up straighter.

The joy of another morning . . . sparkling, brilliant, boisterous. All nature coming to life, awakening, swirling in a dance of life . . . soaring, receding, plunging only to rise again towards the sky. *And God said, Let the waters bring forth abundantly the moving creature that hath soul and fowl that may fly about the earth in the face of the firmament of heaven...* When did I hear these words? All creatures of the air...

Out of the corner of his eye, Peter glanced at John and Michael and Diana, who sat between the two men. Not one of them moved a finger. Not one even blinked. Anne's music had that effect on people. He had experienced this same magic so many times when she was practising. She refused to have anyone else present. Just him. Music was something he and Anne shared. She trusted him completely. He often felt the burden of that trust. After all, who was he to pass judgment on this angel?

"You are my friend," she would answer, trying to get rid of the reservations painted on his face. "You are the only one I trust to tell me the truth." It was a gentle plea as well as affirmation.

He had. Only seldom had he made remarks which made her wince. It was when she attempted to introduce her ego into a phrase. You don't own the music, he would say, the music owns you. Until now. Now the music was hers. If there was anyone who could find a way to separate the two, then he or she was better than I am, he mused.

Anne seemed frozen in immobility. Was she still playing? Am I hearing her bow dancing arpeggios with such ease just to amuse us? No, Anne wasn't frozen. It had been he who had wanted her to stop. To play no more. He refused to share her with this crowd. But jealous nature would not release her. It drew her inexorably into her mysteries.

...ephemeral dragonflies gliding on gossamer wings rose, carried on the breath of a forgotten zephyr, a sigh of a girl in an emerald dress, a winged fairy, a squadron of nymphs, mysterious, following her every turn, lithe, prancing, her feet barely touching the grass, playing . . . rising, and falling, only to alight, silently, on wild petals, swaying, barely, in tune, in tempo . . . allegro ma non tanto....

...rising again . . . allegro, joyfully, allegro ma non troppo, light-heartedly . . . tiny feet whisking across the water, ripples, a tremolo . . . her tiny feet skimming across the furrows between the crests, little, shimmering....

...beyond a crown of a forlorn willow weeping good-bye . . . a whole forest, echoing firs, pines, hemlocks....

...weeping good-bye . . . to Anne still standing, still so far, inaccessible.

Anne, come back . . . come back....

The roar was deafening. People were standing – all of them. People cried. Then they shouted – then cried again. Diana took a step towards Peter, put her arms about his neck, kissed him on the cheek.

"This could never have happened without you. Thank you. Thank you so much...."

Just then Anne looked down from the stage. For the briefest of moments their eyes met. Her smile told him the rest. It
said the same thing Diana had just said. And more.

The press was cautious. The offer from the famed Montreal
Symphony Orchestra was not. The Music Director would very
much like to hear Anne play. When could it by arranged? The
orchestra was having rehearsals every Monday and Tuesday
morning at eleven. Perhaps Ms. Howell might find it convenient
to drop in?

The letter was signed by the conductor himself.

"What do you think, Peter?" Anne asked.

She'd called Peter at the MNI, and Peter had returned her
call an hour later. His residency was still very demanding on his
time. For one more year he would have to give the Neuro all his
attention. Almost all. John Brent would accept no less.

"You cannot serve two gods, my boy," John had told him.
"Believe me, it just cannot be done."

John was right, of course. Peter met with Anne often after
nine in the evening and they would play and talk music till midnight or beyond. At seven the next day Peter would be at the
Neuro, waiting for John to make their rounds. He was never late.
Never.

Anne resented his dedication to the Neuro, just a bit, but she
never admitted her weakness to him. Also, she had never attempted to have him compromise his career for her sake. On
her part, whatever Peter taught her by the time they met next, she
had it mastered. Actually, she didn't find it so much work as
pleasure. She'd also listened to the recordings, the CDs, the
tapes, even some old 78s, of all the great performers who had
ever played all the great concertos. All of them. She could distinguish one performer from another after hearing just a single
phrase. Her ear was that good.

She asked Peter if he thought that she was ready to accept
the invitation from the MSO. "Really, Peter, really, I don't

know," she insisted when he wanted to leave the decision in her hands.

"What do your parents think?" he asked.

"Parents?" she sounded surprised. "How could they possibly help me?"

Peter shook his head. "Anne," he began in his most persuasive tone of voice, the kind he normally reserved for patients who had lost faith in their own recovery. "Accepting the invitation is not just a question of your musical maturity or even virtuosity. It is going to affect your whole life, and therefore theirs... Didn't you think of that?"

The telephone was silent for a longer time.

"I'm sorry Peter. You see . . . I'm still such a child. Shall I see you tonight?"

"I'll be there at nine."

"Come at eight and have dinner with us."

"Once again, did you ask your parents?"

"I'll cook the supper myself!"

"Then I'll eat at McDonald's," he said in a grave voice.

"Pig!" was her parting shot.

John Brent's eyes were glued to the photographs of the MRI he had taken last week. It was just a routine check, but once a tumour had been diagnosed, no matter how well removed, no matter if it had been benign or otherwise, John insisted on an annual check at least for the first few years following the excision. In matters of the brain, there was simply no room for error. In Anne's case, the operation had taken place well before her brain had stopped growing. There was no way to predict if the tumour had been a factor in her occasional erratic behaviour, or perhaps, just perhaps, her behaviour had contributed to the tumour. Last week Michael had been pressing him for, what he called, a final diagnosis.

"Surely," he'd said, "you can't expect Anne to go through life with the Damoclean sword hanging, literally, over her head."

"Surely, my friend," John countered, "you must realize that no matter what gigantic steps neurology and genetics have taken over the last decade, we are still just scratching the surface."

John caught his breath. A wrong choice of words, he realized. Scratching or scraping the surface of the frontal lobes of the cerebellum was what the primitive neurosurgeons did, not so long ago. In the United States they'd started the practice in 1936. They'd called it lobotomy. Before they'd given up on this barbaric procedure, as recently as 1951, over 18,000 lobotomies had been performed in the United States alone, and many more throughout the world. Thank God we've finally emerged from the Middle Ages, he sighed silently.

John could hardly tell Michael that in the brain the distinction between a benign and a malignant tumour was not as immediately, or exclusively, important as it might have been in other parts of the body. He had spent some time assuring his friend that he need not worry, as Anne's tumour was not cancerous. What he hadn't told Michael was that, had there been a lesion resulting from the removal of the tumour, it might still exert pressure on the vital centre of her brain. No matter how big your skull, the space within is still a very confined area. Should there be even a minute lesion, it would have to be removed or shrunk.

"A skull is a skull. Once sealed it seems protected?" Michael's tone was questioning.

"Its component parts differ greatly from man to man. There are twenty-six bones of the skull, which are, to a degree, in constant motion. There is the expansion and contraction of the two hemispheres. There is the motion of the membrane and the cerebrospinal fluid that bathes the brain tissue. There is...."

"I get the point. Points. Lots of them. So once a brain has been tampered with...?"

"No one has tampered with Anne's brain, Mike." There was fatigue showing on John's face. It was never easy. "Life is change. You tamper with your brain each time you convert a memory into words. Each time you speak. Or move a finger."

"Diana said that."

"What?"

"That life is change. Then, when change ceases, that's because you're dead."

"Well, good for her."

Michael wasn't quite fair. He was a self-confessed hater of prophecy, and now he expected his friend to prophesy what might or might not happen to Anne, or to her brain. He realized, belatedly, that he was barking up the wrong tree. He recalled a similar discussion with John some time ago.

"There are 300 trillion cells in an average body," John had told him. "And of these, some ten million are replaced every second of your life. Every cell is exposed to dangers inherent in our ignorance. Like radiation from all sorts of sources, like the intake of chemicals, like inhaling polluted air . . . I am telling you, Mike, sometimes I wonder how we all manage to survive a single day. I am telling you," he repeated in exasperation, "it's a veritable miracle!"

And then John remembered something Diana had said.

"I don't believe we are created unto the image and likeness of God. Our bodies are. We are indivisible from God Himself. We are the mode for His expression. Our bodies are just the means. His means."

Some people are clever, Michael thought. How come I don't have insights like that? And then he also recalled what John had told him many years ago.

"You are a left-hemisphere man."

By now Michael knew that John had been talking about the hemispheres of the brain. 'You are rational, logical, you process your information step by step.' Whereas Diana and Anne were of the right hemisphere. Spontaneous, creative, intuitive. And now Diana is showing mystical insights, and Anne an extraordinary musical talent. What about me, he wondered? He thought he had been dealt the wrong hand.

"So where do we go from here?" he asked after a little while.

"We don't go anywhere. We enjoy today. Now. This is not a scourge, this is the fascination of life. We never know what tomorrow might bring."

Finally, there was something on which they could agree.

Michael tried to imagine the alternative. He imagined knowing everything he wanted to know about tomorrow. And the day after. And the day after that. What utter boredom! It would be like watching a movie on TV, without participating in anything. Devoid of feeling, of any challenge, of the need for courage, will power, even a deeper thought... Life would be an exercise in futility. No matter what I did, the future wouldn't change, he mused.

And at this particular moment he began to understand how Diana managed to stay calm in moments of great tension. She didn't want to change the future, she wanted to live it. With all its unknowns, all its challenges.

"Thank you, John," he said at long last. "I think I am just beginning to grow up."

He couldn't even begin to imagine how far he still had to go.

"**The** Max Bruch? Pyotr Il'yich Tchaikovsky, I can play him better than I can pronounce him. And what of Felix Mendelssohn, or Johannes Brahms. Of course, there is my beloved Sibelius. Dear Jean, dear Julius Christian...."

They all sounded like her dear, personal friends. Peter suspected that, when alone, she thought of them all in first names only. Dear Max, or Pyotr, or Felix.

She had also read all about them. All of them. Detailed biographies, trying to get into the minds of these great composers, perhaps their souls. She needed to know what all those messengers of the gods had felt when those divine notes flowed through them, through their hearts onto the lined paper. She sighed deeply, probably tearing herself away from Jean's study. Then she looked at Peter, a silent plea in her eyes.

"There is also the Ludwig von Beethoven opus 61, in E, which made the young Yehudi famous. There are all the Mozart concertos, the Vivaldis, the Wieniawski and the Stravinsky and the Paganinis, first and the second...." her voice trailed off.

"Easy girl. Easy...."

It is much easier to pick from two or three than from dozens. Peter did his best to force Anne to take another deep breath. He had never seen her so nervous. In fact, he didn't recall ever seeing her nervous at all. Whenever Anne appeared to have some sort of emotional problem, she tended to seize up. She would withdraw, exclude the outside world from her inner reality, deal with whatever affected her adversely, even if only emotionally, and then return, calm and collected to the mundane world that we, mere mortals, have been destined to live in. She had choices the rest of us seemed to lack. And now, with the pending Montreal Symphony interview, her biggest worry was not how well she might play any one movement from any one concerto, only which one to select.

Even when Peter had been recognized as a child prodigy, he had never had to face such problems. By the time he was eleven, his future already hung in doubt. As a virtuoso, that is. At five he had been praised, admittedly only by the local musicians, as the next Misha Elman. Or Heifetz. Or Perlman. Or even Yehudi Menuhin. They were all brilliant. He, as a boy, had showed the same promise.

Only....

Only whatever gift we are given is only as good as the recipient of that gift. Some years later he had tried to assess what had gone wrong. Overtly, he'd just stopped practising. But there must have been more than that. At least he hoped that there was. He did not want to feel the weight of having wasted a gift. A rare, very rare gift. Even as Anne was now reading biographies of great men and women from all walks of life, he had concentrated on what he dubbed the prodigy syndrome.

His interest was not so much in how successful those children had become in later years, but how they had achieved their success. His interest broadened to those born not only without an easily defined talent, but also with apparent limitations. The more he'd read, the more fascinated he had become by his study.

Leonardo da Vinci and Winston Churchill, had both been dyslexic. They could read only with great difficulty. So had a number of multimillionaires of the entertainment industry. Tom Cruise, Cher, Whoopi Goldberg, Henry Winkler, to mention a few. All extremely successful people in their chosen professions. To Peter's knowledge, no one had ever accused any of them of being child prodigies. He also discovered that Albert Einstein and Virginia Woolf had been unable to speak until they were three years old.

"I think," he confided to Diana, sharing his findings during one of the Friday dinners, "I might still have a chance."

Recently, Peter had become a regular at the Howell family dinners. Frankly, Anne had once refused to eat unless he too was invited. Anne was very slim. Diana had no choice. As for Peter, well, his family lived in Toronto, and eating with Dr. John Brent was an undeniable added attraction for him.

Not that I need one... he grinned at his own thoughts.

And then there was August Rodin, who was so inept at reading and math that his teachers discouraged his parents from allowing him to partake even in his interest in arts. That misanthropic, not to say myopic, foresight apparently didn't stop young Rodin from becoming one of the world's greatest and most beloved sculptors.

It had been after one such eye-opening discovery that Peter had begun to research the workings of the human mind. He'd never stopped. John Brent regarded him among the top researchers at the Neuro.

"So, what do you think? Whom should I choose?" Anne repeated. Peter, who had been miles away, came back to the girl and her violin.

No one could accuse Anne of not practising. Whatever her innate talents, she improved on them until they sparkled like rare diamonds. No technical passage was too difficult for her. No harmonic complexity too complex. She worked on it until she won. She always won. Nothing would sway her from her single-mindedness until the desired result was reached.

'Those who have little, even that shall be taken away from them. Those who have much, much shall be given to them,' Gabriel had told him when he'd mentioned Anne's talent to him. It had taken nearly a year for Peter to understand that

Gabriel had transliterated a phrase from the New Testament. Peter strongly suspected that Gabriel had been referring not to Anne's talent *per se*, but to her ability to stay on an even keel. On being single-minded. On hard work.

"Don't think about it, Anne," he said at last. "Have I told you the story about Bach?"

"I wasn't thinking about playing him..." she replied instantly. She wanted an answer but was afraid of commitment.

"I wasn't suggesting that you should. The story about Bach might amuse you. He was once asked how he managed to put such magnificent emotion into his interpretations. Into his music. Bach had replied that it takes only three prerequisites: Technique, technique and, of course, technique. 'But, Master,' the admirer had interrupted, 'your music is so full of emotion!' 'Ah, yes,' Bach had replied. 'Once you acquire the three prerequisites you must forget all about them. What is left is just pure emotion.'" Peter strongly suspected that in Bach's story the words emotion and love were synonymous.

After a moment or two, Anne's face began to relax.

"You don't want me to think about the audition." It was as much a question as a statement of fact.

She was growing in wisdom as well as in beauty.

* * * * *

Chapter 15.

Gabriel

The last time, which was a good three years ago, that Michael had attempted to trace Gabriel's tracks in Toronto, he hadn't gotten very far. John Brent had given him two addresses where Gabriel had been usefully employed. Both hospitals had provided written affidavits of Gabriel's professional qualifications, Provincial affiliation, and exemplary conduct in the execution of his duties. Other than that, no one seemed to know anything about him.

What Michael found interesting was that at the two hospitals in which Gabriel had served immediately prior to applying for a position at Michael's house, he had spent a mere sixteen months at one hospital and four months at the other. Before that, there was no trace of him. It was as though he hadn't lived.

One day, Michael had decided to press Gabriel for a satisfactory answer.

"Is there something you would rather I didn't know, Gabriel? Is there a dark cloud lurking in your past?" Michael had asked him. He also remembered Gabriel's reply.

"Yes, Sir," Gabriel had said and returned to his room. So much for explicit information, Michael mused. In a way,

Gabriel had confirmed some sort of shadow preceding his present existence, but he had also made it abundantly clear that he
was not prepared to volunteer any details.

Some months later Michael had tried again.

"Wouldn't you like to take some time off? I mean to visit
your family or your friends?"

"No, thank you, Sir. I am quite happy here."

Again it sounded like a polite dismissal.

Michael was fully aware that he had no right to intrude on
Gabriel's private life. Certainly not on his distant past. But the
more Michael tried to dismiss the matter from his mind, the
more various questions returned with renewed force. Finally
he'd called John.

"After all, John, it is you who recommended him to us."
He had no idea why exactly he chose to be so aggressive.

"Has he done something wrong?" John asked, his voice as
light as Michael's was heavy.

"No, of course not."

"Well, then...?"

"It's eating me up," Michael confessed.

"Well then, ask him again." With that John hung up. He
had enough on his plate without his friend's hysteria.

Then, one day, just after the first snow, Gabriel slipped on
the steps leading to the garden and twisted his ankle. Though he
vehemently denied being incapacitated, Michael saw him winc-
ing each time he placed his considerable bulk on his right foot.
Perhaps due to the years Gabriel had spent working at various
hospitals, nothing would induce him to see a doctor.

"You are going to sit down, Gabby, right here, and we shall
all take turns in looking after you," Michael declared.

Diana and Anne enthusiastically approved this irrefutable
proclamation. In fact, the following Friday, John and Peter
joined in smothering Gabriel with good intentions. No matter
how painful an expression Gabriel put on his face, and this had
nothing to do with his ankle, all five of them persisted in serving
the major domo his meals, drinks, and entertaining him with the
latest titbits percolating by grapevine from town. It could be

said that never before had so many talked about so little with so few. Another week of such TLC, and Gabriel was likely to become seriously ill.

"If you allow me to go back to my duties, Sir, I shall be happy to tell you about my past," he said on the fourth day following his accident.

The offer was too good to miss. That very afternoon, Michael suggested that Diana take Anne shopping for Anne's next evening gown, in case her MSO interview proved successful. There are few women who can refuse such an offer. Immediately after lunch the ladies left, and Michael settled down in front of Gabriel with a pot of coffee.

"What is it that you would like to know?" Gabriel asked innocently. He looked resigned to his fate.

"How come no one knows anything about you – other than the two hospital employment references you've provided?"

"Whatever do you mean, Sir?"

Michael gave Gabriel a long look. Gabriel smiled, nodded, and dropped both hands, in abject resignation, on the padded arms of his chair.

"You got me, Sir," he confessed.

Michael decided to wait. He'd learned that nothing would prompt this mountain of a man to speak against his will.

After a momentary hesitation, Gabriel said, "I killed a man."

This made Michael sit up with a start. Not in a million years would he have suspected anything of this sort coming from this gentle giant. "You're joking, of course," he commented when Gabriel remained silent.

"No, Sir. I did kill a man," he asserted, a distant shadow of sorrow crossing his face. "With my bare hands." This came out as if he were talking to himself.

"So you were in jail?" he coaxed when Gabriel remained silent.

"Oh, no, Sir." There was a suggestion of a smile. "I was in India."

"You were on the lam?"

"In a way, Sir. In a way." There was that vague smile again. "Only I haven't been running from the law, Sir. Rather – from myself."

This was going to take a while. Gabriel's life was slowly unfolding, perhaps for the first time. He was a very private man, it seemed. He was more disposed to offer help than to receive it. Yet Michael had an impression that Gabriel needed this talk. He needed to unload whatever shadows remained of his distant past.

"I was a professional wrestler," he started, this time without prompting. "My stage name was The Avenging Angel."

It was Michael's turn to smile. He'd never followed professional wrestling, but he did think the name strangely appropriate for a man named Gabriel.

"Yes, Sir," Gabriel seemed to be reading his thoughts. "My stage name was very appropriate. Well, professional wrestling is a very special form of entertainment. You can be a very good entertainer and a very bad wrestler. And vice versa. My opponent, that night, was a very good entertainer. He also hadn't taken the physical aspect of the sport with sufficient seriousness. When you are thrown from a height of six feet onto the deck, you are supposed to groan and wince and generally display signs of agony. The Demon, that was my opponent, Sir, The Red Demon, didn't display any of those signs."

Gabriel's eyes appeared to drift to some distant memory long buried in his subconscious. After another pause, he continued.

"In professional wrestling, you must know how to fall. You must practice. You must take the athletic aspect of the entertainment very seriously. My opponent hadn't. I didn't know that. The previous night, the night before the championship match, he'd been out with the boys. The stage hands, not the athletes." Gabriel took a sip of coffee. "He failed to break his fall. His neck snapped. It just snapped, Sir. Like a twig. A dry twig...."

As Gabriel was nearing the end of his story, his voice was becoming more and more quiet. The last words came out in a whisper.

Michael didn't push him. After they'd sat silent for a while, he got up and poured them both more coffee. They shared the silence, now and then taking a sip, looking straight ahead, each lost in private thoughts. Michael was well aware of Gabriel's gentle nature. The accident must have very nearly destroyed him. And then Michael remembered something Gabriel had said.

"You went to India?"

Very slowly the big head atop those enormous shoulders turned towards his host. "India, Sir?"

Michael nodded.

"Ah, yes . . . India." Gabriel looked like he was still years away from the present. He was unloading his memories, perhaps to finally rid himself of them, once and for all. "I needed to get away. They told me that it had been an accident. They expected me to fight, ah . . . perform, again that very same week." Again his eyes drifted to some long gone reality. "I had to get away," he repeated. "I just couldn't...."

For some reason Michael thought it wise not to pursue the matter any further. Not at the time. For a while they sat in silence, each lost in his own thoughts. Then Gabriel raised his enormous frame, bowed stiffly, and left without another word. Michael pretended to look over the daily paper. Twice Gabriel went past Michael on the way to his room. Twice he seemed to hesitate as though about to say something, only to continue on his way. The third time he passed Michael invited him to sit down. The moment he did, they heard joyous barking at the front door.

Anne running into the house, with Diana close at her heels, dissolved any hope of further revelations.

"Anne, the snow! Wipe your feet!"

"It's an exact match, Daddy! An absolutely exact match!"

"I am sure it is," Michael confirmed, having no idea what Anne was talking about. His face must have registered an expression of being lost. Anne assigned it to her announcement. "The dress. It matches my hair exactly. Exactly!"

Diana nodded. "She's right. It's quite amazing. She will look like Lady Godiva when she wears it on stage."

"Ha!" A squeak more than a shout, was followed by Anne clapping her hands and then throwing both arms around her father's neck and plastering kisses on both his cheeks. "Thank you, Daddy, oh, thank you!"

"Thank your mother, pet."

"I did! Really I did!" Anne insisted. All her assurances carried oversized exclamations marks.

Only then did Anne notice Gabriel. The colossus really was invisible, on occasion. She leaned over and planted a kiss on his left cheek, then walked around his outstretched legs to the other side of the armchair and plastered another on the right side, just for good measure. "You will love my new dress, Gabriel!" she announced, not forgetting yet another exclamation mark.

"I am quite sure of that, Miss Anne," Gabriel replied gravely.

Actually, when they were alone Gabriel addressed her by her first name, but never when even one other person was present. Not even in front of her parents. "It just wouldn't do, young lady," he'd told her.

Michael took a long look at his daughter. She's either getting younger or growing up, he mused. He wasn't quite sure. Whichever temporal direction she'd taken, she looked ravishing and ravishingly happy. Maybe she is growing up, he finally decided. Women go wilder over new gowns than do girls.

Suddenly Anne's face lost its glow.

"I won't be able to wear it to my audition, will I?" It was a rhetorical question. "What if I never give another concert?" Her eyes misted with the equal dispatch with which they shed green diamonds of joy.

"You will give many concerts, pet. As many as you want," Diana said immediately. She believed Anne still needed positive reinforcement.

Anne's emotional maturity didn't quite match her musical talent. Behind those often so serious eyes, she was still a girl. A child. Perhaps more so. She had never had the opportunity to grow up as a normal child. Too few friends, no toys to speak of.

Not even dolls. She had been given enough of them, but they just rested in a pile in her bedroom against the wall. There was Fluffy, of course. He was neither a toy nor a friend, yet he was both of these. He must have heard more whispered confessions from her than either Diana or her father. As for Gabriel, no one could be so sure. There was a strange affinity between them that her parents respected. But this relationship was at a different level. Fluffy was the one and only companion she adored. Fluffy and, the last couple of years, Peter. But he, too, was very different. Peter was . . . well, only Anne knew what Peter was.

Two days passed before Michael had another chance to be alone with Gabriel. While his ankle still wasn't well, the major domo did manage to hobble around, slowly, doing practically all of his work, if a fraction slower.

This was the day on which Anne was to attend her audition with the Montreal Symphony Orchestra. As mature as she was trying to be, she'd asked her mother to accompany her. Anne seemed quite unaware of the incredible command she wielded over the music she'd mastered in just two short years. No matter how confident she was, she always found ways to improve on something which, Diana was sure, no one other then herself would have noticed. With the possible exception of Peter. Peter was like her alter ego. It was a very strange friendship. Some-times Diana thought that it was Peter who used her fingers to play the music. They were like brother and sister. Yet, on a number of occasions, Diana had noticed quite different emotions stirring in Anne's as well as in Peter's eyes. There were thirteen years setting them apart. Was that too much, she wondered?

Gabriel had guessed what was coming.

On the day of the audition, Michael announced that he would go to the office late, to give Gabriel a hand with the chores. He didn't explain what chores, and both ladies were too busy and too excited to ask. Gabriel brewed an extra pot of cof-fee, got two cups, and resignedly settled himself in the armchair from which, he guessed, he would be expected to share the next part of his story.

"India," Michael said, the moment the front door closed behind Diana and Anne. Then he added, "Thanks for the coffee. I should have prepared it, you know."

"As I mentioned, Sir, I had to get away." Gabriel didn't waste any time. "First to Calgary, then Vancouver, then, well, the only cargo ship leaving that day went to India. I got the job... they thought I would be good at carrying things. The stevedores are pretty hefty fellows, Sir." There appeared, again, that self-deprecating smile. "I soon discovered that the bulkheads on the ship had not been designed for my height."

Michael nodded his understanding. He could picture the giant hitting every bulkhead in sight.

"I landed in India three months later. En route, we had docked in a number of ports. We were a trading vessel. What with the bulkheads and all, I thought a while on the hard, I mean the mainland, Sir, would do my head some good. For a while I looked for a job. Any job. I wanted to become invisible, which is not easy considering my size. But I had to get away from the roaring crowd, the twinkling lights, the atmosphere of mad abandon."

"I suppose they spoke English there?"

"Some. Enough to get by. The vast majority spoke Hindi and some twenty different versions of it or other dialects. On the east coast at least. But one didn't need great language skills in India. Not for my purposes. Even the great teachers, there, say little. They seem to show, to impart knowledge in a different way – other than giving lectures. I found one man who for three years hadn't said a word. He had a number of followers."

"You were looking for a teacher? A guru or a swami?"

"They are all one and the same, Sir. And no. I wasn't looking for a teacher. Although a teacher found me."

Michael raised both eyebrows.

"That is how it happens, over there, Sir. Perhaps everywhere. They say that when you're ready, the teacher finds you. What you must do, in turn, is recognize him."

His eyes searched for something he'd lost and didn't know how to find it. "When I got to India," he resumed, this time more slowly, "I was still in a state of depression. I had no faith in the future, nor in myself. I'm told that soldiers feel that way when they come home for leave. I suppose killing, I mean the taking of a human life, does it to one."

"And the man helped you?"

"Oh no, Sir. He told me how to help myself. Unless this is what you mean by help."

"And just how did he do that?" Michael, having experienced mood swings of both women in his life, was fascinated by anything related to self-control, particularly the emotional dimension of it, provided that it didn't involve a psychiatrist. He'd lost all faith in them when they'd failed to help Anne in any way.

"He showed me the way to transfer feelings or, better still, states of consciousness. He said that from depression one cannot transform oneself directly to a joyful state. One must first become resigned – he called it acceptance, then submissive – or define one's place in the universe, and finally become indifferent – or detached would be a better word. A sort of the combination of the first two traits. He said that only then can we live a balanced life."

"And what of the joyful state?" Michael prodded.

"Joyful state is what's left over. It is not really a state of becoming, rather that of being."

"Isn't that a static condition?"

"Not really. He claimed that while we remain in our physical bodies, we cannot achieve full bliss, or the state of absolute joy. What we can do is become observers of our other states from a place which is static."

"And he told you that there is such a place?" Michael's twisted smile gave ample comment on his opinion of the eastern guru's methods.

"Once you desire nothing, you have everything, Sir."

"Sounds like something Buddha would say."

"Nevertheless, it is true."

"You think so?"

"No, Sir."

"So there..."

"I mean, Sir, I don't think so. I know it to be true."

For the rest of the morning they talked about Gabriel's eighteen-year search for himself. Before the ladies returned from Place des Arts, Michael also learned that during Gabriel's eighteen-year absence both his parents had died, leaving him with half an inheritance. Apparently two of his brothers had gone to Australia, and they were never heard of again. Only his sister remained. The inheritance wasn't much, but his needs were very small. Provided he was prepared to do what he did now, the money was more than sufficient. In India, he had kept himself going first by working as a porter; then, after carrying numerous sick people to a hospital following a disaster, he had been offered a job in that very hospital. Lifting people was as natural to him as using elaborate hoists was for others. Soon he had been promoted to nurse's assistant, and two years later he'd passed all the exams to become a registered nurse. When he'd returned to Canada, he'd got a job in the first hospital to which he'd applied. After the budgetary cuts in Federal Medicare, he'd changed hospitals. That was about all. Finally, there was very little he could add.

"In North America, I suspect also in Europe, people are too preoccupied with thought. With the thinking process. In the Far East, they are trying to break down this dependency, this addiction to thought, with meditation. At the time, that was a great revelation to me."

Michael rubbed his forehead. Then he had it.

"Is that what you were doing with Anne?"

He recalled seeing his daughter sitting very still, facing Gabriel, saying nothing. For some strange reason Gabriel appeared to know instantly what Michael was talking about.

"Words are a very inefficient means of communication, Sir." A vague smile flitted across his face. Gabriel felt that it was too early to tell Michael that in India he had learned to listen to his heart, rather than to his head. This was why he had accepted the propitious offer from Michael some years ago.

"This is the second time we are talking like this, Sir, and you still don't know me at all. Am I right?" he asked instead.

Michael had to agree. He still had no idea what made the big man tick.

What fascinated Michael was not what Gabriel had said, but what he had left out. It would be another three years before he heard the rest of Gabriel's story.

The ladies returned from the interview in a grim mood. Anne had been asked to play a new piece – one she had neither seen nor heard before. She hated that. Not that she wasn't an excellent sight-reader of music. Peter had made sure that she could read a musical score with the same facility as she could read a novel. To Anne, the notes were letters; bars, words, phrases – sentences. The musical letters, chords, accords, and phrases, variations in duration and volume and tempo were as natural as a nursery rhyme.

But when all was said and done, Anne still lacked confidence. According to Diana, she had played a piece by an unknown Canadian composer from a score thrust before her. A moment later she'd expressed her dissatisfaction, played it again from memory, and then practically walked out.

"There are too many errors in this piece," she muttered, shaking her head in disgust. Anything less than perfect repelled her. She expected no less of herself in her interpretation.

At seven that evening the telephone rang. The man's voice asked for Miss Howell.

"My name is Jorge di Vargas. You played my piece today at Place des Arts. I understand that you didn't like some phrasing. Might you have a few minutes to spare to give me some pointers?"

"I'm sorry, you are...?"

"Just call me Jorge. I'm..."

"...the ah, the composer?"

"Apparently not a very good one."

"I am sorry, I didn't mean to offend you."

"Please don't apologize. When I heard you play the piece again, the second time, from memory, I was astounded. You played it the way I thought I wrote it . . . alas . . . the little black dots, the musical signs . . . are so limited. I would really appreciate a few minutes of your time."

"I am not a composer, ah . . . Jorge. I have no experience. No experience at all, in composition." Now Anne, too, sounded flustered.

"Miss Howell, if I could come by with my tape-recorder, you might care to play the piece for me, just once more. I would take it from there. Please, Miss Howell...."

Anne had never heard a voice as plaintive as the one on the phone. Nor had she ever been address as 'Miss' Howell so many times in a row.

"You want to come over at once?" There was a gasp on the other end of the line. "I still remember the piece. I could play it for you."

"Miss Howell, I don't know how to thank you."

Anne gave him her address and put down the receiver. Seconds later the doorbell rang. A grey-haired man stood at the door, facing Gabriel's bulk.

"Miss Howell?" he asked timidly.

Gabriel let him in. Fifteen minutes later the elderly composer left, shaking his head from side to side, his hands conducting an imaginary orchestra. His face was lit up with happiness. "That's right..." he muttered. "Of course!" He didn't even notice when Gabriel shut the door quietly behind him.

Anne was already on the floor with Fluffy. His head rested on her lap, while she stroked his head and ears. "A nice man," she said to him. "A little deaf but nice...."

Fluffy wagged his tail in total agreement.

* * * * *

Chapter 16

The Stradivarius

Sir Ian Barton sat halfway back from the stage in the Théâtre Maisonneuve of the Place des Arts complex. He sat motionless while Anne played, twice, the same short piece, the Intermezzo, by Jorge di Vargas. In spite of his Spanish heritage, di Vargas was a Canadian through and through. After her performance, not knowing that the great Sir Ian Barton was watching, she smartly walked off stage and left the building. Only after Anne had left did Sir Ian fully understand her second rendition. He took a deep breath and reached for his handkerchief. He wiped his forehead. He had always known that, before he died, he would hear a new star, a new genius who would raise the human awareness of musical beauty.

"At last, after so many years...." he muttered to himself.

His face showed a mixture of admiration, surprise and deep satisfaction. He sat motionless for a long time. People who knew him better would have said that Sir Ian had just found his pearl.

He had allowed di Vargas, the composer, to test the new violinist under his own baton. It was better that way. Sir Ian thought that an unknown violinist, or pianist for that matter, should be tested or judged on playing a new piece. There should be no tradition infringing on a new composition, nor on his or her style. And who better to conduct than the composer. "Get somebody you've never heard. Better still, someone of whom you've never heard," he'd suggested to di Vargas when presented with the sheet music of the Intermezzo. "Otherwise they'll try to make you sound like somebody else."

It was di Vargas who had picked Anne. He had heard her play at the Pollak Hall. She didn't qualify under the strict terms proposed by Sir Ian, but she most certainly was totally unknown. Jorge taught at McGill and had conducted the student orchestra that accompanied Anne in the Sibelius Violin Concerto. They'd needed just one rehearsal. Anne was perfect then. It would have been embarrassing to ask her to come to another practice run. Already on that first occasion, di Vargas had been practically flabbergasted by Anne's virtuosity, but was too busy conducting the orchestra to fully absorb her talent. That came to him only on hearing her for the second time, during the actual performance of the concerto.

Anne had left so quickly that Sir Ian didn't have a chance to meet her. Of course, she had no idea that the great conductor was hiding halfway up the parterre in the murky shadows of the auditorium.

"Her temperament must be that of a true diva," Sir Ian mused, scratching his head. "The good ones are never easy."

He looked around.

Théâtre Maisonneuve was a compromise. Since 1963, until recently, the symphonic concerts had been held in the Salle Wilfrid Pelletier. Although large enough, it was never considered a suitable home for the Montreal Symphony Orchestra. The MSO needed not just space but time for rehearsals, meetings, discussions, practice studios, lectures and such like. The musicians deserved a real home, where they would like to come, even on their days off. Originally, Montreal was going to build a new concert hall for its symphony orchestra. Subsequently, the money that had been designated for the new concert hall had been reallocated for a new sport arena of some sort, and the needs of the

MSO went by the wayside. Some years ago the City Fathers had decided to enlarge the Théâtre Maisonneuve by some five hundred seats, making it reasonably suitable for symphonic performances. Luckily the expansion did wonders for the acoustics.

At long last, the MSO had a home. A permanent home where other shows would not pre-empt its own needs or schedules. A place where the MSO could have regular matinées for children, for students, special performances for young people in general who, one day, would become regular patrons, perhaps even musicians. One had to educate one's audiences these days.

Sir Ian Barton had been brought over from England to breathe new life into the tired orchestra. The orchestra had been plagued by ongoing strife between visiting conductors and the dilettante musicians, encouraged by a union convinced that the primary purpose of music was to make money. Furthermore, the ongoing uncertainty regarding a permanent home for the orchestra had contributed to a certain staleness, a malaise, which had to be expunged if music was to result. Sir Ian had experience in doing just that. He'd made his terms quite simple.

"Obey me or find someone else."

It was nice and simple. When the musicians agreed, Sir Ian contributed $500,000 of his own money to the Symphony's coffers. The union leaders had immediately accused him of influence peddling. Within a week, ninety percent of the musicians had left the union.

"You are my orchestra now. I must look after you," Sir Ian had said just as simply.

The day following Anne's audition at the Théâtre, he picked up the telephone and called Anne directly. He was a man of much music and few words. Diana answered the phone and he asked for Anne.

"Miss Anne? This is Ian Barton," he announced. "I'd like to see you at the Théâtre Maisonneuve tomorrow at nine sharp." And he hung up.

Belatedly he remembered that he had failed to specify if he'd meant morning or evening. No matter, he thought, a lopsided grin making him look like a baroque dragon, we shall now see who is the greater prima donna, she or I. He always thought that an artist who was not a Prima Donna, with capital P&D, is not worth his or her salt. 'If you don't know you are good, how on earth do you expect others to find out?'

Back in England, stories abounded about the great Sir Ian. He had been known among the *cognoscenti* not just for his ear but, in almost equal measure, for his strange behaviour. In fact, his fame grew in direct proportion to his whimsical eccentricities. On one occasion, he is said to have noticed a member of the audience, a portly 'gentleman,' sporting his red braces, his jacket resting on his lap. In the old country, displaying one's suspenders, as they are called there, is considered highly non-u. "One simply doesn't do that, Old Chap, and all that," Sir Ian would say, had anyone dared to ask him.

The culprit was plainly unlucky in his choice of venue to display his uncouth habits. Very unlucky, indeed.

Before the concert, the soloist had asked Sir Ian to extend the pause between the first and second movement of the concerto, to give a fractionally longer respite to his overworked fingers. Rachmaninov *can* be very demanding!

Sir Ian expected the prima donnas to voice their requests, but it was he who would decide just how long the pause should be. Fingers notwithstanding. He said as much to the poor pianist. Something to do with timing and continuity, he explained brusquely.

Yet, when the time came, the pause was unexpectedly extended, more so than the suffering soloist could have hoped for. Sir Ian took the opportunity to take off the jacket of his own evening suit – tails no less – and with an expert cricket arm throw it, ball it, to be precise, at the offensive man's face. He muttered something about not allowing members of *his* audience to catch a cold. His resonant mutter had been heard in the back rows of the parterre. The next day the newspapers had a feast.

"Doctor Barton treats patient in Festival Hall. The patient survives with a bruised ego." "Sir Ian performs a striptease on stage." And so forth. Other commentaries had been less kind to both, the offensive, not to mention offended dawdler, as well as to Sir Ian himself. Regardless of the press's forced witticisms, the public loved him.

It is worth mentioning that Sir Ian regarded all the concert halls in which he conducted as 'his halls', and the audiences had been invariably included in his parental embrace.

The next morning, promptly at nine, Anne knocked on Sir Ian's very private changing room. Hearing no answer she opened the door and made a little curtsy. She came alone, and had never met aristocracy. Sir Ian sat facing the door, as though daring her to take another step. He looked at her sternly for some moments, then rose to his feet, bowed deeply, took two steps forward, and kissed her outstretched hand.

"I'm glad you could come, my dear," he said gently. "Methinks you and I have something in common."

John Brent had done the unspeakable. He'd always considered himself to be a hard-nosed scientist. If anything didn't lend itself to being tested scientifically, then it belonged in the realm of philosophy – not pure science. Not that neurology or even genetics was pure science in the exact sense of the word. The purists called them applied sciences.

"But once you enter molecular, not to mention submolecular, dimension, science is as pure as you can get. And we are up to our neck in genetics which, since the invention of the electron microscope, has brought us into the atomic age. Or to put it more precisely, into the field of pure physics." John was trying to persuade Peter of his righteousness.

"Until the purest of purists ventured into the unknown," Peter put in, not quite knowing where his boss was going.

"Precisely!" John exclaimed.

"Enter the strings..." Peter murmured. He was beginning to guess where John Brent was heading with his argument.

John Brent had recently published a paper in which he questioned the order of evolution. The realm he had tackled dealt exclusively with neurology, yet even so, there was bound to be a hullabaloo. He felt that if it hadn't been for his stature as the Director of the MNI, the article would have never been accepted for publication.

John had dared to question the order of succession, or the chicken and the egg. Peter hadn't, as yet, had a chance to read the article. He'd hear that it was scientifically risqué.

"There once was a time," John continued, "when pure physics ruled supreme. The others, those outside the illustrious ranks of pure scientists, had been deemed philosophers, theologians, speculators, and even, though sometimes grudgingly, authors of science-fiction. Then the physicists stepped out from the confines of their laboratories and introduced themselves as theoretical physicists."

When John Brent talked science, he waxed poetic. He never forgot his roots in physics. Though he no longer served his old mistress, he remained, in his own way, faithful to her. For him physics, pure as against applied physics, let alone biology, physiology and suchlike, remained the basis of all life. Be that as it may, right then, Peter wasn't sure where John was going with his argument.

John Brent had read all he could find about string theory. It was a theory which purported that the atom is not only made up of subatomic particles, such as the electrons, neutrons and protons, but that those in turn are built up of particles still smaller, such as the now famous quarks. String theory came much later and sounded more theoretical than based in fact.

"The human eye cannot see the quarks, no matter how much they are magnified. The best we can hope for is to observe the trails they leave behind when we smash the atoms in accelerators." He looked triumphantly at Peter. He then smiled his best wry smile. "There is another reason for the invisible quarks. If they didn't exist, the theoretical scientists' calculations wouldn't work. Isn't this like putting the chicken before the egg?"

Peter nodded. John's arguments reminded him that he hadn't had time to have eggs for breakfast for a long time.

"Surely," John reasoned, "it is time to stop!"

He's right, Peter thought. I could do with a couple of fried ones, sunny side up....

"Not so, said theoreticians running another hot tub and soaking merrily until another theoretical thought crossed their theoretical mind." Peter remembered reading an article that theoretical physicists were in the habit of luxuriating in hot water and periodically emerging with new theories about the origin of the universe. If only neurosurgery were that easy, he sighed.

John was staring at Peter as though daring him to contradict his argument. Peter quickly nodded. Repeatedly.

"And it did," John resumed seemingly mollified. "A few dozen hot baths later, they came up with a further miniaturization of the completely invisible quarks and claimed that those funny little thingies were composed of vibrating strings of energy. Why were quarks funny?"

"Because of their names?" Peter tried. John continued as if Peter hadn't spoken.

"The theoretical physicists called them: 'up', 'down', 'charm', 'strange', 'top' and 'bottom'. Only the 'ups' weren't up, the 'downs' weren't down. I am sure that they were all 'charm'ing, although the only thing that they all shared was a flavour. Actually no. The theoreticians *claimed* they all had different flavours."

"The theoreticians?"

"The quarks!" John didn't notice that Peter began looking at his watch.

"As for the strings – they had no names!" John announced triumphantly. "What was more, the theory proposed by the theoretical physicists could not be tested under laboratory, nor any other, conditions. They, the theories, belonged in the realm of equally theoretical math. The strings were wiggly vibrations, in constant movement, which accounted for their eventual attraction to each other, thereby causing them to grow into larger bundles of string, and so on, until they reached a size large enough to be tested in a laboratory. Or else added up to a major planet. Or a sun."

John stood up hopefully to deliver his knockout punch. By now Peter was well grounded in the basic chain of physics.

Grosso modo, cells divided into molecules, which divided into atoms, which divided into electrons and protons and neutrons, which split into quarks and suchlike, which could no longer be split but consisted of vibrating strings of energy. Why strings? Because they were two-dimensional. Peter thought all this had something to do with quantum theory which, to the best of his knowledge, no one as yet understood.

"What really happened," John pontificated, "was that physics had moved into the domain of philosophy, and was on the verge of threatening the realm which heretofore belonged only to theology."

"Why the strings?" Peter asked.

"Because the theoretical physicists needed them to come up with the 'theory of everything'. Don't you see? God? Everything? There is nothing outside God, is there? And using strings, their equations worked just fine. Occasionally they had to resort to a dozen new dimensions, all curled up inside themselves, but, they reasoned, that was a small price to pay to know absolutely everything about absolutely nothing."

Assuming Dr. Brent had stated his arguments in his article, Peter wondered why Director John Brent had exposed himself to such untested terrain? After a momentary silence, he asked him.

"Because of Anne," came the unexpected reply.

Peter knew that repeated fMRIs of Anne's brain had given direct indication that that which she did, how she acted, felt or even thought, brought about, or contributed to, direct changes in the arrangement of neurons in her grey matter. Not the other way round. She may have started with a given matrix of grey cells. There was ample evidence, however, that changes occurred in her brain structure, in her neuroconnectors, which, by all accounts, had no business being there. Her extraordinary enlargement of the pons Varolii had no genetic precedent. Her overwhelming desire to coordinate the different and diverse movements of her left and right hand, in perfect unison with her hearing organs, had to be at the nascent point of the changes. By all accounts, desire had to be at the root of the evolutionary leap that appeared to have taken place in Anne's head. Peter wondered if the same was true of everybody, if we all direct our own evolution.

John gave Peter time to analyze the evidence. Then he resumed talking, this time in a quiet, almost deferential voice.

"Unless it can be proven that all violinists, perhaps also pianists and other instrumentalists, who use two hands to perform different yet very complex movements in unison with each other, Anne is a singular mutation. Until proven otherwise, I am forced to conclude that the need she felt brought billions of neurons into play which otherwise would not even be developed. And changed her brain so she could do the things she wanted."

The purpose of the article that John had written was to attract musicians, of any discipline, to submit themselves to a series of fMRIs, so as to establish or destroy this hypothesis. Since such a hypothesis lent itself to laboratory experiments, its findings would be deemed scientific. It would prove that thought, not to mention desire, precedes the evolutionary act as opposed to the traditional theory of being the result of such.

Finally, John had appealed to parents who have reasons to suspect that their children might be particularly gifted musicians. Any child who showed great promise, and was under the age of eleven, would be offered a free fMRI evaluation, and would be re-scanned annually to detect any unusual developments in their brain structures. An early detection of the Genius Syndrome would assure special protection for such children and promote their development in the field of their choice.

"**Watching** your relationship to Anne, Gabby, it strikes me that you would make a wonderful father," Michael said when he and Gabriel found another moment to be alone.

"It is kind of you to say so, Sir. Your daughter is indeed a very special young lady."

"It is I who thank you, Gabriel. What I meant..."

"...to ask me was why I never got married?" He turned his eyes away as though to conceal his embarrassment. "I told you, Sir, that there was a time when I was a wrestler. I fought for money. Accidents happen in professional sport."

Michael's face continued to register a blank.

"I have sustained a rather serious injury, Sir."

Michael was suddenly embarrassed. Gabriel's unaccustomed hedging could only mean groin injury. "I am sorry, Gabriel. Not just . . . well, I am sorry I was so nosy."

"It was a very long time ago, Sir. I don't think about it nowadays."

Until I opened my big mouth, Michael thought.

Silence stretched for some moments. Michael was suddenly afraid to ask anything lest he tread on some very private ground. But there was one thing he had to find out.

"Why did you say that Anne is very special?"

"All children are special, Sir."

Anne was hardly a child any more, and Michael felt sure that there was more to Gabriel's observation. He was not in a habit of bandying pleasantries around. Gabriel sensed Michael's curiosity.

"All children are special," he repeated. "Unfortunately, most of them lose their potential well before they grow up."

"Why would you say that, my friend?" Michael felt a growing friendship towards this man who served him, served his family, and yet maintained a protective stance towards them like a guardian angel.

"Einstein once said that, and I believe I quote him exactly, that it is almost a miracle that modern teaching methods have not strangled the holy curiosity of inquiry; for what this delicate little plant needs more than anything, besides stimulation, is freedom."

"You have an extraordinary memory." Michael's voice carried admiration with a hint of jealousy. Not for the first time he wished he had spent more time on books and fewer hours trying to please his clients.

"That is of no consequence. Anyone can train his or her memory. What is more important is that circumstances have brought about conditions that enabled Miss Anne to be schooled at home. I believe this was the turning point in her young life."

In spite of his previous misgivings, Michael was on the verge of asking Gabriel a hundred more questions. Luckily, a telephone interrupted their tête-à-tête. Gabriel picked up the receiver before Michael even got up.

"The Howell residence, may I help you? Yes, Sir. Probably in about two hours, Sir. Yes, of course. Good-bye, Sir."

"Was it Sir calling?" Michael asked facetiously.

"It was Doctor Brown. He inquired about Miss Anne's audition. I took the liberty of telling Doctor Brown that the young lady will be back in about two hours."

"You think it will take that long?"

"No, Sir. But I rather think that Miss Anne will need a moment or two to relax before she returns Doctor Brown's call."

The man thought of everything. Michael was ready to share his own favourite Einstein quotation when he heard Fluffy rushing to the front door. What he wanted to tell Gabriel was that Einstein had also said that 'Education was what remains after one has forgotten everything one learned in school'. No matter.

At this precise moment they heard the front door opening. Anne walked in, slowly, as though carrying a great weight with her. Indeed, she did.

When Sir Ian had let go of Anne's hand, she was already flabbergasted. She may have looked mature for her age, but no one, not even Peter, had ever kissed her hand before. And certainly not a Sir, a Knight of the Realm, as her mother had called Sir Ian. What was she supposed to do? Curtsey again? Swoon? She swallowed hard instead.

"I trust I didn't keep you waiting, Sir, Sir Ian?" she said as politely as she could.

"Just one will do?"

"One, Sir, Sir Ian?"

"Just one sir, or better still just Ian."

Anne's cheeks acquired a hue that matched her hair. Only now did she understand what her host had meant.

"Oh, I am sorry, Sir."

"Do you want me to address you as Miss Howell, Miss Howell?"

This time they both laughed.

"Sit down and tell me all about yourself, Anne, would you?"

It took another twenty minutes and as many admonitions before Anne, for the first time, addressed Sir Ian without his requisite title.

"We are in the same business, you and I," he explained. "If we are to work together, we must eliminate everything which might hamper our communication."

"Yes, Ian, Sir. I mean..."

"I know, it will come. What can you play for me?"

"What would you like me to play?"

"Whatever comes to your mind. Or better still, to your heart."

Anne took a while tuning her violin. Then, still sitting on a straight-backed chair, she broke into the middle part of the second movement of Beethoven's violin concerto. Sir Ian listened without a single interruption. Finally, she put the violin on her lap.

Sir Ian got up, went to a glass cabinet, and carefully removed a large case. From it he took out another fiddle and gingerly handed it to Anne. She replaced her own in its case and took the new instrument. It needed some tuning. For over a year now, Anne had had perfect pitch. This special gift enabled her to tune the new fiddle without resorting to a tuner or a piano, a fact duly noted by Sir Ian.

"Try the same piece..." he suggested.

The first few notes sounded strange to Anne's ears. The sound was too powerful, too penetrating. She reduced the pressure of her bow and heard herself play the sweetest pianissimo she'd ever heard in her life. She increased the volume, then, with an ad-libbed passage moved into the cadenza. The double stopping, the harmonic arpeggios filled the relatively small room to overflowing. She was so involved with the sound that she hadn't noticed Sir Ian wiping tears forming in his eyes. Suddenly she stopped.

"What is this...?"

"The fiddle? It is a Stradivarius. One of the better ones."

"A real Stradivarius?" Anne's eyes widened in disbelief. "Yes, I suppose it must be. It must be..." Disbelief in her tone rapidly changed to pure adulation.

"I thought you might like it, my girl. I just thought you might..." And then he got up and took the violin from Anne's hands. "Would you like to have it? On loan, of course," he added hastily. "It has been entrusted to me."

"Me? I mean would I? Have it? The violin? I mean the Strad..." She went on babbling for a little while.

"There is a condition, dear Anne. There are always conditions." Sir Ian looked very stern.

She didn't say anything. She thought she would polish his shoes, clean his floors, do anything for a chance to own such a violin even for a day. A single day.

"There are just two conditions. The first is non-negotiable; the second, well, I hope you'll agree. The first is that you may use it for as long as you play it the way you just did. And the second, well, it's more of a favour. Next month, that is to say in three weeks, I want to give a performance of the Brahms Violin concerto in D Major, opus 77. The violinist who was going to play it had two fingers broken in a skiing accident. I hope you don't ski..." he looked at her even more sternly. "Anyway, I would like you to perform the concerto with me."

Anne kept very still, expecting any second to wake up from this enchanting dream. Sir Ian misread her silence.

"You do play the Brahms, don't you?" his face went almost ashen. The programs had already been printed. They would have to announce a different soloist, of course, but this could be done verbally.

"The Brahms? In D Major? Opus...."

"Yes, yes!"

"Yes," she nodded. "I play all the concertos."

"Of course . . . how silly of me." The great man, the Maestro, sat down heavily, still holding on to the Stradivarius. "Oh, I am sorry," he said, looking down at his lap, "This is yours."

When Anne remained frozen in immobility he raised an eyebrow in mock bewilderment. "You do want it, don't you? And play with me the Brahms?"

"Yes, Sir. Yes, Ian. Yes my Knight in Shining Armour."

With this she practically jumped at Sir Ian, put one hand gingerly on the precious violin and the other around the Knight's neck. She proceeded to shower his cheeks, his forehead and his balding head with kisses. Sir Ian was lucky indeed, that Anne was not yet in the habit of wearing any makeup.

"Easy, girl . . . easy now...."

Sir Ian did very little to defend himself. A man in his position should maintain a degree of equanimity and bear the exuberance of the young with appropriate grace and tolerance.

Anne played three more segments from various concertos for Sir Ian. He just sat there, transported into a different reality where, heretofore, only angels had gone. Occasionally a deep sigh escaped his lips. Later he closed his eyes and surreptitiously continued to wipe an occasional tear that annoyingly kept forcing itself in one eye and then the other. By the time Anne stopped playing, he was quite confident the priceless Stradivarius had at last found a worthy sentinel. The Strad and Anne had been made for each other.

It was with the precious cargo of two fiddles, one under each arm, that Anne, still in a bit of a daze, staggered into the living room, as usual without wiping her feet. On this occasion both Diana and Michael decided to forgive her. At least, for as long as she was the keeper of the Stradivarius.

* * * * *

Chapter 17

The World at Her Feet

The popular press had picked up on the article he had written to
the scientific journal and, so far, he had received over fifty requests from hopeful parents, offering their children for the experimental program. John had appointed Peter to be in charge
of it. But Anne remained his most prized discovery. He desperately wanted to maintain his follow-up examinations with her.

He was insisting that before Anne took off on any tour he
have a chance to check on her condition. It was a bit hard to
argue with his logic. In scientific terms, Anne had become an
equation he couldn't solve. Yet, paradoxically, he felt that he
alone had the skills necessary to assure her well-being. No one,
to his or Michael's knowledge, had ever acquired Anne's virtuoso skill in a period of just a little over two years. There are
child prodigies that astound their teachers, or even the world,
with their command of a concerto or two. Anne's repertoire
included just about everything that had ever been composed for
the violin. Anything of value. Furthermore, she played it all by
ear. Completely memorized, usually after a single reading of the
score. It just wasn't normal by any standard available to science.

"I know that normal is dull, often disagreeable, but there is
a time when deviation from what we call normal, i.e. the norm,

could have an adverse effect on her personality," John continued to have his reservations.

"But Anne is not going anywhere, John. She is going to
play right here, in Montreal," Diana insisted.

Peter listened to this exchange in silence. He didn't feel
competent to argue the pros and cons of another follow up examination in John's presence. But he was not about to get away
with silence.

"Peter," Michael broke in, "you might know her better
than any of us. At least from the musical point of view. What
do you say?"

Peter hated passing judgment on someone as dear to him as
Anne. What if he was wrong? Would he be able to live with
himself? "Musically she is definitely not normal," he said,
playing for time.

"There," John said, "what did I tell you?"

But once started Peter would not be shut off. "With all due
respect, Sir, I do not believe that anyone of us has the compe-
tence to judge Anne's musical geni . . . her talent."

"Call it by its name, Peter. To judge her genius. But I
don't propose to judge her. You are right in your opinion. I
want to assure myself that there isn't something that we should
have done, something that might have proven expedient, when
we had a chance." Then, before anyone else had a chance to
express their thoughts, he muttered: "Before it's too late."

"What do you mean? Too late? Too late for what?" Diana sounded on the verge of panic.

"Easy now. As Peter has pointed out, we are treading on
virgin territory here. I know of no one who has ever made such
an astounding progress as Anne has over the last two years.
Don't you feel it is worthy of ah . . . well, of an examination?"

"You mean like a guinea pig?" Diana said, lowering her
voice. She wasn't smiling.

"Diana, you know very well that we all love Anne. No one
would dream of experimenting on her, or anybody else, for that
matter. All I said was that the previous fMRIs indicated very
abnormal, that is to say, very unusual developments in certain
parts of her brain. The results, or the consequences of these de-

velopments, have been astounding. Incredible. I want to make
sure that there is nothing that might hinder her well-being and
her behaviour when faced with the opportunities that, we all expect, are about to be placed before her."

John took a deep breath. He couldn't possibly tell them
that for the first time in his life, he had an opportunity to examine and follow-up on a brain that could well be the most amazing development in his long career. A brain that, before his very
eyes, had developed from an average, even tumourous condition
to one of unprecedented uniqueness.

He was insanely curious. But his scientific hunger notwithstanding, he would not endanger either Anne's life or her sanity
in any way.

Since Anne had come into his care, he had searched for
anything remotely similar to Anne's development. There was
nothing. Not a single case of such an extraordinary growth,
particularly in the area of her pons Varolii, the usually tenuous
link between the two hemispheres of the brain. What's more,
Anne's frontal lobes had achieved the developmental maturity
of a thirty-year-old. Perhaps even surpassed it. The portion of
her frontal lobe on which he'd operated had reached maturity in
half the time needed by a 'normal' adult.

"You are thinking of another fMRI?" asked Michael.

"And that is all." John confirmed.

"No PET scans, no radiation of any sort and no drugs?"
Since Anne's surgery, Michael had read all he could lay his
hands on about the brain scanning technology in order to be
able to ask pertinent questions.

"You have my word."

Diana still didn't look happy. Anne was not a guinea pig,
she kept thinking. Why can't they leave her alone? Don't they
realize how much stress she is facing right now? What, with seeing Sir Ian twice a week, with the concert coming up in eight
days, with the talk of tours and successes... She's only sixteen
years old. Just sweet sixteen.

"What do you say, Diana?" Michael asked. He sounded
on the verge of agreeing.

"No one is listening to me, anyway." She looked and sounded resigned.

"If I may, Diana. As you so kindly remarked earlier, I know Anne fairly well. I think she would want to do a follow-up on the fMRI. She is as curious about what is going on with her life as . . . I suppose, in a way . . . we all are. She has become the centre of our attention. This, too, has placed her under considerable stress. Another fMRI might dispel such extra pressure. We might discover that, since the last scan, she has remained in a stable condition. Don't you think, Diana?"

"I suppose so. Only don't forget she's still only a child. Just a child...."

Anne's relationship with Peter gave John an idea. He knew that Peter had developed an ongoing, for the want of a better word, camaraderie with Anne that could not quite be defined, as yet, as a physical attraction, but it was very close to it. Peter had placed Anne on such a high pedestal that he could hardly reach the Olympian elevation himself. But if anyone could convince Anne about the benefits of an fMRI follow-up, it would be he. And, after all, Peter Brown was a physician dedicated to neurology.

"Perhaps he isn't quite as fanatical as I am," John muttered to himself, "but his commitment to science could not be questioned. And Peter knows that Anne would not be placed in harm's way."

The next day he spoke to Peter.

"I thought you might find out if she would be willing to enter a regular follow-up program. After all, she's not a child anymore and is well capable of making her own decisions."

This wasn't strictly true, not in the legal sense, but in all aspects that mattered, Anne was mature well beyond her biological age. The very next Friday, just before the regular dinner for all her friends, Anne announced that she would be more than happy to continue with the fMRIs, provided they did not interfere with her music.

"The scans are interesting, but music is my life."

Only if the fMRI confirms this supposition, John thought. He meant that only if Anne continued to have a life. They were venturing here into still very unknown territory. For some reason his excitement was dimmed by a strange sense of foreboding. When things were too good to be true, that was usually because they were. For the now, he decided to keep his thoughts to himself.

Sir Ian Barton arrived at the Howell residence by a regular taxi, like a regular guy. He knocked on the door and Gabriel let him in after Fluffy had approved the visitor. Having placed his coat and hat on Gabriel's extended arm, the illustrious guest did not wait to be announced, but tiptoed in the direction, from which most of the noise emanated, and stood there, in the doorway, beaming.

"Surely, it must be Sir Ian," Diana said, her back to the door. "It's almost seven."

Michael, who saw him first, was about to jump to his feet, when Sir Ian's outreached hand stopped him in mid tracks. A moment later, Gabriel, to allow Sir Ian to have his moment of surprise, stoically having taken a roundabout route through the kitchen, filled the dining room door with his bulk, and announced in a voice filled with mock exasperation: "Sir Ian Barton!"

"Spoil sport," was Sir Ian's retort at which everybody rose in unison.

Anne beat everyone to it. She ran towards the impressive figure still standing in the doorway leading to the hall, and planted a kiss on his sallow cheek. The way Sir Ian loved his music, his skin probably hadn't been exposed to the sun for a number of years.

"At least someone takes time to greet me," he grumbled under his breath, yet loud enough for everyone to have heard him. He still spoke with an unmistakable British accent.

"Mother, father, John and Peter," Anne announced in a way of introduction.

"*The* mother?" Sir Ian inquired. "Now I know from whom Anne gets her looks."

In his acquired European, if not exactly British, style, he kissed Diana's hand.

"And the father," he shook Michael's hand while scrutinizing his face. "Ah, the mysteries that our genes enshroud..." It was quite evident that Sir Ian was curious. "What genes the gods have chosen to commingle into Anne's unique conjunction," he muttered, evidently preoccupied with his thoughts on the elusive subject of heredity.

Doctor John Brent was next. Sir Ian assured him of the international renown of the MNI, "Even in the Old Country, my good doctor," and finally he came to Peter.

"So you are the one really responsible for all this," he said, bowing in Anne's direction. "I am sure you will be amply rewarded in heaven, for truly, my dear doctor, it is from heaven that Anne brings us her ineffable euphony."

"Has she been talking, Sir?"

"Incessantly. A great deal of it about you," Sir Ian assured.

Anne had no need to expose her cheeks to the doubtful benefits of the sun. Right now they were almost as red as her hair cascading in one easy swoop onto her shoulders.

"I hope it was nothing bad," Peter replied, also displaying a shade of colour not normally associated with research scientists burning the midnight oil.

Sir Ian pulled Anne to one side of the room. "That colossus who let me in, was that Gabriel?"

"Of course! Who else could look like that?"

"Who indeed. Do you think you might persuade him to meet me? We haven't been properly introduced."

"How lovely!" Anne clapped her hands and pulled Sir Ian's sleeve towards the kitchen. The guest of honour turned his face towards Diana with a helpless expression as if to ask: "What can I do?"

In the kitchen the Maestro approached Gabriel slowly, studying his face all the way from the door of the dining room. They made a truly odd couple. Sir Ian's waist matched

Gabriel's chest. In girth, that is. Both boasted about forty-four inches. Luckily Sir Ian was also quite tall, and his general demeanour enabled him to carry his love of pasta rather well.

Sir Ian offered his hand. He then held Gabriel's in an amazingly firm grip while he continued studying him at some length. Actually only seconds had elapsed, but the two men exchanged something that made them both smile.

"I feel indebted to everyone who contributed to Anne being what she is today. Thank you, Gabriel."

And then Gabriel said something that sounded strange, even to Anne's ears. "I leave her in your hands, Sir Ian. Look after her well."

For some reason Anne thought that Gabriel almost added '...for me'. 'Look after her well for me.' She had never realized just how precious she had become to Gabriel. All of a sudden she recalled the many minutes, even hours, she had spent just sitting with him, staring into his eyes, soaking up his wisdom. So many hours.... Now that music had consumed her every minute, she had forgotten that her journey to the present had not been an easy one. We all tend to remember only the best. Something to do with our instinct of self-preservation. Preservation not just of our bodies, our physiques, but of our minds and hearts. Perhaps, our souls. It was John who had removed her tumour, but it was Gabriel who helped her heal.

Her eyes caught Gabriel's for just an instant. In that singular moment she knew that whatever fate, or Sir Ian for that matter, had in store for her, Gabriel would always be there to protect her. Somehow.

Dinner was filled with family warmth. By means of his unorthodox entry Sir Ian had succeeded in putting everyone at ease. He was well aware that he tended to dominate any gathering – a man who must command, with a tiny baton, upwards of seventy aspiring prima-donnas, must have this inherent ability. He had to make sure that he didn't dwarf others with the profusion of his social charms, or even an elaborate turn of phrase. During dinner he told them anecdotes from around the world, some funny, some bordering on anguish.

"Music is like that. Great are her rewards, yet she is a demanding mistress. She commands all that serve her with a velvet glove drawn misleadingly over an iron fist. But woe to him, or her," he glanced momentarily at Anne, "who does not commit their total being. I suspect that music, real music, is the nearest we can approach to divinity while still here, on earth."

Thus he concluded one of his stories. He spoke of music with a distant expression in his eyes, as though admiring an unattainable woman, a Euterpe and Terpsichore rolled into a single entity, with himself, like Erato, singing her praises. Though Sir Ian would never admit it, he was an incurable romantic. He married early, divorced soon after, and since had fallen passionately in love with every beautiful woman he'd ever met. And he met many.

Before leaving, he presented Diana with a ticket for the Royal Box at the Théâtre for the concert next week.

"There are six seats in the loge," he mentioned. "I hope I can tempt all of you to attend. I promise you a night you won't soon forget." With that he went through the farewells in reverse order, not forgetting, in fact starting with Gabriel who happened to be conveniently around at the time.

"Thank you, my friend," he murmured, reaching up to place his hand on Gabriel's shoulder. "I promise you I will."

"What was all that about?" Michael asked after the great man had left. For some minutes his presence continued to linger in the living room.

"A complex character," Peter offered. "I would love to have him as a friend, but wouldn't like to cross swords with him."

Anne winked at her mother. She smiled.

"How do you like my Ian?" she asked.

For some strange reason only now did they all realize that Anne was the only one who had addressed Sir Ian as Ian. How strange, they all thought. Except for Gabriel. He thought it was just as it should be.

The month following Anne's debut on the stage of Théâtre Maisonneuve was as hectic as any in Anne's young life. She rose early, went to bed late. She worked as she had never worked before. It was never a question of her performance. It was always the problem of the orchestra rising to her level. Of meeting her demanding standards. Sir Ian Barton did his best to call her only when absolutely necessary. Even that occurred more often than he would have wanted. Once again, Anne was becoming noticeably tense.

"You must learn to relax, my dear. Leave the orchestra to me. I'll bully them until they do you justice. Trust me," he repeated many a time, adding all sorts of other assurances.

Sir Ian was right. He usually was.

As for Jorge di Vargas's *Intermezzo*, it was the first premiere of a short piece by a Canadian composer to receive accolades from all the professional critics. But poor Jorge would never be sure if it was due to the quality of his composition or to what Anne had done with it. He strongly suspected the latter, although, eventually, the two really became one. As for the performance of the Brahm's Concerto, well... There were only two things that separated it from all the other performances in Montreal. First, it was the soloist herself. And the second was almost as unique. Anne's very last note was followed by deadly silence. Whether people had refused to accept that the concerto was over, or whether they were just swept into a different reality, no one would ever know. But it wasn't until virtually the whole audience had risen to their feet that the first hands joined in applause. The applause lasted until Anne had returned to the stage a dozen times, bowed and sent kisses, then climbed to the conductor's podium to kiss the conductor, which act, needless to say, invoked another storm of applause.

Just as Sir Ian had promised, it was a night no one would soon forget.

And this was just the beginning.

John Brent came down himself to pick Anne up and drive her to the Montreal Neurological Institute. Once Anne had told him that she could spare perhaps as many as three hours that afternoon, her availability took precedence over all his other commitments. Even Peter could not extricate himself from his duties, but being a Director carried its privileges.

The patient scheduled, a follow-up case and thus involving no risks other than a slightly bruised ego, had been rescheduled to a later date. Anne submitted to all the boring ritual of scanning with patience and equanimity. Two hours later Peter, who had just finished his duties, drove her home.

Peter had very mixed feelings towards Anne's evidently forthcoming career. He knew that Anne was not yet seventeen. He also knew that the feelings he had for her had nothing to do with her age. He wanted to protect her from the world at large, from the iniquities associated with a life on stage, in so-called show business, no matter how noble in her particular case. He trusted Sir Ian, but he trusted himself more. He was wondering if he should take time off, resign if absolutely necessary, from the MNI and chaperon Anne on the forthcoming Canadian, and planned American, concert tours. Then he realized that the only person from whom Anne might need the protection of a chaperone – was himself.

"I shall miss you," he murmured without looking at her.

"Me too," she replied, also looking away. A slow-moving tear began its tremulous descent down her cheek.

"Will you write? Email?"

She didn't answer. There was something in her throat that would not let her speak. It was true that she was not yet of age, but she had heard about, she'd even seen girls her age running around with boyfriends, smooching in dark doorways, and not-so-dark nooks in the park. She was growing up rapidly in all ways that would, and did, continue to change her from a girl into a woman. Would he ever notice, she wondered? Ever?

There are moments when one's heart takes over the affairs of one's head. Peter pulled over into the Mount Royal lookout. He then almost brutally pulled Anne into his arms and then with contrasting gentleness touched her lips with his own. They sat like that, speechless, barely touching each other's lips, until finally the magnet which drew them together increased in force and their mouths drank of each other's longing.

"I love you, my love, I love you, always have...."

Anne closed her eyes and listened to the words that in her ears sounded like the most beautiful concerto. "Me too," she whispered at long last. So rich when said with her fiddle, so inadequate with words. "Tell me again...." she pleaded.

He did. Many more times.

The next time Sir Ian visited the Howell residence was two years later. He had stolen their daughter and placed the world at her feet. Despite the dangers that novas all too often shine with their exuberant light but for a little while – even the supernova that showed the Magi the way to Bethlehem shone but for a short spell – Sir Ian had taken Anne on a world tour and returned her whole, as promised.

Behind her lay London, Paris, Rome, Madrid, Warsaw, Moscow, Beijing, New Delhi, Rio, Buenos Aires, Santiago, Lima, Mexico, and finally an encore appearance at New York, Chicago, San Francisco and Montreal. Even as tornadoes come suddenly, and pass leaving chaos in their tempestuous paths, so had Anne's tour stirred the world into a tempest of musical activity.

After the single visits to Toronto, Ottawa and Vancouver, the news of the musical phenomenon had spread like wild fire.

They hadn't been just concerts. There had been radio, and television, and recording sessions lasting well into the night. There had been masses of CDs, masses of personal appearances in universities, conservatories of music – everywhere she could inspire with her music or even just with her presence. Anne had given of herself holding nothing back. She, and Sir Ian with her if sometimes from a distance of a thousand miles, had been on a mission, a crusade to show people the meaning of true music. In an age when rhythmic noise went for musical genius, Anne brought music to the world such as it had once known. But she did much more than that. She pointed to the wonders that still lay ahead in the future. She showed them music wherein melody and harmony and purity of sound were a reason for being.

In her last ten performances, while Anne had played inside the standing-room-only concert halls, speakers had been installed for the music to filter to the crowds that stood outside, often in rain or sleet. Crowds hungry for the echo of the divine, which descended to earth to share the unknown, the esoteric, the ineffable.

Sir Ian drove Anne home in his own limousine.

Diana, Michael, John and Peter stood at the front door when his driver pulled up in front of their house. Fluffy stayed back. Perhaps he was afraid that the doors would open and, yet again, Anne wouldn't be there. When the chauffeur opened the sedan door, Sir Ian emerged first from the darkened interior. He was half the man they'd met two years ago. There was power in his posture yet it now came from a gaunt frame of a man in his early sixties. He turned around and offered his hand to his protégée.

Diana caught her breath.

Two years ago, they had bid God's speed to a girl with a girlish gait in her step. From the limousine emerged a woman. A beautiful woman who bore an invisible weight on her shoulders. She walked rather than ran to take her mother into her arms. Then father. Then John and Peter. She offered each of them her cheek to kiss, her smile to enjoy. She was not the Anne they all knew and loved. She was the world-famous, magnificent, incomparable Miss Anne Howell, the violinist extraordinary. She was a goddess who shared her light with them.

And there was great sadness in her eyes.

* * * * *

Chapter 18

Flowers for Algernon

The first three concerts in Canada, the lightning tour of the
United States, and the first two performances in Europe – London and Paris – were wonderful. Anne flew back from each one
of them. There were hours of joyful talk, stories of throngs of
people following her car as she left the concert hall for her hotel.
Stories of children offering her flowers at the end of each performance; of encores played to standing audiences. The exuberance of the patrons created an atmosphere that kept her going, maintained her on a high.

At the beginning she wasn't alone. There was Sir Ian Barton. He was her friend and protector. Her guardian angel. But
mostly a friend.

But that was just in the beginning.

Later, flying alone, to and from each performance, proved
too much for Anne. Diana, Michael and even Peter took turns to
visit her in various cities, even though their time together, and
alone, was usually limited to just two or three hours. The family
visits, wonderful as they were, imposed additional burden on
Anne's free time. Anne desperately needed, as we all do, at least
some precious moments to be alone. She had not yet learned to
detach herself from the needs of others. No matter how close to
her heart.

While Sir Ian Barton conducted the first seven performances in North America, he had his obligations at his new home,
the Théâtre Maisonneuve, the home of his *Orchestre Sym-
phonique de Montréal*. His schedule made it impossible for him
to be with Anne more than at occasional concerts, continents
apart, where he insisted on taking the baton, not because he was
needed, but because he needed Anne, even as her public did.
He, too, was under her spell and needed what drug addicts call –
a fix.

Early on, innumerable calls, e-mails and postcards told Diana and Michael and especially Peter where she was, what she
did, what she had played. Then that, too, proved too much.
Anne was an icon, a goddess already then, after the third or
fourth concert. Her time was no longer her own.

In Madrid she was welcomed at the airport, the Aeropuerto
de Barajas, by an army of paparazzi, who surrounded her right at
the exit gate and followed her to her hotel. There they waited
patiently for her to emerge to eat, to put her head outside the
limits of the hotel's grounds. God forbid she should take a walk
to see the city where she was to perform the next day. The paparazzi had already decided that she belonged to them, for their
private use and manipulation. She was swept away by limousine,
supposedly one arranged for her, but one that had been instead
substituted by the press barons, who whisked her away for an
'exclusive' interview, thereby stealing an edge over other news-
grabbers, and scoring a scoop over the competition.

The same treatment was afforded her from the moment she
arrived at the Warsaw Frederic Chopin International Airport, still
locally known as the Okecie. The same routine followed at the
Sherementyevo International Airport in Moscow, and even at the
Capital Airport in Beijing, where her hosts provided her with a
military escort all the way to the hotel. In fact, in the Peoples'
Republic of China, a fully armed sentinel, fully decked in a Mao
tunic, stood at her door and wouldn't allow anyone to so much
as knock on it unless they could prove a legitimate authority to
do so.

First mobbed, then a prisoner, Anne took it all in her youthful stride. Or so it seemed. No one seemed to notice that her

reactions, her smiles, nods, even the manner in which she walked, were all becoming vaguely robotic. Her only escape was her violin, provided she shared it with thousands.

There were those few moments when Anne was allowed to step out onto the balcony and tour the city with her eyes. There she would breathe the free air of the forty-second floor, while, unbeknownst to her, telescopic cameras were snapping her pictures. She was even escorted to her meals by a guide, pleasant enough, but a woman who didn't take her eyes from her for a single second of Anne's stay in China. There were press conferences, interviews with a number of promising Chinese violinists, who bowed deeply before her even as she reached out to embrace them.

In New Delhi she was caught up in a traffic jam for three hours. It was the only time she could actually be alone, except for her escort, of course, again a pleasant enough man, who unfortunately couldn't stop talking about his own daughter who was, 'just like Miss Howell, an aspiring violinist'. Anne had long since stopped 'aspiring' to anything, except to a moment of freedom, a private phone-call to her father or mother, or . . . Peter. Even then she heard a strange echo on the line, a sure telltale sign that the 'private' line was being listened to, and a recording would probably be sold to some local rag, waiting their turn to make her life more public. She now belonged to the world.

Rio de Janeiro, Buenos Aires, Santiago in Chile, Lima in Peru, Mexico City, were no better. Finally her triumphant return to New York, and then to Chicago and San Francisco broke the camel's back. The screech of police sirens, which apparently mistook her for a visiting dignitary or some obnoxious rock star, never left her between the airports and the hotels, the hotels and the concert halls, or any of her countless public appearances.

At long last, Sir Ian picked her up in his personal limousine at the Pearson Airport in Toronto and had his driver take them both, by a circuitous path to autoroute 401, and finally to a motel off the beaten track. Anne had a night's sleep, and then breakfast, without flash bulbs or rolling camcorders. Later that morning they went directly to her home in Westmount. They weren't followed.

Sir Ian Barton did all that was possible for him to do. In every capital city he, through his secretary, arranged for a chaperon, for the want of a better word, to be waiting for her. He made sure that Anne was never alone, that plainclothes detectives, who had been told to stay in the shadows and not make their presence known unless it proved absolutely necessary, had further protected her from harm.

Anne was safe enough. Unfortunately, too safe.

Her flights had been pre-booked, all first class, her hotels likewise, all transportation arranged to take her to whatever destination. She was pampered to within an inch of her life. No brand new Faberge Egg on its maiden voyage to the throne of the Tsars of Russia had ever been treated with such care and dedication. She was the principal jewel in Sir Ian Barton's crown. She was his pride and glory, his treasure, the daughter he'd never had. He discovered, all too late, that he still didn't 'have' her. Or at least didn't own her. Not even as a father owns a daughter. He couldn't say 'my' Anne, because by then she belonged to all people and to nobody. To no one in particular. Not even to herself. Now, the world owned her. All of her. Not just her talent, her music, but her every word, every smile, every inclination of her head, a gesture, a sigh, whatever sign of life. Every expression on her face, every grimace she showed was meticulously recorded for posterity.

Anne, without fully realizing it, had become a prisoner of her own talent, her genius, and her muse. There was no mother or father to lean on, no Gabriel to stare into her eyes, not even Peter to hold her close as in that so brief moment parked on the lookout of Mount Royal. Once again, she had reverted to the feelings she'd once had, as a child, when imprisoned in that dismal room on the third floor of the walk-up apartment on St. Laurent. Quite unconsciously, she began erecting mental and emotional barriers between herself and the outside world. She had to – to retain her sanity. To remain even partially rational. Towards the end of the triumphant tour she began to hide behind those barriers, in a plight of growing loneliness.

Once again, her only escape was music itself.

"Darling, darling, I missed you so much," Diana whimpered, hugging her, holding onto her, pulling her bodily to herself, refusing to let her go. Like all the people she'd met over these past two years. They, too, refused to let her go.

"I missed you too, mother. Very much." Her smile was mechanical. She could paint it on her face and maintain it there for hours at a time.

"Hello, dad, I missed you..." she told her father. Michael waited his turn to take possession of the apple of his eye. This, too, she had said mechanically, using the remnants of affection that still lingered, barely, outside the realm of music.

"Uncle John, how nice to see you."

"Hello, Peter..."

He was standing in line, waiting, waiting so patiently, so many months, years, just to touch her. And now that she was here he found it difficult to take her in his arms. It was not a reticence brought about by her parents' presence. He'd past that long ago. They'd been fully aware how he felt about their daughter for some time. They had no objections. He was good and able and reliable, and most of all, a good friend. There were thirteen years between them, but, Michael reasoned, Anne needed someone more mature to look after her.

"Hello Anne..."

It was so inadequate. 'Hello?'

A meaningless expression of a perfunctory greeting. Long time no see? Two, three days at most. That is what a hello is for. Not to sate the longing that took sleep from his eyes many a night. 'I missed you too, more than I can say'. That was it. It was more than he could say. Much more. There were no words he could utter that would tell her how he felt. Did she sense that? Could she sense anything outside the domain which she had entered?

"How are you, Anne?" Another banal question.

"I'm fine, Peter, how are you?"

"I'm fine..." No, I am not fine. I hurt. I hurt badly.

I know, Peter. I know. I know . . . what can I do?

What can you do, Anne?

None of it had been spoken but their eyes exchanged not the joy of homecoming but something that lingered at the very edge of an abyss, which their love for each other refused to span. Refused? Or couldn't. Not yet. Perhaps later? Tomorrow? Yes, it will be tomorrow . . . or the day after.

Questions. Many questions.

"I think I am tired, Peter. I think . . . I think you know that?"

"Yes Anne. I think I know that. "

And he let go her hand, her body held in a quick, almost impersonal embrace. He needed her for himself, not shared with millions of people the world over. Just for himself. Did she know that?

More questions.

The next moment Anne saw Gabriel standing at the door to the dining room. It seemed unreal that a man his size could have remained invisible until now. She hadn't moved, but their eyes met. He was the only one who could trap and sustain the attention in her eyes. She stood, motionless, drinking something that seemed to smoulder in Gabriel's eyes, like dying coals being fed with new fire. It could have been a mere moment, perhaps ten seconds, but the next instant a different smile erased the previous mechanical grimace from her face. She walked up to Gabriel and held her head against his massive chest. When she looked up, two tiny tears rolled down her cheek. She wiped them against his chest.

"I couldn't have done it without you, Gabriel," she murmured, only for his ears to hear.

"The power is not from me, little one," Gabriel said as quietly. "The power is always within you."

When Anne turned to face her parents, she looked a little different. A portion, no matter how minute, of the old Anne had just returned. Older, more mature, but still, the old Anne. She looked around the room, her hair following the movement of her head in long flowing swoops.

"How lovely," she said. "How very lovely. You kept it just the way it was." There was genuine wonder in her voice. "How lovely," she repeated. Everything else had changed. Everything.

Only then did they all notice Sir Ian standing in the doorway to the hall. He had remained in the anteroom to give the family a chance to reconcile these last two years. At least on the surface. Sir Ian, or just simply Ian, was the nearest she'd had to family on at least a small portion of her triumphant procession. Someone who treated her like a person, not a goddess to be held in constant awe. Dear Ian, she thought. He knows what happened to me. He knew even before I first left Montreal.

The Howells greeted Sir Ian like a member of the family. Although he had dropped in only a few times to see them during Anne's absence, he'd kept them abreast of all her activities, locations, and the programs she had played. He'd called with reports whenever he could.

"Come, Ian," Diana said, offering him her cheek. "Sit down. We must all sit down."

They hardly realized that everyone had remained standing for the last fifteen or twenty minutes. There was something wrong. Something had changed which no one could quite understand. Perhaps they had all been waiting for things to get back to normal. They didn't. They couldn't.

Nor could Fluffy.

He waited patiently in the corridor to be noticed. He didn't dare approach Anne. She was too different.

When the weather gets cold, the retirees flee to Florida, bears climb into their dens to hibernate, and frogs hide deep in muddy soil or underwater. But not all frogs. For a human kidney or heart to survive until installed in a recipient, the organs must be packed in a special solution and kept surrounded with ice. But they cannot be frozen. Freezing would cause the ice crystal to destroy the cells. There is, however, a type of frog, as well as some caterpillars and even painted turtles, which can freeze.

The frog eats voraciously, storing starch in its liver. It converts most of it into glucose, which then acts as antifreeze. If a human did that, he or she would die promptly of lethal diabetes. But in a frog this condition keeps as much as 35% of its body from freezing. Deep inside. Sixty-five percent of its body water freezes, but the natural antifreeze protects its inner organs. Our genomes are very similar, but we are very different from frogs. Even genetically speaking.

A frog is able to thaw back to life in hours after being an ice cube for months.

We can't. We are different.

Just how different we are was a question John had been asking himself for some time now. Or at least, ever since he'd met Anne. We could not freeze any part of the human brain for deferred study. Not yet?

There was a story John remembered reading a long time ago. 'Flowers for Algernon', by the otherwise not very well know author, Daniel Kayes. It was a novella that in 1959 had won the Hugo Award. Algernon, a simpleton, becomes extra-clever as a result of a brain operation, which previously had been successfully attempted only on animals. However, the effects of the operation do not last and, all too soon, Algernon reverts to his previous state of mental disassociation; he reverts to being a simpleton.

John Brent had performed a number of operations which had resulted in marked improvements in the mental abilities of his patients. Alas, only some of the improvements had lasted. There seemed an element in scientific diagnosis over which neurosurgeons had little or no control. It was that elusive state we recognize as consciousness. It seemed that our mental or intellectual condition is not the cause of, but rather the result of this state, of our consciousness. And this state, this consciousness which has nothing to do with our waken state, manifests through the instrument at its disposal, in this case the human brain. It is not the by-product or the result of the workings of our brain but, if anything, it is the causative factor. Lately, John leaned towards defining consciousness as an aspect of approximately six trillion electrochemical reactions that occur in our nervous system per second. Static electricity is omnipresent, even in the air we breathe. He sought to find a common denominator for the omnipresent energy and consciousness that manifests in all living matter. In his intellectual ramblings, he unwittingly stressed the word omnipresent.

The point of the story that attracted John's attention was that Algernon, once separated from the accepted norm of the human race, had become desperately alone. As a result of the operation he reached levels of IQ quite unattainable by the rest of us. His new abilities, well beyond what we define as genius, placed an even greater barrier between him and the rest of the human race than his original shortcomings. He was much more alone than he had ever been as a mere simpleton.

Anne's operation may well have put wheels in motion that resulted, over time, in her incredible musical ability. She became an instrument through which the heavenly music poured down onto the earth, onto the willing and hungry ears of mere mortals.

If one could but freeze her and unfreeze her into a different reality, John mused. As he stood welcoming Anne back from her concert tour, he had never felt quite so helpless.

And then he, too, met Gabriel's eyes. For a second or two he couldn't look away. A strange thought crossed his mind. He thought he knew what had happened to Anne. A human being cannot be alone. No matter how brilliant, how clever, even how good or compassionate. He or she deprived of the sense of belonging lost something that makes us human. Perhaps that was why God had created man. And woman. He just couldn't stand being alone. Is this the divine trait that we, humans, just cannot do without?

In three days Anne was scheduled to give her final concert of the World Tour in Montreal. Then, she was due for a rest. Before Sir Ian left, she asked him if they might forego the usual rehearsals.

"I've made a lot of recordings of the Max Bruch. Do you think you might manage without me?"

Sir Ian was stunned. Never in his illustrious carrier had he been asked such a question. He, the conductor, determined the necessity of rehearsals. 'As many as needed', was his motto.

But then he looked at Anne. This was not a normal request. Not by any normal standards. He thought again. It was true that, theoretically, he knew exactly how she would play the Max Bruch. He knew every individual expression, her favourite tempi, her occasional exaggerated legatos. Her particular interpretation had long been deeply inscribed in his mind, in fact, in his heart. He always thought that the reason Anne's interpretations had been different from all the others was that she played the way the composer would have written the piece had ink and paper offered sufficient means of transferring what they had heard in their souls, and not what was possible to put down on paper. What rebelled against Anne's request was his ego.

"Of course, my dear. Just as you like," he said softly.

And in that moment, for the first time in his life he felt that he wasn't just her conductor but that she truly became the daughter he'd never had. His concession was an act of pure love. Love rising above personal considerations.

"Of course, my dear," he repeated as though listening to his own voice in disbelief.

It had all happened too quickly.

The original tour had been planned for Canada only. Then, the United States became a natural extension of the Canadian tour. Three weeks suddenly grew into eight. London and Paris seemed like a natural progression. And then, once in Europe, Sir Ian Barton, for the first time in his life, lost control of events. Offers came from all parts of Europe, China, Australia, Japan, India, South Africa, Brazil... Sir Ian couldn't remem-

ber them all. The force of Anne's music took on the intensity
of a global tsunami. The waves rolled over continents, over the
established protocols. Rules were broken, visas appeared on a
moment's notice, programs established with great care were cancelled or postponed to make room and give priority to Anne. It
couldn't last. The universal forces had to dissipate themselves in
the ocean of human desire. Sir Ian cried at the thought of this
happening. He was glad he had a chance to offer Anne, perhaps
his final gift. His pride.

Anne's final concert of the World Tour was, as had been expected, a resounding success. Her affair with the world began
and ended in Montreal. *"Come il faut,"* claimed the French Canadian press. *"Une vraie Québécoise,"* read the headline of another *journal*, stating proudly, among many flowery accolades,
that Anne had been born and bred in the heart of French Canada. If it hadn't been for this fact, she would never have
achieved such sublime quality, the article implied to anyone who
bothered to read it.

The force of Likewise the English language *Gazette* stressed her Anglo-
Saxon heritage, allowing that the English race had never produced such an outstanding artist. The Ottawa press simply stated
that Anne was a National Treasure, and should be shared equally
by the whole country. By all Canadians.

"Who said that Chauvinism was dead?" Michael asked no
one in particular scanning the headlines on the Internet.

Whatever the parochial claims, the commentaries on her
performance appeared in newspapers throughout Canada. From
coast to coast to coast. She was recognized as a National Hero
and a Canadian Idol, not of the screeching, jerking, drum-
beating variety, but of the type one must truly worship from the
bottom of one's heart.

"She's unique among the unique," said the conductor of
the National Philharmonic Orchestra in Ottawa. "A jewel, a rare
diamond...."

There was no end to the raves.

"She's grown, darling," Michael whispered, holding on to Diana's hand. "Children always grow up," he tried lamely. He knew full well that the change in Anne was much more than just a gap of two years.

There was an unreal air about it all.

Anne was always smiling, always friendly, perfectly patient in recounting for the tenth or twentieth time the same stories; to her mother, her father, and Peter and even John when he dropped in twice in three days, just to listen to her talk.

"Really," she insisted. "All I did was to play my violin."

Somehow those words always sounded absurdly inadequate.

At the final concert there was an air of reserved expectation and excitement. The program was reversed. Traditionally, the violin concerto is played before the intermission. It is preceded by some introductory *oeuvre*, usually by a local composer, like the di Vargas *Intermezzo*, and followed, after the break, by a symphony. With Anne, this was impossible. In Rio de Janeiro, more than a year ago, the conductor had wisely decided to change the established order. After her performance in New Delhi, it had proven impossible to maintain any order after she had finished her performance. Following a moment or two of flabbergasted awe, people had erupted into such a display of adulation that it had taken more than an hour to quiet them down. In Rio, and ever since, Anne's performance was the final piece on the program.

In the Royal Box, where Peter, John and the Howells sat as Sir Ian's guests, everyone shed tears of joy, of elation, of euphoria at being transported to a reality they hardly suspected existed. Anne took many curtain calls and then walked quickly, alone, to Sir Ian Barton's dressing room. There she placed the Stradivarius carefully in the glass cabinet from which it had once come.

For a little while she stood looking at the magnificent violin which, at least in part, had made her famous. She touched it once more, as one would touch a lover one would never see again.

A solitary tear rolled from her eye. Then another. And then her chest heaved in convulsive spasms of the agony of the final farewell.

Anne never played another note.

* * * *

THE AVATAR SYNDROME

*"But the Lord is in his holy temple:
let all the earth keep silence before him."*

Habakkuk

Chapter 19

The End of an Era

"**We** can do virtually anything. We can raise men to be as gods or smash them to the level of beasts. We can make men smarter or turn them into whimpering imbeciles. We can even reconstitute portions of their brain with genetic manipulation. We can make them experience moments of great pleasure by releasing scores of endorphins, even if we cannot as yet sustain such a function, nor give man control over it. We can do all this, but we cannot make man happy. Man or woman. Not for any sustained period of time. Their emotional well-being is still beyond the reach of our science, our technology."

John and Peter were sitting in John's office, their faces drawn, eyes trying to avoid each other. They were talking neurology, but both were thinking of Anne. Following recent discoveries, there were virtually no limits to their neurosurgical skills. Embryonic stemcells, introduced surgically into contaminated portions of the brain, were now capable of regenerating damaged areas. Most cancers of the brain had been virtually eliminated. Over time, the neurosurgeons could make the mentally feeble, or even retarded men, into intellectual giants. Comparatively speaking. At least they would be able to fully enjoy their lives. Intellectually, that is. For many it was a resurrection. They had become self-sufficient, contributing members of society, often for the first time in their lives.

"They can even become taxpayers," John had once explained to both, the Federal and the Provincial Ministers of Health.

At the time, this single statement was justification for the bureaucrats to approve additional funds. John had kept his promise. Under his expertise, scores of dependents had metamorphosed into providers, and to the politicians that translated into people from whom they could squeeze taxes. Yet, the part of the brain which appeared to control our emotions – isolated and identified for some time – remained an enigma. The new knowledge of where it was did not take the researchers any closer to being able to influence its functioning. So far, surgeons had been able to induce abundant pleasure, but not, paradoxically, happiness.

"Perhaps they were right. Perhaps we are four in one..." Peter mused.

"Are you drifting towards mysticism?"

Peter was alluding to the subject they had been discussing last Friday, during their usual dinner at the Howells. Diana had offered them a symbolic interpretation of the Four Horses in the Apocalypse of Saint John.

"The horses are white, black, red and pale – corresponding to man's spiritual, mental, emotional and physical aspects. But it is but a single rider who must control all of them," she'd said. Or something like that.

"How can this possibly help us?" Peter questioned his own premise. "Until I find imprints of hoofs on the grey matter, I doubt that it will."

"Hoofs . . . if we could only identify individual emotions," John mused.

At the time Diana had sounded much surer of her ground than either of the physicians now felt of theirs. They had spent hours, mostly at night, pouring over Anne's MRIs and CTs, only to conclude that they had no idea what lay at the root of Anne's mood swings. Only a day after her last concert, her elation had simmered and died. It evaporated into thin air. No lingering euphoria. Nothing. This time she had not slipped into a coma, but she might as well have done so. She was like a being devoid of the red horse of the Apocalypse. There was the physical body, the intellect, and that was it. Unless we define the white horse as the presence of life itself, then that, too, was virtually missing. She tarried rather than lived.

Michael and Diana, and later on Peter and John, had all learned about Anne returning the Stradivarius a week after the concert. Sir Ian came one evening, unannounced. He found Diana and Michael sitting listlessly, as though at a wake, their heads bowed low, dejected, feeding on each other's despondency. Sir Ian told them that he had issued a press release, which claimed that Anne had left town for an undisclosed destination. They had already read his statement, that morning, in the Montreal Gazette:

"If any one of you attempts to discover her location,
he or she will permanently lose all rights to a personal
interview with me. Miss Howell deserves a rest after
she has given her all to all of us."

Brief as usual.

There was the usual journalistic commentary to the effect that "Sir Ian spoke sternly to a gathering of reporters, daring anyone to question the wisdom of his statement. There was some disgruntled murmuring," the article claimed, "but most of the reporters had nodded their heads in understanding, including this reporter." Apparently the paparazzi had disbanded without further questions. Sir Ian wondered if he would ever again get a rave write-up from this bunch.

The Maestro was hoping against hope that, given time, given a good rest, Anne would reconsider her move. For the moment it seemed that Anne had no intention of ever performing again. Her furtive return of the Stradivarius spoke volumes. Some may have thought that she had chosen to stop playing before her fingers could produce a single imperfect note. Before her genius could come into question. Yet Sir Ian seriously doubted if any such thought had ever crossed her mind. Not even the fear of an ultimately waning talent could be her true motivation. There must have been something else. Something lay much deeper, at the very core of her being. Sir Ian had ample experience with great musicians suddenly freezing up. Debilitating stage fright and a creative cramp akin to writer's block. A physical, mental and emotional inability to continue. Or to start again, for that matter. Sometimes it lasted for years.

Any and all attempts he'd initiated to talk to Anne had failed. Diana was also trying daily; Michael, when he thought he might have a chance. For three days Peter did not even gain access to her room, let alone to her heart. Finally Gabriel gave him a nod.

"Don't expect much, Sir," he murmured, but Peter hardly heard him. He was inside the doors before she had a chance to change her mind. He found Anne sitting down on the floor, her back propped up against a wall, seemingly relaxed. Fluffy's enormous head rested on her lap. Neither of them looked up when he came in.

"Is there anything I can do, darling?"

He had purposely addressed her with this term of endearment in the hope of finding an echo of that evening, now such a long time ago, when she had virtually swooned in his arms. This time, Anne didn't move. He was greeted with silence, accompanied by a blank stare, while her lips remained in a fixed grimace of a flat, emotionless smile.

If the colour of her hair could be quantified in a jar, beauty saloons would make fortunes in transposing its innate flame. Or the emerald of her eyes. Peter blinked hard.

She made the air he breathed unique by her presence.

Since the day after the concert, Anne hadn't left her room. Except to use the bathroom, she had remained in a self-imposed seclusion admitting only Gabriel, whom she allowed to serve her with light meals. When Michael or Diana put their foot in the door, she ignored them. If either spoke to her, they would listen only to their own voice. In every sense but the physical, Anne was absent. She seemed so far away that neither human voice nor any emotion could reach her.

Before Sir Ian left that evening, he inquired about John and Peter. Michael directed him to the Institute. The next day Sir Ian asked for and was granted an interview in John's office.

"You know why I am here," he began.

"Yes, Sir Ian. I guess that you are worried about Anne's condition."

"Not exactly. I don't know if I should be worried," he replied. When John looked up in disbelief, Sir Ian continued. "In my profession, emotional breakdowns are a lot more common than any one outside of the so-called 'show business' can possibly imagine. Stress is obviously at the root of them all. Do you think it might be more than that? I understand you once operated on her frontal lobe."

"It was a minor, benign tumour. The operation was highly successful. There are no after-effects that might be related to it."

"And yet...?"

John took a deep breath. "Perhaps we should call Peter in. I'll see if he's free." He pressed a button on his console. Peter's voice answered at once.

"Yes, Sir?"

"I have Sir Ian here. Can you spare a few minutes?"

While waiting for Peter, John recounted, briefly, their findings regarding the frontal lobe development and the extraordinary widening of the pons Varolii. Sir Ian listened, his eyes glued to John's face. There was almost a painful concentration on his face.

"Neither of the two anomalies could be reasonably considered to be at the root of her present condition, Ian," John pronounced the word 'anomalies' with a slight shrug of his shoulders. "We have been racking our brains for...."

"This is *terra incognita* for me, my friend. But you assure me that these unusual developments cannot be responsible for her present condition?" Sir Ian's tone of voice sounded like a statement, yet it left room for confirmation.

"The brain is *terra incognita* for all of us. We have learned an enormous amount in recent years, but, alas, I feel that we have a great many unknowns still ahead of us."

There was pain in John's eyes. He had to admit that his chosen profession, the expertise which had taken him a lifetime to acquire, that had made him world-famous, led him nowhere. Not where Anne was concerned.

Peter knocked and entered, still wearing his green O.R. coat. He'd finished an operation a few minutes ago and hadn't had time to change. Usually Dr. Brent meant 'at once'. Yet when he was directed to sit down on the sofa next to Sir Ian, the two men remained silent.

Finally he had to ask: "It's about Anne?"

The question was rhetorical.

The two older men nodded in unison. The problem was that neither of them had any idea what questions to ask. There were just too many unknowns. In neurosurgery, or neurology for that matter, questions are usually directed at specifics. There were none. Only nebulous symptoms. A whole array of them. Yet none of them seemed to have a neurological origin, and, of late, neurosurgeons tended to reject anything that they could not detect with sophisticated equipment.

John and Peter had both thought of calling in their psychiatric team, but what could they have told them? An eighteen-year-old woman, having worked like a slave for two years, now refused to play her fiddle. Hardly a dangerously neurotic condition. So she doesn't talk much. So many of us should talk less. Anne didn't talk at all. Wasn't it within her rights? One had to know, *really* know Anne before, in order to appreciate the difference in her. The explosive abundance of life in her music, the....

"It happened once before," Peter started again. "She was barely ten, at the time. I believe it either preceded or followed her first operation."

"The minor tumour?" Sir Ian offered.

"Yes," Peter confirmed, but there was a hesitation in his voice. He didn't know if he should divulge to Sir Ian details about her abduction.

"There is more, isn't there, young man." It wasn't a question. It was a statement of fact. Peter looked at John who nodded.

"Anne was abducted for three or four months. Soon after her return she entered a state of, what was described at the time as, extreme detachment. It was as though her body were still here, but the rest of her was missing. Her personality, her emotions, her... essence were all gone." Peter glanced at John for confirmation.

"Yes, Peter. That was also my impression."

So much had happened during these last eight years. The new wing of the MNI had long been completed, new laboratories boasted brand new, state-of-the-art equipment – the envy of the medical world. Peter had passed his final exams in neurosurgery. But somehow it always came back to Anne. It was as though she were the fulcrum around which their personal and even professional lives rotated in slow motion. No matter what alacrity the rest of John or Peter's life commanded, she was the one constant. A constant that kept changing. It didn't make any sense.

"What happened?"

"We don't really know. But we do know that Anne seems to possess a protective mechanism which enables her to live through incredibly taxing experiences and yet, in time, return whole and hale."

"As she was before I took her under my wing?"

This time there was nothing commanding about Sir Ian's voice. It was soft, on the verge of trembling. Peter suddenly realized that Sir Ian loved Anne in a very special way.

"I should tell you, Ian, she was not quite the same girl after her experience. I don't mean the abduction. I'm referring to the time period before and after her withdrawal. Like a new phase or chapter. We, the . . . experts, can't really understand it."

Three weeks and three days after that meeting Anne agreed to submit herself to a thorough neurological examination. John

found the door to her room ajar and had asked her. She had
nodded. That was all. He wasn't sure she'd heard him properly
and repeated his question. She nodded again.

John advised Diana and Michael of her decision. They
nodded also. Diana was too tired to raise objections, and Michael was prepared to try anything to recover his daughter.

"Just bring her back to us, John," he muttered. Yet his
words were accompanied by a slight shrug. Not a shrug of indifference, but of resignation. There was an eerie *déja vu* about
the whole affair. A return to the unpleasant helplessness they'd
experienced so many years ago.

John returned that same evening to the Institute and began
making the arrangements. He and Peter drew up a schedule and
within a few days managed to rearrange other appointments to
make room for Anne. It may not have been all that fair to other
patients, some of whom had been waiting for weeks, but, well,
there was only one Anne. "Besides," John grinned at the
thought, "ten years ago, the waiting time would have been
months, if not years."

"We may all be unique," Peter muttered. "But some of us
are more unique than others."

He and John waited for the fateful day to arrive with a degree of trepidation. For the first time since his student days,
John was actually nervous. He had no idea why. He felt that he
was about to witness something that he had never seen before.
Perhaps no one had. Nor ever would again.

Anne arrived with her mother and father, walking between
them as between two sentinels. She was quite used to that. She
had spent months, years, walking between sentries, who didn't
dare take their eyes off her. They walked with measured steps as
one does in a procession or perhaps a funeral – slowly, befitting
the gravity of the occasion.

Anne felt neither. Neither the gravity nor the sense of the
situation. She knew that she had to go through the tests in order
to be left alone. At least for a while. That's all she asked for.
To be left alone. Quite alone.

John and Peter came down to the lobby together to escort
Anne to John's office. They were hoping to talk to her, to get

her thoughts on what was causing her present state of apparent inertia. She was neither in a trance nor in any self induced artificial state of mental or even emotional indolence. She had said so much over these last two years with her music, she probably thought she deserved to recharge her batteries. Assuming they hadn't run completely dry.

Anne was not unhappy.

Hi, Peter – hi Uncle John, her eyes said. I wonder why they cannot hear me. Gabriel always did. I wonder where Gabriel is. Gabriel? Can you hear me?

She had put her emotions in neutral gear, neither enjoying nor regretting this action. Her moments of great passion, a passion that had swept the civilized world, were behind her. Of those, she had none left. People, thousands of them, perhaps millions – if one took into account all the CDs, were all wrong. The vast majority were under the impression that it was her flawless technique that had captured their collective hearts. But one cannot capture a heart with a technique. No matter how flawless. Bach had taught her that. Bach and Peter. Poor Peter. He didn't deserve any of this.

This was the first fleeting emotion that crossed her awareness since . . . since centuries ago. *Since the last composer I played had died.* Once again.

No. Technique alone cannot capture the heart.

She watched thoughts float across the screen of her consciousness. Technique might capture one's mind, one's sense of judgment, one's intellect, but not one's heart. The heart is swept along by a flow of emotions so powerful that even a long time after experiencing such an influx, one remains still each time one recalls being submerged in the midst of it, once again. It is not a mental decision. Not even an act of will. It is a wave, a tidal wave that covers your reality with the overtones of heaven itself. It is like being in love and loving all rolled into one. An emotion so consuming as to negate everything in your life up to that moment, and leaving a permanent mark on the rest of it. It is the gift of Avatar, an emissary of the gods, of a realm that lies beyond the mind and even beyond human emotions, as understood by the average man and woman.

This may account for the moments of silence that had enveloped her audiences after her every performance. The thunder of applause only followed when people returned from the nameless realm that lies beyond all that is mundane, where time stops, and the very act of becoming is suspended to be absorbed into the bliss of being. Anne had been, and was, perfectly aware that she had been no more than an emissary. She, too, had to return back to earth, to smile and bow to her audience, to thank them for sharing this moment with her.

"All I do is to play my violin," she'd once assured her family and her friends. How inadequate it had sounded then. Yet, she thought, it was true. Always. That was all she ever did. She just played her violin.

And now she would play it no more.

All she had ever heard of, all that was ever composed for the violin that she judged worthwhile, she had already played and recorded for people to enjoy. That was also her pleasure – a pleasure for her. Her duty lay elsewhere. She had had to enter the soul of every single composer; enter the inner substance of his being still suspended in the ethers, and play that which they had been given to pass on to the world. It hadn't been the notes and the musical signs on a piece of lined paper. It had never been that. Every composer, indeed every artist, is an emissary of God. They are sent to earth to show people what heaven is really like. Yet few of them ever manage to convey the true essence of the celestial glory, although Mozart may have just succeeded, seemingly with the last breath of his life. But that, at least in the movie *Amadeus*, only through the diligence of Salieri. Thanks to the old if jealous fellow-composer, Mozart's vision of heaven became immortalized in his incomparable Requiem. There had been other fragments of the indivisible heaven, of infinity, of the elusive Source, that other composers, painters, sculptors, poets, sometimes even unknown artists, had managed to recreate for people to absorb. And in those precious moments, those universal grains had become reintegrated into that which is, and always has been, and will forever remain – whole.

Fragments of eternity suspended in the Eternal Now.

But no one had ever done what Anne had managed to do in just two years. Every time she had played, not just her wondrous Stradivarius but she, herself, had become no more than an instrument through which the Ineffable filled human hearts with joy. It had drained her of her life-force, of her mind and emotions to such a degree that now she felt empty.

"Wait, little one," Gabriel told her. "Have patience."

She believed him. It seemed to her that Gabriel alone knew what had happened. It could not have been explained in words. Not to people who had awareness of their becoming confined just to the physical reality. She had entered the inner chamber of her heart, now seemingly empty, and pulled the gates tightly behind her. There, quite alone, she waited.

She waited. For as long as it would take. After all, she was no more than an instrument herself. She knew not what might be in store for her. None of us ever knows.

John had decided to run the PET scan, and the CT, simultaneously. The images, when coupled together, would allow him to determine the precise nature and location of any changes that occurred in her brain, if any had occurred since the last follow-up scans of two years ago. Essentially, the PET scan would show *what*, while the CT displayed *where*. The combined images assured that John, assisted by Peter, would detect any brain disorder connected with blood supply, the rate of glucose absorption by the cells, and abnormal circulation. Later the fMRI would confirm their findings.

Anne was John's prime guinea pig.

Of course, neither John nor Peter ever thought of her in those terms. But there was no escaping the fact that both neurosurgeons had been fascinated by the workings of Anne's brain for eight years now. Regardless of how they felt about her on a personal level, Anne was unique.

Perhaps it needs mentioning that it was only thanks to Anne having been listed as a research subject that she could take advantage of the services and equipment the MNI had to offer. As some years ago Dr. John Brent had attempted to explain to the Right Honourable Jean Courtier – then the Federal Minister of Health – that neurology was and remained an extremely expensive hobby. Private clinics, hoping to bask in the reflected glory of the Montreal Neurological Institute, charged something in the order of $3000 for each scan. Little wonder. The equipment they had to provide ran close to $3,000,000 per unit. The Director of the Institute had to remain judicious in the allocation of such valuable possessions.

Anne looked perfectly relaxed. Her reflexes were all normal, as was her body temperature, her breathing, her blood pressure and all the major and minor vital signs. She moved her fingers, legs, blinked her eyes on command. She also responded with the movement of her eyes: up and down for yes, left to right for no. She had to. She still wasn't talking.

Couldn't, or didn't want to?

They tried to determine which by asking pointed questions to which there was no yes-or-no answer. They both maintained a close watch on all her involuntary signs. Neither her pulse nor her perspiration nor any other change indicated that she'd experienced the slightest stress through her inability or unwillingness to answer verbally. Now that they knew this, they had no idea what it meant.

Finally it was time. Peter gently lifted Anne's arm and injected the FDG dye, the fluorodeoxyglucose, into a small vein. She didn't even twitch.

She lay there, on the retractable table, relaxed, as though just waiting for the boring routine to be over.

In a desperate search for answers to non-formulated questions, John and Peter had decided to scan Anne's whole body. The last brain scan had not revealed anything new. Perhaps, they reasoned, the answer lay elsewhere. Anne's PET scan would indicate the chemical functioning of her organs and tissues at the cellular level, while the CT and MRI would display the anatomical structure. The dye injected into her arms was actually radioactive, but its half-life was very short – so short that, by the time Anne's scan was complete, the dye would have become inert. Usually surgeons used the PET scans to detect various forms of cancer, but it also served, for instance, to expose possible hints of an undiagnosed dementia. They were grasping at straws.

John took a deep breath. He glanced at Peter, nodded, and pressed the green button.

Very slowly Anne's body began sliding towards the round opening of the machine. Once again she felt free, as she had felt so recently in her room, at home, as she had felt once, a long, long time ago. A tiny smile, like the wisp of an afterthought, widened the very corners of her full lips. The movement was duly noted by the scanners. At that very moment, she thought she saw Gabriel bending over her body, looking into her eyes, telling her not to worry. She wasn't. Not any more. Not now that Gabriel was here.

He would not allow anyone to harm her. Ever.

* * * * *

Chapter 20

The Final Follow-up

Diana had her second breakdown two days after John told her that he and his colleagues would like to keep Anne for a few days at the Institute. He purposely didn't say hospital. A hospital catered to people that were sick. And Anne? Well, no one could determine if there was anything really wrong with her.

"Just a few days to make sure," he assured her.

Sure of what? He was glad no one had asked.

It wasn't just a question of scanning her brain or, for that matter, her whole body. Those scanners, the CTs and the MRIs, were extremely valuable diagnostic tools. What John and his specially selected medical team wanted was to control her diet, her environment, and make sure that she fasted the requisite period before any scanning procedures. They wanted to monitor all her vital signs and a thousand-and-one other minor elements that were possible to detect only under controlled laboratory conditions. Anne was an anomaly, a miracle of individuality, but she was also their most treasured research project.

Had John said anything like that, it would have sounded impersonal. It wasn't. Really. There was no one who felt more like a daughter to him than Anne did. He'd known her for years. Since she was little.

John wasn't about to tell Diana the whole story. After all, she was in no position to help and, frankly, in no condition to fully understand John's reasoning. The matter was complex, yet at the same time the symptoms were so unique that he wanted to repeat the fMRI a few more times, in twenty-four-hour cycles, to seek confirmation of his diagnosis. Anne was no more an aggregate of symptoms. In the MNI files her condition was referred to as the Howell Syndrome. Unique unto itself.

Of course, at home she had Fluffy....

But at the Institute her room would be replete with flowers, as it had been, years ago, during her previous stay. Not just from Michael and himself, but from Peter and now from Sir Ian, who also felt the need to make her stay as pleasant as possible. She invoked such a response from people. There was some question, however, whether Anne, in her present state of mind, could be aware of any of this.

"Please, Diana, you must promise me that you won't worry. I only want what I believe is best for Anne," John added, seeing Diana's frown.

To be quite honest, he'd lied. He had no idea what was best for Anne. Where he did speak the truth was that only a prolonged series of scans might reveal the neurological mystery that Anne's brain suggested. Or else, he mused, to compound it.

There was no Friday dinner that week.

The mood didn't lend itself to a social gathering. Instead, John and Peter dropped in during their rare spare moments. Sir Ian had twice visited Diana at home while Michael was still at the office. The Maestro's evenings remained busy. He, too, looked drawn, strangely emaciated, as if it were he, not Anne, who had already spent time in the hospital. Not just his rotund waistline but his larger-than-life, overpowering demeanour was diminished. The robust silhouette commanding obedience and respect had given way to squinting eyes, a slight stoop, and a look of concern on his face.

"I'm sure she'll be all right, Diana," he offered. They had all said that to her. Sir Ian's voice didn't carry much conviction, either. He knew of breakdowns with very unpredicted consequences. That's what artists were – unpredictable. Great artists more so.

In a way, Michael was lucky. As fate would have it, his firm had just landed a multi-million-dollar engineering project that was to be carried out on a fast-track basis. The schedule left him little time to wallow in self-pity. He worked long hours, worked hard, and was glad of it. Each time he stopped, even for a quick bite, or a cup of coffee, his thoughts drifted to Anne. He also visited her daily. She certainly gave no impression that she was suffering in any way. She just was. Suspended between realities.

The last time he went to see his daughter, he recalled her face as it had looked at the top of Mount Gargas in France. Her eyes shining, her whole countenance bathed in the bright orange rays of the rising sun – euphoric, angelic... For an instant he thought he saw her lips move. But it was just a smile, a little broader, and then it was gone again. Yet, some of it seemed to linger.

Michael really was lucky.

Recently, whether at home or in his office, his memory carried images of his daughter as she was, had been, before she went on the concert tour. Bubbling with life, a strange air of youthful innocence mixed with mature passion for her violin. That was the image that returned to him, again and again, whenever he stopped for a breather. It wasn't so bad after all. Except when he had too much free time to think. Then his practical mind drew him into the reality he was trying so hard to suppress.

He needed all his strength to look after Diana.

The day after Anne left for the MNI, Fluffy disappeared. Michael reported his loss to the local police, had his secretary print leaflets which he, himself pasted on local lampposts. All to no avail. Two days later, John Brent saw a dog, looking very much like Fluffy, sniffing the entrance door at the MNI. When he called him, Fluffy came to him, wagging his bushy tail. Using the escape staircase, John broke all hospital rules and took the lonely stray up to his office. When Anne saw him through her half-closed eyes half an hour later, John thought she might speak. She opened her mouth, and for the briefest instant her old angelic smile widened her mouth. And then she was gone again.

John took Fluffy back home. The sterile conditions of the Institute did not lend themselves to the presence of animals. 'Other than human,' he grinned. When John got to the Howells, Gabriel fed him, and then spent a good ten minutes looking into Fluffy's eyes. After this peculiar staring session, Fluffy, apparently relaxed, lay down and went to sleep. He must have been exhausted. From that moment on, Fluffy didn't go out of the house, except to the garden. Dogs must do that. But apparently he had lost interest in walking the streets, in meeting other dogs, or even just for running around. Like Anne, he had entered a state of abeyance. He waited in silence.

Nevertheless, when Diana became particularly listless, Fluffy would drag his body to her armchair and put his massive head on her lap. Or curl up at her feet. They seemed to share the same feelings, the same longing which others could suppress with work but the two of them had to conquer by will alone.

Doctors Brent, Brown and Martin – the latter a specialist in nuclear medicine, poured over the scans. They had all been present during the actual scanning process. The screens, there and then, had displayed multiple images. They watched them anxiously to spot indications of abnormalities. There were none. Nor in the 'rest' of her body. Anne seemed to be in perfect physical condition.

She just didn't talk or have any appreciable emotional reactions to anything.

Next came the analysis of the computerized images. The CT, and later the MRI. Anne's brain was unusual. But the characteristics that set her apart had been known for two years. The structure of the frontal lobe and the extraordinary development of the pons Varolii were not new. The cellular structure was perfectly normal. The neural complexity was perhaps a little more developed, as was the apparent density of the billions of neurons that somehow managed to accommodate themselves inside her

perfectly normal cranium. What seemed somewhat more impressive was how Anne managed to contain all of them within
her membrane. Not that she had done it at the conscious level,
of course.

But she had done it.

One aspect of the scan appeared a little strange, namely that
which indicated the overall neural activity. Normally, certain
areas of the brain light up when specific organs or senses come
into play. In Anne's case, the overall activity was well above
normal, but there was no noticeable specific or selective neural
response. It was as though Anne had switched off the connections to her body, or even to her sensory inputs, while revving up
her subliminal activity. As though she were experiencing an ongoing, continuous, absorbing dream. Her brain was super-active
but it seemed to function independently of her body, which, as
such, provided minimal response.

Even as John followed the computer images, his mind, incongruously, drifted to something he'd read so many years ago
. . . *for I am fearfully and wonderfully made . . . my substance
was not hid from thee, when I was made in secret, and curiously
wrought in the lowest parts of the earth.* Had the ancients known
something that we are still striving to rediscover? John rubbed
his tired eyes. He was not a religious man. Like most people
brought up in Québec he had left his religious schooling in his
youth.

Where it belongs, he reminded himself, concentrating on
the computer screen.

There was no question of undue pressures on the membrane that would normally result in severe headaches. There
were no localized abnormal neural densities that might cause
distorted vision, or interfere with any of the senses. As for her
speech centre, it seemed as normal as in any other brain he'd
ever scanned.

"Is there anything that hurts you, Anne?" Peter asked,
bending over to watch her eyes. Lateral movement of her irises
denied any such thing.

"Are you sure? Nowhere?" Again the lateral movement.

This time there appeared an intimation of a whimsical smile as if Anne were amused at Peter's apparent desire to find her in pain.

The additional MRIs, conducted in approximately twenty-four-hour periods, added nothing to the team's initial findings. Anne was ready to go home. She had already conquered the world. Now she had conquered medicine.

There were two other 'symptoms' which didn't seem to be of any consequence at the time. Mostly because they didn't concern Anne. At least, there was no apparent reason to connect these occurrences with Anne's presence at the Montreal Neurological Institute.

What happened was that the patients in the rooms adjoining Anne's showed unprecedented and certainly inexplicable improvements. The first, a girl of eleven, had been diagnosed with a malignant tumour below her occipital bone, adjacent to the medulla oblongata. Such tumours are extremely difficult to operate on, as they lie at the point where the spinal column connects with the brain. And they are very likely to spread with astounding speed to other parts of the body. Even if treatment is successful, the survival rate of such patients seldom exceeded five years. Peter had been the admitting physician. He recalled later that, somehow, the girl had learned about her forthcoming demise. Apparently she'd clapped her hands and, with a big grin and in a voice filled with great joy, she'd announced: "I'll see grandma!"

The day before Anne was sent home, the girl was scheduled for neurosurgery. As is customary, immediately before the operation, a final fMRI was conducted to confirm the precise location of the tumour. The surgeons found no trace of it. The tumour had disappeared. The staff double-checked the original CT images. They clearly showed no malignancy. It was as though it had never existed.

The second occurrence was quite different but similar. A professional football player, George, also in the room adjoining Anne's but on the other side, had been waiting for a series of

operations on his spine. He was paralyzed from the neck down
following a powerful tackle. There was a reasonable chance that,
with the MNI's new techniques, a few embryonic stem-cells
could be implanted into three separate segments of his spine, and
with months of intensive physiotherapy, George might, just
might, walk again.

On the day of Anne's departure, the young man visited
Anne, in her room, under his own steam. He just walked into her
room weeks before his scheduled surgery. A nurse, who at the
time, understandably, froze at the sight of him, later reported that
George had thanked Anne for the beautiful dream. That was all.
Then he walked back to his room.

Such events were seldom reported. Each hospital has a
stack of files of these so-called spontaneous remissions. They
are usually assigned to erroneous diagnoses, which is reason
enough not to brag about them. But such remissions do occur,
though seldom to people diagnosed with spinal paralysis.

Even in Lourdes, or Fatima, or La Salette.

The Montreal Neurological Hospital was a considerable
distance from any of them. There was, of course, the shrine at
St. Joseph's, but its miraculous properties appeared dormant for
some time, and their efficacy had never extended beyond the
shrine's immediate area. Yet the two events of 'spontaneous
remission' had taken place under the watchful eyes of an army
of physicians. After an extra day of stringent observations, additional scans and exhaustive questioning, the two patients, from
the two rooms adjoining Anne's, were discharged.

Their files were promptly placed in the subterranean archives. No one mentioned them again. There were lots of patients waiting for the hospital beds. People from across Canada
and around the world sought treatment at the now world-famous
MNI.

Michael took a day off from work just to bring Anne home.
He didn't need to take the whole day – the drive home took no

more than fifteen minutes – but he needed a break. He had been working like a slave to keep his mind occupied.

He later discovered that at the exact time that Anne had left her hospital room, Fluffy woke up, walked up to the front door and stayed there until Gabriel, also inspired, opened the front door at the exact moment of Michael and Anne's arrival. The big man's and Anne's eyes met, momentarily, after which Gabriel allowed himself a strangely satisfied smile.

"Welcome home, Miss Anne," he said, bowing deeply.

Gabriel had never bowed to Anne before. She was young, her manner was youthful, one could say girlish; not conducive to a show of special respect. And now, his show of respect was, to say the least, unusual.

However, these singular events went unnoticed.

Michael led the way to the living room where Diana remained seated in her favourite armchair. In front of her the TV was on, but muted. Diana's expression was that of studied indifference. Anne's condition was an absence; Diana's seemed to be a wilful distancing of herself from the exigencies of everyday life.

Michael bent over Diana to kiss her pallid cheek.

During the last two years, Diana had lost much of her pulchritude. Before the world tour, it had been evident where Anne had gotten her beauty. The same trim figure, the same clear complexion, the mass of hair, which Diana preferred to keep in an elaborate knot at the top of her head while Anne's flowed loosely. In just two years, Diana had become a mere shadow of her former self, of the beautiful woman she once was.

"How are you my dear?" Michael was trying to detect some interest in his wife's demeanour. He found none. "I've brought Anne home, dear," he said, straightening up and motioning behind him.

Diana didn't look up. Just as well as Anne had already withdrawn. She went to her room and sat down. Fluffy followed her, deserting his previous spot at Diana's feet. His mistress was back. Evidently inaccessible to humans, but not to him. No matter how well she was, or wasn't, she was back. This was reason enough to rejoice.

Gabriel watched this series of events with a somewhat puzzled expression. He noted Diana's reaction – or rather lack of it, Anne's prompt withdrawal and Fluffy's act of love. He then also withdrew, silently, towards Anne's bedroom, and for a moment or two regarded his favourite member of the family through the door that Anne had left, as she usually did, ajar. His mind still held the image of Diana's studied indifference. How strange, he thought. How very strange.

"You see, Fluffy, it must really be true. No man is a prophet in his own village," he murmured. "Or woman," he added after a pensive moment.

Fluffy opened one eye and gave a single wag with his tail. Evidently he knew.

At the time, Peter, even more so than John, pressed for keeping Anne in the hospital. At least that way I could see her daily, look at her, perhaps even touch her, he thought. Everything his heart told him about Anne was in direct opposition to the dictates of his highly trained mind. Nevertheless, he would do his utmost to make sure that the tests and the scans which Anne would undergo during those next few days would reveal as much as is humanly possible.

But, in spite of his considerable expertise, or perhaps because of it, he put little faith in the machines. Not generally, but specifically in Anne's case. Since meeting her, so many years ago, he had watched her every move, every step of her development. Not as John had. John Brent surely loved her. But, again, not the way Peter did. Should Anne ask him to give up his freshly acquired Fellowship of the Royal College of Surgeons and Physicians, he would do so without the slightest hesitation. He wouldn't even ask her for a reason. To Peter, Anne was neither a woman nor an unattainable goddess, but a strange amalgam of the two. He was sure that, on this world of some six billion people, he was the only one who had ever held her in his arms. He was the only one who had touched her lips with his own lips.

Tell me again....

Her words he held so precious still rang in his ears. Tell me again . . . tell me again....

He was also sure that he was the only man in the world who had confessed his love for her. Not for her virtuosity, nor her unique interpretation of the great composers, but because she was she and no one else.

And now she lay on the hospital bed, serene, a detached smile on her innocent lips. Peter dismissed the nurse.

"It is I, Anne," he waited for some reaction. "Please, Anne . . . do you remember? That night? On the lookout? Well . . . I still love you. I still do...."

Her irises moved below her eyelids as they would in a REM sleep.

"Happy dreams, my love," he managed to whisper before the nurse came back. She stayed with Anne around the clock. She, or one of her substitutes. No matter. He'd told Anne what he had come to tell her. He was sure that she had heard him.

And now she was home. Peter asked Michael if he could visit her.

"You are part of our family, Peter," Michael replied. "You don't have to ask."

Peter came that evening. He waited for an opportunity and tiptoed into her room. She reclined on her bed, propped up on a number of pillows. Her eyes were closed, the same blissful if hardly discernible smile on her lips. How he loved those lips.

Fluffy lay on the floor. He would have to step over him to reach her. He knew Fluffy would let him, but there was little point. He just wanted to see her. The bedside lamp gave him just enough light to observe her regular breathing, her features relaxed – as usual.

Without thinking he reached over Fluffy and touched her hand. She didn't move. He was about to go when he felt her finger tremble below his touch. He placed his hand under her palm. Her fingers barely moved. But he was sure, quite sure, that he felt a slight squeeze of her hand.

Anne was coming back. He didn't know when or how or why. But Anne, his Anne, was coming back. He wiped his eyes before returning to the sitting room. Yet his face couldn't hide his elation. Michael looked up at him questioningly.

"She's coming back..." Peter whispered. "She is coming back," he repeated louder, surprised at his own words.

* * * * *

Chapter 21

Paparazzi

The circus began around six a.m. Just about the time Gabriel usually got up to spend an hour in the *Siddhasana*, the sitting pose of the spiritually enlightened, wherein the left heel was placed under the perineum while the right foot was laid upon the left thigh. Due to yet another wrestling injury, he had never mastered the *Padmasana*, known in the West as the Lotus Seat. With his usual detachment he ignored the half-dozen cars parked just outside the front door, on both sides of the street, until he finished that which he considered the most important part of his twenty-four hour cycle. Barring accidents, Gabriel would not allow anything to stand in the way of his communion with himself. With atma manifesting in atman. There had been moments, recently, when atman, the divine presence within him, his true Self, seemed to have come, face to face, with Atman. With That which some called the Oversoul. Gabriel called It simply the Source. The individualized Presence meeting Its Source. The particular meeting the Universal. Years had passed before these words began to have meaning for him.

Gabriel had noticed the cars from his upstairs window, where he enjoyed a large room with an *en suite* bathroom. Mr. and Mrs. Howell's master bedroom was at the rear of the house, while Gabriel's faced the front lawn. Anne slept downstairs on the garden side, also with her own bathroom and a large basket for Fluffy.

At precisely seven o'clock, Gabriel took a deep breath, opened his eyes wide, and greeted the day with an affable smile. A second or two later, he heard the alarm clock chime the hour on Mr. Howell's bedside table.

Gabriel showered, dressed with his usual care, and made his way to the kitchen. By the time Mrs. Howell got up, the aroma of fresh coffee induced her to hurry with her perfunctory make-up. The real session in front of her mirror would come later, but a modicum of attention was required when she was to show her face to other people. Even to Gabriel. No matter what mood she was in.

The near collapse she'd experienced only last week seemed to have evaporated into thin air. Not that she'd reverted to her old, youthful self. But in most ways that mattered, she was a functioning, coping individual.

It happened almost overnight. One moment she was a detached, almost depressed woman, seemingly indifferent not only to her appearance but to Michael and the world as a whole. She emerged from her week of trial as a woman who was admittedly older, but pleased with her place in the scheme of things. Years of looking after Anne, almost continuous anxiety for her welfare, trying to protect Michael from everyday worries, had taken their toll. Now it was over. It seemed that she had emerged victorious and ready to face reality. There was only one payment that nature extracted from her. She became prone to sudden bursts of tears. Quite unlike her old self.

Precisely at seven-thirty, they all sat together for breakfast.

Each morning they waited, patiently, for Anne to join them. After waiting for ten minutes, Diana buttered some toast, put a slice of what used to be Anne's favourite cheese on it, and prepared another half-toast with butter and jam. Simultaneously Gabriel poured coffee into her favourite mug, placed both on a tray and took the tray to Anne's room. During the first three days back home, Diana had taken the tray to Anne's room. An hour later it remained untouched. Gabriel had taken over. Somehow, it worked. She ate whatever he brought her. Was it a matter of trust? No one wanted to discuss it. Diana was just glad that Anne was eating. This routine went on for almost two weeks.

"She will join us soon," Michael murmured to his wife. "You will see. Perhaps tomorrow...."

He, too, was getting tired of hoping against hope. Regardless of what Peter had said the week before, Anne did not show any outward signs of returning to the human race. She did perform the minimum of activities she possibly could – a quick wash, a shower every second or third day. She ate a small breakfast and a late afternoon meal of whatever Gabriel prepared for her. She never complained, never asked for anything. If she had been sick, one could consider her an ideal patient. Only Anne wasn't sick. Not by any conventional definition, by any diagnostic procedure available to modern medical science. As long as she didn't talk, there was absolutely no point calling in a psychiatrist. And once she did, there would most probably be no need for one. After all, John had resident psychiatrists at the MNI, and they'd offered no suggestions other than wait and see.

Gabriel had just returned to the table when the front doorbell rang. He excused himself to answer. There was a short scuffle, a single but unnerving growl, and the major-domo returned to the table.

"Who was it, Gabby?" Michael wanted to know.

"The paparazzi, Sir."

"Oh...?"

"They inquired if they could have an interview with Miss Anne."

"And?"

"I said no."

"And the scuffle?"

"I'd say shuffle rather than scuffle, Sir. Two men and one woman were attempting to get past me, Sir."

"I gather they didn't?" This time there was a chuckle at the end of his question.

"No, Sir. Fluffy thought they shouldn't. Would you care for some more coffee?"

This was Saturday and on weekends, although Michael got up at the usual hour, he liked to linger longer over breakfast. Saturday was normally also Gabriel's day off. Usually Gabriel would sit at the dinner table, while Anne and Diana served him his breakfast. Only these weren't normal days.

"That would be nice," Michael nodded. "That would be very nice," he repeated, his mind still preoccupied with Gabriel's cryptic answers.

His mind was mulling over the paparazzi at the front door. They could be a problem. From what he'd heard from Sir Ian, they could be pretty aggressive. Michael picked up the telephone and as quickly put it back. It was much too early to call the Maestro. Sir Ian worked very late hours; often ate dinner after eleven at night.

He tiptoed to Anne's room.

No change. She had already showered; her bathrobe was flung over the back of a chair. Dressed in her favourite dark green overalls, which she usually wore when practising her violin at home, she was once again lying on her bed. As was her habit of late, she was propped up on a number of pillows in a semi-reclined position. Gabriel had already removed the breakfast tray.

Michael was on the point of withdrawing when, from the corner of his eye, he saw movement. He caught his breath in expectation. Anne lowered herself to the floor, her back against the edge of her bed. Her feet slid into a cross-legged position, her back straightened up, and once again she froze in utter immobility. With the same whimsical smile, she looked like a tiny Buddha, content to be alive. Even if she, like Buddha, had her being in a different dimension.

Her half-closed eyes didn't admit much light. If she had seen her father looking at her, she gave no sign. Her body had moved, her inner self remained elsewhere. Perhaps elsewhen? Who could tell where geniuses go when they take time off from our reality? Einstein spoke of muscular shapes, which led to his now famous equation. Saint Francis had floated in a halo of diffused light, just above the ground. There had been other stories

of great discoveries having been made in a dream-like state, akin
to self-hypnosis.

Michael took a step back. He had no idea how long he'd
remained there, just standing, perhaps hoping.

'You are where your attention takes you...' he recalled the
words of a present-day apostle of the inner realm. "I wonder
where she is?" he murmured.

"Wherever her attention took her," Gabriel's voice reached
his ears seemingly from a great distance. He turned his head but
saw no one. My mind is playing tricks on me, he laughed. I
must take things a little bit easier.

The doorbell rang again.

The next moment there was a growl, a bark, a scream and a
whimper. The door slammed so hard that the picture on the wall
went askew. Michael ran to the hall. Fluffy was lying on his
side, licking his front paw. Someone had hit him with a stick or
some other hard item. There was blood just below his knee.

Michael saw red. He ran up to his study, took out his
hunting rifle and ran back toward the front door. He was going
to show them. Before he got halfway to the entrance hall
Gabriel materialized out of nowhere.

"Out of my way!" Michael barked.

Gabriel took Michael by the arm and gently but firmly led
him to the sitting room. A moment later Michael heard police
sirens.

"I took the liberty of calling Sir Ian. I believe he mobi-
lized the police," he explained.

"I want to shoot every one of them!" Michael thundered,
still holding onto his shotgun. "You saw what the bastards did
to Fluffy? What will Anne say?"

"Fluffy will be all right, Sir. Trust me."

"But...."

"Come," Gabriel spoke very softly

Gabriel was right. The moment Fluffy recovered from the
initial shock and pain, he limped back to his mistress. He lay
down in front of Anne, who still remained in a cross-legged position. In no time at all, Fluffy seemed to relax. The pain had
apparently dissipated, the skin closed over the abrasion. Only a

small spot of blood remained on the carpet. Otherwise, no one would have suspected that anything untoward had happened.

The next time Michael looked through the window, there was just one police cruiser parked outside. All the other cars were gone. Michael went outside and stood on the porch looking around. One of the two officers left the cruiser and approached him.

"*Bonjour, Monsieur,*" the officer touched his cap.

"Good morning, officer," Michael replied in English. "Just what is going on here?" he asked. There were still remnants of anger in his voice.

"I would appreciate, Sir, if you didn't come outside just yet."

"I can't come out of my own house?"

"Of course you can, Sir. But we would appreciate if you didn't do so just this minute. We are trying to determine exactly what happened."

So he didn't know. He didn't know that for the last few days, the jewel of the world had been in hiding right here. In this house. Michael found it hard to understand what sway Anne had over her fans. Sir Ian had tried to tell him, but.... For some reason his mind was invaded by something Gabriel had told him a good many years ago. He said that no man is a prophet in his own village. To the world outside Anne may be some sort of a prophet, maybe even a goddess, but not to me.

"Not to me!" he growled through clenched teeth.

Anger was beginning to cloud his judgment. The poor man took a step back. He had no idea what caused Michael's outburst.

"It's my daughter," he said by way of an explanation. "My little girl." Anne being a virtuoso came a distant second. Even an ex-virtuoso. "What do they want from us?" He had his voice under control now.

"That is what we are trying to assess, *Monsieur*. Please give us a few more minutes."

As Michael started turning to go back inside, he saw a few more cars, very non-neighbourly looking vehicles, parked at the first cross-roads. The police could make them leave, but they couldn't make them go far. In Westmount, visitors were not allowed to park on the streets overnight. But this was daylight. After all, this was a free country. He wondered if his own freedom wasn't about to be curtailed.

He was beginning to simmer down when, on turning, he saw more paparazzi cars parked on both sides of the street, further down the road. The cars all faced his house. All his neighbours had garages. Garages and longish driveways. No one ever left his or her car at the curb. But there must have been more than a dozen of them. Even as he watched, two more cars pulled up a few houses down the street. They seemed to exchange words with someone in one of the parked cars, then filed behind the other cars already parked at the curb. This was not going to be much fun. For the first time in his life Michael felt he was in a siege. He also knew how Hollywood stars must feel every day.

"I can only shoot them two at a time," he reflected grimly. And then he shook his head. "My God, what is going on?"

"I would appreciate, Sir, if you could go inside. *Now*, Sir." The officer stressed the word 'now' with the authority of his office.

As Michael closed the door, Gabriel handed him the receiver.

"Sir Ian, Sir," he said.

"Mike? Where have you been? I've been standing naked waiting for you!"

"I'm sorry, Ian, I just popped outside."

"Never mind." Sir Ian had recovered some of his old poise. "I called Inspector Gratton, an old friend of mine. He said he would get the wheels rolling."

"There is a police cruiser outside. The other cars have moved back, about two hundred yards."

"Stay inside and I'll be over as soon as I can. We must powwow."

"That's what the officer asked me to do."

"Good man!" With that Sir Ian hung up.

Michael remained standing, holding on to the telephone. He scratched his head and almost smiled: "Powwow?"

Michael put down the receiver. He turned, looking for Gabriel. He wanted to know just what Gabriel had really told Sir Ian. Did Gabriel know something he'd missed? He looked in the kitchen, then checked on Diana, who had returned to the bedroom to complete her morning ritual. When he heard her shower running, Michael turned and knocked on Gabriel's door. Gently. After all, it was supposed to be his day off.

Silence.

Michael shrugged, returned downstairs, and tiptoed to Anne's room. Fluffy was lying on his side halfway out into the corridor, blocking the half open door. Michael stepped over him and saw Gabriel sitting on the floor, his legs in some sort of a pretzel, facing Anne, who still sat in her cross-legged position. This time both of them were absolutely motionless, though Anne's eyes appeared a little more open. Michael couldn't see Gabriel's face, as his back was to the door.

Michael watched them. Neither of the odd couple moved even a tiniest fraction of an inch. It was as though they had become ossified into a single entity – not so much in space as in time. Or was there really a difference? Maybe Einstein was right. Maybe time is just another dimension.

Why am I thinking of Einstein?

Very quietly, Michael walked back to the sitting room. He noticed that he didn't have his usual Montreal Gazette. The paparazzi must have stolen it. Or just picked it up and forgot to leave it behind. He wanted to switch on the TV, but didn't want to make any noise. It might disturb Anne and Gabriel in whatever they were doing. He peeked again through the front window, then glanced at his watch. It was eight thirty-five. Decent folk should be at home at this time, on a Saturday. Not bothering other folk.

It was too quiet.

Maybe Anne and Gabriel and, more recently, Diana were capable of maintaining long periods of silence, but not he. He needed life. Movement. A human voice. Funny that, he mused. At the office they call me a hermit. Yet here I am looking for company. It suddenly occurred to him to invite the policemen, perhaps one at a time, for a coffee. He dismissed the idea as soon as it came. There were just the two of them against a dozen, or by now possibly many more, paparazzi. What would they do if the reporters resorted to civil disobedience? Would they drag Anne out and carry her on their shoulders? Like an idol in a parody of a Mexican catholic procession?

He sat heavily on the love seat. He tried to imagine Anne sitting next to him. She was wearing a light, flowery dress, her hair swept back by a gust of wind, her eyes sparkling with happiness. Surely, this Anne was still somewhere behind that mask of inexplicable contentment. And what on earth was Gabriel doing there?

"How come I've never asked him what that staring at each other is all about?" He closed his eyes.

"Human language expresses ideas in a linear way."

Michael's eyes flew open. Gabriel was sitting on the chair facing him.

"A series of letters form a word, a series of words, a sentence. We try to communicate ideas in a holistic way. Rather the way you regard a painting, or listen to the lapping of the ocean waves. Better still, the way you recognize a forest. It consists of many trees, but the idea of a forest can be conveyed as a gestalt entity. Likewise, all ideas break down into individual thoughts, but each idea comes into our consciousness all at once."

Gabriel's eyes had a similar sheen Anne's had had, so many times, just after she had played a beautiful piece of music.

"You mean you speak to each other?"

"No, Michael," Gabriel often slipped into the familiar first name when they were alone. "We listen to each other," he said and reached for the telephone. In that instant the instrument started ringing. Michael couldn't be sure which came first.

"It is Inspector Gratton, for you, Sir."

"Mr. Howell? Gratton. Inspector of the Sûreté du Qébec.. I understand Sir Ian already called you. I'm sorry for the trouble you are having. We'll try to settle things as soon as possible." His voice carried hardly a trance of a French accent. It was polite but gruff. Probably too many cigarettes, Michael thought.

"Is there anything I can do?" Michael asked, feeling completely helpless.

"Just stay indoors for a little while longer, Sir. I believe Sir Ian has some ideas. I would rather not discuss them over the telephone."

"Very well, Inspector."

Before Michael could ask any more questions, the line went dead. He glanced at his watch. It was precisely nine o'clock.

At 9:22, Sir Ian arrived at the Howells' in a police cruiser. Inspector Gratton must be a good friend, indeed.

Sir Ian's old self was back. Not that he had recovered his rotund silhouette, but the imposing, almost domineering demeanour was back in full force. This was a man who conducted the world's leading orchestras. He was to civilians, musicians or otherwise, what a three-star general was to an army. The only thing that was truly different about the Maestro, right then, was his attire. He wore jeans, an old corduroy jacket, and something resembling a bandanna around his neck. A tired-looking Panama crowned his head. Somehow, Sir Ian's inherent nobility was visible even without the usual accoutrements of elegance. He'd knocked twice before Gabriel, fast as he was, managed to reach the front door.

"How are you my friend?" Sir Ian asked shaking the hand that Gabriel had extended to take the guest's hat.

"I'm at your service, Sir," Gabriel replied with dignity.

"As I am at yours," Sir Ian replied.

He walked into the sitting room and vigorously shook Michael's hand.

"We don't have much time, Mike." He sat down before being asked. He was panting as though he'd run across the front lawn.

"Just ran to your door, you know? Mustn't be recognized," he added, as though that explained everything.

Michael stared at Sir Ian with disbelief. "I wouldn't recognize you if you walked into me in the middle..."

"Yes, yes. Thank you. These jeans are a bit tight for me, but a year ago I couldn't get into them no matter how hard I tried." He then looked at his watch before again turning his penetrating gaze on Michael. "We must talk," he said, lowering his voice. Then, almost as an afterthought, he asked, "Any change?"

"I'm afraid not. She is physically fine..."

"I understand." Then he looked closely at Michael. "Can she travel?"

"What . . . what do you mean?"

"Relax, Mike. I am not proposing to abduct your daughter and force her to make another world tour. Although . . . never mind." There was a momentary impish gleam in his eye. "I talked with Gratton at some length. We came to the conclusion that it would be best for all parties, and particularly for Anne, if she disappeared for a little while."

Michael remained speechless. "And how is Diana?" Sir Ian asked.

"What? Diana. Ah, yes. I dare say she will be fine the moment Anne comes back. I mean when Anne..."

"I know. We are all hoping."

"You said disappear?"

"I have a friend who has a log cabin at the far end of Lac Pontbriand. That's just north of Rawdon. Ah . . . west, actually. It's not much of a cottage, but it stands on forty acres and my friend goes there hunting for something or other. Or maybe it's fishing? Anyway, the important thing is that he flies there by helicopter."

"What?!"

"It will not attract attention when Anne gets there."

"Anne? By helicopter?"

Sir Ian glanced at his watch again. "At 8.45 this morning. I've discussed the matter with John. I asked him to find a way to excuse Peter from his duties for a few days. A week at most. By then I hope to arrange..."

"What has Peter got to do with any of this?"

"He agreed to look after Anne. Surely, you don't want her to go there without a physician who knows her condition?"

"Anne has no condition..." Yes, she has, he had to admit to himself. It was just that no one had the slightest idea what that condition was. "I see," he finished lamely. "And what do I tell Diana?"

"I would rather leave it in your capable hands," Sir Ian fidgeted uncomfortably. He felt very sorry for Michael's wife, but Anne had to come first.

"And just when would all this take place?" Michael asked.

"If you agree," he glanced at his watch again, "in twenty-three minutes." When Michael didn't react, Sir Ian lowered his voice still further. "I don't suppose you could spare Gabriel for a day or two?"

"Gabriel? What do you want with him?"

"I? Nothing at all. I thought he would be a sort of impromptu bodyguard. And frankly, from what I've heard, he has some means of communicating with Anne, don't you know?"

"Yes, Ian. I know. And he does. Of course he can go. They can all go. That is, if Anne wants to..."

Sir Ian was already up and in search of Gabriel. He explained his plan to the large man. Gabriel nodded and left.

"What's he doing?" Michael was at the end of his tether. When all this was over, he would have to cope with Diana.

"He is talking to Anne."

"She doesn't..."

"I know. But according to Gabriel, he has no problem communicating with her."

"I'll believe anything of Gabby. He is an extraordinary man, did you know that he..."

Gabriel filled the doorway from the corridor leading to the back of the house.

"Miss Anne thinks it is a good idea, Sir. She will be ready in ten minutes."

"How on earth did you do it, Gabriel?" Michael's voice was full of disbelief.

"She chooses not to talk, Sir, but there is nothing wrong with her hearing. I've explained Sir Ian's plan to her and she understood it at once, Sir."

Michael nodded in abject resignation.

"If I may, Sir. I, too, would like to throw a few things together." Gabriel bowed and withdrew without waiting for an answer.

At 9:55, eight police cruisers pulled up in front of the Howell residence. Two minutes later they moved about a hundred feet back, to the left and the right, and blocked access to the street in front of Michael's house. Additional men stood at each house within the restricted area, to make sure no one stepped out onto the street from any of the houses. At 9:56 Anne went to kiss her mother's cheek. Diana remained composed. There were no tears. Anne kissed her father and Sir Ian in quick succession. She bid her farewells in eerie silence, without uttering a single word. At 9:57 Gabriel stood at the front door with two small carrier bags; at least they looked small in his hands. A whirling noise reached them from outside. The helicopter landed in the middle of the street, directly in front of the Howell residence. The space between the maple trees was only just wide enough. Gabriel and Anne walked to the noisy machine. A helping hand pulled Anne inside the cockpit. Gabriel followed immediately. Peter slammed the door shut. At exactly 10 o'clock the helicopter took off and flew directly south.

Michael and Sir Ian sat in the kitchen and took a very unaccustomed shot of vodka.

"I never touch the stuff before noon," Sir Ian affirmed. "God, I needed that," he added elegantly wiping his mouth with his sleeve. "One for the road?"

"God bless," seconded Michael.

Sir Ian's spontaneous responses to the events early this morning were alien to him. Michael needed an orderly schedule outlining the procedures, as a good engineer should. This sudden burst of activity was way over his head. As John Brent would say, he was a left-hemisphere man. His reasoning skills required him to process his information step by step, to have it well structured, logical and preferably written down. There had been no time for any of this. God bless Sir Ian, he thought.

"God bless all of them. And us," he added, raising the glass for the second time. There was something quite euphoric about spontaneity. Strange – but euphoric. He wasn't quite sure what it was, but he liked it. At least, he thought he did.

And just then Diana walked in.

* * * * *

Chapter 22

Mount Calme

Directly across the road from the acreage, on which the log cabin was hidden, was a mountain whose crown was the highest point in the immediate vicinity.   Its name was *Mount Calme*, an aptly named summit of peaceful, bucolic serenity.   During the winter months, hundreds of local skiers, and increasingly outsiders, would schuss and slalom down its rather humble slopes, but now with the summer colours just beginning to turn towards the splendour of Canadian autumn, the serenity of the mountain was palpable.

Just after arriving at eleven o'clock, Anne decided to go for a walk up its gentle slopes. Peter would walk with her. Gabriel would take the cabin's jeep to buy provisions.

"I'll see you in about two hours," Gabriel promised. "If I may say so, Dr. Brown, I would allow Miss Anne a free hand. She has things to work out."

And with this enigmatic advice, Gabriel lifted his bulk into the jeep's driver seat. Even with the seat as far back as it would go, his knees still protruded on both sides of the steering wheel. He looked like an enormous, cumbersome squatting frog.

Rather than driving to Rawdon, Gabriel took the opposite direction, along some unpaved roads, until he came to a store that catered to hunters, quite common in this part of Québec. In

the backwoods, the choice of provisions was limited, and the local people, such as there were, were used to odd characters, who
often flew in from as far as Maine and Connecticut, where apparently the hunting rules were more restrictive.

The flight from Montreal had been so short that Peter
hardly registered it. Once the *Sûreté du Québec* helicopter had
cleared the immediate vicinity of the Howells' house, it had
swerved north, and in a little over twenty minutes and with the
help of GPS had deposited the three of them safely on a little
clearing behind the house.

John had told Peter to do whatever might be necessary to
assure that Anne did not do something that might worsen her
condition. There was not much more that John could have said.
Regardless of his personal involvement, John thought it fair and
proper, indeed mandatory, to look after the MNI's investment in
Anne. Anne had already contributed to the study of the human
brain more than she would ever know. More than anyone
imagined. In fact, only some ten years later, Dr. John Brent,
then semi-retired, would write another dissertation which would,
eventually, give humanity an enormous leap forward.

He would call it, the Avatar Syndrome.

Rising in serpentine curves, the cut-outs through the conif-
erous forest, which served as ski runs during winter, were now
deserted, empty, save for an odd rabbit, or an occasional deer.
Whether Anne was aware of Peter's presence or not was a moot
point. As she climbed the gentle slope, at least gentle until she
began to take shortcuts, she had given no indication that she was
even aware of her surroundings. Normally she would stop to
look at a wild flower, dismiss a buzzing mosquito from her bare
arms, or at least stop, now and then, to admire the view. She did
none of these. The climb, each successive step, appeared to
command all her attention. Peter thought there was a touch of
anxiety with which she tackled the hillside. It was as though she
walked in a sort of composed yet restrained hurry.

Peter was sorry he had forgotten to take any water with him.
While Anne advanced at an ever-increasing pace, he began

huffing and puffing like a man twice his age. The innumerable hours at the Neuro, coupled with his daily visits to the Howells' house, had left him with little to no time for physical exercise. What energies was Anne drawing on to cover the terrain like a trained mountaineer?

The climb wasn't that long. It took about forty minutes to reach the foot of the mountain, admittedly over a terrain which was continuously slopping upwards, but the actual climb Anne had covered in little more than half an hour. Having finally reached the top, she looked a little disenchanted until she turned away from the unfolding view and saw a steep platform rising another fifteen or twenty meters. It served, during winter, for the expert skiers to gather speed before hitting the first slalom gate on the slope below. At the side of the precipitous ramp there was a narrow wooden staircase which rose steeply from the adjacent ground.

Anne ran to the steps and up them at a frantic pace. Peter took a breather before following her. After a minute or two, he did so, even if a lot slower.

As she stood at the top, her eyes travelled over the surrounding countryside. The rolling hills to the south, and particularly the more challenging mountaintops to the north, were already showing signs of the approaching autumn. The tops were covered with conifers, forever green, but their dark pointed heads were already underscored with shades of red sprinkled with amber just beginning to turn into rich gold and pure, if paler, yellow. Toward the south the greens still remained green, but in time, even there the maples would turn fiery red. The birches would remain yellow a while longer and the stubborn pines and firs, intermingled with occasional cedars, would provide a dark-green backdrop against which the multi-hued bouquets would stand out in all their transient, explosive glory.

The long, almost straight line of the smooth surface of *Lac Pontbriand* stretched out below them. As Peter looked, mesmerized, the smooth water shimmered in the glory of the early afternoon sun. A cloud or two crawled lazily from west to east, away from him, along the lake, relaxed, in no hurry to get to their destination. There was peace here, at the top.

"No wonder they call it Mount Calme," he muttered.

"It is glorious . . . so much more peaceful than Mount Gargas," she whispered.

"Mount Gargas?" Peter asked before he realized that he had, for the first time in more than a month, heard Anne's voice. He chose not to comment on her miraculous recovery.

"The mountain top I stood upon above La Salette," she replied in her sweet voice. And then she added something very strange. "There," she said, "you are very close to God. Here, God is very close to you."

It did not matter that he failed to understand what she was saying to him. How sweet it was to hear her voice. He hadn't realized just how much he had missed the sound of her voice.

"I wasn't sick, Peter," she said, as though reading his thoughts. She spoke softly as though her vocal cords were only now regaining their dexterity.

"But..."

"For two years I've been talking a great deal, mostly with my violin. I'd said all I had to say. Since then, anything and everything that left my mouth was to me an extremely painful understatement."

"And now?" he asked, immediately regretting questioning her judgment. It was none of his business when and how she might choose to talk.

"Now we are alone, silly. I'm with you . . . Don't you want me to talk?"

Her voice was teasing. This was the old Anne. The old youthful Anne. He found it hard to believe that she had always been there, just waiting to be alone. Suddenly he remembered her hand giving his a gentle squeeze. She still cares for me, he thought. And, as manly as Peter was, a great tear of joy rolled down his cheek. He looked away towards the distant hills to hide his embarrassment. Anne kindly pretended not to notice.

"Let's go back, Peter. Gabriel will be back soon. He'll need help unloading the car."

That evening Peter called Michael on his cellular to let him and Diana know that Anne had indeed come back.

Diana stood in the doorway, looking at her husband and Sir Ian with surprise in her eyes. The dullness had left them, somewhat, and curiosity had taken over. Sir Ian, buoyed by the two vodkas, jumped to his feet, ran toward Diana, and planted two big kisses on each of her cheeks.

"Why, Sir Ian! I never..."

"Oh, yes, you did, my dear. Oh yes..."

He thought better of it. Lack of sleep, the morning rush, both physical and emotional while organizing Anne's escape, and now the two vodkas on an empty stomach were about to bring him to the edge of making a fool of himself. His flirtatious comment was nothing more than his automatic reaction to a pretty woman.

"By Jove, I had no breakfast this morning," he announced instead, sounding as surprised. "And you forced me to drink that fire-water under such a condition, Michael! Shame on you!"

"Well, actually..."

"You must have brunch with us, Ian. I'll call Gabriel..."

The two men looked at each other. For the next fifteen minutes Sir Ian, with pertinent interruptions from Michael, recounted the events of the early morning. All along Michael thanked his lucky stars for the congenial way in which Diana was accepting the news. Probably, knowing that Anne was under the protection of both, Gabriel and Peter, calmed whatever qualms she may have entertained. "And now, my dear lady, tell me that I haven't earned my breakfast!" the Maestro concluded, challenging Diana to contradict him.

"But it is only ten-thirty," Diana pointed out more than a trifle bewildered.

"It certainly is," Sir Ian affirmed proudly. "I usually get up about this time!"

They went to the kitchen together. Diana soon learned that the Maestro's talents were not limited to conducting aspiring prima donnas, as Sir Ian liked to call his musicians. His culinary skills seemed likewise second to none. When he finally left, about an hour later, the house seemed strangely empty. Or it did until a stone wrapped in paper crashed through the living room window.

"Have you noticed, Peter, that talking in a virtually uninterrupted stream is so common that when someone stops communicating verbally, for just a few days, they are judged to be under the influence of some strange, deadly malady?"

Peter took a deep breath. He was one of the 'judgmental people' she was referring to. There had certainly been many others. Her own parents were, too.

"It is the only way we know how to communicate, dear," was the best he had to offer.

"You should speak to Gabriel. He's taught me a great deal."

At this precise moment they heard the wheels of a car on the gravel outside. Anne sprang to her feet and ran outside to help Gabriel unload the jeep. Compared to her, it was now Peter who was dragging his feet. By the time he got outside, she and Gabriel were already hauling armfuls of provisions through the side door. As Gabriel passed him, he gave him an oversized wink.

"Well done, doctor."

Whatever Peter had felt like today, it was far from being a doctor. Certainly not an accredited member of the illustrious Fellowship of Surgeons and Physicians. "Would you mind awfully not referring to me as 'doctor'?"

The giant raised an eyebrow.

"You've done more than you imagine," Gabriel assured him. "Trust me, Peter, in time you will understand."

Perhaps in time, Peter thought. For now, he was completely at sea.

After lunch, which they took on the small terrace outside the cabin, Peter told Anne about the inexplicable healing at the Neuro, while she'd been there. She listened attentively, even as her eyes drank in the beauty of the Québec countryside. No wonder it used to be called *La Belle Province*.

Rawdon and their cabin lay just at the foot of the Laurentians, *Les Laurentides,* in the district known as *Lanaudière.* The slopes here are gentler, less dramatic, than their bigger sisters to the north; and as the name of Mount Calme implies, the land seems to offer an atmosphere of innate peace.

"The hospital has declared the recoveries spontaneous remissions," Peter concluded, hoping to elicit some sort of reaction from Anne.

"I am sure there are quite a few spontaneous remissions around," Gabriel put in. Then he smiled. "There was a time when people were superstitious. In those days they called such cures miracles."

"And you are saying that they were not?" Peter looked keenly at the giant.

"The magic of today is the science of tomorrow," Gabriel offered.

"Yes, but..."

"But nothing, darling," Anne put her hand on Peter's arm. "There is a great deal we still don't understand. The important thing is to keep learning."

"Shouldn't it be I who tells you that, rather than the other way round?"

"Yes, Peter, it should."

And that was that.

Michael was of two minds: call the police before or after touching the offensive missile. For all he knew, it could hide some sort of explosive that could do him considerable damage. A moment later he shrugged.

"I am becoming hysterical," he chided himself.

The paper that had been wrapped around a large pebble from some misbegotten architect's landscaping project carried a dog-eared message addressed TO THE JAILERS OF OUR ANNE. The letters were all capitals, presumably to protect the identity of the launcher.

MISS HOWELL BELONGS TO ALL OF US.
SHE IS A NATURAL TALENT, A GOD GIVEN TALENT, AND THEREFORE THE WRATH OF GOD WILL FALL ON ANYONE WHO DARES TO KEEP HER TO HIMSELF.

"Why *himself*? Why do they assume that it was a man who'd abducted her?" Michael asked Diana, whose initial pallor was slowly dissipating under the influx of excitement. "Why not 'to herself'?"

"What are you talking about, dear?" she asked instead. She was thinking of the broken pane. Her first reaction was that some children had thrown the rock.

"I'd better call Inspector Gratton, I suppose?"

Not waiting for an answer, Michael dialled the number Sir Ian had given him in case of emergency. "The line is open twenty-four hours a day, you can call anytime," Sir Ian had said.

After the third ring Michael was asked to record his message. He reported, in as few words as possible, about the rock, the paper, and the message. About a half-hour later a police cruiser quietly pulled up in front of the house. It remained there for the next few days. There were no more incidents.

Except for the Internet.

Somehow 'the official owners of Anne's talent' had gotten hold of Michael's email address. He had never attempted to hide it, and it appeared on some of his office stationery. When Michael checked his inbox that afternoon, there were twenty-eight messages, all demanding Anne's release. For some reason, a great many idiots assumed that Michael or his wife, her parents, were keeping their own daughter prisoner. That they were physically restraining her from giving the world what, according to the disgruntled fans, belonged to the world. The next day Michael changed his email address.

The following Friday, Sir Ian and John came to dinner. The summer season was over – the winter had not yet begun. Sir Ian had a few weeks during which his schedule was a bit easier. Almost from the moment the two men arrived, the conversation centred on Anne. The general idea was that the media's attention span usually lasted a maximum of ten days. All the major newsmakers, such as earthquakes, flamboyant Hollywood-type murders, or murderers, cataclysmic inundations and generally events of such newsworthy magnitude, hardly ever remained in the headlines for more than a week. Sir Ian assumed that the same would be true of Anne.

"At best, it will be over by the end of the week, three days from now. At worst, I give it another week, ten days, at the most," he declared pontifically. He had fully recovered his old self.

"I have a better way," John suggested.

He pulled out from his briefcase a manila envelope. From it he extracted a large negative. He held it against the lamp.

"This shows two fingers of a right hand broken in two places each," he said.

"Anne's fingers aren't broken," Michael declared.

"On the contrary. They are already broken," John declared triumphantly.

"Ah! You sneaky devil!" Sir Ian bowed in John's direction. "Quite Machiavellian, my dear Sir. Quite fiendishly Machiavellian!"

"Could anyone tell me what you two are talking about?" Diana's face was a mask of worry and curiosity.

"Your diabolical Doctor proposes, if I am right," Sir Ian glanced at John, "to leak out to our over-zealous paparazzi a rumour that Anne has met with an unfortunate accident . . . perhaps an automobile door closing on her fingers?"

"It so happens that this is exactly how the accident occurred."

"Or a helicopter..."

"What are you two on about!?" Diana was up on her feet.

"Why, nothing, my dear, nothing at all," Michael caught on to the scheme.

"Do you think it will work?"

"We have an orthopaedic doctor on our staff who will testify, under oath – he is a confirmed atheist – that the accident took place on the hospital grounds, in our own car park."

"Bravo!"

"Actually it did. Last Thursday. That is how I got my idea," John confessed.

"Capital, just capital. Are we all agreed? All in favour say I. I!" Sir Ian declared.

"I," John affirmed. "Aye?"

"Michael?"

"I suppose it can't do any harm."

Sir Ian turned to Diana.

"I don't like it but... Fine. If you think it will help," she replied. "I!" she declared, downing the remainder of her glass of Bordeaux.

The article appeared the next day on the front page of the Gazette, La Presse, and two other, minor dailies. The news together with a copy of the negative came 'from confirmed though confidential sources,' of course. The next day, there was no mention of Anne's name anywhere on the front page. The day after, she was mentioned briefly in the entertainment section. The day after that, she was gone completely.

"Ye may be gods, but ye shall die like men or fall like one of the princesses," Michael misquoted the scriptures with relish. He wanted his daughter back. At home. Even if two fingers of her left, or was it right, hand were to be bandaged whenever she walked out for the next few weeks.

Michael would be quite happy if all public memory of Anne died a natural death. Even if she was never to play the fiddle again. Except at home, perhaps. Just for him. And Diana. And for Peter and John. And for Ian, of course.

And, yes, and definitely for Gabby, bless his soul.

Somehow Fluffy had not been included on the list. But later, having realized his omission, Michael was sure that Fluffy would listen with equal pleasure.

They spent the afternoon on the terrace. For a long time all three sat in silence. Anne slept. Gabriel was reading a book, an old copy of the *Origin of Species*. Peter just rested. It seemed incredible that this was the first chance he'd had, in more than two years, to just sit among the trees and dream. He listened to the silence, watched the reflection of the clouds drifting along the surface of the distant water, followed the flight of some geese, probably getting some late practice before their impending departure.

As it got darker, Anne opened her eyes. A little later she began telling them about her trip, some years ago, to La Salette. She didn't mention Lourdes, because she had nothing nice to say about it.

"One night we all climbed to the top of Mount Gargas. I'd seen the stars as one sees them only in the mountains. Away from city lights, from visual or any other noise. It seemed as though we weren't closer to them by a thousand or two thousand meters, but by thousands of light-years. It was there and then, at the top of the mountain, that I realized the scale of man, of a young girl really, and the earth; that I realized my utter insignificance."

The first star twinkled between the treetops, just over the eastern horizon.

"And then I thought of Mozart. And Einstein. And of the Great Masters, and the Avatars . . . And as I stood pondering the scale of the universe, I knew that this very same universe can choose to manifest itself through them, and therefore through you or me, through anyone of us. I thought, right then, that perhaps I, too, might become such an instrument. A channel through which the essence of Whoever or Whatever had designed this incredible jewel stretching over my head might choose to manifest some of Its beauty through me."

Once again they sat in silence, allowing thoughts to flit across their minds, idly. Anne was right. There was no need to talk all the time. Sometimes they would hold on to ideas, images, for a second or two; at other times they would let them drift away, gently, without compulsion, until silence ruled supreme in each of their heads and souls. Peter had never experienced such silence before. Not a silence that reaches one from outside through the ears, but the silence that is born from within. It embraced him as a mother embraces her baby, with infinite care, with an enigmatic love, a sense of unity. He found himself at peace with the world, such as he hadn't known since he was a little boy. If even then....

"I've never had time..." he murmured by way of an excuse.

God lives in the depth of impenetrable silence, he realized, amazed at his discovery.

And this blessed, divine silence stretched into the evening. Slowly, the first stars emerged from the greys of the east, crept upwards until half the sky had turned darker, even as the last rays of the dying sun touched the dark tops of the distant hills receding towards the far, far west.

A lone bird bid them goodnight.

And then there was that peace again. Someone had once called it the peace beyond human understanding. Perhaps. But at this moment, with hardly a thought disturbing his consciousness, Peter imagined that one day, one day soon, he might understand at least some of its mystery. It had to do with submission. And with acceptance. And with blending into the reality and not opposing it. It had to do with becoming one.

After another timeless while, Anne stood up.

"Come," she said, taking his hand in hers and leading him into the house.

Gabriel had already retired.

"Come," she repeated softly so as not to disturb the magic of the night. "Tell me again..." she said softly.

* * * * *

Chapter 23

Gabriel once more

"**There** are two complementary channels of evolution. The first is natural, or along the lines Darwin defined as Natural Selection. Species evolve by mistakes and mutations. If one survives, selection is satisfied and evolution stops, or slows down to an imperceptible rate. If variations keep dying, the process of change continues. There is no doubt that this process is extremely wasteful, brimming with blunders and unmitigated errors. In fact, it is a process of trial and error, heavily weighted towards the error. It is extremely slow. Essentially, if something works well enough to survive, it means that it can withstand whatever evolution or nature may throw at it, or can overcome the prolific errors perpetrated by the system. Hence the wastefulness. If an evolutionary unit or model survives, it is good. If not, well, there are plenty of other models that will try."

Gabriel sat at the end of the dining room table, which, evidently at this moment, had become the head. As seemed appropriate, Michael's, Diana's, Anne's, Peter's and John's heads were all turned towards him. The dinner was over and Anne had insisted that Gabriel join them for coffee and explain.

"Explain what, my dear?" Diana had asked innocently enough.

"Everything, mother. Just about everything," Anne had answered with her usual directness.

Since Anne's return, both physical from Rawdon and spiritual from wherever she'd gone, she had been more inclined to join in conversation, though she still seldom initiated one. But today she'd insisted. She had been asked too many questions, by too many people, to which she could provide no answers. "Ask Gabby," she would say and return to what she had been doing. Usually, some form of contemplation. Finally Michael, at Anne's insistence, did just that. He had asked Gabriel to join them and explain what it was that had happened to Anne.

Gabriel took another deep breath.

"As I am sure we all agree, the purpose of evolution is to assure the survival of our genes. To do so, nature, in order to evolve, appears to rely on increasing the complexity of the re-productive enclaves."

"Complexity?" John challenged. "We cannot fly south like the geese without the aid of a GPS, avoid an object with our eyes closed – like bats, or communicate over considerable dis-tances under water like the whales or dolphins...."

Michael joined in, "What about the cockroaches, which while not nearly as complex as we are, in any department, seem to survive all we can throw at them. Of course, they might not do so well without human assistance. Without us, for instance, they couldn't cross the oceans."

Gabriel appeared quite undeterred. "Those species have evolved to the complexity necessary for their role in nature. Crocodiles haven't changed for millennia because they are per-fectly adapted for what they do. Perfectly complex to the degree necessary for the continuation of their species. We, the human animal, not only modify our bodies through physical and chemical means, but also manipulate our environment. It is our minds that are our tools, and they have not finished evolving." Gabby paused.

"There is one aspect of evolution which we must under-stand," he continued. "It appears, as Darwin also observed, that natural selection is characterized by abject blindness to suffer-ing. The catastrophic eruption of Mount Pelee, the recent Tsu-nami in the Indian Ocean, the earthquakes at Kansu in China, Tokyo, Sicily, Peru, India, each add up to tens of thousands of casualties in hundreds of species, not to mention the toll in the

suffering of the survivors. All such events, and many others, indicate nature's complete indifference to and disregard for the
human lot. Nature or natural selection, just like chaos, has no
sense of right or wrong or purpose that we know of. It simply is.
Unemotional and indifferent. In humans for example, it is
hardly popular knowledge that most human embryos harbour
colossal genetic defects. Most pregnancies quietly fail within
days, or a few weeks, after conception."

"But the church doesn't allow that," Diana put in.

"Indeed, Madam. Neither do many laws. But this is not a
question of choice. The body simply rejects the embryo. Nature
is not sentimental, nor does she recognize religious dictates governing the termination of pregnancies. To repeat, we, as the human animal, indeed just like any animal, simply do not matter."

"Just like the ice ages," Peter piped up. "Millions of species wiped out. Huge changes in speciation and population. We
don't think of them as tragedies. They simply happened."

"We don't care because no humans suffered," Michael
said.

"That's not entirely true, Sir, but you get the idea. Senti-
mentality and suffering are human concepts and have no place
in nature."

"But that's horrible," Diana couldn't contain her disgust.

"Nevertheless, He to whom the various religions refer as
God seems utterly indifferent to the welfare of His creation. Not
even that of the sixth day."

This made Michael look up. "So God created man in his
own image . . . and the evening and the morning were the sixth
day," he quoted from memory. Remnants of Jesuit brainwash-
ing sill lingered in his subconscious.

"So there is no benevolent Being up there, somewhere,
looking after our welfare? Meting out punishments and rewards?" John mused aloud, his tone a little supercilious.
Amusement was evident in his eyes. He, too, recalled a biblical
quotation that confirmed Gabriel's thesis. 'My Father judges no
man,' it said. Yet until Gabriel had pointed out the screaming
paradox, he'd never realized just how far the various Christian

sects had drifted away from the Bible. God judges no man, he pondered the words again. We're on our own.

"Not to my knowledge, Sir. There is no benevolent spirit." Gabriel replied dryly. "And by feeding people a pack of ah . . . mendacities, the various religions of the world are doing us irreparable harm."

"Mendacities?" Anne asked.

"Lies," Michael came to her rescue. He was beginning to get the message. "Fabrications, falsehoods, inventions...."

"You mean you don't believe in God? I thought you contemplated every morning." Michael contrived to sound genuinely surprised.

"Buddha postulated that every man is a Buddha, the Enlightened One, though not yet aware of this truth. In fact, the vast majority of people seem completely unaware of their own potential. They are not yet awakened, as Buddha called it. Jesus of Nazareth stated, quite unequivocally and explicitly, that he and his father, whom he regarded as God, are indeed one and the same. Indivisible. Krishna claimed that he flows in the veins of everything that lives. There have been others who expressed a similar sentiment."

"B-b-but I thought God is good," Diana put in. Her mind was still dallying on Gabriel's previous characterization of evolution. She didn't feel comfortable with the concepts her major domo was stirring up. She liked her world a little simpler, carrying a little more responsibility.

"God is good indeed, Madam. Only we seem to have problems with defining both, God and goodness."

"So?" She sounded a trifle offended.

"The problem is that we, men and women of the twenty-first century, tend to externalize not just god, but good and goodness. Though in essence the three are one. You might say, they are synonyms for each other."

"So you do believe in God?"

Gabriel smiled.

"To answer Madam, at least in part, I do not believe in a judgmental externalization of our responsibilities. I like Lao Tsu's comment on the subject. The Old Master said that, and I quote: 'it is the way of heaven to have no favourites: it is constantly on the side of the good man'. So to answer Madam directly, I would have to say no. I do not believe in God as defined by various religious organizations."

"Define a good man, Gabby?" Anne asked.

"That is a tough order indeed, Miss Anne. There was a certain Nazarene who had been addressed by one of his followers as Good Master. 'Why callest thou me good?' asked the Nazarene. 'There is none good but one, and that is God'." Gabriel looked around at his audience. "He, the Master, had been speaking to simple folk. Now you will ask me to define God...." This time Gabriel grinned. "I shall refer you to Spinoza. He postulated that to define God is to deny God." Gabriel again was examining the faces of all present. "The closest I'd like to come is to say that goodness and god are one and that it is a sense of harmony. That which is in harmony with itself and its environment is good. Even natural selection seems to tend towards it, and humans are no different."

"I read somewhere..." Peter spoke as if he hadn't been listening to the last few exchanges, "I've read that God is what the opposites have in common."

"This would be the concept closest to Lao Tsu's heart," Gabriel said very softly. "Rather like Ahura-Mazda and Ahriman. One incapable of evil, the other by nature treacherous and malignant. The so-called good and evil," Gabriel added with a quizzical smile.

It had taken Gabriel some ten years of search in India to discover the Source. "The true Source of all realities is completely neutral. So much so that it allows all instruments capable of metabolizing the concept of power to exercise their own will for whatever purposes such power was desired. Buddha thought that desire lay at the root of all evil. No desire, no duality. No duality, no problems."

This time the silence lasted a lot longer. Diana was the most disturbed by Gabriel's ideas. She was also the best versed in the scriptures, which she had studied, intensely, when Anne had first begun creating problems. And now, the word 'mirror' struck a distant echo in her memory. It brought her to an expression she'd reread a dozen times, in an attempt to understand it. It was a statement attributed to John of the Apocryphal Acts. 'A lamp am I,' it said, 'to you that perceive me. A mirror am I to you that know me.'

Peter glanced at Anne. He kept glancing at her as though to assure himself that she was still there. He'd promised himself that he would never, never again, let her go. If she chose to go on another world tour, to do anything at all, anywhere, he would go right with her. To the ends of the world. She, in turn, felt his eyes on her and gave him a hardly discernible wink. Then she got up and served everyone some more coffee. For a little while, they all smiled at each other, almost shyly, as though no one was willing to admit to themselves his or her apparent ignorance of the subjects discussed. Finally Peter took it upon himself to revive the conversation.

"At the very beginning you said, Gabby, that there are lots of other channels. Can you expand on that?"

"Yes, Peter. At our level of evolution about six billion of them. And a much greater number coming up to take over, if need be."

"Channels for what?"

"This brings us to the second aspect of evolution. You might call it the spiritual evolution. That which most people regard as God, I prefer to recognize as an inherent, universal predisposition towards order and harmony. Taken as such, there are no emotional connotations attached to the idea. Morality is usually recognized as behaviour which does not offend another person. What is moral for one, however, is amoral or even immoral for another. Ethics are a different story. But those, too, vary from culture to culture."

Diana raised an eyebrow. For her, ethics were Christian ethics. Love thy neighbour . . . do unto others . . . and suchlike. She didn't recognize other systems as ethics only as schisms. She didn't know what exactly to do with Buddha.

"As master Peter said a few moments ago. God is what opposites have in common. Buddha said that god and goodness are one and therefore harmony is that balance. The source is neither good nor bad, right nor wrong, black nor white. Harmony is both simultaneously. Lao Tsu, like Rumi and much later Nietzsche, reached out beyond the concept of moral good and evil. Our predisposition, like natural selection, is always on the side of harmony or goodness. It is up to us to become aware of this predisposition."

"So we cannot benefit from this, ah, predisposition unless we recognize its existence?" Diana's face was showing light dawning after an eternity of persistent dusk.

"Exactly, Madam. What is more, the greater our awareness, the greater channel we become for the efficacy of this universal tendency."

"I always suspected that our ability to recognize the universe is a way in which the universe becomes aware of itself," John said.

"A very apt observation, if I may say so, Sir," Gabriel looked pleased as a teacher would be of his pupil.

Peter sat up, opened his mouth and closed it again. He was thinking of the spontaneous remissions that had taken place at the MNI, with Anne in attendance, so to speak. Maybe what Anne's presence did was to restore order and harmony in both patients? Or at least, somehow may have been instrumental in order and harmony having been restored. Was she merely a channel? An instrument, as Gabriel might say? The idea was too preposterous to be taken seriously, though. After all, he was an accomplished neurosurgeon. On the other hand, isn't this what I do, or try to do, day in and day out at the Neuro? Trying my best to restore order and harmony in my patients?

"I have a long way to go," he murmured.

Anne, sitting next to him, placed her hand on his. She seemed aware of his inner struggle.

"The greater our awareness," Gabriel continued, "the better channels we become."

"So if we seek an outside agency to find . . . to find good, then we are looking..." Her voice trailed off. Diana didn't quite know how to express herself.

"Heaven is within you, said the man so many recognize as God," Gabriel smiled, and then his smile broadened into a grin. "And without you," he added.

"But how much easier to find it within," Diana whispered. And then, as did all the others, she withdrew into her private thoughts.

Anne quietly excused herself. She had seen Fluffy looking at her from his perch just outside her bedroom door. As she neared her room, Fluffy's tail performed a Dervish's dance of joy. For a little while every person at the table ruminated on what had been said. Gabriel, too, thought that perhaps this was enough for a single meal. He was ready to start clearing the table after coffee when John got up and began pacing the room. Finally he stopped behind Gabriel's chair.

"So what about Anne?" he asked bluntly.

Gabriel took yet another deep breath. He was glad that Anne had left the table. Perhaps she'd sensed that, sooner or later, she would become the sole object of discussion. On the other hand, she was the only person truly able to talk about her particular path. He could do little more than speculate. Still, the idea was to help these people to understand her better.

"Anne was lucky..." he began.

This seemingly innocent statement made Anne's parents catch their collective breath in unison. Whatever they each thought of Anne's past, neither would ever dream of describing it as lucky.

'...even as I was when I'd been forced, by my own misplaced sense of guilt, to leave Canada," he reflected, but didn't elaborate any further. "Yes, Anne was lucky. She was given an opportunity early in life to learn what, for centuries, indeed, millennia, people have attempted to learn by sequestering themselves in caves and deserts," Gabriel said wistfully. "To seek enlightenment, awareness of this predisposition, this connection to harmony, in solitude."

Diana turned to stare at Gabriel. He was talking about her little girl.

"Lucky?" she repeated, sounding surprised to the point of ridicule.

"She was abducted, when no more than ten years of age. Already then she was forced, by circumstances beyond her control, to learn how to detach herself . . . or perish. In terms of her mental and emotional sanity, literally – to live or die. She was forced to learn how to withdraw herself, without the benefit of being alone. Ah, yes..." Gabriel's eyes drifted to some long-remembered Himalayan peaks, "she was lucky."

John continued standing behind Gabriel's chair. His face did not show any degree of comprehension. There was one thing, however. John knew from his experience as a physician that difficult things are best learnt when one is young. According to Gabriel, Anne had had that opportunity.

"Are you telling me that her refusal to speak was just that – refusal?"

"No, Sir. Not only that. Any more than you could refuse to operate on her tumour."

"What the devil do you mean by that?"

"Just that, Sir," Gabriel allowed himself a surreptitious smile. "We all respond to our conditioning, to our acquired and conditioned response. You must operate, she must withdraw. They are both conscious actions, yet they are also a great deal more than that."

"Are you trying to tell me that her conditioned response of withdrawal was overriding her conscious will?"

"Not completely. Again, the parallel with your chosen profession is evident. You would only refuse to operate on a patient if you had absolutely no choice. You might think of yourself as incompetent. Or too tired. Or that the previous night you had one drink too many, or . . . The point is that all these reactions might influence you at a subliminal level. And force you to choose not to operate. Being an adult, you would most probably overcome them. And operate anyway. Anne..." he smiled with tacit admiration, "Anne is but a child. She, like all children, listens more closely to her intuition than most adults."

John simmered down, partially, and returned to his chair.

"To fully understand the force with which Anne struggled," Gabby continued, "let us, again, examine the past.

Throughout history there have been men, and occasionally women, who realized that the balancing act, between nature and spirit, could take place only through human intervention. This intuitive knowledge, or suspicion, led them to become hermits, loners, to live apart, to contemplate in search of still greater understanding. This act of detachment was at the root of Buddha's search. Jesus is said to have disappeared for eighteen years. Or at least, we have no record of his endeavours during that time. The isolation provides a reconnection to that spirit. The spirit that would cause you not to operate or that caused Anne to be silent. Anne learned, as I've already mentioned, early in her life that she can reach this state of detachment within a crowd. Or at least, without resorting to having to sequester herself from other people, from the world. She acquired control over her sensory inputs to a degree hardly possible for most of us.

"The moment I put my foot inside your front door," he said, looking at Michael, "I sensed Anne's presence. Her aura, even then, extended to embrace the whole house."

Short breaks of pensive silence were becoming the order of the day. Those moments of mental respite were no longer awkward. They suggested the need for serenity. For slowing down the pace of life. They were needed for the bits and pieces to arrange themselves in specific order in everyone's mind. For the fragments to coalesce into the whole idea.

"Now, I strongly suspect, it is much broader," Gabriel continued very quietly. His tone was akin to reverence. "But she needed help and understanding. It was my humble lot to serve. Anne's ability lay at the source of her brain's evolutionary pattern. By developing pons Varolii, she was able to switch from one hemisphere to another at will, though I can only guess why she would want to. Perhaps it might have been to be able to switch off the part of the brain which responded to speech, or hearing. I doubt if, at the conscious level, she knew herself. Anyway, our two neurologists are vastly more competent than I to answer such questions."

"Are you telling me that her neural development was a by-product of her *modus vivendi*?"

"Isn't everyone's?" Gabriel asked. "Perhaps not the tumour, but the pons?"

"Surely, we act in accord with the configuration of our brain, not the other way around!" John insisted.

"We do, Doctor. After all, whatever is received is received in accordance with our nature."

"Didn't Aquinas say something like that?" Michael butted in.

"That is quite right, Sir. He did. And this is where the Nazarene's dictum comes in at full force. The two are one. I and my father – united. You and your instrument are inseparable, so to speak. You become your instrument, in a way. Anne's mind changed because she needed it to. And Anne changed because her mind changed."

"And with this realization comes Power..." John was thinking of the spontaneous remissions.

A feeling of serenity hovered over the room like an invisible blanket of an early morning's summer haze. It was as though they'd all stopped breathing. Not only that, but they all seemed to be restricting their movements. Even their faces assumed expressions of unfamiliar tranquillity. Simultaneously, a palpable sense of being alive, of life itself, was so much more present than an hour ago, at the beginning of the discussion.

After a long while Peter cleared his throat. "And her music?" he asked, sounding guilty for having broken the silence. He also was sorry Sir Ian couldn't be here today.

"Ah, yes. That was another problem. As we now all agree, we receive in accordance with our capacity to receive. What Thomas failed to tell us was that we are also limited by our capacity for giving."

"I don't understand," Michael confessed.

"Anne's inherent desire to give overrode her ability to do so. Rather like a surgeon who, having performed so many operations, collapses from exhaustion. This, regrettably, was the stage she had reached. During the first two years, before her tour, she had learned to sublimate her ego, in order to do justice to the composers. Later, she leapfrogged this apparent hurdle, by perceiving the intent the composer had had, but had been unable to express with the limitations inherent in a musical score. Even a poet can say only so much with mere words."

Gabriel let them all absorb the importance of this analysis before continuing.

"Music is the product of order and harmony, as the latter word implies. It was the most natural manner in which Anne could find an expression of her understanding, of her inner insights. Remember that Anne had never attempted to verbalize her perceptions. She, like so many great people before her, felt and understood reality holistically. In a gestält fashion. The reality with which she had to deal was never written down for others to read. She had discovered it by her ability to enter the great silence within her being."

In the now recurrent stillness that ensued once more, Diana's tearful spasms, though quiet, filled the whole room like a gentle ripple spreading across a village pond. No one said anything. They all had to deal with their own inability to have been more help to Anne, even in her most difficult moments. After a while, Michael put his arm around Diana's shoulders and pulled her close to his chest. Rather than helping to quench her tears, he only served to release a torrent, which she seemed quite unable to control.

"I . . . I d-d-didn't know..." she whimpered. "I just d-d-didn't kn-n-now...."

"None of us knew, dear. There now . . . let them run..."

Suddenly Michael noticed that Anne was standing behind Diana, behind his arm that he'd dressed over his wife's shoulders. He felt a peculiar sensation; the sort one feels when something very wonderful happens. Like getting a toy under the Christmas tree he had been hoping against hope for when a little boy. The next moment Diana looked up with a big smile.

"What are we doing here?" she asked. "Shouldn't we all be in the sitting room?"

Not only her mood but the tears had evaporated into thin air. As Michael turned to thank Anne, she wasn't there. He wondered if he'd imagined seeing her standing behind his wife's chair.

No one moved. It was apparent that only Diana had benefited from whatever took place. John and Peter, and even Gabriel were sitting still, seemingly lost each in his own thoughts. "I suppose the trigger was La Salette?" Peter asked quietly.

"It seemed so to me also," Gabriel agreed. "That was her first conscious realization of what was already fomenting within her. These things take time."

Peter who'd benefited from the time he'd shared with Gabriel in Rawdon was beginning to understand what it takes to be Anne. "And her music was the first total sublimation of her ego . . . It must have sucked the very life from her."

"It very nearly did. It seems to me, she stopped literally at the very last moment."

"But why? Why must it be so consuming?"

"While here, in the material reality, we all need at least a smidgen of ego to survive. Dualistic reality demands it from us. It is the price we pay for being human. She didn't know that. Remember that all her perceptions have been holistic. Nonverbal. Not broken down into intelligible, laterally structured concepts. They were all more like feelings, like images...."

For the first time Gabriel had also run out of words. Some things just couldn't be described. They had to be experienced.

Peter, too, was groping. "But what of her withdrawal? She seemed so happy, her smile was..."

"...beatific? Yes, Peter. The inner silence to which she had learned to withdraw was and is a place of great bliss. If it weren't for her great love for her parents, for life, she might have remained there forever."

And then Gabriel looked deep into Peter's eyes. "And it is you, my friend, for whom she returned to our reality in Rawdon," he seemed to say. But Peter already knew. His eyes showed a pale reflection of the bliss Gabriel had spoken about.

What Gabriel hadn't told anyone at the table, and Anne herself was still hardly aware of, was that she was becoming the tabernacle of astounding power. Gabriel had seen rare examples of such power in India. When one reaches a certain level of understanding, one can wield power for good or evil with equal facility. Furthermore, both powers are easily demonstrated in the dualistic reality in which we all abide. Few people are willing to understand that that which we call good or evil originates from the same single source. Great philosophers and theologians insist that there is a single source, but assign to it only good attributes. The evil, according to them, emanates from some other source, thus resulting in two deities.

Anne's dilemma lay in the fact that she had obtained access to this power too quickly. She could hardly be expected to handle its awesome consequences.

As far as Gabriel could reach into Anne's subconscious, at present she was capable of restoring order in a considerable radius upon which she directed her attention. She also could, should she want to, play havoc in even distant areas, which she might well already be capable of reducing to a state of primordial chaos. This, Gabriel assumed, must have been why all the great Avatars always insisted on the supremacy of love.

Finally, the dinner, the coffee and Gabriel's discourse were over. Peter knocked on Anne's door. Receiving no answer he bid Diana and Michael goodnight and left with John to be ready for the morning rounds at the Neuro. Those very early morning rounds which enabled both of them to have time later for surgery. To restore order and harmony in their patients, as best they could.

"What do you make of all that?" he asked John as they left the house. They'd decided to walk to the Institute. Lately they'd both been sleeping at the Neuro. With the first rounds at seven a.m. and the last operations often going past nine at night, it would be foolish to waste precious time on travelling to and from their individual apartments.

"It seems that we are all sort of pointless. I must say it doesn't do much for my ego."

"Me, too. But do you really believe that Anne may have influenced those, you know, those spontaneous remissions?"

"Frankly, at this stage I don't know what to think. Only time will tell. But I did have an idea at the time when Gabby told us about her, ah . . . realization. It is a little bit of a subterfuge but, from the medical point of view, it might clear up a lot of questions."

Peter didn't like the sound of it but, it was his boss talking. "Go on," he said dutifully.

"I'd like you to invite Anne, on some pretext, to make a tour of our wards."

Peter bit his lips. "You want to test her?"

John didn't answer. Yet Peter knew that, whatever Dr. Brent may or may not be as a friend, he was first and foremost a scientist. But even as anger was stirring in his veins, an idea stuck him that allowed him to remain true, at least to himself. He decided to partake in the subterfuge. Only, if he were lucky, it wouldn't be Anne but John Brent at the receiving end of it.

It was too dark for John to see Peter's mischievous grin. At any rate, John was still submerged in his own problems, not the least of which was that Gabriel sounded too damn convincing.

*   *   *   *   *

Chapter 24

The Avatar Syndrome

For Diana and Michael, the next few days were distinctly awkward. No matter how hard they both tried to regard their daughter as a normal, ordinary, if very talented girl, it just didn't seem to work. They couldn't shrug off their own seeming inadequacy, not only as compared to the traits that Gabriel had assigned to Anne, so convincingly, but for not having detected any of them on their own.

"My own flesh and blood," Diana repeated from time to time, shaking her head. "Who would have thought?"

"He said that no man is a prophet in his own village. It must be true. It is like not seeing the forest for all the trees, I suppose." It wasn't much, but Michael tried.

"Where is Gabriel?" she suddenly asked.

"As usual," Michael replied.

The 'usual' meant that the major domo was probably sitting in front of Anne, both drifting on some gossamer wings towards an inaccessible reality. At first he found it annoying. That old Gabby was keeping his daughter away from spending more time with him. With her parents. Try as he might, he never really understood what this contemplation business was all about. It must be my left hemisphere, he mused for the umpteenth time, remembering John's many lectures.

"It is only a question of suspending your thought stream, Michael," Gabriel had told him repeatedly. "It takes a bit of practice, but anyone can do it."

Why anyone would want to stop thinking was beyond him. Vegetables don't think. Nor, presumably, do worms and cockroaches. But does that make them happy? Not with a hungry bird around. Gabriel had used the word Avatar in connection with Anne. Michael still had no idea what the word really meant. He'd read all he could get his hands on that he thought was relative to the subject. A messenger of God, he'd read. From Sanskrit *avatâra*, *ava*, down and *tarati* meaning he goes, or passes beyond. They'd spelt it with a small 'a'. Somehow Michael always capitalized the word in his mind. As for the word itself, Michael found it misleading. It sounded a bit as though an Avatar was both, coming and going. Coming down and going beyond. Anyway, on another occasion Gabby had said that we were all avatars. This time he thought of it with a small 'a'. It's all in the mind, he'd thought.

"No, Sir, it reaches beyond the mind," Gabriel had assured him.

Go figure. If it reaches beyond the mind, then how can I possibly understand it? He was ready to give up. I'll just accept her for what she is. Whatever that may be. Little Anne. She was still only five-foot-two. Little. For an emissary of God she was a mere pip-squeak. The most beautiful pip-squeak in the world. Dear Anne....

Months had passed since the paparazzi had shown their true colours in front of the Howell residence. Sir Ian had been right. The media's interest waned quickly enough. They'd left Anne alone. They had new fish to fry. To make life hell for. Whether her reported injury had any influence on their disinterest was hard to tell. They would probably have blown a few gaskets if they'd suspected that Anne might have been in a position to cure herself. Heal, Gabriel called it. Curing comes from without, he'd said. Healing from within.

He missed Sir Ian, a little. Once Ian had given up on Anne resuming her career, he hardly ever dropped in. Now and then, rarely, Michael suspected, just to make sure that Anne hadn't had a change of heart. Music was his life. He couldn't help himself. It was probably his karma. That was what Gabby would have called it. I must stop quoting Gabriel, he told himself.

John and Peter had remained faithful.

All of them looked forward to Friday dinners. Actually, Anne hardly ever stayed long, while Gabriel had reverted to his old habit of not fraternizing with 'the upper classes', as he'd once called the Westmounters. The session over the after-dinner coffee, that night, was evidently going to remain an exception to prove the rule.

Diana had settled down. Whether it was Anne's relaxed behaviour, her daughter's rare but well-chosen kind words, or just the fact that she'd decided to accept things as they were, Michael didn't know. But they did go out on occasion together, all three of them, to the movies, and they had resumed their walks on Mount Royal. Twice Sir Ian had sent them tickets to his Royal Box. Anne had refused to take advantage of his kindness. Michael knew that she loved Ian very much. Perhaps she didn't want to raise false hopes.

Anne, for the most part, remained Anne. She spent most of her time in her room. She also read a lot, went for walks at the Summit Circle, sometimes she'd walk all the way to the top of Mount Royal. Always by herself. Almost. There was a large shadow that seemed to follow her every footstep, in addition to a hairy beast that seldom strayed far from her feet. Yet, contrary to Fluffy, Gabriel managed to melt into the background.

At home, she liked to spend time with Gabriel. Only God knew what they were up to, and He wasn't telling. But whatever they did, the door to Anne's room always remained at least half-open, as though inviting anyone to join them in their semi-solitary wanderings.

"How is she?" Michael would ask now and again, when he happened upon Gabriel leaving her room.

"Growing, Sir," came a terse reply. Terse, almost rude, yet always accompanied with a bow indicating respect.

On one occasion Michael asked him directly why he always found it necessary to bow to everyone he met.

"It is an old Indian custom, Sir," he explained. "I salute that within you which is your true self," he replied, bowing again.

There were occasions, on weekends, when Anne went out with Peter. Not to any social functions, but just to be together. They walked, arm in arm, Peter shortening his step to keep step with her. In his other hand he held onto a short, retractable leash which Fluffy did his best to extend to its maximum length. On one occasion they came across an accident. A car had been speeding along Côte de *Neige* and hit a small dog.

A screech of breaks, a vulgar curse, a painful yelp and it was over. The car sped on.

Anne's face turned pale. She began concentrating to make the dog recover from the hard impact. She tried and tried to will him hale. To no avail. She turned away and hid her face in Peter's chest. Looking over her shoulder, Peter watched the dog shiver, then get up, stretch, and hobble on his way. For a few more steps he limped, then gathered speed and disappeared behind the fence of one of the houses clinging to the mountain. Peter wasn't quite sure what had happened. Nor was Anne.

That evening Peter told Gabriel about the incident.

"The power is within her, Peter, but she has no control over it."

"What?" Peter was even more confused.

"You don't own the power. The power owns you. Its nature is universal. If you are to channel it for whatever cause, you must withdraw your ego. At least, until you learn to act consciously."

"Is that what Avatars do? The great healers, the miracle workers?"

"No two are alike. Bruno Gröning healed people by his mere presence. Arigo, whose full name was Jose Pedro De Freitas, healed thousand of people by performing intricate surgical operations with his penknife – he excised countless tumours, attached loose corneas, extracted innumerable bleeding ulcers, even malignant tumours. As I said, we don't control the power. We learn how we may be of use, and then submit to it."

"And that's what an Avatar does?" Peter refused to let go.

"There are many aspects, or symptoms, which add up to an avatar. We first detect them, then recognize them, by knowing their attributes. They are visible to those who study such matters. 'Face', in Biblical symbolism, stands for the power of recognition, which in turn refers to God's omnipresence. When we meet an Avatar, unusual things begin to happen. It might be the power to operate with a kitchen knife without causing and spreading gangrene. It may be an indescribable talent for music. Or it might be a dog that gets up and walks away when we stop trying to impose our will on him."

Over the last few months, Peter had attempted, albeit lamely, to tell Anne about John's plan to have her walk the wards, while he and John monitored the effects she had on the patients. Somehow Peter felt guilty about making such a proposal. It felt too much like using Anne. He hated using people generally and Anne in particular. Still, he had made a promise. He had to admit that should it be possible to relate Anne's neural development to some kind of healing emissions; it would be an incredible feather in not only John's cap, but in the crown of the Montreal Neurological Institute.

Finally Peter thought that if he were to tell Anne about it quite openly, not in some sort of subterfuge as John had initially suggested, then the shoe would be on the other foot. First, Anne could refuse. And secondly, she might be in a position to control her gift. If gift it was. Such gifts placed undue stress on their recipient. They might prove more a scourge than a joy. Gabriel had told him, some time ago, that both Gröning and Arrigo had come to untimely ends. So did most Avatars.

"It would be a strictly scientific procedure, and it would be carried out practically at your convenience," he assured Anne when he'd finally found courage to tell her about John's request.

When Anne remained silent, he tried to explain further. "We would then compare the MRI and perhaps the PET scans of the before and after of the various patients and draw scientific conclusions. It really would teach us a great deal," he finished, trying to avoid her eyes.

"You both think that I am some sort of a freak?"

"Darling, please don't. John really tries to do as much as he can to help..."

"...himself?" Anne smiled. "I'll do it. But you of all people must know that I have absolutely no control over what you call 'healing power'. It is not like playing my violin, you know. There, I was at least in partial control. Here...?" She left the sentence hanging.

In spite of Anne's limited blessing, Peter delayed the event for as long as he could. It was early spring before he told John that Anne had agreed to visit the Neuro. John told Peter that he would make the arrangements and let him know. He did – within three days.

Anne arrived by herself, finding that Peter was already waiting for her in the lobby. Peter took Anne upstairs to the Director's office. John greeted her warmly, thanked Anne for her kindness in agreeing to this 'experiment', and handed her a white hospital coat.

She glanced at the sofa, at the window. She knew she had a debt to pay. It had nothing to do with money. It was the love John had showered on her right here, in this room, not so many years ago. Yet she knew that if she tried to repay the way John would want her to, it would all come to naught. She found herself in a no-win situation.

"You, my dear, are now an honorary member of my personal staff. Do not be surprised if you heal some people."

If this was a joke, Anne didn't show any signs of amusement. She remained reserved, nervous, as though she had come because she'd been asked but did not really want any part in this charade. After some ten minutes of small talk, all three left John's office.

Anne walked in the middle, with John and Peter taking the two flanks. She had flashes of *déjà vue* of the times when two large men with fixed smiles and extra broad shoulders escorted her, carrying her precious Stradivarius.

This wasn't as bad, or – as good. Right then, Anne felt as if she was being escorted for a protracted execution. Everything in her rebelled against this sort of experiment. And yet, she could not come up with a logical reason why she shouldn't take part in it. What if John did learn something that might help people? What if many might gain even if she and she alone proved to be a loser? Did it really matter that much?

Yes, it does.   Anne glanced at John. For a moment she thought she'd spoken aloud. John looked different. His teeth were tight, his fists clenched.

It's high time I put all this nonsense to bed . . . once and for all.

But they mocked the messengers of God....

Relax darling. It's only a sort of formality.

It will be the joke of the hospital. Miracles??? Ha, ha!

Are there not mockers with me?

It won't be long, darling. Just bear with us a little longer....

I will put all this nonsense behind me – nonsense . . . nonsense . . . nonsense . . . nonsense!

I am as one mocked of his neighbour....

Please, darling, please don't be angry.

Spontaneous remissions? Bah!!!

Be not deceived; God is not mocked: for whatsoever a man soweth, that shall he also reap....

"This is Mr. Marois. He joined us last Monday. It seems that we might be able to excise . . . well, these are medical details," John smiled with compassion at the man before them. The young man couldn't have been more than twenty. Twenty-five at most.

"Hello, sir," Anne's voice was barely above a whisper.

"Hello, Miss?"

The youngster was trying to remember where he'd seen this angel before. It came to him when the procession was three beds away. "She played like an angel. Maybe it is her...."

"Mr. Jones injured his spine skiing. Now that was naughty, wasn't it, son?" John continued the spiel. Anne with Peter behind her walked quite fast, speaking to every third patient or so. As they passed any particular bed, John ticked them off his list.

The next ward was for women.

"Cancer of the womb. Quite common," he said. The MNI wing dealing with oncology had grown considerably during the last few years. Particularly due to unprecedented progress in nanotechnology. "Pity. She's only twenty-two." They were standing some distance away. "Do you want to get closer?"

Anne shook her head.

"She fell down the stairs. A little too much of the good stuff, I'm afraid. We think we can repair her spine to give her the use of her upper body. Her legs...." John didn't finish.

They saw a total of eleven men and seven women. The peculiar thing was that all the patients looked well under thirty. Anne wondered if this was by design or just a coincidence. They all had their life ahead of them. If it hadn't been for whatever brought them here . . . if they were only . . . whole?

Toward the end of their little tour, Anne began leaning heavily on Peter's arm. When looking, even from afar, at the last two patients she felt quite weak. She seemed to be dragging her legs behind her. Peter felt her weight on his arm.

"That will be all, Dr. Brent," he said. Peter's voice carried unaccustomed authority. Even to his own ears his tone sounded strange.

John, surprisingly, nodded and turned toward the door.

"If we could just..." he tried nevertheless.

"No, Dr. Brent. Miss Howell is tired now." Peter sounded quite official as he continued walking towards the corridor. The moment they cleared the ward door Anne virtually collapsed. It was as though her legs had been swept from under her. Peter picked her up in his arms. She was as light as a feather. He carried her all the way to Dr. Brent's office. There he placed her on the settee. Peter looked sorry for having to discharge his precious cargo. Within seconds she opened her eyes.

"I know this place," she said, her voice sounding weak. "I've rested here before...."

"Just take it easy, darling. Don't talk." Peter looked much paler than the girl he'd just carried from the ward.

"What is the matter, Anne? Are you feeling sick?" John's face showed genuine concern. His previously almost lackadaisical manner during the short tour was gone. This was the old John. Uncle John who cared for Anne as he would for his own daughter.

Anne appeared to have read his thoughts.

"I am quite all right, Uncle John," she smiled sweetly. "May I go home now?"

"Why, of course. But shouldn't you rest a little longer?" John knew that some people couldn't stand the sight of blood, others had the same reaction to hospital wards. Something to do with the smell of the antiseptics.

"Do you mind, Sir, if I take her home?" Peter asked, his eyes begging for permission. "I think Jerry can stand in for me. I spoke with him before lunch."

"Of course, Peter. Just leave everything to me. Look after yourself, sweetheart. There's a good girl."

But the little girl couldn't quite look after herself. Peter, his arm around Anne's waist, half carried her to the elevator and then to the taxi. Fifteen minutes later they arrived at the Howell residence. Gabriel, moved by some sort of intuition was at the curb, from which he carried Anne all the way to her bedroom. Peter thanked his lucky stars that Michael was still in the office and Diana had popped out.

"She will be all right now, Peter. She must rest."

Gently but firmly, Gabriel closed the door to Anne's bedroom. Peter continued to look worried, his arms dangling helplessly at each side. "You're sure there's nothing I can do to help?"

"She wasn't quite ready for this. It was too much – too early."

When Peter continued to stand still, looking quite despondent, Gabriel took him by the arm and led him to the sitting room. He pointed Peter to an armchair, and a minute later presented him with a snifter of brandy.

"It is fortified wine," he said with a whimsical smile.

The young ones, he thought. They have so much to learn.

"There are a great many symptoms which constitute the face of an Avatar," Gabriel said slowly after Peter downed the snifter in one swallow. "You, in your profession, Peter, might call it the Avatar Syndrome."

Following Anne's visit to the MNI, John missed the two Friday dinners in succession. "Just too busy," he said when Peter came to pick him up. But it wasn't that. Peter knew the real reason, but he kept it to himself. In fact, Peter had known the initial assessment of the consequences of Anne's visit within two days. He hadn't talked about them out of deference for John Brent. But now that two weeks had passed, he'd decided to tell Michael and Diana what had happened. Anne already knew, even if her knowledge was incomplete. As did Gabriel. Not in terms of detailed facts, but the underlying repercussions. They couldn't have known the details. No one did. The hospital records were still in shambles.

"They are still trying to sort them out," Peter confessed over coffee. "They will get there no doubt; it's just that they are still not sure where to look."

"Just what happened exactly?" Michael, whose scepticism could only be compared to John's, looked uncomfortable.

"As I've said, we are still trying to sort things out."

Anne, who now regularly participated in Friday dinners, was as curious as her parents were. She didn't interrupt, but Peter could see that she needed all her self-control not to rush him along.

"I'd better start at the beginning. Such as it is," Peter began in earnest. "We have one hundred and forty-six resident patients at the Neuro. There are another sixty-eight outpatients, who attend treatments between two and five times a week. So one way or another," Peter continued slowly, "we have two hundred and fourteen patients in our active files. And to answer Michael's question, yes, to date, we have recorded forty-seven spontaneous remissions. At least . . . we think we did."

"What the devil do you mean by that?" Michael said, a hint of anger in his voice.

"Well, we cannot be really one hundred percent sure."

"What?" Michael was about to explode when Diana put her hand on his arm. Since Anne had regained her speech, Diana had recovered her old graceful charm and poise. Once again, he simmered down. At least for the moment.

"We cannot be sure because our computer records have been erased."

Michael opened his mouth but, luckily, no sound emerged. Anne, who was sitting quietly next to Peter, allowed herself a tiny smile. *I will not be mocked*, she remembered vaguely. The phrase came to her out of nowhere.

"All the records?" It was Diana's turn to be surprised.

"No Diana. As far as we can tell, only of those patients who had experienced the ah . . . spontaneous remissions." Peter took a sip of coffee to moisten his dry throat. In contrast, his palms were sweating. When he decided to give Michael and Diana the details of Anne's visit, he hadn't realized how difficult it might become. Not so much the visit itself, but the ramifications.

"So why is there such havoc?"

"Well, at the Neuro, we are all rather busy. There was no one we could have assigned to check all the records. There are volumes of them."

"I still do not see what was the big problem?" she said.

"Don't you see? We can only learn about the spontaneous remissions after we check the records. Neurological cases, other than spinal injuries, are not readily apparent. We need complex scanning devices to arrive at a diagnosis. Short of conducting fresh MRI and PET scans on everyone, we have no way of finding out who were the patients affected by remissions. Until we check their files, we can't be sure who has benefited from . . .

from Anne's presence, and who hasn't. It is not as though people with early stages of a tumour, benign or malignant, give outward signs of their condition."

Michael was still looking sour. He began to realize what Peter had meant by havoc. He knew well enough what problems an electric surge had once created in his own office. And at the Neuro, the erasures had been, apparently, selective. They wouldn't know they had a problem until they actually found it. Alternatively, until they found that they no longer had a particular problem. For the first time since Peter came, Michael's face relaxed. In fact, a lopsided smile lightened his features.

"But Anne saw and talked to only some, what did you say? Eleven men and seven women?" he asked, his voice as calm as it was pugnacious a minute ago.

"Only the last two and one other woman Anne saw benefited from Anne's presence."

The mystery unfolded itself at a slow pace. And a mystery it was such as Michael had never been involved in before. It was so much easier to design multimillion-dollar structures.

"Sorry, Peter. I didn't know..." he mumbled.

"Nor did any one of us. But to get back to the story, we have, as far as we can see, forty-one patients who no longer exhibit symptoms for which they were initially admitted."

"I thought you said forty-seven, Peter?" Anne looked up from her coffee which, until now, she had been studying with great earnestness.

"That is the most perplexing enigma, Anne. Six of the remission-affected patients were nowhere near the Neuro at the time of your visit. They were mostly at their homes, and one, on that particular day, was in Toronto," he said very quietly.

"A coincidence?" Michael offered.

"Weren't they all?"

For a while they all sat quietly, each lost in his and her thoughts. No one appeared to notice Gabriel withdraw, only to return some minutes later with a fresh pot of coffee. The Howells were great coffee drinkers even if, in recent years, they had switched to decaf. No matter, "Java is Java," Michael declared defensively as if he suspected that decaf might have some emasculating effect on him.

Settled once more, Gabriel spoke for the first time.

"Do you have any indication when exactly those remissions occurred?"

For some reason Peter suspected that Gabriel already knew the answer to his own question. Or at least, had a good idea what it might be. "That is the funniest part. As far as we can determine, mostly from nurses' reports of the behaviour of certain patients but also by conducting a number of interviews with the patients themselves, the changes in the way they all felt occurred at almost precisely the same time."

Peter looked at the faces around the table. Michael was absentmindedly examining his nails. He looked nervous. Peter still hadn't told them that some of the computer records hadn't been erased but merely *altered*. The records of the patients in question were still there, only there was no mention in them of any malignancy or organic defects. This added twist, needless to say, in no way helped their cause.

In contrast to her husband, by this time Diana seemed more relaxed than she'd been for a long time. Gabriel contrived to look enigmatic. Only Anne was looking up at him, her eyes large, green and hungry for information. It was becoming evident that she had absolutely no idea of what had really taken place.

"We think it all happened at the precise moment when we'd left the last patient, and Anne collapsed in the corridor."

"She did what? Anne, you fainted?" Diana was up in arms.

"All the spontaneous remissions took place between the moment I picked her up in my arms, and the moment she opened her eyes on John's settee. Three minutes, at most." Peter completed his account, ignoring Diana's interruption. He wiped his forehead with both palms. He was glad it was over. He'd told them, even if he didn't know himself what it all really meant.

Gabriel smiled his most benevolent smile.

"Thank you, Peter," was all he said.

Anne got up, kissed her parents, then Gabriel and finally Peter on his cheek, and went to her room. A moment later she was sitting, cross-legged, her eyes half-closed. If any one had been there to observe her, they would have seen that, within seconds, a tiny, beatific smile appeared on her lips. She was back in her private realm. A realm where order and harmony prevailed. Where no men nor women were ever sick or infirm or angry. Not even unhappy. It was the universe that she knew, intuitively, was as real as the one she had just left. If only for a little while.

"Funny, that," were her last conscious thoughts before she'd suspended all mental activity. "The road here is straight and narrow. And yet people seem to get lost."

With half-closed eyes she smiled at Fluffy already curled up, happily, at her feet. "If only they knew..." she mused and let her soul take her into her true domain.

It seemed more than likely that Fluffy knew.

* * * * *

EPILOGUE

"In an instant rise from time and space
set the world aside and become a world within yourself."

Shabistari
[Secret Garden]

The Face of Avatar

Every third or fourth week, an extended family dinner was held at the Browns. No longer in Westmount, but in a nice little condo, downtown, that during summer months was always replete with flowers. Not just the condo's little terrace, but the whole district. No wonder the developers had named the community *Floralies de la Montagne,* although it was never clear why '*de la Montagne*'. Mount Royal, to which presumably the *montagne* referred, was a good twenty-minute walk away.

When Anne had turned nineteen, she and Peter had tied the knot. Perhaps a little young, but life was short, they hadargued.

"You know, Dad, how little control I have over my future...." Anne had told her father.

From anyone but Anne, such a declaration would have sounded ominous. For Anne, it was just normal.

Meanwhile, Peter continued to walk up the hill, daily, to run his research programs at the Neuro, which, over time, survived the long hush-hush debacle of Anne's visit. As for what actually happened that day, Gabby explained that Anne hadn't cured anyone, nor had she erased any documents, he insisted. What happened was that at times Anne appeared to enter a different reality. In her new state of consciousness, the tumours and other pathological conditions simply do not exist. When she returned to 'normal' awareness, the reality in which she had spent what can only be described as moments of infinity persisted into the world we all regard as the here and now. The patients had evidently been drawn into the vortex that Anne had entered at that particular time. The hospital records didn't exist because the 'patients' had never been sick. John, Peter and Michael preferred not to question Gabriel's explanation. Diana thought it crystal-clear.

Peter still worked under the tutorship of the old Director, Dr. John Brent, though the old war-horse was no longer the Chief of Staff. Running the two functions had proven too much for his old friend. John was much the happier for it. He was more relaxed, particularly since he'd finally accepted that there really are two distinct evolutionary tracks, and his was destined to remain firmly attached to mother Nature. He didn't mind that at all.

"There are no two paths that are suitable for any two people in the world," Gabriel insisted. Whenever the dinner was held at the Browns, good old Gabby would be treated as the guest of honour. It was quite amusing to watch his discomfort when he was afforded the same deference that he invariably bestowed upon others.

"It's a hard cross to bear," he insisted.

"Action equals reaction. You are discharging your karma," Michael quipped.

"No matter," Peter tried to cheer the big man up. "Think of it this way, Gabby, you will go straight to heaven."

It was a long-standing joke between the two. Peter insisted that he had been living in a heavenly state from the day Anne had said yes. Gabriel insisted that Peter wasn't in heaven but that he had discovered heaven within himself. In a way, both of them were right.

The moment Anne had moved out of the Westmount residence, Gabriel had offered his resignation. He was flatly denied such disloyalty.

"And how do you suppose are we going to cope without you?" Diana wanted to know. "And what about the children?"

Anne and now Peter had been officially designated as the children.

"B-b-but...."

For the first and only time Gabriel appeared tongue-tied.

"No ifs or buts," Diana declared.

"But the burden...."

"You have never been a burden, Gabby. You know that very well." And then Diana's voice turned more serious. " I think you know that Anne might need you at any time."

Gabriel didn't try to dissuade her. It would never do, nor would Diana believe him, should he tell her that, of late, it had been he who was drawing on Anne's strength. She had grown phenomenally. When Sir Ian and John ceased having demands on her person, she matured like a diamond to which an invisible hand kept adding polished facets through which her Inner Light shone with unprecedented brilliance. Strangely, there were not many that could see this light. Its ephemeral vibrations were well beyond the visible spectrum. Yet to those that had eyes to see, the light flickered on and off, like the rays of a rising sun caught on the surface of a pond disturbed by a gust of wind.

Gabriel was in the habit of taking long walks, and he often found his feet leading him directly to Anne's condo at the *Floralies*. The two of them would sit on the small terrace, sipping green tea, while Anne, her eyes sparkling like the rarest of emeralds, described to him some of her experiences.

"I saw gods more powerful than any gods anyone ever dreamt of on Earth," she told him. "They played with galaxies for the sheer fun of it. To them, life – as we know it on Earth – seemed of no consequence. They thought nothing of removing a densely populated planet to make room for a more interesting species. It all seemed but a game...."

"More interesting for whom? Them?" he asked.

"Gods, for they acted like gods, are not all they are presumed to be. As long as their reality is based in becoming, they are destined to abide in duality. Their potential for good is balanced by their potential for evil. At least in my eyes. Duality is like that. The universes work continually to re-establish the state of balance."

Gabriel, who had once regarded Anne as his protégée, regarded her with unabashed admiration. There was a time when it had been he who was explaining the mysteries of existence to her. For some time now, the roles had been reversed.

On another such afternoon they sat together, facing each other, as in the old days. Soon Gabriel felt drawn into Anne's reality. His mind was swept clean, his memories erased, his attention entangled in....

...a golden thread running through the heart of all realities stretching into infinity itself....

It seemed incredible that even on primitive Earth there were people, such as Anne, who could unlock such mysteries, he pondered later. "The Avatars?" he thought, but dared not ask.

He'd sensed that when one reached a certain level of evolution, there was nothing to guide one between good and bad . . . between good and evil. *Ye are gods...* he heard his own heartbeat pounding like the arcane drum of Brahma – its reverberation traversing countless aeons of space and time. Aummm, it sang in the depth of silence. Aummm . . . Aummm . . . Aummm . . . repeated the holy syllable . . . *ye are gods....*

"We are all gods," Anne said moments later, "or at least gods in waiting. We are the sole arbiters. We also pay the ultimate price for the abuse of our power. Even Jesus said that the Father judges no man."

"Must there be power?" he asked. Like Sir Ian, Gabriel too, in his own way, was an incurable romantic. He was dreaming of a universe where love alone ruled supreme.

"In material realities yes. Duality prevails. It is the price of becoming," she whispered dreamily. "Surely, Gabby, you wouldn't want to give up the joys of becoming?"

Not for as long as I can sit here with you, he thought.

"It is only through self-awareness that we can realize the awareness of Self," she added.

Is there a difference between being and becoming? Between life and living? And yet the two are indivisible. And in that moment he realized that, for the first time in years, he had become a taker.

"Not so," she said, reading his thoughts with ease. "You must take in order to be able to give. Otherwise you would stand still. We are like tides in a universal ocean of becoming."

Becoming within an ocean of Being....

He bowed to her better judgment.

And then she told him what future she'd seen for the entities populating the Earth. She called people entities – most still unaware of their potential.

"...and after my vision, after I'd experienced the awesome power in the hands of a single individual, I no longer think, I know, that the human brain is not ready, yet, to be given the wiring which would enable members of the human race to wield such authority. I have to make sure that my 'accident' is not duplicated and instilled in others. Not yet."

She called it her accident.

John Brent once said that, in a way, all mutations are accidents. Some, just some, for the better. The lucky ones. John Brent had referred to them as evolutionary mutations. But most did not evolve; indeed, they were steps back. As the Hindu scriptures said: most of us are devolving. In the midst of the age of Kali. The dark age. John had pointed to the proliferation of cancers, of dementia, of Alzheimer, of so many previously unknown diseases that seemed to embrace the masses. 'Sure, we are learning to cure those ailments, but for every one we cure, there are ten more waiting to take their place.' John reached forward to the time when Anne's virtuosity could be installed, surgically, in men and women who desired such gifts.

In his later years, John Brent had become a disconsolate dreamer. He would seldom admit that, when he recalled Anne's experiences, he'd realized, even then, that there might not be that many volunteers for his experiments.

"I might be able to multiply human talents, but who would install the sense of responsibility?" he mused sadly. "All I can do is to increase the human potential, not to direct the course it would take. History is replete with men who abused their talents. Like the so-called great leaders."

Gabriel remembered a sad smile playing at the corners of John's drawn features. "And conscience, I know, cannot be implanted surgically. Not everyone would use their improved potential to add beauty to our world,' he'd said, probably thinking of Anne.

Gabriel shook his head.

Recently, Anne had become increasingly aware of her power and held herself back until she could be sure of not abusing it. So far, she'd remained no more than a channel. She didn't decide who might live or die. The universe decided. God, if you like. But a time would come when she would be the sole arbiter. When her will alone would determine how power would flow through her.

She was still afraid of that day.

On yet another occasion, Anne told Gabriel about her 'world tour'. A least that was what she called it. "Without my violin," she added with a grin.

Gabriel resigned himself to be, once again, left behind by her willingness to enlighten him. Not in the sense of preaching, but merely by her attempt to share with him her inner experiences. In her heart of hearts, she still regarded him as her tutor or at the very least an elder, more experienced brother. In some ways, he probably still was.

"It takes about a millennium or the equivalent of a few earth-days, just to find one's bearing. I was lucky. The very first time it took me a mere year or two."

Even to Gabriel, well versed in Hindu concepts, wherein a day of Brahma, the maha-kalpa, spanned over four billion years, Anne talked about the passage of time in a most incomprehensible way.

"I used my chance to see as much as I could. I saw marvels I'd never dreamt possible. Worlds coming into existence for fractions of a second, evolving to unprecedented heights of technological enlightenment, and then disappearing in the blink of an eye as though they'd never existed. Yet the inhabitants of those worlds experienced billions of years of existence."

"Inhabitants?" Gabriel's eyes were filled with wonder.

"In their particular modes of becoming," Anne explained the seemingly obvious. It wasn't. Gabriel grasped but an inkling of what she was trying to share with him.

"Einstein warned us about that. The quantum theory took us even further," he murmured, doing his best to understand at least some of Anne's concepts. He knew that Einstein had proven time to be a relative concept. It varied with the velocity and the position of the observer. He wondered from what vantage point Anne had been observing her reality. She had advanced so far, so fast.

Anne and Peter periodically visited places where Anne's presence could make a difference. Some such were in Montreal, some in Toronto, some in the hypodermic needle district of Vancouver. Other trips took them to the slums of New York, not that far from where she'd performed her inimitable concertos. For some reason she'd always select communities where few 'rich men' would ever tread. Peter remembered the old biblical saying about the camel and the eye of a needle. It must have had something to do with where your interests were. After all, he also remembered that 'where your treasure is, there will your heart be also.' Something to do with distractions.

Once or twice a year they flew to more distant countries. There she walked, unescorted, amid the danger-fraught favelas of Rio. Anne had spent nights wandering the dismal streets of Calcutta. She had broken bread with the Untouchables in many parts of India.

There were many such places.

The first time that Anne had ventured out at night, under the cloak of darkness, Peter had remained in the hotel, trying not to go crazy worrying about her. But she had insisted on going alone.

"How else can I learn to define my limits, darling. Did you not study your medicine in your room, alone, burning the midnight oil? Well, these are my studies. I am still little more than a student."

Anne had a tremendous advantage over important people. She didn't have to dress to impress anyone. She also didn't need titles. Once she covered her hair, no one could recognize her, no matter what the crowd. Her face was the face of the masses she visited. It was their pain, their concerns, their worries, even their fears that were etched on her features. Among the people, she had always been one of many. No one could tell her apart. Unless one gazed into her eyes.

"But isn't this true of all of us?" she'd asked Peter.

The day after and even during the weeks following her first outing alone, there had been reports of strange occurrences. People not only recovered from some horrendous diseases which only extreme poverty can breed, but they changed their attitudes towards life. It was as though their minds, their characters, their points of view, had been fuelled to take charge of their own lives.

"Is that all you want to do from now on? Just heal people?" He said it as though Anne were doing something very wrong. He loved her dearly, but he'd never understood how she could give up her musical gift to offer solace to some strangers she never even saw. Anne only smiled.

She had seen that in future years there would be a sudden influx of young talents, of musicians and sculptors and painters and poets, who seemed to make their mark in their particular societies. The societies she'd once visited. She had awakened the spark, lit the fire in young hearts to bring beauty to all who searched for it.

That was the nature of her enigmatic healing.

She never stayed in any one place longer than a couple of weeks. Usually less than a week, often for just two or three days. Not only because Peter had to return to his work, but also because Anne felt completely exhausted after every such marauding expedition. Not robbing others but sapping her of her life force. She had chosen to give freely, rather than to heal by premeditation. She still remained an instrument, and nothing more. Rather the way it had been with her music.

As once had been her Stradivarius, now she, herself, had become the instrument.

Eventually Peter learned, and not for the first time, from Gabriel, that although her physical anonymity made her hard to follow, he had learned to detect her aura. It was not something he saw, it was something he sensed. The way some of us sense the smell of danger, only in reverse. He'd also learned to become nearly invisible as he followed his wife at a discreet distance, ready to help at a moment's notice. He was perfectly aware that had Anne wanted to, she could give him the slip. Yet she never admitted that she was aware of his actions. She knew that he needed assurance for his own sake, rather than hers.

On one particular occasion, after Anne had returned to the hotel particularly tired, she also seemed, at the same time, unusually elated.

"What happened?" Peter wanted to know.

"I think I got to them all," she replied.

"All?" Her answer was meaningless. "All who?"

"All who were ready," she answered. Later she explained that whenever she acted as a channel she felt the energy flowing through her. She was aware of both influx and efflux, or effluvium. "I'm hardly aware of my body, only of the flow...."

Peter could but wonder at what she meant. Yet he found her attitude a bit strange.

"Didn't you ever wonder if that . . . that flow doesn't reach people who are undeserving? Who might abuse it? Is it not true that the power you offer can be used both, for good and for evil?" He wasn't quite sure what he meant exactly.

Anne put her hand on his cheek.

"My poor darling," she whispered. "Does the rain fall only on the just? Do the rays of our sun caress only the good and the kind? Why must we always judge those we know nothing about?"

"I only meant...."

"I know what you meant. But that which people call God doesn't work that way. It is the very essence of unconditional giving. People talk often of love. But what they are really doing is trading. I'll love you if... There are always conditions... But that is not love at all. You cannot love and judge at the same time."

"So it's just giving? What if you have nothing left to give?"

"Peter, my love. You are not the giver. Nor am I. You are the channel through which the bounty flows. You do not contribute one iota to the universe. The world is already complete. Whole. You just help to transfer the bounty to those who are ready to receive it."

And once again Peter recalled the phrase Gabriel had assigned to Thomas Aquinas: Whatever is received, is received according to the nature of the recipient.

"What if the recipient is atman?"

"Then you own the whole universe, and the whole universe is within you," she murmured. "That is when you become the ultimate giver...."

Two days later they were back in their condo in Montreal. Peter managed to get home early and caught Anne looking at the old violin she'd once played, before the Stradivarius. All his repressed bitterness at the loss of Anne's talent, or her unwillingness to exercise it, again flooded his heart.

"And you prefer to heal them!" he blurted out uncontrollably.

Anne replaced the violin in its case and led him to the sofa.

"Sit down, Peter," she started, "we need to talk."

Still embarrassed at his remark, he sat dejected, saying nothing. For a while they just sat, Anne waiting for Peter to relax. When she saw his lungs fill deeply with air, she smiled as she would at a child.

"I don't heal people," she said.

"I know," he cut in. "It's the force, or whatever...."

"No, Peter. It is not that, either. Neither I nor the creative Life Force does anything to the men's or women's bodies. If they are missing a leg, that leg remains missing. If they have cancer, then the cancer is still there for as long as the reality in which they dwell is cancerous. It is never the question of their body."

"But at the Neuro you, or that force of yours, healed the seemingly incurable...."

"I am not denying that physical healing *can* take place. But it is not what I do."

For a while there was silence. She took his hands in hers "You heal the blind?"

"No, silly. Of course not. At least I don't think so."

She smiled at the thought. She was sure that among the people she reached there were so many that were blind but could see, and just as many with 20/20 vision but could not see at all.

"No, darling. What I am trying to do is to reach that within them that awakens within their awareness their true nature." When Peter remained silent, she added, "to make them aware of who they really are."

"And that's it? That's all you do?"

"Peter, my love, the potential within all of us is infinite. This is not an adage, a phrase or a clever aphorism, but a statement of indisputable fact. There are many that are on the edge of discovering that truth about themselves . . . all they need is a little help. We, as a race, physically, are on the decline. In spite of the wonders you and John do at the Neuro. In fact, the ever increasing volume of work you have confirms my statement."

"But surely...." Peter felt embarrassed. He'd never looked at it that way. His hours were becoming longer while the numbers of staff also grew exponentially. Since he'd met Anne, two more annexes had been built at the Institute. Three more had been planned. "...if that is so, then what is the point of it all?"

"The point is that while the multitude continues to decline, the individual entities are nearing the next step in their evolution. They are the future wonder children, the wunderkind, the great artists, the musicians, the philosophers, who in turn will help others rise above the masses."

"So we are not all equal?"

"We never were. This question of equality is the greatest fabrication perpetrated by our illustrious leaders. What we share are our possibilities, not the way we put them to use. Boys and girls may be born with equal potential, but fifteen years on, one is an A student, the other is abusing his or her body, her potential, with drugs. They are not equal, though their theoretical potential always has been."

"So we need to maintain our bodies..."

"...in the best condition we can, for our potential to manifest itself."

"So my work is not wasted?"

She drew him towards her and made him hold her close.

"Not now, darling...."

She was joking, but Peter understood what she meant. It was the old Thomas Aquinas theorem again. We all receive according to our nature. *Mens sana in corpore sano.* Even Anne couldn't have played, the way she had, without her Stradivarius. We are all instruments, and Anne enables people to see that. Perhaps, thanks to Anne, one day there will be dozens of Annes and Angelos and Antonios, and other as yet nameless geniuses, touring the world, awakening the longing for beauty and love and passion for the unknown. And bringing heaven to earth.

Perhaps....

On another occasion Sir Ian came to visit *Floralies*. Peter couldn't help but feel sorry for their old friend.

"Would it really hurt you to play the violin again?" Ian asked.

"To play as others play it, of course I could. But what would be the point? I might maintain my quality for another year or two. Perhaps five, or even ten. And then?"

"But surely..." Sir Ian could not reconcile himself to the loss of the talent, to the loss of the gift bestowed upon Anne. He lacked the words to explain it.

"Ian, one cannot serve two masters. I have chosen the greater part. The part that makes me human. Not a genius, not an idol, but human. There is no limit to human endeavour. No ceiling. No restrictive horizon. Is there a greater calling?"

She studied him from under her long eyelashes.

"There is one other thing, my friend," she said slowly, as though thinking aloud. "Countless people give up playing their instruments because they realize that they cannot overcome their limitations. Or, perhaps, that they cannot meet their own aspirations. Peter stopped because he'd stopped improving. I, too, reached as high as I could go...."

There was a touch of sadness in her voice. 'Life is an expression of change in so many ways,' Peter recalled their previous discussions. Anne had reached a plateau. Albeit an Olympian one, but still.... Peter remembered that he'd once suffered from being named a child prodigy. A Wunderkind – just for a year or two. How ludicrous. The novas light up the universe for millions of years, yet from the viewpoint of the earth or better still of 'earthlings', such light is visible for but a brief moment. He thought he understood. Anne needed a light that would never go out.

Never.

Whenever the children returned home, it was always a reason to celebrate. Diana and Michael, and Sir Ian and John, and most of all Fluffy, kissed, embraced and licked Anne, each in his and her way. Peter rejoiced in the love that everyone poured on his wife. Funny, he thought. She not only can give, but is so wonderful at receiving. He remembered when her self-imposed detachment did not allow her to manifest such a predisposition. His wife was growing. And in his small way, so was he.

Diana, determined to become a grandmother, was particularly glad whenever she heard that Anne and Peter were back in town. Since 'the children' had moved out, she had tried her best to fill the void in her life. Having discharged her maternal obligations, which had been none too easy, particularly during Anne's younger years, she now found herself in an emotional vacuum. She'd tried painting, then writing poetry, then attempted to trace her family tree back to the fourth or fifth generation in Middlesex, north of London.

Alas, she found herself devoid of talent, and her ancestors seemed as uninspiring as she'd felt right then. Finally, she channelled her energies into creating a social life: one centred on the restitution of the old custom of High Tea, served with cucumber sandwiches, scones and an assortment of home-made wines. She had not elaborated them herself, but her guests seemed bent on breaking the Provincial budget by resorting to making their own alcoholic concoctions. Blueberry, elderberry and a multitude of other berries helped to raise spirits of the assembled housewives, all suffering from their young having flown the coop.

On special occasions, she served home-made mead.

Within a little over a year, the High Tea fever had swept Westmount, from Sherbrooke street to the Summit Circle, to such a degree that poor Michael had to return to his office in order to escape the effusion of breathless gossip which reverberated in his home, until recently his castle. Though he had officially retired from 'active service', he found innumerable excuses to offer his vast experience to his younger partners. He didn't even charge for his expertise, as long as he was allowed to keep his old office as his haven.

But these escapes didn't last for either of them.

One day, Anne took Diana on a visit to a school that catered to autistic children. Diana never looked back. She spent every spare moment offering herself in whatever capacity she could help. Back home, tired but strangely elated, she found that the distant children had inspired her. She decided to give them a voice. She spent two or three evenings a week writing poetry. Later, she read the verses to Michael. He became her editor, press agent and, not for the first time in his life, her number one admirer.

As for Anne?

There was simply no telling how far her studies would take her. Gabriel said that we could all predict the future, only none of us ever knew when it would happen. Michael, moved by his sardonic humour, simply affirmed that the future is the hardest thing to predict. It did not really matter. Peter and Anne's future was the present.

The future, they agreed, would take care of itself.

* * * * * * *

Acknowledgment

I would be remiss were I not to thank Bryn Symonds and Madeleine Witthoeft for their diligent editing, each in his and her inimitable way. To Francine Clouâtre I owe for her scrutiny of my French. But most of all my gratitude goes to Kate Jones, a lady of uncommon fondness for punctuation, but also blessed with an eagle eye capable of discerning even the tiniest slips in my manuscript. Finally, as always, my gratitude to my wife, Bozena Happach, who put up with being a grass widow for weeks on end.

Sincerely,

Stan J.S. Law

INHOUSEPRESS, MONTREAL, CANADA
http://www.inhousepress.ca
email: inhousepress@sympatico.ca

108367

HEADLESS
WORLD

A sequel to THE AVATAR SYNDROME

The Vatican Incident

A novel by

Stan I.S. Law

INHOUSEPRESS presents the sequel to THE AVATAR SYNDROME
HEADLESS WORLD
Coming soon